Also by Earl Murray
HIGH FREEDOM

"What I like most about Earl's story is his obvious love for the land about which he writes. Reading his work, it's easy to see he's a westerner, one who appreciates the vital importance of caring for the land and preserving it for future generations."

—Lucia St. Clair Robson,
author of *Walk in My Soul*

FREE FLOWS THE RIVER

"There is nothing less than exquisite beauty in the power Murray wields to enfold the reader in the simple, yet explosive, world of his very real characters at the cross-roads of their culture."

—Terry C. Johnston

"Depicts the remarkable inner awareness that distinguishes Native American life. He shows the intermingling of the spirit world with what's generally perceived as reality."

—Lucia St. Clair Robson,
author of *Walk in My Soul*

"A powerful drama, brimming with triumph and tragedy. *Free Flows the River* is Big Medicine.

—Richard S. Wheeler,
Spur Award-winning author of *Fool's Coach*

TOR BOOKS
by
Earl Murray

FREE FLOWS THE RIVER
HIGH FREEDOM

SONG OF WOVOKA

A NOVEL BY

EARL MURRAY

A TOM DOHERTY ASSOCIATES BOOK
NEW YORK

SONG OF WOVOKA

Cover art by Paul Maughan
Maps by Victoria Murray
Book design by Christine Aebi/Neuwirth & Associates

A Tor Book
Published by Tom Doherty Associates, Inc.
175 Fifth Avenue
New York, N.Y. 10010

Tor® is a registered trademark of Tom Doherty Associates, Inc.

ISBN: 0-812-52091-2

First edition: July 1992

Printed in the United States of America

0 9 8 7 6 5 4 3 2 1

To my wonderful wife Victoria,
the love of my life,
who came to me on a mountain morning.

And for Paul; her son, and now, my son.

ACKNOWLEDGMENTS

During the writing of this novel, I received a great amount of information from a great number of people. With some I had lengthy discussions concerning volumes of historical data; with others merely a sentence or two was passed. In all cases, the value to me was tremendous.

I wish to extend my heartfelt appreciation to my editor, Harriet McDougal. Her support and assistance was immeasureable.

Sincerest thanks go also to: Faith Bad Bear, Buffalo Bill Historical Museum, Cody, Wyoming; Ronnie Clincher (Wounded Robe), Oglala Artist, Laurel, Montana; Jeanne Eder, Associate Professor of History, Western Montana College, Dillon, Montana; Dr. C. Adrian Heidenreich, Professor of Native American Studies and Anthropology, Eastern Montana College, Billings, Montana; Father Tom Rochford, S.J., Editor, *Jesuit Bulletin*, St. Louis, Missouri; and Brother Simon, Archives Curator, Red Cloud Indian School, Pine Ridge, S.D.

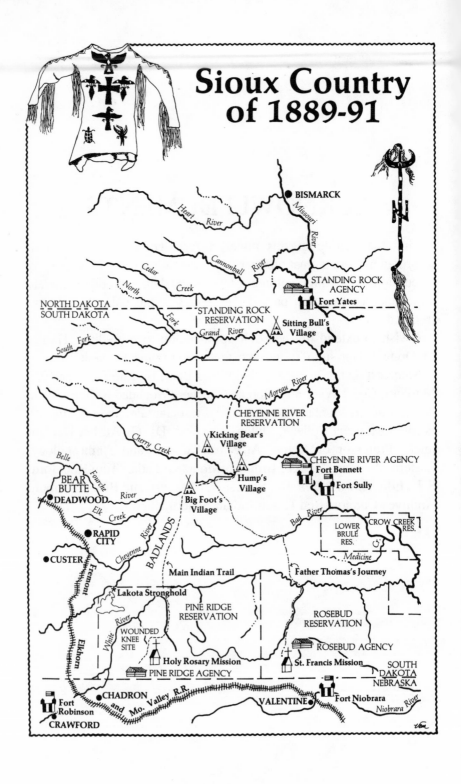

Sioux Country of 1889-91

BISMARCK

Heart River

Cannonball River

Cedar Creek

North Fork

Missouri River

STANDING ROCK AGENCY
Fort Yates

NORTH DAKOTA
SOUTH DAKOTA

South Fork

STANDING ROCK RESERVATION

Grand River

Sitting Bull's Village

Moreau River

CHEYENNE RIVER RESERVATION

Cherry Creek

Kicking Bear's Village

CHEYENNE RIVER AGENCY
Fort Bennett

Belle Fourche

BEAR BUTTE
DEADWOOD

River

Elk Creek

Hump's Village

Fort Sully

Big Foot's Village

RAPID CITY

Cheyenne River

BADLANDS

Bad River

LOWER BRULÉ RES.

CROW CREEK RES.

CUSTER

Fremont

Main Indian Trail

Father Thomas's Journey

Medicine Cr.

Lakota Stronghold

PINE RIDGE RESERVATION

ROSEBUD RESERVATION

White River

WOUNDED KNEE SITE

Elkhorn

Holy Rosary Mission

PINE RIDGE AGENCY

ROSEBUD AGENCY

St. Francis Mission

SOUTH DAKOTA
NEBRASKA

CHADRON

and Mo. Valley R.R.

Fort Robinson

VALENTINE

Fort Niobrara

Niobrara River

CRAWFORD

*Lakota Stronghold

PART I
January, 1889

Mother, come home; Mother, come home.
My little brother goes about always crying,
My little brother goes about always crying,
Mother, come home; Mother, come home.

Lakota Women's
Ghost Dance Song

ONE

THE TWO men presented an unlikely appearance: a Catholic priest on his first trip into the West and an Unkpapa Sioux man, returning to his home for the first time in seventeen years. They stood in the aisle of a New Year's Day train running west from Council Bluffs, Iowa, each insisting the other have the privilege of the window seat.

They stood nearly the same medium height, both slim, yet sturdily built. The priest's deep blue eyes and reddish-blond hair contrasted sharply with his black Jesuit cassock. The conductor called "All aboard!" for the last time, and the train lurched into motion. The Sioux man sat down in the aisle seat, and the priest sat down next to the window.

The train was filled with westbound passengers eager to view the solar eclipse expected later in the morning. Although the Sioux man was dressed neatly, no one had wanted to sit next to him. The priest, being the last aboard, had found the aisle seat next to the Sioux the only seat left unoccupied. The Sioux man had risen to offer his choice seat out of respect.

Startled by the articulate insistence from one in braids and buckskin, the priest stared at the Sioux man. "I'll be able to see the eclipse just fine," he said. "Is that why you're being so kind?"

"You don't want to look at the eclipse," the Sioux man said. "It will make you blind."

"Yes, I suppose you are right," the priest acknowledged with a laugh. "So why were you so persistent?"

"I felt that if I were kind to you, maybe they wouldn't make me ride back in the luggage car."

"Oh, I see," the priest said.

"Yes, they do that," the Sioux man continued. "When they crossed our lands, the railroad said we could ride the Iron Horse for free. They just didn't tell us where we would be put."

"That isn't quite fair, is it?"

"Not many things in life are fair," the Sioux said. "But now I won't have to worry about my death." He looked at the priest, a smile beaming from his dark eyes. "I've heard that those who are good and follow the Black Robes' medicine are to be favored in the next life."

The priest raised an eyebrow. "I've never heard it put that way before."

"Isn't that the idea, though?"

"Is that what you believe?"

"That's why I gave you the seat."

The priest laughed and extended his hand in introduction. "My name is Father Mark Thomas. I'll do what I can for you, but don't expect any miracles."

"I am Shining Horse, and I've received my share of miracles already," the Sioux man said. "So I won't expect you to perform any in my behalf. But for my people . . . well, that's another matter."

"What do you mean?" Father Thomas asked.

"It's going to take a great many miracles to keep my people from losing everything they have," Shining Horse said. "It is a very trying time. Everything is changing, and not for the better. So maybe you're right. Maybe you haven't got the right connections to be of much help to my people. I'm not certain that the white man's god cares that much."

"There is only one God," Father Thomas said. "He represents all races."

"I noticed you said *represents* and not *serves*," Shining Horse said. "I am of the opinion that the white race pushes into line first, and if there's anything left, everyone else must fight for it."

Father Thomas studied him without comment.

"Are you shocked by my words?" Shining Horse asked. "Does it surprise you that I can tell you these things so well in your own tongue?"

"I would be lying if I said otherwise," Father Thomas admitted. "I have no doubt that you are well educated."

"I was taken when I was eight and sent to school at Carlisle. I didn't know anything about Pennsylvania or any of the lands east of my home. A rich family wanted to make me into a *Wasichu*, a white man, and decided I should be James Williams. I was James Williams while I lived back there and went to their schools. Now I'm Shining Horse once again, and on my way back home to my people."

"You are very articulate, Shining Horse. What made you decide to come back out here?"

"No matter how well I speak the *Wasichu* tongue, I will always be of red skin. The two worlds are very different. I don't know if they will ever be one. Certainly not in my lifetime."

"Won't coming back be a bigger change for you than when you left as a child?"

"It might be so," Shining Horse acknowledged. "I just hope I can remember my own tongue. You don't speak Lakota, do you?"

Father Thomas chuckled. "I must admit that I know very

little about your race. But that is all going to change. Very soon."

"I would bet that you're being sent to a mission."

"Yes, as a matter of fact," Father Thomas said, "I'm going to St. Francis Mission on the Rosebud to learn from the priests already there." He pulled a letter from his pocket. "I have orders from my new Provincial, in St. Louis, to bring the word of God to your people."

"I know it is an honor among Black Robes to go on missions," Shining Horse said, "but do you really know what you are in for?"

"What do you mean?"

"My people already know about the Black Robes. They have seen your kind and heard your words. Those who have not welcomed you never will."

"Yes, but that is why I wanted to come out here," Father Thomas said. "I believe I can reach those among your people who have shunned others." He opened the letter. "In fact, my orders state that I am 'to bring the word of Jesus Christ to those on the Sioux reservation who are the farthest away from God.'"

"There are many who will not embrace the *Wasichu* god," Shining Horse said. "A great many."

"Where are they living?" Father Thomas asked.

Shining Horse shrugged. "All over the reservation."

"But who are the farthest from God?"

"Maybe the Minneconjou on Cheyenne River. Yes, Kicking Bear and his people on Cherry Creek do not have a mission. Sitanka, the one they call Big Foot, has asked for a mission. But Kicking Bear does not want anything to do with the *Wasichu* god."

"It sounds to me like your people are divided," Father Thomas said. "They don't all hold the same views?"

"There is a lot of bitterness among my people now," Shining Horse replied. "Your government has decided to pick the men among our leaders who best suit its needs and to give them the power to speak and sign papers for the entire Lakota nation. That does not sit well with the older leaders. They are the ones who are keeping the old ways alive. This has caused infighting among my people."

"But that is not the fault of spiritual people, such as myself," Father Thomas said.

Shining Horse chuckled. "They don't tell you much before you come out here, do they? You men of the *Wasichu* god have your own wars."

"What do you mean?" Father Thomas asked again.

"The Catholics and the Episcopals have a war going between themselves," Shining Horse said. "They both want the exclusive rights to force the *Wasichu* god on my people. I know about that. Too many different speakers for the same white man's god."

"How do you know so much about what's going on out here?" Father Thomas asked. "I thought you told me you haven't been back since you were a child."

"I made it a point to talk to the delegations who have traveled to the eastern lands over the years," Shining Horse explained. "There have been a number of them, from many different tribes. They come to try to settle some legal dispute, usually a treaty that has been broken. I know what's happening out here."

"I'm afraid I don't know enough about the situation," Father Thomas said. "With God's help, I will do as much good as I can."

"You had better have your god teach you the ways of a warrior," Shining Horse told him. "You won't do any good at Cheyenne River unless you learn how my people think."

"I'm sure I'll be learning more of what you've talked about," Father Thomas said. "I will be given a lot of instruction at St. Francis."

Both men looked out the window as a long shadow began moving across the landscape. Slowly the shadow grew longer as the moon's path took it closer to the sun. Everyone on the train began talking excitedly. Everyone except Shining Horse.

"The eclipse has begun," Father Thomas said. "Aren't you interested in things scientific?"

"I have already seen a great many things scientific," Shining Horse replied. "Including the Iron Horse, which destroyed the buffalo hunting grounds. I do not feel that this event we are now watching should be classified as scientific."

"You are a hard man to please," Father Thomas said. "Very hard, indeed."

"You will see that I am pretty open-minded compared to the others," Shining Horse said. "When you reach Cherry Creek, you ask Kicking Bear and his people what they thought of the sun turning black. I'm certain they will not call it a scientific event. They will call it a bad time, a time when the sun deserted them. Some will be angry, some will be sad. All of them will be changed, and *that* is what you will have to deal with."

Mako sica, the Badlands, locked in frozen white, showed no signs of life but for a lone Minneconjou Sioux woman riding horseback through the lower reaches of Big White River. Those who knew Fawn-That-Goes-Dancing were not surprised at her taking off alone in the dead of winter, having no fear of either the elements or the prospect of not eating until she reached her destination. But many found surprise in the reason for her journey.

Fawn was torn. She had received a letter from the Holy Rosary Mission at Pine Ridge, written and signed by a Black Robe, announcing that her mother, along with another woman, was to be married on the third day of January in front of the *Wasichu* god. Fawn had spent a day in the hills shedding bitter tears. It had been hard enough to see her mother leave the summer before to live with an Oglala man at Pine Ridge; but Fawn had never dreamed that Sees-the-Bull-Rolling would make her mother travel the White Man's Road.

Fawn dismounted at a small spring, her face turned against

a sharp northerly breeze. She rubbed her hands together briskly, working the circulation through numbed fingers. After dislodging a large, pointed rock from the hillside, she slammed it through the brittle ice at the mouth of the spring, then stepped back while Jumper, her red pinto pony, sucked noisily from the thin flow, his nostrils flaring in the cold.

Fawn pulled the remnants of a tattered woolen blanket closer around her shoulders. Underneath, she wore an old, loosely fitted deerskin dress given to her by her mother on the eve of her first marriage. Her legs and feet were covered with cowhide leggings and moccasins, her feet wrapped in rags for added measure against the cold.

Maybe she was getting too old for this. Maybe she should have stayed back in the village at Cherry Creek and not risked the trek across *Mako sica* alone. Her younger brother, Catches Lance, had said he would ride with her and bring his closest friend, a warrior of mixed Sioux and Negro blood named Tangled Hair. Though Tangled Hair had argued they should go, Catches Lance had changed his mind and unsaddled his pony at the last minute.

Nothing, aside from death itself, would have stopped Fawn from going to Pine Ridge. She did not want her mother to think she no longer cared for her, even though her mother had decided to travel the White Man's Road and leave her old customs behind. Fawn missed her mother and had wanted to see her badly enough to ride off alone into the cold.

With the coming of the warm moons, Fawn would see the end of her thirtieth winter. Though she maintained her youthful beauty, to her the count of her years might as well be fifty, or even sixty or seventy. For her, time had no meaning now; there was nothing to bring joy, nothing to look forward to. Most of the old ways and traditions were gone, pushed behind with the sweeping movement of the *Wasichu* into Lakota lands. She was among the last of those holding out against the changes, living in Kicking Bear's camp on Cherry

Creek, doing the best she could to survive and still maintain the teachings she had learned as a child.

She would pass those teachings on to her two small children. Besides her mother and her younger brother, they were all the family she had left. Her father and two other brothers had been killed in warfare against Bluecoat soldiers in the fight at Rosebud River, prior to the famous battle at the Greasy Grass, the Little Bighorn. At Greasy Grass she had suffered the loss of her first husband. One more had fallen to the Bluecoats after that, and her third had died in a stupid, drunken fight with his own brother.

During her marriages, Fawn had borne six children. Four of them had already crossed over from sickness. The two youngest, Hawk, who was eight, and Little Star, four, were now her entire life. She had left them with Catches Lance and his wife, Night Bird, who was her best friend.

Though Night Bird had yet to conceive, she treated Fawn's children as if they were her own. Like Fawn herself, she divided her rations for them, and sewed and beaded clothes to fit them from muslin meant for her own use. Not a day went by when Night Bird didn't give them both some form of present, even if it were as small as a playing stick.

Fawn considered Night Bird as she would a younger sister. They often talked well into the night, sharing their lives and their views of the future. Night Bird had told her there was no sense in riding down to Pine Ridge and had begged her not to go. Night Bird had once called Fawn's mother her own mother, but she would do that no more. She wouldn't accept anyone who turned to the White Man's Road, no matter how good a friend she had been in the past.

Fawn turned her head and held her breath against a sudden blast of arctic air. Shot with needles of frost, the wind stung like fire against her exposed skin. She wanted to cry out, but if she did, the air would only find the deepest recesses of her lungs and bring more misery.

When she was young, the cold hadn't dealt her the pain it

now did. In those days, she reasoned, she had eaten better, and the times had been, if not entirely peaceful, at least happier. There had been buffalo to hunt and free space in which to live. All that was now gone. For this reason, she could not blame her brother for his seeming indifference toward their mother's marriage.

Fawn wondered now if she shouldn't have taken Night Bird's advice. She felt weak and numbed from the cold. She hadn't eaten for over a full day, and she hadn't filled her stomach for nearly a moon's passing. The villages all over the Great Sioux Reservation had fallen into famine, as the latest shipment of beef from the agencies had been under half the ration. The people had been left to scrounge for whatever they could find. The buffalo were gone; the deer and the antelope were scarce. Now jackrabbits were tracked down by the people and dug out of hiding. Children cried continuously from hunger, even the children among those who, like her mother, had given in entirely to the *Wasichu* conquerors.

Although she felt deep hunger, Fawn considered herself lucky. Unlike many other adults, and a great number of babies and toddlers, she did not have a distended stomach. There were many among her people who needed the nourishment more than she, including the young, who must live to carry on the Sioux nation. Many of the people had given up hope and now awaited the end. Too much had happened. It seemed unlikely that the people who were once the strongest tribe on the plains would ever have fallen to this.

When her pony was finished at the spring, Fawn drank slowly of the cold water. She wiped her lips and mouths, careful not to leave dampness and invite frostbite. She looked up at the sun. She felt something, a change perhaps, but saw no reason to think that the weather might soften soon.

She climbed back on her pony. The sunshine began to dim in a mysterious way and a fear she had never known gripped her. A dark shadow crept quickly over the land, engulfing the broken hills and deep ravines, changing the day into night.

Fawn wondered if the sun were dying and all life might be coming to an end. She thought she had prepared herself for the end; she had been certain she could face a Bluecoat soldier's bullet, or the slow, painful death of malnutrition. But this kind of death would be something she had had no way of preparing for.

Fawn did not look at the sun. She did not want to watch the life force that had sustained her people for countless generations sing its last song. Instead, she got down from her pony and stretched her arms skyward. She began to sing her death song, praying to the Powers that her life be taken quickly and that she be allowed to live in peace after crossing over. She prayed for the quick and painless deaths of her brother, and of Night Bird; of her children, and of all her people. When the sun died, nothing on the Earth Mother could possibly live.

One thing that puzzled her was the fact that her pony merely stood in place, awaiting her return to his back. The horse showed no fright whatsoever. Fawn began to think that if there were cause for alarm, Jumper would certainly feel it.

She stood in the cold, trying to get a feel for what had happened. Though it had become as dark as nightfall, the sensations were entirely different from when the sun went down to sleep. The air hadn't changed, as it did when the sun left; and though stars appeared, they did not glimmer as they did when night was real.

As the darkness settled into its thickest period, Fawn took a deep breath. Though the temperature hadn't changed, the air seemed somehow warmer to her. She realized that something was telling her not to be afraid, yet the panic wouldn't leave her. Somehow she felt that she was to experience something she didn't want to see, something that would terrify her.

Suddenly a presence began to surround her, as if a huge spirit person had come to stand beside her and envelop her to hold her in one place. Fawn's breath caught in her throat. She dropped the reins and started to run blindly through the darkness. She ran and yelled, stumbling and falling. Still, she could not shake the presence that seemed to grow ever stronger around her.

Screaming in terror, Fawn tumbled down a steep bank, bouncing over rocks and brush, rolling for what seemed like an eternity, until she came to rest at the bottom.

She discovered that she could not rise. She seemed to be held fast to the ground, incapable of even lifting her head. In fact, it felt to her as if she were sinking into the snow around her, down past the snow and into the soil, deeper and deeper into the ground.

TWO

FAWN SUDDENLY felt as if she were standing. She did not remember rising, or even partially recovering from her terror and the tumble into the ravine. Yet she felt fine. There was no fright, nor any cold that taxed her body.

Everything felt wonderful. The darkness around her seemed to have fractures in it, where she could see things with daylight attached to them. Most things were good to look at, but something she focused on troubled her deeply.

It was her own body, lying just at her feet.

Fawn continued to stare. She lifted her arms and ran her hands over herself. Nothing seemed any different to her, yet there she was, lying on her back in the snow, and here she was as well, standing upright, as if she were two separate, yet identical, people.

But that wasn't possible. How could this be happening? Who was the person on the ground who resembled her so closely?

"Don't be frightened," came a voice from beside her.

Before she even turned, Fawn recognized the voice as that of her mother. But how could her mother be here, in *Mako sica*, when she awaited her wedding at Pine Ridge?

"You know how I have always helped you through hard times," her mother's voice continued. "I want you to listen to me very carefully now."

Fawn turned. Her mother, appearing as a young woman, smiled and put a hand on her shoulder. Fawn didn't know whether to be frightened or happy; both feelings flooded over her at the same time.

"There are things you must learn today," her mother said. "I understand your feelings right now. Everything that you once knew has suddenly changed for you. Your life won't be the same after this. But you have been chosen."

"Mother," Fawn said, "you look like you are very young. Why is this? Where are we?"

"None of that matters now. I don't have much time to spend with you, so you must listen."

"But I don't understand what has happened to me. Am I dead?"

"Only for a short time. Do not worry."

Fawn's eyes widened. "How can I die for just a short time?"

"Do you know how the medicine people talk of visiting the spirit world?" her mother asked.

"Yes," Fawn answered, "but I have not studied the ways of medicine."

"Perhaps not, but the ancestors have willed it that you should learn some things that only medicine people know. Things that are Truth. Things that you will need to help you understand what is to come."

"What are you saying?" Fawn asked, still confused. "Are you having the same dream as I? Is that why you look so young? Are we truly in the spirit world?"

"I do not want you to wonder so much about what has happened and where you are that you won't listen," her mother said impatiently. "You must relax and act as you did when you followed me around as a child. Can you do that?"

"But I am not a child."

"I'm not asking you to *be* a child. I want you to listen *as if* you were a child."

"Yes, I will do that," Fawn said. "Where are we going?"

"I will do the talking," her mother said, holding out her hand. "You just do the listening."

Fawn turned and stared at her body for a moment, then followed her mother, hand in hand, across *Mako sica*. While she moved as if walking, she felt as if her feet were drifting just above the ground. The hills seemed cheerier, and though part of the country was still cloaked in winter, much of the landscape was deeply colored in shades of green and sage-gray, as though after a long spring rain. She wondered if she wasn't somehow seeing through time.

Fawn pulled away from her mother's grasp. "Let me see what it's like to travel on my own," she said.

As she began to wonder how the country looked just before the snows came, suddenly parts of the landscape took on the reds and yellows of fall. Amazed, Fawn began to wish that the entire area might be shrouded in springtime. Before her eyes, the landscape changed to green. Incredible! Maybe it should snow, she thought, and immediately large flakes began to fall.

It occurred to her then that she had the power to see what she wished to see, to change what she wished to change. Reality could be bent and shaped by mere thought. She felt herself move around the landscape, across great distances at a time. It took no effort to go anywhere she wanted, only the desire to be there.

Suddenly the adventure ended. Her mother had called her back by thought.

"Enough of the playing, Fawn," her mother cautioned her. "You cannot get too used to this, lest you have a hard time going back. Besides, we have little time."

"Why do I have to go back? Why can't I stay here with you?"

"That is not my decision to make."

Fawn suddenly realized that she had asked something for herself, something totally in her own behalf, without even considering her children. She wondered why she hadn't been concerned about their welfare. It hadn't even occurred to her. She remembered the way her emotions would take over when she was in the other world, and suddenly she felt very selfish.

"Don't concern yourself with what your life is like back there," her mother said, reading her thoughts. "It is more important now that you watch and listen very carefully. You can do what's best for your children when you do what's best for yourself."

Fawn felt her mother's hand in hers again. She became aware that they had left Lakota lands and were crossing plains and valleys she had never seen before, and a desert that held little visible life. Her mother brought them to a place at the base of a range of mountains. A great number of Indian people were gathered there, from numerous tribes, speaking in many languages. Everyone was excited. They stopped their talking when a well-built man raised his hands to the sky and led them in prayer.

"I can't hear him," Fawn told her mother.

"It is not time for you to hear him," her mother said, leading her up close to the man. "What I want you to do is to look at this man and tell me what you feel."

When the prayer was ended everyone sat down to listen to the man speak. Fawn looked around, noting that even though she and her mother were standing right beside him, no one noticed them.

"There are many thousands watching this man, yet none of them sees us," Fawn observed. "We truly are in the spirit world."

"What do you think of him?" her mother pressed. "What do you see in his heart?"

"He is a kind man who has seen a lot of injustice," Fawn

answered. "He wants to make things right for all Indian people, and he believes that he has found the way. I can't hear him, yet I know that is what he wants. How can I know this?"

"You are *feeling* him, not listening to him," her mother explained. "There is a difference. Always remember to feel while you listen, as you did as a child."

"I believe he wishes to have things good for Indian people everywhere," Fawn said. "Who is this man?"

"His name is Wovoka. He is Paiute. You will learn more of him in time, my daughter. Right now there are more lessons."

Again Fawn placed her hand within her mother's and they traveled back over the desert and the hills and valleys until they had returned to *Mako sica*. The cold moons had come once again; but instead of seeing a vast open filled only with snow, Fawn stood with her mother on a high table of land amidst an encampment of thousands of her people.

"Our people are headed into a very dark time," Fawn heard her mother say. "This has already begun, as you know, but the darkness will become even worse. You will see things here that I cannot explain. You must watch and listen carefully."

Fawn suddenly discovered herself standing beside her mother within a huge circle of dancers. The people were of all ages and both genders. They were singing, shuffling together through the snow in a clockwise motion, turning like a huge wheel spinning slowly through time.

Most of the warriors wore a garment that Fawn had never seen before, a type of long-tailed shirt covered with painted images. The animal medicine symbols stood out to her, specific in their size and design. Magpies and crows were the most common, along with eagles and turtles. Most of them were painted red, and they bore two other main symbols: Christian crosses, and stars and stripes from the American flag.

A large number of the women had the same designs painted on their dresses, which were usually made of muslin and embellished with beadwork designs. The women danced with the men, and some of them placed small children and newborn infants into the circle.

"The very young are so close to the spirit world," Fawn's mother said. "You know this, but you can see that there are images gathering around the children. See them?"

Fawn's breath caught in her throat. Faces were beginning to form in the air, faces of dead warriors from the past. One of them even looked like the man whom she had married and then lost not long after at Little Bighorn.

"How can that be?" Fawn asked her mother. "I hardly believe this is possible. It looks so real, as if it is happening now."

"It is real," her mother said. "They are dancing to bring back the old times. That is what they want to do."

Fawn wondered how this dance was connected with the Paiute man who had kept the attention of so many thousands back near the mountains. She realized that some of the people listening to the Paiute had worn the same kind of shirt she now saw on the dancers.

"Do you mean that the Paiute told them to dance, told them to bring back the happy times that you said you had lived as a child?"

"Those are the times the people want to make return," Fawn's mother said. "They want to see the *Wasichu* leave the plains and mountains. Then the buffalo will come back, along with all those who have crossed over. They want everyone to come back and live happily."

"How can they make that happen?" Fawn asked. "Just by dancing?"

"It is foretold," Fawn's mother said, "that the buffalo will some day return and that *Wankantanka* will give the land back to the Indian peoples. The man you saw near the mountains has heard this from the Ancestors. He has told everyone that these things will happen if they dance and treat one another well, even the white man. There can be no war. Fighting will not do it. Just goodness. Just dancing."

Fawn stared, watching the dancers in disbelief. There were so many passing in front of her that she realized she never saw the same one twice. And as they passed, she noticed a change that was gradually occurring. Their faces had once been happy and resolute, held in belief that what they were dancing for would come to pass. Now the faces were drawn with anger and bitterness. Many of them wore blood on their garments; their eyes were hollowed out, their spirits gone.

Fawn wondered what had happened to them, and what the blood meant. She saw many rifles and knives, and even the older weapons: bows and arrows, and lances. A large tree, covered with weapons and animal effigies, appeared in the middle of the circle. The dancers appeared to be driven by rage, not by faith or hope. They wanted to kill, not to be peaceful.

As more and more dancers filed past, Fawn became frightened. Many began to fall to the ground and moan, or to flop around as though something unseen might be pulling at them. Those who remained dancing seemed to be very tired, close to collapse. It was obvious that they had been dancing endlessly.

"I do not think the Paiute man wanted this," Fawn said, filled with despair. "How did it happen?"

Fawn's mother answered matter-of-factly, "You will have to live through this, my daughter. You will have to grow to understand how it came to pass."

Fawn became more frightened. She realized now that she knew a great many of these people, including the two children—her own—dancing on each side of Night Bird.

Fawn started for her children, but her mother held her back. "You can do nothing," she told Fawn. "You cannot change anything."

Fawn tried to pull away. "But I want to talk with them."

"They don't know you're here," her mother explained. "It is no different than when we were in the Paiute's camp. No one can see or hear you. It will do no good to go up to them. Leave them alone."

"I don't understand. My children are crying. I must help them!"

"It is not for you to understand. Look at the other children. Aren't many of them crying as well?"

Fawn stood beside her mother, her eyes filled with tears, her hands reaching out to Hawk and Little Star. Suddenly everything exploded and the dancers were flung into the air, turning and twisting like leaves in the wind. Fawn screamed.

"Listen to me," her mother said. "Get rid of your fear and hear me."

"What happened?" Fawn screamed, watching bodies drift skyward, higher and higher. "Where are my children?"

"Fawn, why aren't you listening to me?"

"Mother, I don't see my children! I'm afraid for them. I must look for them."

"Do you understand that you do not have the power to stop what you see, or to deliver your children from it?"

"Yes," Fawn sobbed. "But I don't want my children to die! I don't want that!"

"What is the main thing I told you as a child? What did I tell you to do above all else?"

"You told me to believe in *Wankantanka* and to trust in His ways."

"It is one thing to be frightened for your children," Fawn's mother told her. "It is another thing to look to *Wankantanka* with your fear and offer it up to Him. You must leave your children in His hands."

Tears streamed down Fawn's face. The bodies had floated far and away, up into the clouds. She turned to her mother. "I don't know what to do. I feel lost and confused."

"I have come to tell you that *Wankantanka* is the one to listen to. Always. No one else. If you will listen, He will speak to you. He will always be there for you. Do you remember this from when you were a child?"

"I learned from you as a child that it is foolish to try to change things that cannot be changed," Fawn said. "I also learned that there are some things that can be changed but that I must be wise and know which they are."

"What do you think about changing what you have seen? Do you think you can change what they want to do?"

"I think that is why I am so frightened," Fawn replied. "I believe I cannot change what I see, even where my children are concerned. I feel that I must leave it alone. I want to believe that everything will turn out well, but I also know that *Wankantanka* works in ways I cannot understand. Things will be bad, but I know I must keep my faith that everything happens as it does for a good reason. It is important that I learn from whatever comes to pass."

Fawn's mother smiled. "Your words are wise, my daughter. That is a good sign. That means you will be a good mother and a good woman, no matter what happens. It will be very hard, but you must remember what you just said to me. I know now that I have taught you well."

"I didn't see Catches Lance, though," Fawn said. "Was he among the dancers?"

"It is time for you to return," Fawn's mother said.

"Return to where? I don't want to leave you."

"You must go back. I know you will not forget me."

"But I want to ask you some more questions about what we just saw. What about Catches Lance?"

Fawn found herself standing on cold feet, looking up the hill through the darkness, still asking her mother about Catches Lance, tears still streaming down her face. She wiped them away, looking around at the same time for her mother. All she could see and feel was the darkness around her, laden with snow and cold. Nothing was the same as just a few moments before. Everything was as it had been when she rolled down the hill. She had somehow returned to the world she had known before her fall.

Fawn trembled. Her body ached from the tumble down the

slope and from the intense cold, now numbing her clear through. She knew better than to call for her mother, for now it seemed as if what had happened couldn't be real. It had to have been some form of dream. Yet the images were so strong, it seemed as though she had been awake.

Overhead, the dark shadow that had covered the land began to move on. Sunlight gradually returned, revealing the same mass of frozen wasteland she had first entered. Fawn wanted to rejoice, but she shivered instead. She wanted to welcome the sun back to life, but her own life now seemed at the edge of ending. Still dazed and confused from her experience with her mother, together with her physical suffering, Fawn began to wonder if she hadn't died and been sent to a place of continual winter.

She decided that she must at least get out of *Mako sica* to know whether she had crossed over or not. She tried to climb up the steep slope but found the soil too frozen for her to gain a foothold. Yet somehow she would have to regain the small flat just above and find her pony.

She tried repeatedly to climb the frozen slope, but slid back down each time. At last she sat down at the bottom and huddled in her thin blanket, tears once again staining her cheeks.

She looked to the sun for help. Far out, crossing in front of the round ball of gold, were the broad, gliding wings of an eagle. Suddenly her mood changed, and she rose to her feet. She watched the movements of the eagle as it drifted gradually lower in the sky.

The bird began to turn through the clear, frigid blue. It sailed seemingly without effort, its wings partially folded, descending slowly downward. Fawn dropped her blanket and stretched her arms up toward the sky. She called out to the eagle, now gliding almost overhead. It crossed over a short way out from her, its shadow slipping across her face.

She turned with the bird and watched it disappear over the hill. Her body suddenly felt comfortable again, much as it had when she had been with her mother. She picked up her blanket and smiled.

Just then her eye caught the movement of riders at the top of a ridge where the bird had flown, and her mouth fell open. She recognized the lead rider as Catches Lance. Behind him rode Tangled Hair, leading a packhorse laden with firewood.

Catches Lance had already spotted her and her pony. He and Tangled Hair began to negotiate a trail that would bring them down to the little spring. Fawn waved and shouted to them anyway, then breathed a sigh of relief as Catches Lance hurried his pony to the edge of the steep hill and slid off to lean over.

"How did you get way down there?" he called.

"I fell in the dark, when the sun went to bed during the day," Fawn replied. "How will you get me back up?"

Tangled Hair jumped from his pony and took a horsehair rope from his saddle. He threw one end down the slope to Fawn and tied the other end around the saddle horn. He told Fawn to hang on to the rope tightly and he would have his horse pull her up the hill.

Fawn knew Tangled Hair very well. He was the son of a black soldier and an Arapaho woman. His mother had later married a Minneconjou man, but neither she nor the man had been happy in the marriage and she had returned to her people. Not caring to move away from Catches Lance, his best friend, Tangled Hair had accepted an invitation to stay with Catches Lance and his mother and live among Kicking Bear's Minneconjou on Cherry Creek.

In the beginning, Fawn hadn't cared much for Tangled Hair. She didn't understand why her brother and mother had allowed him to impose on them. But gradually she relaxed her judgment and saw him more as an unsure young man than as a brash and pompous warrior. She knew that although he had gained honors as a Sioux warrior and had been accepted as a member of the Lakota people, he remained deeply insecure.

Fawn eventually realized, too, that Tangled Hair had stayed behind mainly to try to win her over rather than to be with her brother. This became obvious when he began playing a love flute for her. Night and day, the music would flow through the hills. He had wanted her badly. Though Fawn was older than he, she knew that fact would never deter him.

While she had always respected his persistence, she was certain that she would never have any desire for Tangled Hair. There were many young women who desired him, though, and it had always seemed odd to her that he had never chosen to divert his attentions to someone nearer his own age.

Fawn realized that Tangled Hair might persist forever in his quest for her and that helping her today would make him even bolder. Despite that, she was overjoyed to see him. She was glad to see both him and Catches Lance. Without their coming when they did, she would certainly have died at the bottom of the draw and joined her mother permanently in that land she had just left.

THREE

THE ECLIPSE passed and sunlight returned. The event left the train passengers excitedly conversing, giving them a topic of interest over the long stretches of white that lay between stops.

Father Thomas had turned to reading from a small bible. Next to him, Shining Horse reached into his buckskin coat and pulled out a copy of *The Complete Works of St. John of the Cross.*

Father Thomas noticed the title and his eyes widened. "Where in the world did you get that?" he asked.

Shining Horse turned from his reading. "I once considered becoming a priest, a Black Robe like you. But I decided it would be a waste of my life."

Father Thomas stared at him. "You once wanted to become a priest?"

"I wanted to do good among my people and help them learn the White Man's Road. I thought that by becoming a Black Robe, I could teach my people and be accepted by the

Wasichu. Now I know better. I would never have been accepted in the white man's world, and my people wouldn't have listened to me."

"You can't say that," Father Thomas said. "You should have gone ahead with your plans. You could have had the opportunity to do what I'm doing. Think of that, working with your own people. You could have opened a lot of doors for them."

Shining Horse shook his head. "You have to understand; those words work for white people, not for red people. You can want a lot of things as a red man, and can be qualified to have them, but you won't be blessed that way in the white man's world."

"I thought you said you were taken in by a white family. Weren't you shown the conveniences of modern life?"

"Conveniences don't make a person happy," Shining Horse pointed out. "Even though the family treated me well and tried to make me feel welcome, I could never become a part of that kind of life. Even if I had wanted to, I wouldn't have been given a chance. I will always think of that family, and of how much they wanted me to be like them. But it just wasn't possible."

Father Thomas thought for a moment. "If you were given all those opportunities, how could you not take advantage of them?"

Shining Horse said, "I had all I wanted in the open spaces where I lived. I didn't see moving to a foreign place as an opportunity. It was closer to a bad dream."

"What did their friends and neighbors think of you?"

"At first I was something of a novelty. Their name was Markson, and they were pleased to introduce me around. Finally the Marksons realized that they were being laughed at. After a while, the interest in me dwindled, and people couldn't understand why the Marksons didn't just get rid of me."

"That they didn't send you away speaks well of them," Father Thomas commented.

"I'll agree with that," Shining Horse said. "I've often thought that Mr. Markson had a great deal of character. He was a lawyer, and his business suffered, but he told me I could stay as long as I wished, that he would even adopt me. He and his wife are brave people. So you can see, I don't hate the white man, just his ways."

Father Thomas took a deep breath. "I know the road is hard, no matter the color of the skin. Once I have established the mission, I plan to help your people grow and become productive members of society."

"They already *are* productive members of society," Shining Horse said impatiently. "I don't think you've been listening. It just happens to be the wrong society. Nothing is going to stop this change from coming over my people. It will be like some kind of terrible storm that will tear their lodges from their resting places on the Earth Mother and scatter the people to the Sacred Winds, which have now turned against them."

"You really make it sound bad," Father Thomas said. "How can it be so bleak?"

"Make up your own mind when you get there."

"Instead of the end, maybe you can see it as a new opportunity for your people," Father Thomas suggested. "New and better homes. An easier life-style than what was afforded by just living off the land."

Out of respect, Shining Horse held back a cynical smile. "Where are my people going to get these new houses and this easier life-style?"

"They'll have to learn to produce things for themselves, just like the farmers do who are moving West. They can sell crops for money and buy the things they need."

Shining Horse shook his head. "My people have never been farmers. They don't know how to farm, and they don't want to learn."

"I don't understand."

"My people feel that it is a grave sin to tear into the Earth

Mother with a plow and to churn the grasses upside down. You know the word—sacrilege."

"You can't feed a lot of people unless you use the land in some way," Father Thomas argued.

"My people were always fed by the land," Shining Horse pointed out. "We didn't have to try to change everything to suit ourselves. We were given what we needed, without trying to constantly make everything over. We had a fine life harvesting what grows naturally."

Shining Horse pointed out the window, past Father Thomas and toward a series of rolling hills. Father Thomas looked out.

"Before I could walk, my father placed me on a pony. It was just after daybreak, and my father led the pony to the top of a hill, such as one of those. For the first time, I could see out over a great distance. I was thrilled. I could see clear to where the sun was coming up, and there were buffalo scattered all over, in a large herd. My father told me to remember what I saw, for I would not see many sights like that after I grew up. We stayed there most of the morning and I didn't want to leave. But finally we had to go, and he wept all the way back down the hill to the village."

"It sounds to me like your father was a loving and kind man," Father Thomas said.

"He still is," Shining Horse said. "His name is Sitting Bull. Did you ever hear of him?"

Father Thomas's eyes widened. "Yes, I've heard of him. Wasn't it he who killed Custer at the Little Bighorn?"

Shining Horse hid a smile. "That's what the newspapers printed."

"I take it the story was not accurate."

"I seldom find anything accurate in newsprint."

"Perhaps the papers were misinformed," Father Thomas said.

"Yes, they were. But I believe they could have learned the

truth had they been willing to seek it. Printing lies sells papers."

"You have to believe they're doing the best they can with what they've got," Father Thomas said. "The truth can be very elusive at times."

"Not really," Shining Horse disagreed. "It's there for everybody to see if they want to look for it. But you won't find it in the newspapers, because truth is hard to sell."

Father Thomas turned and stared out the window for a time, looking across endless miles of snowbound plains. Barren and cold, the territory as far as the eye could see seemed inhospitable to all forms of life. Still, isolated clusters of homesteads dotted the white landscape, thin plumes of smoke rising out of stone chimneys into the cold.

Up the line, he would disembark for a period of time at Fort Kearney. There he would meet with other priests who were being sent to missions in the West. They were all to be briefed on what to expect and given a tour of the fort in order to gain a feel of the military and the structure of the reservation system. Father Thomas felt certain that he would be learning it from one side only.

He wondered as he mused how he could possibly have found someone like Shining Horse, the first real Sioux Indian he had ever met, a man more educated than many whites he knew. How could he use the information he was gathering from this man in his quest to bring the word of God to those who hadn't had Shining Horse's opportunity? The trip had merely begun and already the surprises were many.

Father Thomas turned from the window. Shining Horse was sitting peacefully, staring ahead of him.

"What did your father think of your going East to study?" Father Thomas asked.

"He didn't have any more choice in the matter than I," Shining Horse said. "I believe he thought I should have fought harder against it, though."

"Will I be serving your father?"

"My father is at Standing Rock, not on Cheyenne River," Shining Horse said. "Don't go to talk to him. Don't waste your time. He hates the *Wasichu*."

"Does he know what forgiveness is all about?"

Shining Horse studied the priest. "You wouldn't understand. You have never had to live through the grief of losing a wife and children to Bluecoat soldiers. My father has enough anger in him to fill twenty men. And you think *you're* going to rid him of it?"

"What are you going to do when you get back among your people?" Father Thomas asked.

"I am going to be a Lakota warrior once again. I am going to take the money I was given by the Marksons and I am going to buy a horse. Then I am going to use the rest of the money for food and supplies. I will go back to my father with something to show for my time gone besides knowing the *Wasichu* tongue."

"You once wanted to be a priest," Father Thomas said. "Do you still feel that you would like to serve God?"

"I will serve God in my own way."

"No, I mean, will you help me? Will you teach me your ways, so I can help your people?"

"It's been a long time since I've seen my father," Shining Horse said, "but I'm certain that he would never divert from the old ways."

"Maybe he would if he were to hear you speak," Father Thomas suggested. "You have learned a lot about the white culture. Take what's good in it and teach it to your people."

"I would have a hard time finding enough to teach that is good," Shining Horse said. "Can you tell me what is good?"

"We all have to look to God for what is good," Father Thomas said after some thought. "We have to expect Him to bless us."

"And that brings us right back to where we started," Shining Horse said. "My people are wondering why they haven't been blessed lately. What do you want me to tell them? What do *you* expect to tell them?"

Father Thomas pointed to the book in Shining Horse's hand. "What have you learned from that? Doesn't that have some answers for you?"

"This book is interesting," Shining Horse said, "but it tells me nothing more than what my father told me when I was a child. He said to go out into the hills and listen. Feel the wind and learn from the changes in the sky. Watch the birds and wonder at the miracle of the seasons. He said to know and learn from every living thing—trees, flowers, everything—for *Wankantanka* speaks through even the rocks.

"This man, St. John, has listened, and he has heard and felt many things. But I don't believe anyone told him to speak with everything he saw. The white culture does not revere the Earth Mother the way my people do. The white man does not know how to combine the messages from both Earth Mother and Father Sky. I can tell you that there are many among my people who are greater than this man."

Father Thomas closed his bible and squeezed it tightly between his fingers, staring hard at Shining Horse, who stared back, unblinking. Finally the priest looked out the window and took a deep breath. When he turned back to Shining Horse, his voice was calculated as he said, "If you have any men among your people greater than St. John of the Cross, I would like to meet them."

"You will," Shining Horse said. "And when you do, I am certain you will feel their spiritual power. You will know what I am saying."

Father Thomas took another deep breath. "Will you introduce me to them?"

"Do you want to meet them for who they are, or do you want to try to change them to your way of thinking?" Shining Horse asked.

"If they are as strong spiritually as you say they are, they will surely see that I bring them the word of God."

"Then you certainly don't need me," Shining Horse said. "If you are as strong as you believe you are, then they will prepare a feast for you and listen to you day and night without interruption. They will ask you to lead them and to give them your blessing. As for me, I've seen both sides very clearly. I know the ways the *Wasichu* use their god to control their own people. That is why I am returning to these lands. As bad as the conditions are, at least my heart will be at peace again."

"It seems as though I can't convert you," Father Thomas said, "even though you seem to know almost as much about my religion as I do. You aren't about to give me a chance to show you who I really am, are you?"

"I know who you really are," Shining Horse said. "I do not believe that your heart is bad, just blind."

"You don't think I can see?" Father Thomas asked, taken aback again. "You don't think I know the word of God?"

"I believe that you have learned the word of God from someone else," Shining Horse replied. "You have been taught to listen to the words of others in order to know what is right. That is not the way. Among our people, we learn early that *Wankantanka* speaks to each of us in the manner He wishes to have us hear Him. We are not obliged to obey what another thinks is best for us. How can another know what is best for you?"

Father Thomas again became angry. "What makes you think you know how I have learned?"

"You have been made to listen to Black Robes high in authority and to read from the books they give you. They tell you what to take as truth even though you do not always believe them. Is that not right?"

Father Thomas was speechless.

"I told you, I once tried to become a Black Robe," Shining Horse said. "I wanted to bring the story of the Bleeding Chief, Jesus Christ, to my people. I wasn't allowed. But now I am glad, for I wouldn't have done things the way you do. I guess they knew that. And I also know that if you want to make friends among my people, you will have to do things differently."

"You make it sound impossible," Father Thomas said. "But there are already missions established at Pine Ridge and on the Rosebud. You can't be right about all of your people. Some of them must want to change."

"My people have been driven to change," Shining Horse pointed out. "It is not of their choosing. All they want now is to be left alone and to have someone keep the promises that were made to them."

"I do not intend to lie to anyone," Father Thomas said.

"I did not say that you would," Shining Horse said. "But for as long as the *Wasichu* has been in our lands, my people have been lied to. How will that change? How are you going to stop the government in Washington from doing just as it wants? How are you going to make my people believe that you are someone special who has come to help them? Nothing will change with your coming."

"Why do you keep speaking about earthly matters?" Father Thomas asked. "I told you before, and you know it well, that I am on a spiritual journey."

Shining Horse smiled. "Are you going to tell them you're making this journey for you, or for them?"

"For them, of course."

"Then listen to me." Shining Horse was now utterly serious. "You'd better consider a very important point before you meet my people. Jesus Christ is who you will speak to them of, and my people all know for certain that this man was very brave. What they will want to know is why he died the way he did, why your own people killed the most important man in their religion and then made him a hero. Can you answer that?"

"Can't you see?" Father Thomas asked. "Christ died so that all men can be free of sin."

"I already told you, my people have no concept of sin, not

as you Black Robes teach it. I asked if you could explain why Christ died so they can understand."

After some thought, Father Thomas said, "I don't know.

"Then you'd better turn around and go back where you came from," Shining Horse advised. "Up to now, all that my people have heard from the Black Robes is how sinful they are. Unless you have something different to say and can help them end their misery at the hands of the government agents, you will do no good. You will only make matters worse."

"I still want you to help me," Father Thomas said. "I won't give up, you know."

Shining Horse smiled warmly. "Yes, you are a fighter." He held up the book on St. John of the Cross. "Have you read this?"

"I've been aware of it for some time," Father Thomas said. "I was assigned part of it to read in the seminary. But I've never had a chance to read it thoroughly."

Shining Horse placed the book in the priest's hands. "I've read it twice. I keep it only because I've learned a lot of the English language from it. You read it. If you tell my people that there are those among the *Wasichu* who journey into the hills to listen, you will have to say no more. Most of your battle will be won."

The train slowed, preparing for the stop at Fort Kearney. Father Thomas thanked Shining Horse for the book. "I wish I didn't have to depart," he said. "I would like more time with you. I am going to have to look you up when I finish this book."

"Don't worry about that," Shining Horse said. "Keep it."

The train eased to a stop. Outside in the snow, people waiting for the train wished one another a happy new year.

"It has been a great pleasure meeting you and talking with you," Father Thomas told Shining Horse. "In fact, it has been nothing short of a blessing from God." He held the book up. "Until we meet again."

* * *

Fawn looked up into the sky, feeling a lightness about her once again. Catches Lance shouted down to her, and she reached for the end of the rope that Tangled Hair had thrown down the slope.

"You will owe me for this," Tangled Hair called down to her. He smiled. "Maybe a new pair of moccasins."

Fawn took the rope and held it tightly, trying to walk along the slope as Tangled Hair's pony began hauling her up the hill. The snowy ascent proved too slippery for traction, and Fawn fell, slamming her side into the frozen ground. She thought it odd that the blow did not stun her more than it did, or cause her pain.

She held fast to the rope, drifting off again into a dream. This time she saw a warrior whom she did not know standing before a large crowd of her people and reading the words from a letter. The warrior was tall and strong and sure of himself, and she felt good at seeing him. But she had no idea of who he might be.

This warrior seemed to know her, and he watched her carefully as he read. She could not hear him, though. As it had been when she was with her mother, she could see only the reactions of the people, all of whom listened intently, cheering at his words from time to time.

It bothered her that no sound came to her. Only vision, and . . . yes, feeling. Feeling was the most important facet of the entire experience. She remembered her mother's words and began to feel, realizing that what Tangled Hair was reading made everyone around him sit up with new animation in their faces. Those who were hungry smiled, those who were sick raised their arms for joy. Whatever Tangled Hair was reading, it made the entire village listen closely.

The pony finished dragging Fawn to the top of the slope, and she discovered herself lying on her back, staring up at Tangled Hair and her brother, both of whom studied her with great concern.

"I told you not to go to Pine Ridge alone," Catches Lance scolded, rubbing her feet with his hands. "Now what if you can't walk again?"

"I can walk," she insisted. "Let me up."

"You just stay down," Catches Lance ordered. "We will build a fire and eat something. You must wait to get your strength back."

"But I feel good, and I feel warm."

"She must be freezing to death," Tangled Hair told Catches Lance with concern. "They say you feel warm when you are close to death from the cold."

"I am nowhere near death," Fawn argued. "I tell you both, I feel very good."

Catches Lance reached down into the cloth around Fawn's feet, and his face registered confusion. He touched her legs and hands, and reached up to feel her face.

"Your body should be like ice, but you feel far warmer than I do." He turned to Tangled Hair, who looked on with interest.

"Did you meet *Wankantanka*?" Tangled Hair asked. "That would be the only thing that would keep you from becoming cold on a day like this."

Fawn did not know how to answer. Still dazed from her experience, she looked up at Tangled Hair. "Maybe," she said. "I don't know, but maybe that is what happened."

"I do not know what has happened," Catches Lance said, "but you do not seem like the same sister who left Cheyenne River. In fact, you do not seem like anyone I know. Maybe it is hunger. Let's see what you are like after you have eaten."

Fawn looked into her brother's face. His concern was deep. She didn't know what to tell him, for she couldn't begin to understand herself what had taken place. Maybe he was right; maybe her hunger had caused all of this. She would eat, and then she would see if her world became the same once again.

FOUR

FAWN SAT up and watched while Catches Lance selected a spot and scraped snow from the ground. Tangled Hair brought firewood from the packhorse and soon there was a warm blaze going. Fawn didn't feel like getting close to the fire. Her senses seemed more alert than she could ever remember, and her body felt the most comfortable it had been in many months.

The three of them shared the hindquarters of a coyote that Catches Lance had shot earlier in the day. The meat was stringy, but after it was heated over the fire, Fawn thought it as good as anything she had tasted in a long time.

Although the meal afforded each of them only a few bites, it would give them enough strength to reach Pine Ridge. Once there, they would share the remainder of the coyote with whoever was most in need of food.

Fawn began to contemplate her experience, which seemed to her now something from the distant past. She had had many dreams that seemed very real, but none of them had been anything like this. Possibly, as Tangled Hair had suggested, she had met *Wankantanka*. But likely that hadn't happened. No one ever came back to life in this world after a meeting with Him.

She wanted to believe that her experience had been an unusual dream, that possibly she had merely recalled some occasion she had shared with her mother as a small child. She could not remember any dreams she had had where children had appeared, though. She couldn't answer the many questions that now troubled her regarding her children and their dancing in the circle. Up to that time, the experience had been a cheerful one. But when the visions of the dance had come, her feelings had turned to fear and concern.

This made her realize that she had been with her mother in a state much stronger than that of a normal dream. As much as she wanted to downplay the event, Fawn realized that something very unusual had happened to her during the darkening of the sun. She had traveled somewhere with her mother to see something that would be of great importance to her in the near future. She couldn't understand why her mother had chosen such a way to show her these things. Why couldn't her mother just tell them to her when she reached Pine Ridge?

Other questions concerned her, including the length of time she had been with her mother. It seemed they had traveled far and had seen much over a period of many moons. But that wasn't possible. Fawn realized, in listening to her brother and Tangled Hair, that the length of time the sun had been darkened couldn't have been that long. To hear them discussing it, Fawn believed it hadn't lasted even as long as the time since they had seen her from the top of the hill and had come down to save her.

This had to be true, she reasoned, or she would certainly have frozen to death. Very long in this cold and a person would die quickly. She couldn't understand why her body wasn't close to death anyway. In reality, exposure for just a short period of time without moving should have slowed her blood to barely flowing at all. Yet her body functioned perfectly. She was as comfortable as she had ever been in her life.

"How do you feel now?" Catches Lance asked her. "You are lucky to be alive. I hope you don't want to ever do something like this again."

"I did not want to leave for Pine Ridge without you," Fawn said. "But what choice did I have? You told me you weren't coming."

"It doesn't matter," Catches Lance said. "I don't think any of it matters now. The sun died and brought darkness to our lands. Though the light came back, we have lost our lives."

"I am not so certain," Fawn argued. "After the daylight returned, I saw an eagle. It flew over you and Tangled Hair, toward the East. That is where new light comes from. I don't believe that we all have to die."

"We might as well," Catches Lance argued, tossing aside a piece of coyote bone. "We have nothing to eat, and now we must kill the Sacred Dog to live. *Wankantanka* does not favor us."

"Did you not hear me?" Fawn asked her brother. "I told you that I saw an eagle. It is a good omen." She looked to Tangled Hair, who merely shrugged.

Fawn studied her brother. She wondered if he had decided to go down to the wedding from a sense of obligation rather than from really wanting to see their mother. "Are you angry at me, Catches Lance?" she asked. "Or do you wish our mother would give up the idea of taking the White Man's Road?"

"What does it matter now?" he asked. "Soon there will be no one left to say they were born a Lakota."

"That will not happen," Fawn said. "Do not say things like that."

"What is to keep that from happening?" Catches Lance asked. "There is no food. We are told to grow food, but the land here is barren. We couldn't make anything grow if we wished to. And there are never enough provisions."

"We will find a way," Fawn said. "Our people have always found a way to survive."

"It is time we got onto our ponies," Tangled Hair said, "or we may not survive. The true darkness will soon be upon us, and we have used up most of our wood. The cold will sneak through our clothing and into our bones. We must reach Pine Ridge or we will all be food for the wolves before the sun comes again."

Tangled Hair helped Fawn catch her pony while Catches Lance gathered scraps of sage wood and whatever else he could find to help replenish what they had used. It would be late before they reached Pine Ridge, and they would likely need to stop once to warm up.

Tangled Hair and Catches Lance watered their ponies at the spring while Fawn stared out over the Badlands. Her life and the lives of those around her seemed to be changing fast, yet she had no anxiety. Instead, the deep warmth she had felt right after the experience with her mother lingered. It filled her with hope.

Catches Lance led her pony to her. "What are you smiling about?" he asked angrily. "We are risking our lives to see our mother turn to the *Wasichu* god and you are happy about it."

Fawn turned to him. "Happy? I don't think you understand. I wasn't happy."

"I saw you smiling," Catches Lance argued.

"I don't think it was happiness I was feeling," Fawn told him. "Possibly it was a form of contentment I haven't ever felt before. It is something that words cannot describe."

"Has the cold frozen your brain?"

"No. I told you, I saw an eagle."

"You act like you want to fly away with the eagle, to go somewhere you can't reach," Catches Lance observed. "It is like you were at a place and you want to go back to it but you cannot. Are you thinking of spring?"

Fawn climbed onto Jumper. "Perhaps that is it," she replied. "Maybe that is the best way to describe it."

She noticed Catches Lance staring at her as if he didn't know her any longer. She now realized how much different she must seem to him. The forceful, impatient sister he had always known had suddenly become relaxed and mild-mannered. She didn't know what to tell him; it wasn't something that could easily be put into words. She just realized that, after today, Catches Lance wouldn't know her in the same way ever again.

She knew that Tangled Hair also wondered about her. He had thought of her as someone whom he might be able to persuade to love him. Now he was worried about her. He certainly sensed everything that Catches Lance did, and he couldn't understand it, either. They would all ride the rest of the way to Pine Ridge together, each wondering what the others were thinking.

A sudden breeze caused Fawn to turn her head. The breeze settled just as suddenly, and a small white feather with black bars drifted down in front of her face. It settled into her pony's mane. She picked up the feather. She realized that it had come from the wing of a snowy owl. The wing feathers were the smallest of feathers, the ones that allowed the bird to fly silently. Her people called them breath feathers.

Fawn looked around; no owl was in sight. Catches Lance and Tangled Hair had already started the journey again. She let the feather go into the breeze.

As she settled her pony into line behind Tangled Hair, she felt renewed in a sense, yet saddened at the same time. It confused her deeply. Something had taken place that had changed her drastically from the woman who had left the camp on Cherry Creek to be with her mother. She was not even the same Fawn-That-Goes-Dancing who had broken ice for her horse just a short time ago, a time that now seemed distant, behind the passing of many, many winters.

*   *   *

The midmorning sun could not penetrate the cold that had settled over the land. Fawn rode into the Pine Ridge Agency with Catches Lance and Tangled Hair to the camps of some four thousand Oglalas scattered along the bottom. Already a huge line had formed behind a number of wagons loaded with beans, flour, coffee, hardtack, and other foods. Rations day had brought everyone out into the snow to gain some measure of provision against the harsh weather.

At the front of the line, the agent began the distribution. Fawn knew the routine well, for the same method was used at the Cheyenne River Agency. The older men, each the head of a household, were called in alphabetical order to receive the rations for their families. Gone was the importance of structural order practiced in the old days, where the men of distinction were at the forefront of activities. Now the agents decided who was important among the people.

To survive, the people were forced to take food in any way it was given to them. Though the Lakota women had always taken care of the food chores, the older men had learned to carry the rations back to the dwellings, where the women took over. For a time, the older men had refused to partake in rations day, but they soon saw that if they did not conform to what was expected, they would lose their allotments.

Fawn scanned the massive gathering for her mother. It was hopeless. After a brief discussion, she went toward the front of the line, while Catches Lance and Tangled Hair rode their ponies along the stream of cold and hungry Oglalas, their backs turned to the sharp wind.

Fawn dismounted and waited near the front of the line. Aboard the wagons, laborers tossed rations down into a pile. One of the workers, dressed in a worn buffalo-hide coat, tossed a bag of beans that split open upon impact with the ground. He laughed and spit a stream of tobacco juice into the scattered beans.

One of the other workers, a mixed blood, jumped him, and

the two fought their way down off the end of the wagon, ripping a sack of flour in the process. The foreman yelled for them to break it up and dismissed the mixed-blood worker on the spot. The laborer in the buffalo coat smirked and spat again, staining the flour that was spilling from the back of the wagon into the snow.

Fawn still could not find her mother. Finally she asked a woman near her own age if she knew a man named Sees-the-Bull-Rolling and a woman named Goes-to-River.

"Was this woman to be made a member of the Black Robe religion tomorrow?" the woman asked.

"Yes, that is right," Fawn said. "Do you know her?"

"I am a Brulé from over on the Rosebud," the woman said. "I arrived yesterday with my mother and others of my people. My mother is to be in the same ceremony."

"I have come down from Cherry Creek," Fawn said. "My mother should be here."

The Brulé woman hesitated. Fawn knew that something was wrong. She could feel it; she could see it in the woman's eyes.

A sudden gust of wind made both women duck their heads. When Fawn looked up, she saw a small white feather with black bars floating in the air between them. The Brulé woman saw it also and quickly looked down as it drifted past them and settled in the snow.

"Do you know where my mother is now?" Fawn asked, her voice filled with urgency. It was another breath feather from a snowy owl.

The Brulé woman kept her head down. "I am sorry to be the one who must tell you this," she said. "Your mother died of the coughing sickness. They say she crossed over just as the sun turned dark."

Fawn stumbled back in shock. "What? She has died?"

"I am sorry," the Brulé woman said again. "I know Sees-the-Bull-Rolling is keeping her somewhere. No one has told the agent, so that the Black Robes will not know. Everyone knew you would want to leave her body open to the sky, in the old way."

Dazed, Fawn turned away from the woman and struggled to mount her pony. Catches Lance and Tangled Hair rode up from the back of the line. From the look on Catches Lance's face, Fawn knew he had received the same news.

"Have you heard?" he asked her.

Fawn nodded, tears streaming down her face. "Did you learn where Sees-the-Bull-Rolling is keeping her?"

"Yes," Catches Lance said. His voice was choked. "We will go there."

They found Sees-the-Bull-Rolling sitting at the edge of the creek, staring out across the plains to where a bank of heavy white clouds had gathered.

"Where is my mother?" Fawn asked, jumping down from her pony.

Sees-the-Bull-Rolling pointed into a heavy stand of wild rose and snowberry. "She is wrapped in a blanket."

Fawn hurried into the brush and exposed her mother's face. She wailed and hugged her mother, while Catches Lance and Tangled Hair looked on.

Sees-the-Bull-Rolling pointed to the north. "See, the storm has come to take her," he said. "She wants to be with the wind, even if it is cold."

"She did not wish to turn to the *Wasichu* god," Fawn said bitterly. "She chose death instead."

"Fawn, that is not fair," Catches Lance said. "It was our mother's decision to change. You cannot blame Sees-the-Bull-Rolling."

Fawn covered her mother's face with the blanket and stood up. She took a deep breath and looked toward the north.

"I just wanted to talk to her, to understand what I have been feeling about her. That's all."

"She is in a better place now," Sees-the-Bull-Rolling said. "A place where things are like they used to be. She was a good woman, and that is why *Wankantanka* has taken her to be with Him."

Fawn turned to Catches Lance. "I see no reason for us to remain here any longer. I wish to take our mother to a place where she will rest in peace, before the agent discovers that she has died."

"A storm is coming," Catches Lance said. "We have to wait."

"Maybe you have to wait," Fawn said, "but I do not have to, and neither does our mother. She will not fall into the hands of the Black Robes."

That evening, under cover of darkness and heavy snowfall, Fawn wiped tears from her cheeks and checked one last time to be certain that her mother's body was secured tightly to the travois. Catches Lance and Tangled Hair were on their ponies, waiting.

Sees-the-Bull-Rolling did not have the strength to accompany them. His days as a warrior were over. He himself now looked toward the end, when he would be reunited with Goes-to-River on the Other Side.

Sees-the-Bull-Rolling had given Fawn a knife to use in cutting off her hair and in making gashes in her lower legs. She would perform her act of mourning along the trail when they were safely away from Pine Ridge. Fawn knew very well that she and her brother could both get themselves in trouble if they were caught mourning in the old way. Both the Episcopal and Catholic missionaries forbade the practice, and the agents strictly enforced their wishes.

Fawn's behavior in stealing off with her mother was not unusual. Often members of a family would sneak the body away to be honored in the manner they saw fit. Placing the body in a tree or on a scaffold was certainly taking a great risk, for if the agent or any of the missionaries happened to find it, they would remove it and place it in the ground.

Neither Fawn nor Catches Lance worried about any of the *Wasichu* finding their mother. They were going into *Mako sica* once again, far enough out and off the main trail that only a wanderer would find the body. There were few wanderers among the *Wasichu,* for they found little comfort off by themselves.

Fawn mounted her pony. Sees-the-Bull-Rolling gave Goes-to-River a last kiss on the forehead before covering her face against the snow. Catches Lance and Tangled Hair made sure the fresh firewood they had been given was well secured on the packhorses for the ride north. Sees-the-Bull-Rolling wished them well and stood back while they rode off into the snow and darkness.

They journeyed throughout the night, following a trail down Wounded Knee Creek. They reached the mouth of the creek, where it fed into Big White River, and built a fire. As the sun rose, the wind stopped and the snow fell straight down, huge flakes that landed soft against the face. The temperature had risen substantially. The three placed the travois in the branches of a large cottonwood at the mouth of the creek.

While singing a mourning song, Fawn took the knife Sees-the-Bull-Rolling had given her and hacked at her hair. Dark handfuls scattered in the snow at her feet and were soon mixed with blood as she placed the blade against the calves of her legs and carved downward. Catches Lance took out his own knife and brushed snow from the face of a flat rock. He placed the palm of his hand down and in a single, quick stroke, severed the last joint from the little finger on his left hand.

Fawn felt uneasy at leaving her mother's body behind. She looked back often as they rode up out of the bottom toward the main trail that would lead north to Cheyenne River. Though it remained in the recesses of her mind, she did not dwell on the unusual dream she had had involving her mother. She decided that her mother had come to her immediately after passing to say good-bye. There was nothing unusual in that. Many talked of seeing the spirits of loved ones who were dying.

Still, she could not dislodge the feelings she had had during the experience. The impression of her mother as a young woman remained very clear. Traveling with her and seeing the changes of season had brought her great warmth. The rest of the experience now seemed hazy, as if it might not have happened.

The scenes she had witnessed near the end of her experience had been too vivid for an ordinary dream, though, and the people too real. Seeing her children and Night Bird during the strange dance brought back strong feelings. She wondered if thinking about it hard enough might not take her back into the dream. She didn't want that to happen ever again.

Despite what she wanted to believe, Fawn realized that her experience with her mother had been meant to prepare her for something. She felt this strongly as she watched the sun move higher into the winter sky. She couldn't say how soon this would happen, but it couldn't be far off. Many questions surfaced in her mind, questions that could be answered only by her mother. All she could do was wait.

FIVE

SHINING HORSE discovered Rapid City to be much more than he had imagined. After spending but a few hours in town, there was little doubt in his mind that the *Wasichu* had settled for good. Rapid City was now a hub of expansion. There were more people arriving to look for opportunity than there was housing available.

The permanence of stone and brick had replaced the tents and pine logs of the gold rush. Instead of miners and frontier transients, farmers and ranchers frequented newly established lumber and feed mills. Doctors and lawyers had placed signs in prominent places. There was even a college. The world of the *Wasichu* had settled fully and permanently within the Black Hills.

When Shining Horse had left for Carlisle, there had still been hope among some factions of the Lakota that the Black Hills would some day come back to the people. But most agreed that with the killing of Long Hair Custer and his Bluecoats at the Greasy Grass, more angry soldiers would simply come to take the place of the fallen. The Lakota people could only see more bloodshed ahead.

Then the Oglala chief, Red Cloud, had signed a treaty, believing he had guaranteed peace between the Oglalas and the whites. The treaty had been interpreted by the government to mean that the Sioux nation had given up its sacred hills. This angered the Minneconjou and the Unkpapas greatly. Not one from either of their tribal divisions had been consulted, yet they had lost the home of their ancestors. Now bad feelings ran deep.

Shining Horse expected to be treated much the same in Rapid City as he had been on the train. After Father Thomas had disembarked, the passengers had glared at him openly. Many asked the conductor to remove him. A few had even asked him where he had stolen the clothes he was wearing.

Though other Indians had come and gone, Shining Horse had been the object of particular derision. The white passengers were not comfortable at seeing him dressed up, and certainly not with braids hanging down his back. In their minds he was an Indian, with no business acting civilized.

Where he could have become angry, Shining Horse only laughed to himself. These people insisted that Indians become like them, but not too much like them. Indians must forget what they had learned from their grandparents and take on all the *Wasichu* values presented to them, and do it immediately. But they certainly shouldn't rise to anywhere near the lowest class of *Wasichu*. Any Indian who managed to somehow adapt to the new culture, and adapt well, was deemed arrogant and precocious.

Shining Horse realized it would have been no different had he taken the northern line through Bismarck. It certainly would have been the shortest link to Fort Yates and Standing Rock. But he wanted to learn what had taken place in the area since his childhood, and for that reason he had chosen the route through Nebraska and the connection north into the Black Hills. He wanted to be able to tell his people just how many of the *Wasichu* had come into the country and what their plans might be.

During the remainder of his train ride, Shining Horse had thought often about Father Thomas. Maybe he shouldn't have told him he had once wanted to become a Black Robe. It had been a dirty trick. But he had wanted to see Father Thomas's reaction. Certainly the priest hadn't scoffed at the idea, and it had been pleasing to hear a *Wasichu* encourage him to work hard for his dreams. If it were only that easy.

No question, the priest had a strong heart and a strong mind to match. If he could use them together, Shining Horse thought, he would make many friends among the Lakota.

Shining Horse hoped that Father Thomas had gained some idea of the difficulties that lay ahead for him. Had the priest been with him now, he would certainly see first-hand the problems the Lakota people faced.

As he walked the downtown area of Rapid City, Shining Horse was well aware of the eyes that followed his every movement. Most citizens crossed the street to avoid him. Despite his neat appearance, he was sorely out of place. He belonged among the others, across the tracks, eking survival out of dumps at the edge of the city.

Though he hadn't discussed it with Father Thomas, Shining Horse had been given a good sum of money by the family he had lived with in the East. That didn't matter to the businesses in Rapid City. Indians were not allowed to enter shops and stores. Those who had something to trade for liquor or goods could go to the back door.

After trying unsuccessfully to purchase a meal or register at a hotel, Shining Horse bought a thick blanket at a back door and spent the night in a cave a few miles above town. The next morning he returned.

In the middle of town, Shining Horse watched a large group of citizens gather at the foot of a platform. The platform was trimmed in red, white and blue, and an American flag whipped in the morning breeze. A group of dignitaries took their places behind a table on the platform; the crowd yelled and clapped. The mayor of the city stood up and raised his hand for silence.

"It is indeed a pleasure to see you all here today," he said. "As you know, we are petitioning to become the fortieth state in the Union." A huge cheer arose. "It is wonderful, isn't it?"

Shining Horse listened while the mayor talked about the growth of the city and the prosperous years ahead. Shining Horse was preparing to leave when he heard mention of a land commission, which was to be discussed by another dignitary. He decided to wait, but he was approached by three large men. Each carried a heavy revolver, and the smallest also held a Springfield rifle. The biggest one wore a thick beard, while the other two were stubbled by a few days' growth. The smallest of the three was badly pockmarked. Shining Horse guessed that he had survived smallpox.

"What do you think you're doing, standing there?" the biggest one asked.

"He can't speak English," the little one said. He raised his hand clumsily in the signal to leave, to go away.

"You should learn sign better than that if you want to talk with your hands," Shining Horse suggested.

The three were taken aback by Shining Horse's fluent English. He knew better than to challenge them any further, but he wanted information.

"The mayor said someone would speak about a land commission," Shining Horse said. "Do you men know anything about it?"

All three smirked. The big one answered, "You can go back and tell your Injun friends to get ready for a land cut. You got too much as it is, and you ain't doing nothing with it."

"Who is heading up the commission?" Shining Horse asked.

"Gen'l Crook," the big one answered. "You know who he is?"

"George Crook?" Shining Horse asked.

"That's the one," the big man replied. "I suggest you go and tell your stinkin' friends all about it. Now!"

Shining Horse walked away. The little one started to follow, and Shining Horse turned to meet him.

"Wasn't you one of those who killed Custer?" the little one asked.

"I wasn't old enough then to kill Custer," Shining Horse told him, "or I would have."

The little one looked startled. The big one called to him from behind. "Grady, you get back here with us. We don't want no commotion taking place now, not with all the goings on. It'll wait."

The little one glared at Shining Horse. "You'd best not be around when the festivities are over," he said. "I'll come lookin' for you."

Shining Horse walked away. At a livery stable at the edge of town he picked out a small bay mare, choosing a good bridle and saddle.

"You'd better have two hundred bucks if you want to leave with that horse and tack," the livery man said.

Shining Horse knew the man was asking twice what the horse and gear were worth, but it would do no good to argue.

Shining Horse pointed into a corral. "I'll need those three mules, also."

"That'll be two hundred more. Them's fine animals."

Shining Horse peeled off the bills. "And here's twenty extra. If you charge everyone like that, business can't be too good."

"You makin' fun of me, Injun?"

"Do you want the money or not?" Shining Horse asked. "You're not the only one around here with horses and mules for sale."

The man studied the money in his hand. "Where'd you get all this?"

"You got more than your share," Shining Horse said, his

tone firm and even. "I'm not in the mood for much more today, so mind your own business."

The livery man took two steps back and watched Shining Horse saddle the bay mare. Shining Horse then tied the mules together in single file and led them out of the corral.

He bought food supplies from three different stores, packing the mules to the limit. He had no use for all the money that he was carrying, and the food would help his people. He knew without a doubt that they sorely needed all the help they could get.

He took the back trails out of the area, realizing that he could be robbed, possibly killed, at any time. Certainly the livery owner had spread the word that an Indian was loose with a wad of money. He would ride continuously until he reached the mouth of Elk Creek, or Cheyenne River. Very few traveled out from Rapid City toward the reservation.

Shining Horse had seen more than he wanted to in less than two days. The most important bit of news was that another land commission was on its way. It appeared that the politicians were folding to the will of the people, who demanded more Indian lands for homesteading and farming.

Shining Horse knew for certain that his place now was to help his people fight the commission. The Black Hills had been taken from them, and now even more land would go the way of signatures on meaningless paper. If the Lakota people were forced to give up more, something was bound to happen. Something bad for both sides.

Fawn, riding behind Catches Lance and Tangled Hair, urged her pony on toward Cherry Creek, crossing the expanse of winter plains, the wind coming and going. She stayed within herself, wondering at how her life had changed so quickly and so drastically. Nothing from here on would ever be the same for her.

Her main concern at the present was over the way that

Catches Lance seemed to have changed. She could not understand this, and it troubled her deeply.

Although their mother had decided to go down to Pine Ridge with Sees-the-Bull-Rolling and live with his people, Fawn had not passed judgment against either of them. Now she was beginning to see that Catches Lance had always been angry about it but had never said anything. Among the Lakota, it was the custom that the man live with his wife's people. Sees-the-Bull-Rolling should have come up from Pine Ridge to be with their mother among the Minneconjou on Cherry Creek.

Fawn realized that none of that mattered now. Her mother had passed on, and no amount of wondering about her decision during this life would change anything. It bothered Fawn that her brother chose to carry his anger, even now after her death, but she knew full well that it was not her place to try to talk him out of it. She had her life to live now, and so did he.

In a couple of days they would again be on Cherry Creek. Fawn hoped to be able to straighten things out with Catches Lance before then. There was enough to deal with day-to-day without adding more.

As they crossed over a ridge, Tangled Hair spotted a small herd of deer just ahead, browsing on sagebrush. He pulled out his rifle and pointed. "If you two will stay here where they can see you, I will sneak around behind them and get us some food."

"I will wait a while, then go forward a way," Catches Lance told him. "You take them from behind, and I will get as many as I can from the side."

Catches Lance held Tangled Hair's pony and the pack-horse, while Tangled Hair dismounted and began to circle around the deer. Fawn and Catches Lance also dismounted, tied the horses to sagebrush and stood quietly, being careful not to spook the herd.

"I will give him some time before I go," Catches Lance said. "*Wankantanka* has looked upon us with favor this day."

"We will have meat to take back to the village," Fawn said, watching the deer browse hungrily. "More meat than we have had in a long while."

"That is good," Catches Lance said, "but I am worried that you will not be able to rejoice near the cooking fire."

Fawn turned to him. "What do you mean?"

"You seem unusually troubled that our mother has passed over," he said. "Yet you are not surprised. How did you know?"

"I just wanted to see her," Fawn said. "I did not want her to die."

"I believe there is more to it than what you tell me," Catches Lance continued. "You acted at the tree as if she were a young woman and you but a small child. You mourn as if you needed her as a child might."

"Maybe you should be more sorrowful about her death," Fawn suggested. "She made her choice to go with Sees-the-Bull-Rolling without pressure from him."

"I know that I should not concern myself with that," Catches Lance said. "But if she had stayed with us, maybe she would not have died."

"She crossed over because it was her time. How could we have changed that?"

"We could have taken care of her!" Catches Lance snapped. "Nobody down there would help her. She was not even on the rolls."

"That is unfair, Catches Lance," Fawn said. "I am certain that Sees-the-Bull-Rolling and his family did all they could. Besides, he is right, she is better off on the Other Side."

Catches Lance frowned. "That is a strange thing to say. What has happened? Your mind is different since the sun turned dark."

"Yes, I am different since the sun turned dark," Fawn

admitted. "It is something I cannot understand at this time. I will talk to you about it when I know what I am feeling."

"Did you hurt your head when you fell down the hill?"

"I told you, I will talk with you when I understand my feelings better."

Catches Lance stared at her. "Good. When will that be?"

"Why are you pushing me? This matter will take time. Something happened that frightened me and caused me to wonder a great deal about life."

"What happened?" Catches Lance insisted.

"I told you, I don't know what it means."

"I'm not asking you what it means. I just want to know what happened to you."

"I do not know if I am ready, or even if I should tell you," she said. "It seemed comforting, yet frightening. I am very confused."

"All the more reason you should tell me," Catches Lance insisted, forgetting about the deer. "After all, I am your brother and it is our mother we are talking about here. And it did have to do with our mother, didn't it?"

"Yes, it did," Fawn said. "When the sun turned dark, I fell down the hill and something happened. I had a strange dream, where I saw our mother. She was a young woman, as young as when I was a child, before you were born. She showed me many things. Some of them were not pleasant."

"What do you mean? What did she show you?"

"It was as if I traveled with her to times and places that have not yet happened," Fawn explained. "I saw our people dancing in very large circles. They wore uniquely painted clothing. It was very strange, very frightening."

Catches Lance frowned. "Dancing? You mean dancing for war?"

"It wasn't supposed to be for war. At first it seemed as if the dance was for peace. Later everyone was angry. They were waving weapons and using the dance wrongly. It seemed as if the dance had become one of war, when it should have been used for peace. It was a dance I have never seen before. Everyone was doing it."

"How did you know the dance was for peace and not for war?" Catches Lance asked.

"I learned about it from our mother," Fawn answered. "She told me that this dance would come to our people from a Messiah who lives to the west."

"A *Wanekia*? A savior?"

"Yes, he was a special man," Fawn replied. "He was talking to a great many people, teaching them. I don't know what I am supposed to do."

"That is a strange dream," Catches Lance said, his face lined with concern. "Did you learn the dance?"

"No, I did not dance at all. But I saw my children—"

"They were dancing and you weren't?"

The lines in Fawn's face deepened. "I certainly do not understand what I saw."

"I believe you saw our mother just after she crossed over," Catches Lance suggested. "She must have had good reason for showing you these things. How come you didn't say something about it when we found you at the bottom of the hill?"

"Even though I know that what happened to me was real," Fawn said, "I don't want to believe it. Can you see how hard it is?"

"Yes, I can see that it is very hard," Catches Lance said. "Suddenly I feel very strange, also. Thinking about the dancing bothers me. I feel something happening inside me."

"Are you afraid?" Fawn asked.

"Yes, I am afraid. I don't even know why, but I am afraid."

A shot rang through the winter air. One of the deer jumped and scrambled crazily from the herd before tumbling head-first into the snow. Startled, Fawn and Catches Lance turned to see the herd bounding away. In the distance, Tangled Hair continued to shoot. One more deer fell. Catches Lance ran out from the horses and took a wild shot, but the herd was out of range.

Tangled Hair trotted over to where Fawn and Catches Lance awaited him. He caught his breath and stared at Catches Lance in confusion. "Why didn't you sneak out toward the deer and get ready to shoot?" he demanded.

"I don't know," Catches Lance answered. "I wasn't ready, I guess."

"I gave you plenty of time to get into position. I waited until I was certain you would be ready. What were you doing?"

"I said I just didn't get there in time!" Catches Lance said angrily. "Didn't you hear me the first time? What is wrong with your ears?"

Tangled Hair gritted his teeth. He turned and snatched his pony's reins loose from the sagebrush and jumped into the saddle. He took a last look at Catches Lance and kicked the pony into a gallop toward the fallen deer.

"Maybe you shouldn't have talked so sternly to him," Fawn told Catches Lance. "He has no idea of what we were talking about."

"Did you want me to tell him?"

"I just mean that you could have told him we were talking about important things and forgot about the deer. You wouldn't have had to tell him any more than that."

"I don't owe him any reasons for what I do," Catches Lance said. "Nor do I owe you any reasons, either."

"No, but you do owe people common courtesy."

"Sometimes I cannot understand you," Catches Lance told her as he jumped atop his pony. "Maybe you care for Tangled Hair more than you show. Maybe you care for him more than you do for your own brother. I know that our mother cared for him more than she did for me. Now she isn't alive to do that anymore and you think you have to. Is that it?"

Catches Lance kicked his pony into a gallop, leaving Fawn dumbfounded. She saw Tangled Hair, standing with his hands on his hips near one of the fallen deer, watch Catches

Lance disappear over the brow of the hill. Fawn untied the packhorse and mounted her own pony. As she rode toward Tangled Hair, she wondered what had made her brother so angry. It was true that their mother had given Tangled Hair a lot of things, but only to make him feel as welcome as her own children. Perhaps, she finally concluded, her brother was jealous that their mother hadn't appeared to him also after her death.

Fawn helped Tangled Hair tie one of the deer over the packhorse. She then offered her own pony to carry the other deer.

"That means you will have to ride behind me on my horse," Tangled Hair told her. "What will the people in the village think when we ride in?"

"They will think it was necessary to get both deer back, that is all," Fawn said matter-of-factly. "I don't think that is the important problem right now. Do you?"

"No," Tangled Hair agreed. "What happened to your brother? He is acting crazy."

"We talked about our mother," Fawn said. "He forgot to help you stalk the deer, and maybe now he is feeling sorry."

Tangled Hair tested the last knot and climbed on his pony. "There is more to it than you have told me," he said. "You have changed. When we found you after the sun died, I was certain you were different."

Fawn grasped Tangled Hair's extended hand and swung up behind him. "It is true. Something happened to me when the sun died, but I cannot discuss it with you."

"I see," Tangled Hair said. "I would bet that you talked about it with Catches Lance."

"Yes."

"That might be the reason for what he just did, but there is something else happening to him. He became different even before the sun turned dark and your mother died. He has been changing for some time now."

"What do you think is happening to him?"

"It is almost as if the Catches Lance I knew as a child and a young warrior has died," Tangled Hair replied. "He has grown very different. He angers much more easily than he used to. And he complains about everything. It seems that he has begun to rot away inside, as if he wants to die."

"I have noticed the same thing," Fawn said. "He seemed not to care too much about our mother's death. I can't believe it's just because she moved to Pine Ridge. He doesn't seem to care about anything. That is not like him."

Tangled Hair looked far up the trail, where Catches Lance was urging his horse up a slope. Catches Lance had gained a lot of ground on them and it was apparent that he didn't intend to wait for them.

"Yes, the friend I once knew so well is no longer," Tangled Hair told Fawn. "I will still love him, but I don't think anything will ever be the same."

SIX

SHINING HORSE sat the small bay pony atop a snow-swept ridge above Sitting Bull's camp. It had been many years since he had been outside for very long in such cold. His hands and face were numb, his toes and feet still smarting from the pounding he had given them just a short time before. Had he not dismounted periodically to walk and keep his blood flowing, his hands and feet would have frozen before now.

Throughout his ride, Shining Horse had thought back on his days of growing up, but the scene before him certainly did not remind him of his days as a child. The banks along Grand River were lined with makeshift cabin dwellings and lodges built of patched and rotting canvas. There were no meat racks present, no display of medicine and war shields beside the dwellings. Very little of the past had been retained.

Smoke rose and hung in the thick cold, but there was no smell of cooking fires. Horses ranged out in the hills, well beyond camp, foraging for scant wisps of grass through the snow. No one watched them, as there was no longer any threat of raids from neighboring enemies. Those days were gone. Other than the smoke and a few children scampering among the lodges, the village might well have been vacant.

In Shining Horse's boyhood, his father's lodge had been painted with many animal and elemental power signs, symbolizing the strength of the man's dwelling and the Lakota people as a whole. Now his father had a cabin, and it was distinguished from the others only by its size. The walls of the cabin depicted nothing sacred; Shining Horse realized that Sitting Bull would never paint any kind of designs on the cabin, for he would never give the *Wasichu* way of life any of his own power.

Shining Horse had by now grown to accept the fact that his people had become destitute. But he was still not prepared for what he saw. Though he believed he had done everything he could to prepare himself for all of this, he reeled from shock. He could remember as a child how families proudly offered feasts for the entire camp and then took their turns in attending feasts held by other families. Now *pte*, the buffalo, the Sacred Giver of Life, had all but completely vanished from the plains, leaving the Lakota totally dependent on the conquering *Wasichu* for food.

As Shining Horse rode down toward the village, he thought about the words he would say to his father. So much had changed. Would the great spiritual leader even remember him? It had been many winters since the death of Shining Horse's mother, when Sitting Bull had brought Shining Horse into his lodge to be raised by his wives. Many warriors had been killed by Bluecoats, and many children had gained new fathers in a similar fashion.

Shining Horse had always wondered why Sitting Bull had taken him in. A number of other families would have been happy to raise him, but Sitting Bull had insisted. Though he had been very young, Shining Horse could remember Sitting Bull's disappointment at seeing him go East. But he had told his father that he would be back some day. This was that day.

As he neared the village, a group of young men mounted their ponies, each with a rifle that he waved in the air. They charged out of the village at him, and Shining Horse held his hand out in peace.

This didn't stop them. They circled him, shouting and waving their rifles. Shining Horse wondered if he would be killed. Their yells increased as they neared him. When they were nearly upon him, he threw open his arms and shouted at the top of his lungs.

"*Hoka hey!* It is a good day to die!"

The warriors reined in their ponies. The lead warrior appeared to be under twenty winters in age. He rode up close to Shining Horse and studied him and the bay mare. "He is no Bluecoat scout," the warrior told the others. "He is one of our people. He just doesn't know that he rides a Bluecoat horse."

The young warrior looked very much like a boy with whom Shining Horse had often played before he had been taken to Carlisle. He could not recall the young warrior's name. Struggling with his own language, Shining Horse asked, "Are you a brother to one who used to be called Swims Funny?"

The young warrior looked surprised. "Yes, my older brother, who has crossed over, was once called Swims Funny. You knew him? Who are you?"

"I am Shining Horse, son of Sitting Bull. I left as a child to go to the East and attend the *Wasichu* schools. Now I have come back. Why would you think I was a Bluecoat scout?"

The warrior's eyes narrowed as he studied Shining Horse. "I am not sure of that," he said. "No son of Sitting Bull would ride a Bluecoat horse out to our village."

Shining Horse looked down and ran his fingers through the hair on the mare's left shoulder. Indeed, his pony had at one time been branded with the letters US. To add to the shock, he could see a faint 7 burned in underneath the larger letters.

The brand was well grown over with hair, but sharp eyes

could certainly tell the mark. He felt foolish. He realized that he should have been more careful in selecting his horse.

Shining Horse turned back to the warriors. "I have shown myself to be blind in overlooking this brand, but I can assure you, I have seen many things. I smelled the blood and tasted the dust that day at the Greasy Grass. I lost my blood father in Medicine Tail Coulee, so there is no Bluecoat blood in me."

The young warrior leaned forward toward Shining Horse. "You say you were at the Greasy Grass?"

"Your brother and I were together that day," Shining Horse told him. "We ran up on the hill after the battle. I found a Bluecoat rifle with *Wasichu* writing on the stock. The writing said, 'Dolly.' I gave it to Swims Funny. He tied a hawk feather to the trigger guard."

The warriors began talking among themselves. The young warrior nodded. "Yes, you were my brother's good friend. He talked much about you, and how he missed you after you were taken to school. I am called Bob-tailed Cat."

"My good friend can be proud of his younger brother," Shining Horse said. "Whatever happened to the rifle?"

"I had to hide it," Bob-tailed Cat replied. "We all had to hide rifles taken at the Greasy Grass. The Bluecoats who put us on reservations would hang anyone they found with a rifle taken at that battle."

"A lot of things have happened because of that day," Shining Horse said.

"Then you should know better than to ride a Bluecoat horse into camp," Bob-tailed Cat said. "Especially a horse with that kind of mark on it. Do you know what the agent would say if he saw that horse?"

"I can guess," Shining Horse said. "He would likely want to punish its owner for having killed a Bluecoat at the Greasy Grass fight. But after all these winters have passed?"

"Yes," Bob-tailed Cat said, "even after all these winters. No one will ever forget that day. I know this, and I was only half your age at the time."

"I am certain of one thing," Shining Horse said. "I believe I can solve the problem I have brought with me, and at the same time, ease the hunger here, at least for a while."

"That could well be your only salvation," Bob-tailed Cat said. "I hope you can stay, and the others with me feel the same. But it is not for us to make that decision. You must face the man who took you in to be his son. It is he who will decide whether you should stay or go."

Shining Horse reined his pony in among the young warriors, leading the pack mules behind, as he was escorted into camp. By now a number of villagers had emerged from their lodges to watch. Waiting for him was Sitting Bull, who greeted Shining Horse with a hard stare.

"As I have told the others," Shining Horse said after dismounting, "I came back to rejoin my people. I did not intend to bring trouble of any kind."

"Why would a man ride a Bluecoat horse into an Unkpapa village if he didn't want to make trouble?" Sitting Bull asked.

"The horse is for the cook fires," Shining Horse said, "not for the agent's eyes."

"I thought maybe you had come back to try to talk me into taking the White Man's Road," Sitting Bull said. "But I certainly know you wouldn't begin that by riding a Bluecoat horse."

Shining Horse smiled. There had been a hidden benefit in his mistake. "I guess I would make a poor diplomat."

Shining Horse noticed how Sitting Bull studied him, the piercing eyes absorbing his entire being. This did not bother Shining Horse, but only lent encouragement to the hope that his father remembered him. This hope was fulfilled by the faint hint of a smile from Sitting Bull, which quickly disappeared.

Sitting Bull did not say anything for a long time, but merely continued to study Shining Horse. As Shining Horse remembered, his father was slow to speak, careful to define each word before he presented it aloud. He wanted no misunderstanding; he said nothing that he hadn't calculated beforehand.

Except for features hardened by age and anger, Shining Horse noticed little change in his father. Still sturdy and rugged, the legendary leader's near six-foot frame held the same power his son remembered as a child, the same posture of unquestioned authority. Sitting Bull led the Unkpapa people only, but all members of the Sioux nation, each and every one, knew him and respected him.

There were those who felt that he was too old and his ideas too antiquated to lead the people any longer, but none of them had ever been able to take away his power. Those who were loyal looked up to him as a pillar of strength, holding their nation atop his strong shoulders.

The *Wasichu* had been quick to label Sitting Bull a troublemaker. It had been widely spread in print that he would kill at a moment's notice, for no good reason. His fame among the whites had come largely from newsprint following the Custer fight. Over the years, the legends had grown darker than even the most condemning of the war tales. To most of the settled white population, Sitting Bull represented the last threat to civilization.

Those who knew him well would not argue to the contrary. Yet his anger at what had happened to his people was not maniacal or in any way uncontrolled. His reserve in the face of white arrogance was exemplary, even under extreme conditions. He had never lowered himself to impulsive behavior, and he never would. It seemed odd to Shining Horse that the strong and numerous *Wasichu* should be so frightened of a man who wanted nothing more than to be left alone.

Shining Horse had read about his father's trips into the East, placing himself on exhibition so that people might view this wild and untamed savage. He had read much about his father's celebrated performances with Buffalo Bill. Shining Horse perceived most of the fanfare as amusing, if not downright ludicrous. If his father had done half as much as had been printed, he must have had little time for rest.

The man he now saw in front of him was still the parent and leader he had looked up to as a child. Shining Horse was eager to ask about events since his leaving for the East, but that would come in due time.

"Well," Sitting Bull said, "are you going to let my people eat what you have brought for them?"

"Yes," Shining Horse said. "I must say, though, that I was given the money I bought the provisions with. It was a present from the people I lived with."

"You were presented money by a *Wasichu*? Surely not for the purpose of feeding your people."

"They wanted me to have a good start out here. They did not tell me how I must spend it. Their attitude was kind."

"Do you believe you are getting off to a good start?"

"I hope so," Shining Horse replied.

Shining Horse watched while the horse and the pack mules were unloaded. After three shots, the animals lay still in the snow while the villagers danced around them. Then the butchering began. Shining Horse had never seen anything like it, anywhere. They scavenged the horse and mules like wild animals. During his days as a child, he had seen some hard times, but they had produced nothing like this. Even the time of the locusts, which he remembered well, had not caused such misery.

Shining Horse realized that what he had brought would appease their hunger for only a few days. Still, anything of substance was a cause for rejoicing.

Sitting Bull studied his son. "Is it as you envisioned?"

"Worse," Shining Horse replied. "Much worse."

"Come," Sitting Bull said. "We have much to talk about."

Shining Horse followed Sitting Bull to his cabin, noting that his father's limp had grown more pronounced. Twenty-four winters had passed since Sitting Bull had felt the sting of a Crow warrior's bullet along the sole of his left foot. The injury had never healed properly. Now each time that Sitting Bull walked over the Earth Mother, he was reminded of that horse-stealing raid.

Sitting Bull led the way into his two-room log dwelling. His two remaining wives, Seen-By-Her-Nation and Four Times, were talking. Sitting Bull spoke softly to them. Four Times, the younger of the two by a good many winters, bowed and left the cabin. Seen-By-Her-Nation studied Shining Horse for a moment and then followed behind.

"This is not a home," Sitting Bull said, gesturing toward the walls of the cabin. "Maybe someday I will again live in a lodge made of the sacred covering of *pte*. I am already tired of logs. I miss the old days."

An open stone firepit just outside the door served as the cooking area, while a small iron cookstove sat unused in the corner. The two women set a kettle to boiling and after reentering the cabin for an old parfleche, placed thin strips of dried beef in the water. Then they retreated to their own adjacent one-room cabin.

Although his father didn't show it, Shining Horse knew he was offering all he had. The strips of beef had been stored next to his medicine items and had likely been there for some time. A guest had to be offered something, even if it was the last food on hand.

Before he sat down, Sitting Bull lit a red pipe. He stepped outside and offered smoke to Earth and Sky and the Four Directions, then limped back inside to a three-legged wooden chair. He puffed long and hard before turning the pipe toward Shining Horse, who took it, smoked and handed it back to his father.

"You have been given many things," Sitting Bull said. "You have learned the *Wasichu* ways. Why would you come back into a world where the people are nearly dead?"

"These are my true people," Shining Horse answered without hesitation. "In the world of the *Wasichu*, everyone seems to be alive, but their spirits are dead."

"I did not know how to feel about you that day they took you and the others," Sitting Bull said. "There was nothing I could do. Do you feel anger toward me?"

"Of what use is anger?" Shining Horse asked. "You could not stop them. They came, with the Bluecoats, and picked us. I don't even know what happened to the others."

"Some have returned here," Sitting Bull said. "Some of them now work for the *Wasichu* agents."

"What about the schools they have started among our people?" Shining Horse asked. "Has there been trouble because of them?"

"You know how it is," Sitting Bull said. "They chop off the braids of the little ones so they will look like *Wasichu*. They beat them if they speak the Lakota tongue. Our children are afraid."

"I was very lucky," Shining Horse said. "The family that helped me let me wear my hair in any manner I wished. I was never beaten."

"How about at Carlisle?" Sitting Bull asked.

"I believe those people rescued me from that place," Shining Horse said. "I cannot say why, but I do know that *Wankantanka* lives among the whites, also."

Sitting Bull smoked the pipe and handed it to Shining Horse. "I still wish I had stopped them from taking you."

"Maybe you thought when the *Wasichu* teachers took us that things would go better for everyone," Shining Horse said.

"You know me better than that," Sitting Bull said. "I knew that nothing would go well for our people, ever, as long as the *Wasichu* lived in our lands. They have come and are doing what they want, no matter what they have said about leaving us alone."

"I have met people back there who are willing to help us," Shining Horse said. "Lawyers who want to make the *Wasichu* obey their own legal documents. There is a group called the National Indian Defense Association. Sometime soon a woman named Catherine Weldon will be coming out here to talk to the agents about the conditions here."

"She will have to be a very good talker," Sitting Bull said. "The agent at Standing Rock, White Hair McLaughlin, has no more use for me than I have for him. He holds me here, without allowing me even to go and visit relatives. I might as well be dead."

"The people who want to help us, they all know about McLaughlin," Shining Horse said. "It is hoped that he can be removed."

"There are *Wasichu* who care about us?"

"Yes, and they are good people. But they are few, and it will be hard."

"That is the problem," Sitting Bull said. "All that is good is too scarce. It will take too long to change things. I will not see it."

"Maybe you will," Shining Horse encouraged him. "Maybe it will happen sooner than you think."

"I am getting old," Sitting Bull said. "I can do little now but make White Hair angry. I hope these people you speak of can do some good, but White Hair and the others are powerful. They have men behind them who want to see our people die off like leaves before the cold moons. As long as I am alive, that will not happen."

"The National Indian Defense Association wants to make things better for our people," Shining Horse said. "We must do all we can to help them."

"What can we do?" Sitting Bull asked. "We are prisoners in our own lands."

"Maybe this Catherine Weldon can do some good," Shining Horse said.

"Do the *Wasichu* give the women a strong voice?" Sitting Bull asked. "I did not know that."

"Some women have strong voices in any camp," Shining Horse pointed out. "Catherine Weldon is such a woman."

"It will surprise me greatly if this woman can get rid of

White Hair," Sitting Bull said. "I believe that the *Wasichu* will never leave, but will become ever stronger. Unless something kills them all. There are so many, it would take an act from *Wankantanka*."

"There is other important news that I heard in Rapid City," Shining Horse said. "I learned that another land commission will be coming out to try to buy lands from our people."

"That did not work before," Sitting Bull said. "They must make three fourths of our warriors sign their papers."

"This time it will be different," Shining Horse said, passing the pipe back. "The one you called Three Stars Crook will be among them."

Sitting Bull seemed to be staring into the bowl of the pipe, his face etched with concern. "Yes, that will present a problem," he said. "We must hold a council and discuss it."

"We have to unite our people," Shining Horse said. "It is important that we all think the same and act as one to keep our lands intact."

Sitting Bull sang a song and passed the pipe to Shining Horse once again. They smoked and talked further, discussing what would happen to the Lakota if the land commission succeeded in getting the reservation reduced. Shining Horse vowed to do all he could to unite the seven major tribes of the Lakota nation against further loss of land. Being taken from his people as a child had been hard, but he knew that this would be even harder. And it would possibly be the most important thing he would ever do for his people.

SEVEN

FAWN RODE behind Tangled Hair into the Minneconjou village on Cherry Creek. She felt naked
without her long hair, and the calves of her legs throbbed with
pain. The gashes would heal, she knew, and form scars over
the other wounds from past deaths. But a very different
wound had opened within her since the argument with
Catches Lance.

The villagers welcomed them with shouts of glee. Catches
Lance, who had arrived a good deal earlier, watched from
afar. While Tangled Hair unloaded the deer, Fawn hurried to
her brother's lodge, where she found Hawk and Little Star
tucked snugly into ragged robes, sleeping soundly.

Night Bird, who had been quietly beading a pair of
moccasins, hugged Fawn in welcome. Catches Lance had
already informed her of their mother's death, and she had
expected Fawn to return with short hair and wounds of
mourning.

Fawn knelt and awakened her children gently. They

jumped from their robes and threw themselves into her arms, crying loudly.

"They have been worried about you," Night Bird told Fawn. "Ever since the sun turned dark, they have been saying that you might not return. They felt death near you."

"It was my mother," Fawn explained, soothing the children. "My mother crossed over at the time of the sun's darkening."

"I am sorry about that," Night Bird said. "I know she was to be married, and maybe she would have been happy, but I am certain she is living much better on the Other Side."

Fawn thought momentarily about her experience on the Other Side. She wanted to tell Night Bird the things she had seen and felt, but held back. She knew that Night Bird wouldn't understand. A vision of Night Bird holding the hands of Hawk and Little Star, one on each side while they danced in the huge circle, now flashed through Fawn's head. She gasped, and Night Bird looked at her strangely. She pulled herself together. This wasn't the time to discuss it.

"Are you all right?" Night Bird asked. "You appear very worried."

"Things are changing so fast," Fawn said, holding her children. "It troubles me."

"You are right," Night Bird agreed. "And now even more trouble has started . . . between our own chiefs. Big Foot came up from his village to see Kicking Bear while you were gone, and they argued."

Fawn knew that Big Foot had been pressing the agent for some time to begin a mission and a school on Cheyenne River. Big Foot had tried to show the *Wasichu* that he respected their ways by planting corn. Kicking Bear was adamantly opposed to anything that had to do with the *Wasichu*, and Big Foot had lost his respect. Since Big Foot was his wife's uncle, the matter grew ever more complicated.

"What happened between them?" Fawn asked.

Night Bird took a deep breath. "Big Foot told Kicking Bear that a Black Robe is coming to live among us."

"No, that can't be," Fawn said.

"Yes, it is said to be true," Night Bird said. "Others have heard this as well. The Black Robe is to come up to us from the mission among the Brulé on the Rosebud."

"Does he know that our people do not want him?" Fawn asked.

"No one knows anything except that he is coming," Night Bird said. "Some say that we must take him or we will not be given rations. It is said that some of the agents refuse to hand out rations to those who do not accept the *Wasichu* religion."

"Then maybe that is what will happen here as well," Fawn said. "The *Wasichu* wish to change us in any way they can."

"These are the worst times our people have ever known, and all because of the *Wasichu*," Night Bird said, her voice turning hard. "I wish they had never come into our lands. I wish our people in the old days had turned them all back and killed everyone who tried to stay."

Fawn listened to her friend's words with concern. Night Bird had grown increasingly bitter. She was small, with better than average looks, but now she spent all her time in seething anger at the Lakota condition. Fawn was certain that had she been male, she would now be leading a revolt.

Listening to Night Bird made Fawn wonder whether she herself might soon become as angry. Before her vision in the Badlands, she could have easily done so. But now she realized that anger wouldn't change anything that was to come. They could protest, as they had been doing, but the *Wasichu* would have their own way in the end.

Fawn realized that it was better for the body and the mind to remain calm. Perhaps it was the experience with her mother that brought her to this realization. Life had been very hard for all of them ever since the fight at the Greasy Grass. But having seen her mother young and happy had led her to believe that nothing could be accomplished by worrying about the future. Disturbing the present moment was nothing but a waste of time and thought.

Fawn tried to comfort Night Bird. "Times will get better, you will see. Spring will bring new grass and game of all kinds."

Night Bird frowned. "What? *You*, of all people, are telling me that you can see good times ahead? That doesn't sound like you."

"I can't tell you why I believe that," Fawn said. "I can only tell you that I feel it is true."

"That is but a dream, Fawn," Night Bird said. "A dream that makes the heart sing, but one that cannot come true."

"Who knows what the warm moons will bring? Maybe something new will come to us."

"You are beginning to sound like Kicking Bear. He has told the village that he went away from his body when the sun turned dark and he learned that better times are ahead. I can't believe that."

Fawn stared at Night Bird. "What did you say? Kicking Bear had a dream?"

"I don't know what it was," Night Bird said, her anger rising again. "But it can't be real. Nothing is real but the *Wasichu*. They are worse than the locusts that came when we were small children. I can still remember them, buzzing until I thought I would go crazy, so thick that the sun was darkened, just like it was this time. When they were gone, the grass had been cleaved off to the roots. It was two winters before the buffalo returned. We had to travel into Crow lands and fight to hunt. Do you remember that?"

"Yes," Fawn said. "It was indeed hard for a time."

"That is what the *Wasichu* are doing to our people," Night Bird said. "Yet they will not leave. They only grow stronger. They keep chopping at us, right down to our roots. How can we live?" Her eyes filled with tears and she covered her face with her hands.

Fawn let her children go and held her friend for a time. She could see no end to Night Bird's anger and despair, yet Night Bird had just spoken of a vision seen by Kicking Bear during the dark time of the sun. It sounded to Fawn as though she and the camp leader had had a similar experience. Maybe in time she could discuss it with him. It was important now that she get Night Bird and her children out to where the village gathered for the feast.

"Tangled Hair killed two deer," Fawn said. "Let us all go and join in the eating."

"I do not feel like eating," Night Bird said.

"How can you not feel like eating?" Fawn asked.

"There are many problems," Night Bird replied. "Why did Catches Lance ride in ahead of you and Tangled Hair?"

"I do not have the answer," Fawn said. "He became angry partway through the trip back and left us. I thought that maybe he would talk to you about it."

"He only said that you had changed, and not for the better," Night Bird said. "He left before I could ask him what he meant. I haven't seen him since. I think he is angry with me, also."

"No, I cannot believe that he is," Fawn said. "He is in mourning for our mother, that is all. Do not worry. Come with us now."

"You take Hawk and Little Star out to the feast," Night Bird said. "I don't feel like doing anything but staying here in the lodge."

"It would do you good to eat something," Fawn argued. "It would help you feel better."

"Please, go without me," Night Bird insisted.

"I worry about your health," Fawn told her sister-in-law. "You cannot stay strong if you do not eat. And these deer are very good, much better than the rations."

"Bring something back for me," Night Bird said. "I don't know why, really, but I do want to live."

"Of course you want to live," Fawn said, putting an arm around her. "We all want to live."

Fawn hurried her children out to where the village elders were overseeing the feasting. Hunger had reduced even the strongest to quarreling over places in line. The bitter cold, combined with bad rations, had caused considerable misery among the Minneconjou and the few Sans Arcs, Two Kettle, and Blackfeet Lakota camped along Cheyenne River. On the last rations day, the beans had been so stale that they would not soak up water, and the flour had been black with mold. Tangled Hair's deer would assuage some of their misery for the time being.

The people tore open the two carcasses and devoured them totally, consuming the entrails and body organs cold, without even the thought of waiting until they had been cooked. Those organs that had become partially frozen had been tossed onto hot coals, with meat cut from the back and legs, and were being eaten half raw.

Children, together with young adults and warriors, were fed the greater share, as they represented the Lakota future. Mothers with babies at their breasts were also given priority. Though many of these women would still not be able to save their infants, at least they might live to bear more children.

The older warriors and women, although hungry too, took heart in watching the deer meat disappear into the mouths of those who needed it most. One warrior especially enjoyed watching the proceedings: the tall and experienced warrior named Kicking Bear. This sudden good fortune gave a recent prophecy of his a sound measure of reality.

Fawn talked with other villagers about Kicking Bear's experience, learning that Night Bird had been right. After watching the sun disappear and then reappear, Kicking Bear had come to believe that his people were to see a new time in their lives. He believed that the sun had merely grown old and died and that a new sun had come to take its place.

He had spread the word that a spotted eagle had appeared to him, flying against the new sun, an omen of good fortune for the Lakota. Instead of fear and discouragement, Kicking Bear had begun to call for renewed hope. He seemed certain that something glorious was going to happen very soon.

Kicking Bear deemed that the arrival of meat to feed the hungry was the beginning of good times again. It would not be long, he told everyone, before more game came to the Lakota people, so they would not have to depend on the *Wasichu* rations to satisfy their hunger.

Fawn knew Kicking Bear well and often wondered how long it would be before the volatile warrior led an uprising against the hated *Wasichu* conquerors. Strong convictions ran deep through his family line. A first cousin of the famed Crazy Horse, Kicking Bear admired the great warrior's courage and aspired to make the same kind of name for himself among the Lakota.

Nearly twelve winters had passed since Crazy Horse had been murdered by a Bluecoat soldier, but the vision of this proud cousin remained strong within Kicking Bear's mind. As a main force among his people, Crazy Horse had been lured to Fort Robinson, Nebraska, under the guise of talking in council. He had seen the deception early and had fought to stay out of the stockade. There had been too many soldiers, and a Bluecoat bayonet had taken his life.

When the news had reached Kicking Bear, he had grieved the great warrior's murder with a promise to secure vengeance at any cost. Later, Crazy Horse's medicine bundle had come to him so that he might carry it into battle as his own. Though very few ever saw the small rawhide bag containing a sacred stone, it was widely known that Crazy Horse's mother had given the bag to Kicking Bear in person. Many believed that she hoped the medicine once given by the Powers to her son might live on in her nephew.

Fawn watched Kicking Bear give Tangled Hair two good horses for having brought food to the village. There weren't many things a warrior could do these days to show courage and valor. Feeding the village, by whatever means, brought considerable honor.

As Fawn watched her children fight with other children for every scrap available, she realized that she could easily go back to her anger. She had learned long ago that the words of the *Wasichu* were meaningless, that they contained no truth. Nothing the white people said could be taken seriously. She could not count the times her people had been lied to, and she did not want to think about it.

Fawn realized that the only way to cope with all this was to leave it in the hands of *Wankantanka*. She could even see her mother smiling now, assuring her that she was right to let go of it. But it wouldn't be easy. The hardest part of winter had just arrived, and the village had very little food. These two deer were only a short-term solution. Many among the old and the very young had already become sick. They would die before spring, as would others after them.

Fawn took a thin slice of tenderloin back for Night Bird. Hawk and Little Star followed, Hawk holding tightly to a small bone. He had promised to let Little Star suck on it when the hunger pangs became unbearable. Fawn made a small fire, careful not to use too much wood. The children fell asleep immediately, Hawk clutching the deer bone in one hand and his little sister with the other.

As the fire died down, Fawn stared into the coals. Though she fought herself, she began to question her new attitude of perseverance. How could things improve? Where would relief come from? Certainly the agent would not help them, and he was the only link between them and the *Wasichu* government.

Unlike Night Bird, Fawn did not want to see all *Wasichu* killed. She had come to understand that honorable men existed among the whites. But unlike her own people, where honor was rewarded, the *Wasichu* did not consider those who were good to others as fit leaders. They were pushed down, while those who held the power were merciless tyrants.

Fawn began to think of her mother again. She lay back in her robes and closed her eyes. Maybe she could recapture the feeling that had come to her in *Mako sica* when the sun had turned dark. She lay still for a long time, relaxing herself, calling in her mind for her mother, envisioning her. Nothing happened.

Fawn sat up. She wanted to scream. Where was her mother when she needed her? She looked over at her children, shadows from the fire dancing against their sleeping faces. They rested soundly, fed and content in the knowledge that their mother had returned. Nothing else mattered. Nothing else now but to rest. Nothing else but to survive.

After a deep breath, Fawn lay down again. She was no longer a child, and she could no longer depend on her mother to comfort her, at least not in the same sense that her children depended on her. No, she must be the strong one now. And she didn't have to be alone, she thought as a warm feeling flooded her. She wouldn't be alone as long as she remembered what her mother had taught her: *Wankantanka* would always be there.

All eyes were on Shining Horse as the sun rose fully in the cold eastern sky. A number of warriors, as well as the council elders, waited in the council lodge for the signal from Sitting Bull that this very important day would begin. Shining Horse would tell them of all he had heard in the *Wasichu* settlement of Rapid City.

Shining Horse entered the large council lodge and accepted the purifying smoke offered by the attendant at the door. After cleansing himself with the odors of sage and sweetgrass, he took his place at the right hand of his father. The others watched him intently.

The matter to be discussed merited the consideration of every prominent elder and warrior. It affected the entire Lakota nation, but each band would deal with the issue within its own structure. Shining Horse's arrival in camp had aroused even more anger in Sitting Bull and his followers toward the hated *Wasichu*. His son's news that the whites were preparing to acquire more portions of the Great Sioux Reservation demanded immediate action.

Although the snows of the cold moons would control the lands for a good time yet, the *Wasichu* would certainly come with their papers and lies as soon as the grass turned green again. Since the *Wasichu* plot to take the lands hadn't worked in the two previous summers, the Lakota people had hoped

that there would be no more pressure. But Sitting Bull, for
one, had known that the *Wasichu* would not give up until all
the lands were gone and the Lakota people were left with
nothing. All hoped that in this council a definite plan would
emerge that would protect the people's rights.

To be certain the Powers would hear its prayers for guidance,
the council had followed traditional guidelines. It assembled in
a lodge constructed especially for the occasion. Four families
had combined their lodges to make enough room for those in
attendance to sit in a large circle, as in the old days. Council
members would rise and address the group from the center of
the circle, each member taking as long as needed to make his
point. Food would be placed outside the door periodically, but
the lodge would otherwise be undisturbed until the men
emerged after their important decisions had been made.

The members of the council had seated themselves cross-
legged, ready for a long session. The majority of them were
Sitting Bull's most loyal followers, a group called the Silent
Eaters. This group had been formed as a social dining society
by members of an important warrior society known as the
Midnight Stronghearts. The Silent Eaters were the last bas-
tion of strength against the overpowering *Wasichu* tide.

Along with the other council members, Shining Horse
raised his hands, palms upward, toward the center of the
circle. His eyes followed the smoke of the central fire, now
laced with sage and sweetgrass, to where it drifted out the
hole in the roof of the lodge. Sitting Bull then offered the
sacred pipe to Earth and Sky and the Four Directions and
began a prayer:

"We call upon You this day, *Wankantanka*, Great Holy One
who sees over all, One who brings life to all. We call upon You
for guidance, for wisdom and understanding. Hear us, Your
children, in our time of need. Hear us and bring to our hearts
Your holy way. Show us how to live and what to do to make
You happy with us again."

As the prayer continued, Shining Horse noted the marked

difference between these words and the prayers he had heard as a child. In those days the Lakota were facing greater and greater adversity, but there had been no feeling that *Wankantanka* had deserted them or otherwise wanted to punish them.

Shining Horse realized that since his departure to be educated, Lakota life had taken a very different turn. The struggle for hunting grounds had passed with the wanton slaughter of *pte*. Now the sacred buffalo was gone, and the Lakota faced a similar fate. The end of their way of life seemed trivial compared to the very real possibility of extinction.

Sitting Bull finished the prayer, asking for the highest wisdom and guidance for all of the council members, invoking *Wankantanka* on behalf of each one. The fire rose in a straight column toward the top of the lodge, without the aid of more wood. Sitting Bull nodded in satisfaction; *Wankantanka* had come to be with them.

Shining Horse felt one with the group, joined in mind and spirit with each of the others, pulled together into a circle as one collective mind. It was a feeling he had known often as a child while playing and eating with others his own age. He had never known it as a young man or as an adult. He was glad he had come back.

As the pipe was passed around the circle, Shining Horse considered the possible loss of more reservation land. Such a loss would certainly further demoralize the Lakota people, while giving the whites an even firmer foothold in the region. With the movement afoot to force the Lakota to farm their sacred lands, it could happen that the *Wasichu* government would decrease rations.

If this happened and the cold settled in hard again during the following winter, even more of the Lakota people would starve and die of sickness. That would be too much to bear. The Lakota would never let themselves be exterminated. There would be a strong revolt before that happened. A very strong revolt.

EIGHT

THE PIPE circled the council and finally reached Shining Horse. He smoked and handed it to Sitting Bull.

"It is fitting," Sitting Bull said, "that you begin by telling us how it is in your heart."

Shining Horse looked around the council. He recognized many who had been just horse tenders when he had left for the East. Many had witnessed battle for the first time at the Greasy Grass. Now they were mature in the ways of life, hard ways for all of them.

Bob-tailed Cat, the youngest of the warriors in the council, watched him with the most interest. It was he who had first met Shining Horse, thinking to scare this stranger riding a horse marked with the brand of the Bluecoat army. It was Bob-tailed Cat who had discovered that Shining Horse did not scare easily. *Hoka hey!* Every day was a good day to die.

Shining Horse stood and began speaking, telling of his days as a child among the Unkpapa Lakota. "I learned to ride and to swim and to walk long distances without water so that as a man I might better serve my true people," he said. "But I was not able to do that for a very long time. As you know, I was taken to learn the ways of the *Wasichu* and to become one of them. I did not want to do this, but went because I was made to go."

Shining Horse paused to sense the general feeling of the group toward him. Many had always believed that he went because he wanted to become white and go against his father. He had heard that opinion from a number of people since his return. Most of those who spoke in this way had no idea of his circumstances.

"I will not tell you what happened during the years I was gone, because you know how the *Wasichu* feels toward his red brother," Shining Horse continued. "I will say that the family I lived with did not act like that toward me. They loved me."

A few murmurs arose among the council members.

"It is true," Shining Horse said. "There are those among the *Wasichu* who know love, no matter the color of the skin. But I did not return here to dwell on them. I came back because I wanted to live with my true people. I wanted to get away from the many *Wasichu* who spat on me and told me I had no business living among them. Now I am going to thank them, for by learning their tongue and their ways, I can better help us all."

Again more murmurs arose. Shining Horse realized that many had no use for the White Man's Road in any form. Bob-tailed Cat was the foremost among the younger warriors with this conviction. His ambition was to become like Sitting Bull, who was considered the strongest among those filled with disgust for the White Man's Road.

Though Shining Horse had just spoken in behalf of the *Wasichu* who had given him a home in the East, he noted no hint of disapproval from Sitting Bull. Perhaps, in his travels with the showman Buffalo Bill, Sitting Bull had himself met a few *Wasichu* who could be called honorable.

But the vast majority of the *Wasichu* who had come into these lands did not care for the Lakota people, or for any Indian people for that matter.

"In the *Wasichu* village called Rapid City, I learned that the Great Sioux Reservation is again in danger of being divided," Shining Horse said. "Since the *Wasichu* did not succeed the first time, they are bound to try again. But this time they will be using different tactics than before. They won't be coming with unknown dignitaries, people whom you won't even listen to. Instead, they will be sending one of their leaders whom you have all trusted in the past. They will be sending a Bluecoat officer named George Crook. The one called Three Stars."

Cries of shock and surprise rose from the council. Three Stars Crook, the Gray Fox, as he was often known, had gained a great measure of respect among the plains tribes, and especially among the Lakota. He had the reputation as being the single *Wasichu* whose words were never false. If he came to talk to the Lakota people, what he said would be believed. This development would divide the people even more.

As Shining Horse had expected, the council began earnest discussion. One by one, each member rose to give his opinion, first declaring his past history as a member of the Unkpapa band and as a Lakota warrior, including honors taken in battle.

During these narratives, more attention was given to battles with old enemies than to fights with Bluecoat soldiers, save for the Custer encounter at the Greasy Grass. The Crow and Arikara and the Pawnee were brought up often, as members of these tribes had enlisted as scouts for the Bluecoat armies. The Lakota had fought these tribes for many generations, and it seemed proper to spit on them now.

Even more important than the war deeds was the advice given. Most declared that the people must be warned against listening to any *Wasichu*, no matter his reputation. The concern over Three Stars Crook was apparent as the warriors, in turn, proclaimed that the people should not even gather to listen to propositions of any kind for taking their lands. The *Wasichu* would make promises to them of a better future as long as they gave up more land. They would come offering the *Wasichu* money in exchange for the land. There would be many promises, as always, but none of them should be believed.

Some members of the council disagreed. They were not convinced that Three Stars Crook would bring trouble. These men were of the opinion that Crook's arrival could actually mean better times for the Lakota people. They were not met with jeers or mockery, but allowed to have their say. Arguments between individuals would be heard only after everyone had spoken.

Shining Horse watched his father's face darken with ever more concern. The Lakota people were already divided over following the White Man's Road. To Sitting Bull, this circumstance would serve to divide them more deeply than ever.

The only council member who did not speak was Bob-tailed Cat. He had never dealt with Three Stars Crook, and he had little knowledge of the battles and skirmishes the men talked about. Out of respect, he chose only to listen.

Shining Horse thought it fitting that Bob-tailed Cat allow the others to discuss the matter. Everyone knew his opinion, and everyone knew how bravely his father had fought against the Bluecoats. All Bob-tailed Cat wished was to live the way his father had lived, something that he knew would be next to impossible. The world of the Lakota had changed more since he had been born than in any other time of the people's history. There seemed little doubt but that it would change even more.

Discussion lasted all day, throughout the night and into the early morning of the following day. As the council neared its conclusion, Shining Horse offered to take the news down to the camps along Cherry Creek and Cheyenne River. Kicking Bear and his people on Cherry Creek would likely vote to stay away from Three Stars Crook, while Big Foot's band would be divided, as would Hump's group at the mouth of Cherry Creek.

There would certainly be those who would want to believe the promises, want to believe in an end to their misery. Shining Horse hoped to convince them that by giving in, they would only be increasing their misery. To the *Wasichu* government, less reservation land meant less responsibility, and certainly less attention to Lakota problems.

Sitting Bull had just begun to speak again on how they might unite the Lakota nation when someone just outside the council lodge began yelling for him to come out.

"Metal Breasts!" one of the council members said. "I know the voice of the chief, Afraid-of-Bear."

The council members began to talk among themselves. Shining Horse turned to Sitting Bull, who explained that Afraid-of-Bear was the chief of the Metal Breasts, the Indian police force, warriors hired by James McLaughlin to enforce agency rules against their own people. Afraid-of-Bear was a farmer who lived a short distance to the north and did everything the way the *Wasichu* wished. He had been picked to be the leader of the Metal Breasts because he would do as he was told, even though it might bring his people suffering.

"He is a Yanktonnais," Sitting Bull explained. "They and the agent call him Bull Head."

The yelling outside continued. One of the council members peered past the door flap. "Yes, it is Afraid-of-Bear," he said. "And the bad one, Shaved Head, is with him. They have brought six others."

"Those sucking dogs!" another council member snarled. "How dare they interrupt a council in session!"

Other voices rose in anger. Outside, the other Indian police joined Bull Head in yelling for Sitting Bull. Many of the council members wanted to go out and punish them for their rudeness.

"I, for one, would like to pull them down from their

ponies," one council member said, "and make them walk back
to where they came from, like the children they are."

Many shouted their approval. Sitting Bull raised his hand
for silence. "Do not let a Metal Breast cause you to lose your
heads. They are not warrior quality and must do what White
Hair says. You stay inside. I will go out and see what he
wants."

"I will go with you," Shining Horse offered. "I believe I
know why he's here."

Shining Horse followed Sitting Bull outside the lodge. Bull
Head and the others, in their blue uniforms and with shiny
badges, stood out plainly. By this time, Bull Head was yelling
louder. He was leaning over his horse, slapping the lodge wall
with his quirt.

"What is so urgent that you lose respect for a council?"
Sitting Bull asked him.

Bull Head pointed to Shining Horse. "He has not yet
checked in with White Hair. We have orders to bring him to
the agency."

"I will gladly go," Shining Horse said in a pleasant voice.
"Why is there all this fuss?"

"Anyone who comes or goes from this reservation must see
White Hair first," Bull Head shouted. "You have not done
that."

"I will go," Shining Horse said. "There is no need for
trouble."

Bull Head turned to Sitting Bull. "Have everyone come out
of the council lodge. I want to see if you are hiding anyone
else in there."

Sitting Bull called for the council members to come out.
One by one, they passed the door flap and stood behind
Sitting Bull with their arms crossed. Bull Head instructed
Shaved Head to dismount and take a look inside the lodge.

"They don't have to do that," Bob-tailed Cat said. "Have
they no thought of respect?"

"Let them look," Sitting Bull said. "They are but children.

They have no coups and they need to do something to make themselves feel brave."

While Shaved Head searched the council lodge, Shining Horse studied Bull Head. The policeman appeared close to his own age. His hair, and the hair of all the other policemen with him, was cut short, clearly defining their decision to follow the White Man's Road. To a Lakota of the old ways, hair was sacred and a sign of strength. To cut it off was to lose one's power.

Shaved Head came out of the lodge and hurried to the side of Bull Head's pony. "The lodge is empty." Younger than the other Metal Breasts, and mean in appearance, he had especially close-cropped hair.

"Go tell White Hair that we have him and that we will bring him in right away," Bull Head told him.

Shaved Head nodded and selected two others to ride with him. When they were gone, Bull Head turned to Shining Horse. "We will go now."

"I will get a few of my things," Shining Horse said.

Bull Head leaned forward off his horse. "I said we will go. Now!"

"He will get what he needs first," Sitting Bull told Bull Head. "Do you understand?"

Bull Head saw that the faces of his fellow policemen had become strained. A number of young Unkpapa warriors had surrounded them and were awaiting Sitting Bull's command to attack.

"Do you understand, Afraid-of-Bear?" Sitting Bull asked again.

Bull Head glared at Sitting Bull. "I will tell White Hair about this. Things will not go good for you."

"Things will never be good between us," Sitting Bull said. "You cannot make things any worse. You cannot do anything unless you kiss White Hair's genitals first."

Bull Head squeezed his quirt until the muscles in his hand

stood out like ropes. "There will come a day when you will wish you hadn't talked to me that way."

"You are not a smart man to come into my village and pound on my council lodge," Sitting Bull reminded him. "Maybe you had better think before you come back."

"That man has to come with us," one of the policemen said. "White Hair will send soldiers after him if he does not obey."

"Go back to your mother's breast," Sitting Bull told him. "Speak up only after you have become wiser."

"I told you I would come with you," Shining Horse said. "When did I say I wouldn't come?"

Bull Head sat on his horse, glaring. None of the policemen spoke.

Bob-tailed Cat, along with another warrior named Long Hand, walked over to Shining Horse. "We are going with him," he said to Bull Head. "We will hear what White Hair has to say."

"White Hair did not ask for any but the new man who rode into your camp," Bull Head said.

"It does not matter what White Hair *asked* for," Bob-tailed Cat said. "He will see all of us or he will not see any of us."

Bob-tailed Cat called for his pony and for ponies for Shining Horse and Long Hand. Shining Horse went into Sitting Bull's cabin to gather some winter clothes. Sitting Bull followed him.

"Now you see how it is here," he told Shining Horse. "Our own people want to kill one another."

"The Unkpapas have never gotten along with the Yanktonnais," Shining Horse said.

"Disagreements are one thing," Sitting Bull said, "but murder is another."

"Yes, I can see that the agent has used old feuds to control the people," Shining Horse said, starting for the door. "I admire the way you hold your temper and the way you keep the others from doing foolish things."

"It may not always be so," Sitting Bull said. "Have a safe ride."

Shining Horse would not see James McLaughlin until far after sunrise the following morning. The forty-mile ride to the agency lasted well into the evening, and then Shining Horse was told that he and his companions would have to find a place to spend the night.

Shining Horse secured permission from an officer to use an abandoned tack shed at Fort Yates, just across the road from the agency. Had the weather been colder, he and the others might have suffered severely. As it was, they made a fire outside the shed and discussed the insanity that was growing like a mold across the underbelly of the Lakota people.

Long Hand tended to the fire. Bull Head and the rest of the Metal Breasts despised him. It was no secret that they would kill him if they thought they could get away with it. Long Hand had surprised a Metal Breast trying to steal one of his rifles. In the ensuing fight, Long Hand had broken the policeman's arm. The only witnesses had been Long Hand's two grown nephews, who testified that Long Hand had acted to save his life. The Metal Breasts did not have the nerve to try to arrest Long Hand.

Shining Horse remembered Long Hand as an older boy who had lost his father and two brothers at the Greasy Grass. Ever since that day, Long Hand had disliked the color blue. The Metal Breast whom Long Hand had maimed had been wearing a blue shirt with a yellow scarf around his neck.

Long Hand had brought a supply of beef pemmican and now he passed out handfuls of it to Shining Horse and Bob-tailed Cat. "The rage is growing within our people as each day passes," he said as he chewed. "We are doing ourselves a great deal of harm. Because our people turn against the *Wasichu*, we are forced to turn against ourselves to appease our anger."

"It will be an even greater problem when Three Stars Crook

arrives with his land commission," Shining Horse said. "He will have everyone fighting. It is my hope that we can unite before Crook gets here."

"That will be very hard," Long Hand said. "The different agents will not allow us to visit one another. They never do. We cannot go anywhere."

"He is telling you just a small part of the problem," Bob-tailed Cat put in. "Some agents are better than others, but they all work to make themselves rich men. They swindle us out of our rations and our beef. They make deals with robbers and thieves, taking what rightfully belongs to the Lakota people."

"It is hard enough that we cannot live in the old ways," Long Hand said, "and that the agents mistreat us. Now we must put up with our own kind turning against us. The Metal Breasts are of the Nakota nation and not either the Dakota or the Lakota, but they should still respect us as brothers. Anyone who will come and pound on a council lodge has lost all respect for his people. He has lost respect for himself."

"That was truly a bad thing," Shining Horse agreed. "I am not hurting any of them by being here. White Hair McLaughlin must have some sort of plan to try to make my father very angry. I don't know why he would dislike my father that much."

"Sitting Bull will never take the White Man's Road," Long Hand said. "That makes White Hair angry. Sitting Bull is a far smarter man than White Hair, and much more honest in his ways. That makes White Hair even angrier."

"White Hair does not know of honor," Bob-tailed Cat put in. "He wants things to go his way and he will scheme until he has turned us all against one another."

"Are the people under other agencies having as much trouble as we are here?" Shining Horse asked.

"Feelings are growing divided in all the villages," Long Hand said. "Many are beginning to think about taking the White Man's Road. They feel that the old ways are dead and that we cannot survive unless we bow our heads to the *Wasichu*. There is even strife among the Metal Breasts. Some want to retain honor, while others do not care anymore. Agents like White Hair choose the dishonorable ones for their leaders."

"You will soon see what manner of man White Hair truly is," Bob-tailed Cat told Shining Horse. "Everything that Long Hand has told you is true. White Hair is married to a woman who is mixed Yanktonnai and *Wasichu*. Now she wants to be all *Wasichu*. She wants to be just like the women who are married to the Bluecoat officers at the fort."

"They will never accept her," Shining Horse said. "No matter how nicely she dresses or how well she speaks the *Wasichu* tongue, they will turn away from her. I can say that from experience."

"What you have to remember," Long Hand said, "is that there is a private war between White Hair and Sitting Bull. White Hair is pushing your father, hoping that he will do something foolish."

"My father is too smart for that," Shining Horse said. "His medicine is much stronger than anything an agent can understand."

"This is true," Long Hand said. "But maybe White Hair wants to use somebody who understands Sitting Bull's medicine. Maybe he now has a plan to use you in his battle against your father."

"Let him try," Shining Horse said. "I have met many *Wasichu* who are like him. And they are all in high places. I know their ways. Let him try to pit me against my father. I will use some of his own tricks on him."

NINE

THE FOLLOWING morning Shining Horse was escorted into the agency by Bull Head, Shaved Head, and two other Indian police. Long Hand and Bob-tailed Cat were told to wait outside.

James McLaughlin, sitting behind his desk, was dressed in a dark suit and a white shirt buttoned tight at the neck. Though coated with oil, his thick white hair bristled. His eyebrows pinched together over his nose.

He lit a cigar and stood up through a haze of smoke. "I've been wanting to meet you," he said to Shining Horse, extending his hand.

Shining Horse took McLaughlin's hand. He noticed that McLaughlin looked more concerned than friendly.

"You should be very proud, after all you've accomplished," McLaughlin continued. "Not many of your people can boast that they attended Carlisle and were then taken for a higher education beyond that."

"It wasn't of my choosing," Shining Horse said.

"Are you sorry you spent that time back there?"

"No," Shining Horse said. "I'm glad I've learned what I have about your people."

"You don't sound very impressed."

"I'm not."

Bull Head and the other Metal Breasts, holding their Spencer rifles across their chests, stared at Shining Horse.

McLaughlin grunted and stepped past Shining Horse. A stout man, he moved across the room with authority, his pudgy face lined with concentration. He stopped at an open window and looked out, exhaling a cloud of smoke.

"It's no secret that your father and I don't get along," he said. "I was hoping you would give me the benefit of the doubt and hear what I have to say."

"I'm listening."

McLaughlin turned back from the window. "My job is to do the best I can for your people. That is just what I am doing. But your father is standing in the way."

"I can't change my father," Shining Horse said. "His values were formed a long time before you got here."

"Yes, but he is not educated," McLaughlin said. "You are. You can tell your people that they must take the White Man's Road. They have no choice."

"I didn't come out here to change my father's mind, or the minds of those who follow him," Shining Horse said. "I came out here to help save as much of our lands and heritage as possible."

"You had better tell them what will surely happen," McLaughlin said. "You had better tell them the government will take more of their land and that they should get the most for it while they can."

"My people do not want *Wasichu* money," Shining Horse said. "They want their land and their way of life back. That's all."

"It's too late for that," McLaughlin said. "Homesteaders and cattlemen are pushing Congress for more land out here.

They'll get it. I don't like all I see happening, but I can't stop it."

"Can you show me any letters you have written to Congress protesting it?" Shining Horse asked.

McLaughlin bit down hard on his cigar. "I do my job the way I see fit. I don't have to answer to you for that."

"So my father is right about you, then," Shining Horse said. "You talk like you want to help my people, yet all you are really doing is making a name for yourself."

McLaughlin's face turned a deep red. "I thought you were a reasonable man. I thought I could make you see that you could rise above your father and become someone important on this reservation. But I see that I was wrong."

"I just want my people treated fairly," Shining Horse said. "What I see coming is more empty promises and more land taken away from them."

"You're no different than your father, are you?" McLaughlin said. "You're going to be as bull-headed as he is. Well, I tell you, neither you nor your father will win. You ought to think about that."

"My father is a great man among the Lakota people," Shining Horse said. "Many throughout the reservation respect him highly. They will listen to him. You know that."

"I can see that we're both wasting our time," McLaughlin said. "So I'm going to tell it to you straight. Your father is on the way out. There are new leaders coming in. Young leaders. Progressive leaders. I had hoped you would be one of these important men and that you could help me ease your father out of the picture."

"My father is in the picture for good," Shining Horse said. "He is the backbone of the Lakota culture. You could never displace him. You would have to kill him to do that."

McLaughlin grunted again and looked out the window at neighboring Fort Yates. "You see those soldiers across the way?" he asked, pointing with his cigar. "They have come to ensure a new life out here for decent men and women. If you and your father think you can behave like savages forever, you're both sadly mistaken. You're standing in the path of civilization."

"Maybe you are forgetting, my people were here first," Shining Horse said.

McLaughlin's breath quickened. "In case you haven't noticed, a lot has changed since you left here. Your people have been given ample opportunity to use the land right. So far, they have failed to do so. It is imperative that the land is used properly, farmed, made to produce the most it can. That means your people will have to sell it to those who can make good use of it."

"Not unless you can get three fourths of the Lakota men of legal age to sign an agreement," Shining Horse said. "That won't happen."

"Yes it will," McLaughlin said confidently. "You think you can stop what's happening here, but you can't. Educated or not, you're Indian, just like your father."

"If you think so little of us, why did you bother to marry a Sioux woman?" Shining Horse asked.

"You leave my wife out of this! She does not claim to be of your race."

Shining Horse stared. It was hard to know whether to laugh at McLaughlin or to take pity on the man. "How can you or she, either one, deny her race?" he asked.

"She's more of the white race than she is of yours!" McLaughlin snapped. "I don't want you to speak of her again."

"I'm through with this talk," Shining Horse said. "I have better things to do."

"I'll tell you when I'm through with you," McLaughlin retorted. "I would throw you in the stockade but it's full."

Shining Horse wasn't listening. He was halfway to the door.

McLaughlin turned to the police. "Seize him!"

Bull Head started to turn his rifle toward Shining Horse. With his left hand, Shining Horse grabbed the barrel and shoved it away, then slammed his right fist into Bull Head's jaw. Bull Head reeled backward into the wall. Before Shaved Head and the other police could react, Shining Horse had turned the Spencer on McLaughlin.

Shaved Head and the other Metal Breasts, rifles cocked, looked to McLaughlin for instructions. McLaughlin held the cigar tight between his teeth, staring down the barrel.

"*Hoka hey*," Shining Horse said. "It's a good day to die! For all of us."

"Put the rifle down," McLaughlin ordered. "You haven't got a chance."

"Neither have you," Shining Horse told him. "Just think, they will have to bring someone else in to take your place. Someone else who will say that he was the one who got the bold Lakota nation to do things his way. You'll just be buried in the ground and forgotten."

McLaughlin's face hardened with rage. "You won't get a half mile from here. My police will see to that."

"I thought you much smarter than that," Shining Horse said. "Crook and the others will be coming with the land commission before very long. Killing me would create a political scene that would bury you just as sure as if you were actually in the ground."

McLaughlin ordered Shaved Head and the other police to lower their weapons. Shining Horse thanked Bull Head for the rifle and started out the door. Shining Horse turned and brought the butt of the rifle squarely into Bull Head's face, breaking his nose.

"He's not a good choice to lead your police," Shining Horse told McLaughlin. "He makes poor decisions."

"You're the one who has made the poor decision," McLaughlin shouted. "You should never have come to my agency. But now that you're here, you're bound. Your name was never taken off the tribal rolls. You had better not set foot off this reservation or I'll issue a warrant for your arrest so fast you won't know what happened. Do you understand?"

"I don't think *you* understand, White Hair," Shining Horse said. He now spoke Lakota. "As you have said, I am much like my father. I will live free until I die. Neither you nor anyone else can take that away from me."

"Just remember what I said," McLaughlin repeated. "You had better not break any laws. I'll have you behind bars for the rest of your life."

"There is something you should remember, White Hair," Shining Horse warned. "It might appear to others that you are taking care of the Indians here, but you do not have me fooled. There are people coming to see my father who have a lot of questions to ask you."

McLaughlin stormed over to his desk and jerked open a drawer. "There isn't anyone coming to see your father that I won't know about first," he said furiously, holding up a handful of letters.

Shining Horse was shocked. "You are intercepting my father's mail?" he asked. "That is illegal."

"Your father cannot read or write English," McLaughlin said. "Those of us who seek the best for him are just making sure he gets good messages, not negative ones."

"Why don't you let him decide that?" Shining Horse said, stepping forward for the letters.

"Oh, no," McLaughlin said. "You aren't a certified mail carrier. I would be breaking the law if I gave these to you. Your father has to come up here in person to get them."

"How many do you have?"

"That's none of your business. If your father wants to know, he has to come up here and see for himself."

"Very well. But I thank you for showing those letters to me. You will certainly wish you hadn't later on."

McLaughlin frowned again. Shining Horse glanced at Bull Head, who was sitting on the floor holding his nose. Shaved Head and the others glared as Shining Horse shouldered past. Outside, he met Long Hand and Bob-tailed Cat, waiting with the ponies. They had heard the commotion inside the agency.

"We were just about to come in," Long Hand said. "But we saw White Hair trembling at the window. We could see that you needed no help with him."

Shining Horse mounted. "White Hair hates me even more than he does my father," he told them. "I know a lot about him and what he is doing here. I am a marked man."

The sun had fallen when Shining Horse and the other two reached Sitting Bull's village. The weather had changed and the smell of snow was in the evening air.

As Shining Horse and his companions dismounted, large flakes began to drift down.

Sitting Bull met them. "I have prepared a sweat lodge for the three of you," he said. "You have had a bad time with White Hair."

Shining Horse knew better than to be surprised at anything his father might say. Sitting Bull's powerful medicine was known among all the Lakota. Shining Horse fully expected his father to know every word that had been exchanged at the agency. Sitting Bull was known for somehow becoming aware of events he wished to know about, as clearly as if he had actually been there himself.

There were many stories of how the old medicine man had pointed out to those who had been away things that they had said or done. His visions were many, the most famous being that of the Bluecoats he had seen falling from the sky before Custer's defeat at the Greasy Grass, turned upside down as they fell. Sitting Bull had described *Wankantanka*'s gift of Custer and his Bluecoat soldiers descending into the massive Lakota village on the Little Bighorn.

Now Sitting Bull packed a pipe with tobacco while singing a sacred song. When he had finished with the song, he turned to Shining Horse. "I don't have to tell you, but things could have been very bad for you today," he said. "You must be careful with your emotions. I have other sons, but I don't want to lose any of you."

"I'm sorry," Shining Horse said. "I could not control myself. He made me very angry."

"I can understand how he could easily make you angry," Sitting Bull said. "Until this morning, you had not met White Hair. After knowing him for just a short time, you could see what his plans are for our people. I do not fault you for getting angry, but don't press for trouble next time."

"He has been keeping letters from you," Shining Horse said. "That is very wrong."

"I know he has," Sitting Bull said. "Others have seen him looking at writings addressed to me. This will be taken care of in time. You must not lose control."

Shining Horse took a deep breath. He knew his father meant that he must listen to White Hair until he was finished, no matter how hard it was to hear. To try to take power from such a man was to make a lifetime enemy.

"I have learned," Shining Horse told his father. "I will be a better warrior next time."

"Do not let there be a next time," Sitting Bull advised. "White Hair will not tolerate having you near him. He is the kind of man who will have you killed if he can."

Shining Horse had thought about this during the ride back to the village. If he stayed here even until morning, he might not get away when daylight came. By then Bull Head and the other Metal Breasts would be back to keep an eye on him, to keep him trapped. Shining Horse stripped for the sweat. The air was cold and the snow hit like tiny cold feathers against his skin.

Shining Horse turned to his father. "I must take word to Three Stars Crook and the land commission right away."

"A bad storm is coming," Sitting Bull said. "When the blowing snow has passed, my wives will pack food for you. Go first to the Minneconjou, Kicking Bear's village on Cherry Creek. You will get good support from him. I will give you a buffalo calfskin vest that was made for me. It is sacred. And I will give you one of my best ponies. Kicking Bear will know you bring important news."

Shining Horse entered the sweat lodge and sat in the cleansing steam with Long Hand and Bob-tailed Cat. They sang songs for their people, and Shining Horse asked *Wankantanka's* forgiveness for having become so angry at White Hair McLaughlin. He wondered what would have happened had he actually used the rifle on the agent. He would have been killed also, he saw, and no doubt the act would have brought more suffering and misery to the Lakota people.

He also sought power and wisdom for the mission he was undertaking: to spend the remainder of the cold moons telling all of the Lakota about the new land commission. If Crook succeeded, the people would be separated from one another, making it difficult to keep in contact. Everyone must unite.

Long Hand and Bob-tailed Cat left the lodge. Shining Horse remained in the steamy darkness, trying to see what lay ahead for him. All was black, as black as the robe of the priest who had ridden the train with him. He couldn't know what was to come until it happened.

Then he stepped out of the sweat lodge. The creek was frozen over, except for a deep hole where flowing springs ran from the hillside. He waded into the icy water and lowered himself in to the neck. For a moment he couldn't breathe.

The snowflakes had grown thicker and the wind began tossing them into flurries. Father Thomas again came to his mind. The Black Robe he had met on the train must now be somewhere in Lakota lands, working to persuade people to hear his words about the *Wasichu* god. As dedicated as Father Thomas was to his ideals, he must surely be having success.

Shining Horse climbed out of the water and wrapped himself in a blanket that Sitting Bull had left for him. The wind began to whistle through the cottonwoods. His father had said it would be a strong, but quick, storm. Shining Horse wished that the trouble that lay ahead for his people would pass just as quickly. But he knew better. It would come as strong as a bad storm, and it would not go away for a very long time.

PART II

February, 1889–August, 1889

Father, I come;
Mother, I come;
Brother, I come;
Father, give us back our arrows.

Lakota Warriors'
Ghost Dance Song

TEN

FATHER THOMAS placed wood into the fireplace in the mission school at St. Francis and listened to a small Brulé Sioux boy struggle to recite the Confiteor for his teacher. Outside, the sun descended in the west, behind a strong winter storm that holed down from the north. Darkness inside the school was broken by the light of the fireplace and two lanterns on the teacher's desk.

The other children shifted nervously in their seats as the boy worked to recite the prayer. He had first to formulate the words within his head in his own language, then translate them somehow into English. His teacher, Father Joseph Lindebner, waited impatiently.

Father Thomas stoked the wood into flames. It would seem hard enough, he thought to himself, for any child to begin to understand the complexities of the prayer, even if taught to him in his native tongue. Father Thomas was certain that the small boy hadn't even begun to grasp English yet.

Father Lindebner drew in a deep breath and told the boy to

stop, that he was ruining the prayer. The boy lowered his head. The only sound in the room was the crackling of the fire.

Short and stocky in stature, with demanding small eyes set beneath bushy graying eyebrows, Father Lindebner presented an imposing figure as he stroked a thick beard and moved angrily around his desk and over to the shaking boy.

"You must repeat after me," Father Lindebner began in English heavily laden with a thick German accent. "I believe in Gott, the Faatter Almighty . . . well?"

"Father, the sun is nearly down," Father Thomas broke in. "We don't want the children trying to find their way home in this storm after dark."

Though most of the children could not totally understand what Father Thomas had said, his tone of voice made them turn and stare at him. The sound was neither gruff nor demanding. The statement had been made clearly and with conviction. They knew instinctively that Father Thomas had interceded in their behalf.

Father Lindebner snapped, "Dismissed!" and waved his stout arm toward the door. Father Thomas stood and smiled at the inquisitive faces of the children, who hurried past him and out into the winter storm.

When the classroom had emptied, Father Thomas watched Father Lindebner scratching notes at his desk. The teacher's arm was stiff, his hand muscles taut, jamming the quill pen into the paper as he completed an entry.

Father Thomas noted Father Lindebner's wrath, but he showed no fear. He saw no excuse for intimidating small children. He did not agree with the philosophy that the Indians should never be allowed to speak their native tongue, especially in class. Father Thomas knew that if he were forced to view this scene much longer, he would have to overstep his authority for the sake of the children, even if it meant a lot of friction with his superiors.

Father Thomas and Father Lindebner had disagreed at

almost every turn. In Father Thomas's mind, that would not change. The Mission Superior at St. Francis School and Mission was Father Florentine Digmann, who had ridden over to Holy Rosary Mission at Pine Ridge to assist in a number of marriages. He was also to baptize a number of Indians and make certain that the sister mission was running smoothly. He had been gone since before Father Thomas's arrival, and Father Lindebner had been left in charge as the local superior.

Father Lindebner continued to make notes, pausing frequently to glare up at Father Thomas. Father Thomas turned to a window and watched the children plowing through drifts of blowing snow, helping one another up when they fell, their faces turned against the raw wind. Their clothes, thin and tattered, were soon caked with crusted white. Before long they disappeared into the deeping twilight toward their homes.

Behind him, Father Lindebner had risen from his desk and was approaching him, clearing his throat. He began a dissertation on the necessity of discipline among pagan children. Father Thomas heard instead a voice within his head, the voice of Shining Horse as they had journeyed on the train, speaking to him of a life his people had once known. This life had been taken from them, and a harsh and cruel reality had taken its place.

Shining Horse had told him that winters on the open plains were fierce and that before the reservation system, his people had normally migrated to the shelter of the Black Hills. They followed the game animals, as the animals always knew the best places to survive. Shining Horse was of the opinion that the Great Father in Washington had purposefully placed his people out in the open, where the cold wind would freeze the life from them so there would be no more Lakota.

At the time, Father Thomas had thought Shining Horse might be exaggerating to make his point. The truth appeared to be much starker. The Lakota people not only fought the

bitter cold, but also malnutrition. Father Thomas had witnessed rations day and realized that the flour, stale beans, and
hardtack were not enough to sustain health—and yet the
people were not allowed to go into the Black Hills and hunt
game. To Father Thomas, this seemed totally inhumane.

Father Thomas had had no satisfaction from looking into
the affairs of the agency. The agent had told him that beyond
the mission and the school, all else that went on was none of
his business. Any information he needed would come from
his superiors. Father Lindebner and the other priests had told
him that he had acted without authority. The mission did not
meddle in government affairs. The food supply was a government matter. Their place was not to question government
authority, but to save as many Lakota souls as possible.

Father Thomas turned from the window as Father Lindebner fairly barked in his thick, broken dialect: "Are you
listening, Faatter Thomas?"

"Yes, certainly," Father Thomas replied.

"Can you tell me, then, why you question my authority?"

"I'm only wondering why you have to be so harsh with the
children," Father Thomas said. "I don't agree with the physical punishment I'm seeing here. What do you have against
these people?"

"These people have to learn the word of Gott, Faatter
Thomas," Father Lindebner said angrily. "They have to learn
it at a very young age. Yes, just as we did. I am troubled that
these poor souls are slow to grasp the truth, but we must still
work ourselves hart to bring salvation to them. We must work
very hart, Faatter Thomas."

"Perhaps your zeal confuses them," Father Thomas suggested.

Father Lindebner's heavy eyebrows descended into a
frown. "I have been chosen by Gott for this work, Faatter
Thomas. This is my classroom, and I will have you to let me
teach as I see fit. And I will dismiss when I see fit. Do you
understand?"

"My apologies, Father. I only thought—"

"Maybe that's the trouble," Father Lindebner broke in. "Maybe you don't know what to think about all this. Gott knows, you're confused."

"Confused?"

"Faatter Thomas, you haven't been here long enough to know these people and what they need. But you've got all kinds of things to tell me. All of them are wrong. I will tell you this. Don't you know why you came here? Don't you know what to do for these poor savages?"

"I will agree that they are poor," Father Thomas spoke up. "But I hardly see them as savages."

"You don't see them as savages?"

"No, Father, I don't."

Father Lindebner placed his hands behind his back, a furrow above his thick eyebrows. "That is your problem, is it not, Faatter Thomas? You cannot see. You cannot see at all. You think these people are the same as us."

"How are they different?"

Father Lindebner threw up his hands, then stomped to the window and glared out into the darkness. "You have seen how they live. Little better than the beasts of the field. They ride their horses and visit each other. They will not do anything else. They will not watch our brothers as they farm and plant vegetables for winter use."

"It is my understanding that they have always hunted game and picked wild fruit," Father Thomas pointed out. "You can't expect them to just change overnight."

"But there are many who *will* not change," Father Lindebner argued. "I believe they do not know the soil as they should. They will not work it and plant. Gott knows they will not do honest work. They don't know how to take care of themselves."

"I'll bet they were doing fine on their own before the expansion came out here," Father Thomas said. "I guess we know what happened then, don't we?"

"Ah! That is it!" Father Lindebner said, throwing his hands up again. "You have come to ruin the hard work. I will tell this to Faatter Digmann when he comes back. I will tell him you are not obedient."

"I have not disobeyed you!" Father Thomas protested. "Does a disagreement constitute disobedience?"

Father Lindebner seethed with rage. "I have worked hard with the other Faatters, and with the Sisters and Brothers, to bring these people the gospel of our Lord, Jesus. Now you come and try to tell me the work is no good."

"I'm just suggesting–"

"I have not been here long," Father Lindebner broke in, "but much longer than you. I have gotten a good many of the savages here to look for Gott. As for those on Cheyenne River, where you believe you are supposed to minister, they have nothing but pagan hearts. You are more like them than you are like a priest. How do you expect to go among those poor lost souls and bring them the word of Christ?"

Father Thomas studied Father Lindebner for a moment. "Did you come here of your own accord?" he asked. "Did you really want to be a missionary, or are you doing this because you believe it will make you a better Jesuit?"

Father Lindebner turned, his face taut beneath his heavy beard. "I do what I am told, Faatter Thomas, and I do not ask all the questions. I am obedient, as you should be. I told you, I was sent by Gott to this place. I will honor Gott's decision."

"Maybe you will honor God's decision," Father Thomas observed, "but it doesn't seem like you are happy doing it. Why don't you apply for a transfer?"

"Nonsense!" Father Lindebner blared. "Utter nonsense! Rubbish!"

"Some people are better with children than others, that's all," Father Thomas said.

"You should not have transferred from your province," Father Lindebner said. "You should be doing other work. This is not for you."

"I did not know I was going to be told to teach the word of God in this fashion," Father Thomas said. "Had I known, I would never have applied for this province. But since I am here, I am even more fully aware that this is where I belong and what I should be doing. But I'll never use a ruler on a child. You, nor anybody else, will make me do that."

Father Lindebner pulled on a dark wool overcoat and threw an equally dark muffler around his neck. He lifted the two lanterns and handed one to Father Thomas.

"The others are waiting for us to eat," he said. "You had better spend the night praying to the Sacred Heart of Jesus. For obedience."

Father Thomas took the lantern and set it on the window-sill. "You go ahead, Father. I will stay here until the fire dies down."

"You should come right now."

"A little later. I'll be along. Don't wait for me to eat."

Father Lindebner grunted. He said nothing more as he strode to the door and out into the cold.

Father Thomas stoked the coals in the fireplace, breaking them down into small, glowing pieces. One by one, they began to burn out.

As he stared at the flickering embers, he considered his mission to bring the gospel to the Minneconjou of Kicking Bear's camp. He didn't believe the way he taught the children to be a matter of obedience. His mission was to bring them the words of Jesus Christ. He couldn't do that by making them afraid of him.

Father Thomas knew about fear. The eldest of eight children, he was often beaten by his alcoholic father. There was never any predicting when it might occur. The only reality was that it would occur.

Other than the strict enforcement of English and the physical punishment, Father Thomas thought the mission at St. Francis to be exemplary. The food was not better than that the Lakota were given. In fact, the missionaries made it a point not to eat better.

Though the living quarters were better than the Indians' small log cabins and run-down lodges, they were not furnished lavishly. Nothing more than a cot for sleeping and a few wooden chairs were found in any of the rooms.

Father Thomas realized that his responsibility to deliver the word of Christ to the Minneconjou would bring great change to him. He would celebrate his thirty-fourth birthday in less than a week. Since his arrival at St. Francis, he had read well into the book Shining Horse had given him. St. John of the Cross had been a true mystic in the sense that he had devoted his life to God and had opened his mind to receive grace. In doing so, the saint had discovered that the true road to God varied with the individual.

In his reading, Father Thomas had thought that Shining Horse could very well be right in stating that many among the Sioux were equally as spiritual. Shining Horse had pointed out that among his people, each learned to reach the Godhead in his or her own way. Elders were there for instruction and support, but never to control. Each person had charge of his or her own spiritual growth.

Father Thomas had not been taught this at all. Once you decided to become a priest, you obeyed without question the orders given you. You had to have faith that your superiors were directed by God in selecting your place of work. Choosing to become a missionary was an honorable goal. It was also the avenue of most freedom. Father Thomas knew that this life among the Plains Indians was meant for him.

After seeing how the Brulé lived, Father Thomas believed that he could reach the Minneconjou. He must certainly start by learning their language. It was preposterous to assume they would gain any knowledge of the gospel unless they could first realize the meaning of the words. His observations had told him that even those among the Sioux who had totally accepted Catholicism had no concept of how the teachings of Christ paralleled their own lives.

In fact, they had been taught to the contrary. They had been made to believe that nothing of their previous beliefs held any merit. They must start over. They must put aside all of the teachings they had considered sacred since early childhood. They had been led to believe that none of that wisdom could be retained, that they had heretofore led lives as terrible sinners.

Though he had been among these people for little more than two weeks, Father Thomas had already gained a healthy respect for their ability to cope with hardship. He realized that their lives could never have been easy, even under the most optimal of conditions. At best, he concluded, they had enjoyed periods of comfort during the days when the buffalo were plenty. Life had been a struggle for them, but they had been happy doing things the way they wished, without interference.

Then had come the movement West. For the Sioux, the change had been rapid and drastic. Father Thomas saw that the methods employed in teaching these people had likely done more to confuse them than to convert them. It seemed that those who had become Catholic had done so merely in the hope of gaining a measure of safety from the government and improving their impoverished lives.

Father Thomas laid the stoker to rest near the fireplace and shrugged into his heavy topcoat. He picked up the lantern and stepped out into the storm. Darkness was complete. The snow blew fine and sharp, like tiny needles pricking the skin.

As he started toward the living quarters, he heard something over the sound of blowing snow. Faint, yet discernible, it was a child crying. He lifted the lantern and turned into the wind, looking to where the children had vanished, their tracks already filled in as if they had never been there.

Father Thomas listened intently. Had it been the wind? No, the crying came again. He began working his way toward the sound, down the path from the school toward the lodges. He surged through snow past his knees, the lantern swinging with each gust of wind. The crying continued, driving him faster toward the village. If they lost a child in this storm, he would never forgive himself.

The crying grew louder, but it seemed to be coming from more than one direction. Father Thomas now wondered if more than one child might be calling for help. He turned a full circle in the storm, hearing the crying all around him.

"What is happening?" he asked himself. "My mind must be playing tricks on me."

Through blasts of snow, Father Thomas saw a light coming toward him. A woman wrapped in a muslin blanket, her hair caked with snow, held a torch up to his face. She wailed at him in Lakota.

Another woman, younger, hurried up behind her and took the torch from the first woman, who sank down into the snow and sobbed.

"I speak the *Wasichu* tongue," the younger woman told Father Thomas. "This woman is my older cousin. Did you come out to help her?"

"Is she looking for the children?" he asked.

"Yes, she comes out into the cold often."

"I heard a child, or children, crying," Father Thomas said. "Did all of the children make it back from school?"

"Yes, all the children from the school are safe."

"Then who is crying out here?"

"It happened the winter past, not this one," the young woman explained. "They were her twin sons, just four winters old. They got lost coming from the school. They are not at rest. She still looks for them."

Father Thomas stared at the young woman. "What do you mean? Are you saying that her children died and she still looks for them? Didn't they find them?"

The young woman stared curiously at the priest. "Yes, they found them." She stooped to raise her cousin. "I must get her back to her lodge. She wants to come out in every storm to look for them. One time she will die."

Father Thomas assisted the women back toward the lodges. He continued to look around, listening intently again, certain he still heard crying.

"Can't you hear that?" he asked the young woman. "Where are they?"

"You are new here," she replied. "I haven't seen you before."

"I am Father Thomas. I have come to be here for a short while. Then I will go up to the Minneconjous on Cherry Creek."

"I am Little Buffalo Woman," she said. "I would like you to find a certain woman for me when you get to Kicking Bear's village. I have something I want to give her, if you will take it for me. Her name is Fawn-That-Goes-Dancing."

"I would be happy to take whatever it is," Father Thomas said. "I don't know how soon I'll be leaving, but I'll take it up to this woman."

"It is just a small skin bag with something in it for her," Little Buffalo Woman said. "She does not even know me well, but I know that she must be given the bag. It is not too big for you to carry."

"I will take it for you," Father Thomas said again. "But right now I am worried about the children. When we get this woman back to her lodge, are we coming back to look for the children?"

Little Buffalo Woman stopped. She told the crying woman to stand up by herself for a moment. She wiped snow from her face and held the torch up so that she could see Father Thomas's eyes. "Can you put the children at rest?" she asked. "Can you help them cross over?"

Father Thomas thought for a moment before he replied. "Are you saying that these children are dead but they still cry?"

"Are there no spirits in the world of the *Wasichu*?" Little

Buffalo Woman asked. "The other Black Robes here speak of the Holy Spirit. But they don't seem to know of any other spirits. Are you the same? Don't you understand?"

Father Thomas stared. Little Buffalo Woman had said that the children had died in a storm the previous year. He didn't want to believe he had heard their spirits still crying.

Little Buffalo Woman saw his frightened look. "They will not harm you," she said. "They are lost and do not know they are dead. Some of our medicine people have been able to reach them and talk to them, but the children will not leave their mother. I had only hoped that you could help the children go on to the Other Side."

"I know how to help people before they die," Father Thomas said, "but I have never tried to talk to a spirit. I wouldn't know what to say or do."

"I understand." Little Buffalo Woman turned and took hold of her cousin's arm. The three of them entered the village.

Once he was among the lodges, Father Thomas noticed that there was crying everywhere. Little Buffalo Woman explained that the children often cried at this time of night from hunger. It was hardest after dark, when the temperature dropped and the cold crept into the lodges.

Father Thomas wanted to believe that his experience with the crying in the storm had been nothing more than the voices of these hungry children carrying out from the village. Certainly this was what he had heard, he reasoned, not lost souls coming back to wail.

At the woman's lodge, Little Buffalo Woman spoke while she settled the older woman into her robes and stroked her back until she fell asleep. "She will not eat at times like this," she explained. "From the time each storm begins until the snow stops falling, she will not touch food."

"How is it that she is still alive?" Father Thomas asked.

"You will have to ask *Wankantanka*. Only the One Above has

kept her alive, for whatever reasons, for this woman certainly should have crossed over from hunger by now."

"She isn't even that thin," Father Thomas observed. "You appear more gaunt than she does."

"This is true," Little Buffalo Woman said. "Maybe you will learn why this is so if you ever speak to *Wankantanka*. He has made the decision to keep her alive. Maybe she has displeased Him and is being made to suffer."

"She will be rewarded in the end," Father Thomas said. "Will you come for me when she is near death so that I might give her the last rites?"

Little Buffalo Woman frowned. "I do not give permission on behalf of others. This is not our way. It is up to her."

"Maybe she will not be capable of speaking for herself. Will you ask her?"

"I will see if she remembers you and I will tell her of your wishes. Do not look for me to carry her word to you, though. It will be her decision."

"That is fair," Father Thomas said.

Little Buffalo Woman studied him. "You must feel that you have strong medicine to talk to your god so he will make things good for a dying person. If so, how come you cannot help that person after death?"

"That is not something generally practiced by my people," Father Thomas said. "We pray to the angel and saints on behalf of the dead we loved, but we don't speak to the dead themselves."

"So what have you come to these lands for?" Little Buffalo Woman asked.

"To help the living. To prepare them to meet God at death."

"Things are not good for me," Little Buffalo Woman said, "but it is Wailing Woman who needs help more than I." She pointed to her friend, lying deep in troubled sleep. "She has lost everyone. Her husband and all of her brothers and sisters, all gone. Three children died of sickness, and last winter her two remaining children, the twins, froze to death in a storm. She could have used one like you a long time ago."

"It is especially people like her who need help," Father Thomas said. "That is why I have come."

Father Thomas and Little Buffalo Woman looked up as the entrance flap opened. A small and sharp-featured warrior entered and balked at seeing Father Thomas. He scowled and turned his eyes to Little Buffalo Woman.

"I see you are here again," he said to her in Lakota.

"You knew I would be here," Little Buffalo Woman said.

Father Thomas recognized the man as one of the Brulé leaders, a warrior named Short Bull. The warrior had been pointed out earlier in the week by one of the other priests, who had said that this man had no use for the mission or the school. He continually talked against any changes in the old way of life and had gathered into a group all those who agreed with him.

There was talk among the missionaries that Short Bull would soon be moving his followers away, into an area of their own, much as Kicking Bear had separated those Minneconjou who wished to follow him away from Big Foot's main camp on Cheyenne River. Short Bull would soon be a leader against any type of assimilation.

It was obvious to Father Thomas from Short Bull's glare that the Brulé chief would be demanding that he leave. He wished now that he hadn't lingered. The way that Short Bull's face had knotted into anger, Father Thomas feared that both he and Little Buffalo Woman were in grave danger.

ELEVEN

SHORT BULL stood near the door flap waiting for Little Buffalo Woman to join him. When she did not move, he stepped past Father Thomas to look her square in the face. They spoke in Lakota.

"My war-brother is worried about his wife," he said. "You know that his back troubles him when the cold comes. He wants you to know that he wonders why you go out into the storms. What if you get lost?"

"That will not happen," Little Buffalo Woman assured him. She pointed to the sleeping woman. "I must help her whenever I can. My husband knows that."

Short Bull glanced quickly at Father Thomas. His close-set eyes emitted hatred. "Why did you send for a Black Robe?"

"He came on his own, to help," Little Buffalo Woman answered. "He is new at the mission."

"Tell him he is not welcome," Short Bull said.

Father Thomas could understand almost none of the words, but their meaning was clear.

"I don't want to make trouble for you," he told Little Buffalo Woman. "Maybe I should go."

"Stay until I have finished with Short Bull," she said.

Short Bull knew no English. He grew angrier at having been excluded from the conversation. He now glared at Little Buffalo Woman.

"Why are you speaking with him?" he demanded.

"He helped me get Wailing Woman back to her bed," Little Buffalo Woman said. "He is not a bad man."

Short Bull spat on the ground. "All *Wasichu* are bad! When are you going back to your lodge?"

"If you wake Wailing Woman, I will have to stay longer," Little Buffalo Woman said. "She needs sleep. You can tell my husband that I will come very soon."

"He will be angry that you didn't come with me."

"I will be along soon, Short Bull. He understands, even though you don't."

"I will tell him that you have invited a Black Robe, that you decided to follow the *Wasichu* god."

"Tell him what you want, Short Bull," Little Buffalo Woman said. "I'm not going back with you."

Short Bull pushed through the door flap, back out into the storm.

Little Buffalo Woman looked at Father Thomas sadly. "You see how it is with many of my people. They hate all *Wasichu*, even the holy men."

"I am sorry this is the case," Father Thomas said. "Maybe in time I can persuade them to listen to me."

"Maybe," Little Buffalo Woman said, "but likely not. You will have to suffer for the wrongs of your people. No matter how honest you may be, many of the Lakota will not trust you, especially Kicking Bear's people. These are the ones you seek to reach, but these are the ones who will resist you the hardest."

"Could you help me?" Father Thomas asked. "Someone like

you could speak in my behalf. You could help me a great deal."

Little Buffalo Woman studied him. "I will consider it only if you can help my friend," she said. "If you will learn how to reach her crying children and get them to cross over where they belong, then I will know you are a strong and wise Black Robe, with sacred medicine. If your god teaches you this, then I will know that helping you is good."

"You ask a lot of me," Father Thomas said, picking up the lantern. "I know that God will help me answer your challenge, though, and I pray that I will be equal to the task."

"You will have to be more than equal to reach Kicking Bear's people," Little Buffalo Woman told him. "You will have to be far ahead of any Black Robe who has ever come into these lands."

"I will be leaving for Kicking Bear's village before long," Father Thomas said. "I will come back and get the little bag before I go. Is there anything you can tell me that might help me reach those people?"

"I think you know how to reach them," Little Buffalo Woman said. "Always speak straight, as you have with me, and you will gain their respect. They may not accept your medicine for a time, or ever, but they will respect you."

"Thank you," Father Thomas said. "I will return for the little bag in the next couple of days." He looked once more at the woman asleep in her robes. "Tell her I will pray for her children."

Father Thomas left the lodge and stepped out into the winter night. The storm had eased up, and the blowing snow had settled into high drifts. He picked his way around many of them before he reached the mission school. Just outside, he met Father Lindebner and another priest, along with three brothers.

Father Lindebner's voice was thick with irritation. "Where did you go? We were set to start looking for you."

"I have had an interesting time," Father Thomas announced. "As soon as the weather opens, I am going up to Kicking Bear's village. I have found a woman here who has connections up there. I have a contact I can work from."

"You will wait until Faatter Digmann returns first," Father Lindebner ordered. "You cannot go making decisions yourself."

"Yes, but I am supposed to go up there in time anyway," Father Thomas said. "I just wanted to say that I feel more confident now."

"What makes you so certain you are supposed to go up there?" Father Lindebner demanded.

"My orders," Father Thomas said. "The letter with my orders says I am to bring the word of Christ to those who are not yet attending a mission church."

"I have the letter," Father Lindebner said. "It says you are to bring the word of God to the Sioux. It says nothing about which of them you teach."

"How did you get my letter?" Father Thomas asked.

"It was lying on your bett," Father Lindebner replied. "You were supposed to give it to me anyway."

Father Lindebner turned and began to lead the other priest and the brothers back to the rectory. Father Thomas hurried up next to him and held his lantern up. "I'm still assigned to open up Cheyenne River, aren't I?" he asked.

"I cannot say," Father Lindebner replied. "That is not up to me. Faatter Digmann will make the final decision when he returns from Pine Ridge."

"Final decision? But Cheyenne River is my reason for coming out here. I know that in my heart."

Father Lindebner walked through the snow without speaking.

"I must go as soon as I can," Father Thomas said. "What if an Episcopal mission has already started?"

Father Lindebner raised a hand into the winter air. "Faatter Thomas, I will discuss the matter with you no further."

Father Thomas fell in behind him. The brothers broke off

and disappeared into the darkness toward their own quarters. Father Lindebner spoke to the other priest at the door of the rectory and ignored Father Thomas completely.

That Father Lindebner did not care for him did not bother Father Thomas in the least. What concerned him was the fact that the older priest could very easily be planning to keep him from going up to Kicking Bear's village. Father Lindebner required absolute obedience; Father Thomas believed he had not disobeyed Father Lindebner, not even once. Arguments did not qualify as disobedience.

But Father Lindebner saw things differently. As a result, his report of Father Thomas's first month at the mission would not be good. In fact, Father Thomas worried, the report might be bad enough to warrant reconsideration of his mere presence on the reservation. After all, a priest who couldn't do as he was told, and in proper order, would not be capable of keeping wild Indians in line. With the friction that now existed between them, Father Thomas realized that Father Lindebner would never consider him competent to carry the word of God to anyone, much less to such a camp as Kicking Bear's.

Father Thomas kicked snow from his boots before entering the rectory. He took one last look out into the darkness. A voice inside told him to turn and go back to the village, that his time at St. Francis was over. He made his way directly to his sleeping quarters, where he sat with his head in his hands, agonizing over the decision he had already made. He would leave. Tonight.

Father Thomas began packing his few belongings. One hand wanted to stuff his clothes inside the leather bag as fast as possible, while the other hand wanted to tear the clothes out and set the bag in the corner. He stopped in the middle of his work and closed his eyes.

"Sacred Heart of Jesus, I beg for guidance. I am not a disobedient son. I want to do your work. I want to go where I know my orders are directing me. I want to do the right thing."

Suddenly Father Lindebner burst into the room. "One of the priests said you are packing," he said. "What is this?"

Father Thomas looked up and frowned. "I didn't hear you knock, Father."

"I said, what are you doing?" Father Lindebner demanded. Other priests began to gather behind him.

"It is time for me to leave," Father Thomas said. "I must go where my orders have dictated. I know I am meant to work among the Minneconjou."

"What! You can't do that!"

"I can and I must," Father Thomas said. "I was ordered to go there."

"Ordered?" Father Lindebner echoed. "I give you the orders now."

"My obedience belongs to my mission," Father Thomas said. He picked up his bag. "Now, if you will excuse me."

Father Lindebner stood blocking the door. "I won't let you go. You are a disgrace to Gott Almighty."

Father Thomas took a deep breath. "Father Lindebner, I'm going through that door, one way or another."

"You wouldn't do that!"

"Are you going to let me pass, Father?"

Father Lindebner stepped aside, yelling at Father Thomas for his disobedience. The other priests asked Father Thomas to reconsider. Father Thomas bundled himself into his thick coat and stepped from the rectory out into the winter night.

Father Thomas stood a distance from the rectory and looked toward the shadowed cluster of ragged lodges along the creek. The storm had passed entirely and the clouds had departed. The snow, sculpted by the wind into smooth and frozen banks, gleamed in the light of a near-full moon.

Tonight he had forced a dramatic change in his life. He knew he would fight with his conscience over his decision. But in his heart, he knew he was right. In actuality, Father Lindebner had given him no choice. Had he stayed in the rectory with the others, even until the morning, Father Thomas knew that he would never have gotten the chance to leave.

Going up to Cheyenne River was the reason he had come to this land, to teach the last holdouts against the white man's god. Nothing could change his mission to do that. Now he would begin his journey to the Minneconjou without the blessings of his superiors. But he still considered himself a man of God, and he would do his best to convey holy scripture to those who would hear him.

Father Thomas felt confident in his ability to reach them. He had come to learn that they weren't the ignorant savages many would have him believe, and he knew that with the right approach, they would listen. It wouldn't be easy, but he was certain that he would gather a good number into his fold. But first he had to get there. Whether or not he made it in this weather, with no extra clothing or supplies, was up to God.

First he would get the small skin bag from Little Buffalo Woman, which he would take up to Cherry Creek for the woman named Fawn-That-Goes-Dancing. With any luck, he wouldn't have to begin his journey tonight, having no idea of where he was going. He hoped he would be allowed to keep the fire going in Wailing Woman's lodge and maybe get a little sleep before he departed in the morning.

Father Thomas had no idea of how he might find Little Buffalo Woman again or the lodge where Wailing Woman lived. He would just have to look around the village until he found one or the other.

Without so much as a look back, he began to march toward the lodges. The frozen trail crunched under his feet. He listened intently, but he could hear no crying voices, only his own heavy breathing in the frosty night air. Nothing, in fact, appeared quite the same. He wondered how he would be welcomed this time.

As he entered the camp, wondering if anyone knew he was

present, he heard the voice of Short Bull, who came up behind him.

"No, no!" Father Thomas yelled in English. Little Buffalo Woman, who hurried up behind him, talked to her brother-in-law in Sioux until he settled down.

"He cannot understand why you have come back," she said. "He thinks you want to steal something."

Father Thomas, his breath vaporizing, stepped back from the approaching Short Bull. Little Buffalo Woman spoke in Lakota and Short Bull stopped, apparently demanding an explanation.

"I don't steal," Father Thomas said. "Tell him that."

Little Buffalo Woman translated for Short Bull, whose mood seemed to darken even more. When he was finished with his reply, Little Buffalo Woman cleared her throat.

"He says he knows that you did not come back to spend the night with Wailing Woman, or with any other woman," she told Father Thomas. "He says that you Black Robes do not know what to do with a woman. So you must have come to take something you liked and wanted for yourself."

"I came back to get whatever it is you wanted me to give to your friend on Cherry Creek," Father Thomas said. "I'm leaving for there tonight."

"Tonight?"

"Yes. I can no longer stay with the other priests. It is time for me to leave. I cannot wait."

Little Buffalo Woman told Short Bull the news. He studied Father Thomas up and down, then said something to Little Buffalo Woman. He stared at Father Thomas a short time longer and walked away.

"Short Bull believes it would be best if you left just before first light," Little Buffalo Woman said. "You should get what rest you can in Wailing Woman's lodge."

"I thought he was worried about me stealing," Father Thomas said. "Why would he trust me in Wailing Woman's lodge?"

"He believes you now," Little Buffalo Woman said. "He knows that you came for the bundle I have for Fawn-That-Goes-Dancing. He thinks you are a brave man for deciding to leave, even though the cold could kill you."

Confused by Short Bull's change of heart, Father Thomas followed Little Buffalo Woman to Wailing Woman's lodge. Inside, she helped him arrange a bed for himself on the opposite side of the lodge from the sleeping woman.

"I want to thank you for offering to take the bundle to Fawn-That-Goes-Dancing," Little Buffalo Woman said. "She is not expecting it, and she might not even remember me, but it is very important."

"I understand," Father Thomas said.

"Do you think you can survive three to four days of walking in this weather?" she asked.

"I can survive it," he answered with conviction. "I didn't come all the way out here to die the first winter."

Little Buffalo Woman smiled. "No, I don't think you did."

From outside came the sound of a horse snorting. Little Buffalo Woman peeked out of the door flap. "Stay here," she told Father Thomas. "I'll be right back."

Father Thomas waited, listening to the muffled voices outside the lodge. Wailing Woman turned over in her bed and fell back asleep. Little Buffalo Woman returned and sat down next to Father Thomas, smiling broadly.

"You won't have to walk up to the Minneconjou village," she said. "Short Bull says you should be riding, not walking."

"Short Bull gave me a horse?" Father Thomas asked.

"One of his finest ponies," Little Buffalo Woman said. "He says you are a brave man and if you are to die, it should be on a good pony."

"I have nothing to trade him."

"It is a gift," Little Buffalo Woman said. "He has packed enough provisions for two small meals a day. If you want more than that, he said you will have to find game."

"I can't take the food," Father Thomas said. "Your people need it far more than I do."

"It is a gift," Little Buffalo Woman said again. "Take it with honor. It was given to you in honor. You are a strong and special man to have gained Short Bull's respect so quickly. Just be gone at first light so the other Black Robes do not try to stop you."

Little Buffalo Woman stood up and started for the door.

"I don't know how to thank you," Father Thomas said. "You have done a great deal for me."

"Just give the little pouch to Fawn-That-Goes-Dancing," Little Buffalo Woman said. "That will be enough thanks."

"I surely will," Father Thomas said. His eyes stayed with Little Buffalo Woman for a long moment. "I hope things get better for you and your people."

"*Wankantanka* works in strange ways," she told him. "I do not worry. Good luck to you."

Little Buffalo Woman slipped past the door flap. Father Thomas stared at the spot where she had been standing as if her essence were still there, warm and soft against the patched lining of the lodge. He thought about her words, that God works in mysterious ways. How many times had he heard that from priests and others of his own religion? He realized that the Lakota people certainly knew about the Supreme Being, though they worshiped in a different way, a way that was not acceptable to the white culture.

Father Thomas tossed a couple of sticks into the fire and lay down on his side, watching the flames grow from the wood. He felt as though he was at the start of an awakening of sorts, the first stages of an insightful knowledge about God that he hadn't felt before. He had come to bring the teachings of Christ to a people who were supposed to be ignorant of God's ways. He would have to think very hard to tell them something they didn't already know.

He wondered at the irony of his situation. He had been around good people all of his life and had met any number of kindly bishops during his time in the seminary, but he hadn't truly learned the meaning of charity until tonight. He had been given a horse and food as a gift by a rebellious Sioux leader who despised Black Robes and all they stood for. Yet this embittered man was willing to show his utmost respect. It was hard to understand someone who treated an enemy with that kind of regard.

As Father Thomas closed his eyes to sleep, he realized that he had truly been blessed. God certainly was watching over him. Perhaps He had sent Little Buffalo Woman to speak in his behalf. She didn't know him at all, yet she had gone to great lengths to help him.

Something about her would stay with him. It seemed ironic that he should come to these cold, open plains to find an angel dressed in ragged muslin.

TWELVE

THE SNOW had softened, and the morning sun brought birdsong from the cottonwoods along the river. The bitter winds had left, at least for a time. Here and there, men and boys were riding, while the women of the village walked along the river and talked about their lives.

Fawn sat on a blanket and watched as Catches Lance led a gentle mare across the hillside. Little Star sat atop the pony, holding on to the mane and shouting with glee, kicking the horse's sides boldly.

Night Bird sat next to Fawn, amused. Hawk stood a little way from Fawn, yelling, "It's my turn, Little Star! You got to ride long enough. Catches Lance, tell Little Star that it's my turn!"

"You just got off the pony, Hawk," Fawn reminded him. "Come, sit down and be quiet or you will lose your next turn."

Hawk grudgingly obeyed. He made snowballs and lobbed them down the slope. They began to fall closer and closer to the mare.

"Stop throwing snowballs, Hawk!" Little Star yelled. "Mother, make him quit."

Fawn asked Hawk to behave himself. He got up, found another place a ways distant, and sat down. He placed his elbows on his knees and rested his chin in his hands. Soon he was gazing out across the open bottom, dreaming of the day he could ride as long as he wished and wouldn't have to share his pony with anyone.

Night Bird smiled at Fawn. "There are not enough gentle horses in the herd for the young to learn on. But soon your son will be riding a fine pony."

"Yes," Fawn said. "Hawk is growing up quickly. Maybe Catches Lance can find him a pony before long."

"Catches Lance enjoys being with your children," Night Bird said. "Maybe in time I can give him a son of his own."

"Yes, you will, in time," Fawn said. "That will be a happy day for everyone. I feel the warmer weather is a good sign."

Fawn felt thankful that the warmer weather had come, but she was even more grateful that she and Catches Lance had begun to talk together once again. Hawk and Little Star had asked Catches Lance to take them riding just that morning, so it had actually been the children who had gotten Catches Lance to talking. Though he wouldn't tell Fawn what was really bothering him, at least they had begun communicating.

Night Bird was relieved, too. During the time that Catches Lance would not speak with Fawn, there had also been tension between herself and Catches Lance. It had been Tangled Hair's anger at Catches Lance that had helped to change things. Tangled Hair had made Catches Lance understand that both his wife and his sister were worried about his behavior.

But Tangled Hair's outburst had further eroded his friendship with Catches Lance. The two had been inseparable as youngsters until, in their early adolescence, Tangled Hair's mother had gone back to her people, the Arapaho, and the resultant burden on Goes-to-River had caused friction.

Catches Lance had voiced his opinion that his mother was overdoing her attention to Tangled Hair and neglecting Fawn and him. Tangled Hair didn't deserve any special favors just because he had chosen not to go with his own mother. Fawn had never shared those feelings and had been unable to understand Catches Lance's behavior. She still couldn't understand it.

Despite all this, Tangled Hair had remained true to his friend. But after Catches Lance's mother had left, and especially since their recent trip to Pine Ridge, Tangled Hair had begun to feel that he didn't deserve any more blame.

Tangled Hair had left three days before to seek power. He had said he did not know how long he would be gone, but not to worry about him. The weather was warm and he would be fine. Before he left, he told Catches Lance, "Open your eyes and see how you have hurt your sister's feelings."

Catches Lance had sulked for two full days. Then Hawk and Little Star had asked to go riding. Seemingly, Catches Lance had opened up. Fawn hoped that when the children were through riding, she could speak with him at length.

Night Bird's humor had brightened considerably. She had renewed hope for the two of them, but she realized that their reconciliation would take time and work. "Maybe Catches Lance is finally beginning to find himself," she said. "Your mother's death left him very confused about things. But I don't think he should have been angry at you."

"I want my brother to be happy," Fawn said. "I will always help him if I can, but he must find contentment on his own."

"It will be a time yet before he can be content," Night Bird said. "Sometimes I think that he believes your mother would still be alive if she hadn't moved down to Pine Ridge."

"That is foolish," Fawn said. "We could not have saved her from the coughing sickness."

"No, he believes that up here she would not have gotten sick," Night Bird said. "He thinks that Sees-the-Bull-Rolling took her down there to spite him."

"I know that he did not want her to be married, not to anyone," Fawn said. "That made it hard for Sees-the-Bull-Rolling to make friends with him. Catches Lance was very angry when he asked her to leave us and become a follower of the Black Robes."

"Yes, but your mother made the decision to move down there herself," Night Bird pointed out. "He should not blame Sees-the-Bull-Rolling."

"It is over and cannot be changed," Fawn said. "Catches Lance is foolish to remain angry. I just hope he can get over it."

Night Bird looked into the distance, then lowered her eyes to the ground.

"What is it?" Fawn asked.

"I believe there is something more serious bothering my husband, but he won't discuss it with me."

"What do you believe it is?"

"Tangled Hair told me that Catches Lance wants to be heard as a strong voice among the Minneconjou," Night Bird said. "But Kicking Bear will not recognize him. I believe that is making Catches Lance angry, also."

"Catches Lance has always wanted to distinguish himself," Fawn said. "But the old days are gone and he cannot prove himself by warring and taking horses from enemies, as was once done. He will have to be content with the way things are."

"I am worried," Night Bird said. "I fear that he will want to prove himself in some way. I hope he does not try to talk back to Kicking Bear. The people will not be on his side. Kicking Bear is too powerful."

"I wish we had the old ways back," Fawn said. "Then he could lead a war party, if that is what he wished to do. Things would be settled in the old ways."

"Not everyone wishes for the old days, not like they used to," Night Bird said. "There are some who are talking about taking the White Man's Road. They might move to Big Foot's village before long. There are getting to be more of them, you know."

"I realize this," Fawn said. "I cannot understand why they would make that kind of choice."

"They believe that the *Wasichu* will feed them. They believe that if they act right, they will be given good clothes and food, and live well."

"Do they think that the rags the Black Robes hand out are good clothes? Don't they know they are getting cast-off *Wasichu* garments? That makes them beggars. Is that what they want?"

"You know how hard it is to talk to someone who is hungry," Night Bird said. "You will do anything to stop your children from crying."

Hawk stood up and came over. "Is it my turn to ride yet?" he asked.

"Yes," Fawn said. "You may take a turn."

"Can I take the mare and ride alone this time?" he asked. "I have ridden her alone before. I won't get hurt."

Fawn hesitated.

"Please?" Hawk begged. "I won't go very far. Just down the hill to the bottom and back up. Please? She won't try to take off with me. I won't let her."

"If you promise not to kick her in the sides," Fawn said. "I don't want you falling off."

"I have to kick her or she won't go," Hawk said. "I won't kick her hard, though. I promise."

"Tell Catches Lance I said you could ride alone," Fawn told him. She called after him to be careful as he shot across the hill to meet Catches Lance, waving and yelling.

"Hawk is a very strong boy," Night Bird said. "I'll bet that in the old days he would have counted coup before he reached eighteen winters."

"You are probably right," Fawn said. "But we will never know for sure. There are no more buffalo and no more quests for glory. Hawk will never know what that was like, except to hear the elders tell their stories."

Fawn's memories had blossomed to vivid life since the experience with her mother. Even the strong, wonderful feelings of those lost days came back to her. Any time she wished, she could envision her mother, looking young, a broad smile on her face, walking with her along a river, telling her about the ducks and geese, and the shore birds that waded the shallows searching for food.

When the warriors went off into enemy lands, it was a custom for the women to spend their days on hilltops looking for signs of their return. Fawn remembered standing thus with her mother, looking out with her from a high point, often seeing a herd of buffalo grazing in the distance.

Fawn marveled at the clarity of the memory. Nothing could compare to a clear spring morning, when the yellow-breasted birds were singing in the foreground and she was looking far out across the backs of the shaggy beasts, a rolling brown tide in the vast grassy distance.

It saddened Fawn to realize that this sight was forever gone. At the same time, she knew that it was better to remember and feel warm at the memory than to disturb the beauty of the moment with outrage at a loss that couldn't be remedied. Maybe this was the way she was meant to think of those times: to be happy that she had a clear mind to see and feel the things she would never experience again.

Down on the bottom, Hawk was attempting to kick the old mare into a gallop. He could get only a fast trot out of her. Still, he yelled war songs he had heard the elders singing.

"That Hawk is a bold one," Catches Lance said as he carried Little Star over and sat down next to Night Bird. "He would ride clear to the Black Hills if he could."

Little Star was pouting. "It isn't fair that Hawk gets to take another turn so soon," she said. "My turn wasn't over yet."

"You'll get another chance to ride." Catches Lance began to poke her gently in the ribs with a finger. "You must be sure to never go to sleep while you ride. You aren't asleep, are you? Let me make certain."

Little Star squirmed and giggled while Catches Lance tickled her ribs. Night Bird laughed. Fawn turned her eyes to the distance, once again thinking of the circle of dancers she had seen in her odd dream when the sun turned dark. She saw Night Bird and Hawk and Little Star, but none of them were laughing. Their faces were worn with fatigue.

Since her experience, Fawn had thought of all kinds of questions she wished she had asked her mother at the time. She wondered if these questions would ever be answered, or if she could call on her mother and have another experience. It seemed more likely now that her mother had shown her all this when she did so that Fawn might have time to contemplate the meaning of her visions; it had not necessarily been to show her everyone who would be involved with them. After all, she had not seen herself among the dancers.

Nor had she seen Catches Lance. She wondered about this. Perhaps Catches Lance had been viewing the dancers from somewhere nearby.

The sight of Hawk and Little Star in the circle continued to bother her. She couldn't forget how nervous her children had appeared. Night Bird had been holding them very tightly, her face etched with deep concentration. Fawn wanted to believe that the deep lines in her sister-in-law's face had come from dancing for a long time, not from the extreme worry that had seemed to be there.

Each time she thought about the dancers, she realized a little more of the truth. There had been a sense of urgency to the scene, as if all of the people were reaching for something, were dancing so that some dream might come true.

It was common for her people to dance in order to ensure that some event might come to pass, such as a successful buffalo hunt, or a successful raid on an enemy. This dance, for whatever its purpose, appeared to be just as important as any of the old dances. Maybe more so.

Fawn noticed Night Bird watching her now. Catches Lance and Little Star were walking down the hill toward Hawk and the mare.

"What is it, Fawn?" Night Bird asked. "You look deeply troubled. Is something wrong?"

"No," she lied. "Is Catches Lance taking Little Star for another ride?"

"Yes," Night Bird answered. "Don't you remember him asking? You told him to go ahead, but to bring both of them back to the lodge before long."

"Did I say that?"

"Yes, you did. But your eyes were glassy."

"I must have been dreaming," Fawn said.

Night Bird was staring at her when a camp crier announced the entrance of someone into the village. They looked off toward the north to see a lone rider approaching. He rode a beautiful black stallion and wore a buffalo calfskin vest decorated with eagle feathers.

"He must be someone special," Night Bird said. "He is wearing the shirt of a leader."

Fawn called down to Catches Lance, who had already seen what was going on. He let the mare loose and waited while Fawn and Night Bird came down the hill.

"Do you suppose that rider has come to be a new leader among our people?" Hawk asked.

"I don't know why he has come," Fawn replied. "Maybe we will know before long."

They hurried together toward the center of the village, where the rider was sitting the black stallion. Everyone watched while Kicking Bear came out of his lodge and invited the warrior down from his horse.

As the warrior dismounted, Fawn realized that he hadn't lived among his people for some time. He spoke halting Lakota, and he was too well fed to have been living on the reservation. Still, he was greeted with respect, and Fawn heard him say to Kicking Bear that he had come from Sitting Bull's village on Grand River.

"I am Shining Horse, son of Sitting Bull," he said. "My father has sent me to your village to tell you what I know of things to come."

"You are welcome here," Kicking Bear said. "The old wise one, Sitting Bull, must believe you can help us."

"I can help all the Lakota people," Shining Horse said. "I bring important news to all the villages about those who will come again to take our lands. We must unite against them. When you are ready, I will speak to your council."

The newcomer intrigued Fawn. She stood nearby and realized that he had felt her gaze. He turned to look at her and stared momentarily.

"Come," Kicking Bear told Shining Horse. "We will begin the council right away."

Shining Horse followed Kicking Bear to his lodge. The camp buzzed with conversation as village elders entered their own lodges to change into their ceremonial clothing.

"I am going back to the lodge and warm some broth," Night Bird said. "The air is getting colder again."

Hawk and Little Star asked to go along. Fawn gave them permission and they hurried away with Night Bird. When they had left, Fawn turned to see Catches Lance watching the warrior and Kicking Bear as they talked near the council lodge.

"What do you suppose he knows about the future of the Lakota?" he asked Fawn.

"I don't know," Fawn said. "He has to be special to be wearing eagle feathers given to him by Sitting Bull."

"Didn't you hear him say he was Sitting Bull's son?" Catches Lance asked.

"Yes, I heard," Fawn replied. "But that does not matter. No man of Sitting Bull's stature would place eagle feathers on another in that manner unless he was very special."

Tangled Hair joined them, having just come down from the

hills. Fawn and Catches Lance were surprised to see him. "I have already learned some things," Tangled Hair said. "It was time to come down."

"You have power already?" Catches Lance asked. "I do not believe you can have learned much in such a short time."

"Why should it worry you one way or the other?" Tangled Hair asked. "It has to do with my power, not yours. You can seek your own power any time you wish."

Catches Lance pointed to where Shining Horse was being escorted into the council lodge. "This warrior is an honored son of Sitting Bull," he told Tangled Hair. "He has been in the *Wasichu* lands and knows much about their race. It is said that he can beat the *Wasichu* at their own game. He is going to take news to all the villages on the reservation. I am going to go with him."

"What are you talking about?" Fawn asked. "No one asked you to go along."

"He will want me along," Catches Lance said. "There is much territory to cover, and I can help him cross it."

Catches Lance left to catch his best pony. Fawn told Tangled Hair that this was the first she had heard of her brother leaving with the warrior who had just come into camp.

"I don't understand it," Fawn said. "He doesn't even know that warrior."

"Catches Lance is in need of being recognized," Tangled Hair said. "Maybe he thinks he can go with this warrior and be honored for it."

"What if the warrior does not want him along? Then Catches Lance will become angry."

"Catches Lance is already angry. And he seems to be getting angrier. Maybe the warrior will take him along and it will be good for him."

"I hope so," Fawn said. "Something good has to happen for Catches Lance before long, or I fear he will do something that will be bad for everyone."

THIRTEEN

SHINING HORSE told the council everything he had told his father, and how he had come to know it. Then the warriors took turns telling of their war deeds before they gave their views on the upcoming land commission. All were in favor of fighting it.

After that discussion, Shining Horse brought up the fact that White Hair McLaughlin had been tampering with Sitting Bull's mail. Those in the council immediately became suspicious that their agent might be doing the same thing.

"I cannot say that your agent is doing that," Shining Horse told them. "So it would not be good to confront him with it. Even if he were, he would have to deny it. I mention this only because there were a number of letters. Someone has been trying to reach my father."

"Do you have any idea of what the letters said?" Kicking Bear asked.

"No idea," Shining Horse replied. "I think it is important to think about who would want to reach my father, and possibly you, too, Kicking Bear. Maybe there are many who are not getting their mail for some reason."

"What would the *Wasichu* have to hide from us?" one of the council members asked.

"I can't think of anything," Shining Horse said. "Perhaps it is just White Hair who is doing this to my father."

"I have relatives among the Arapaho," Kicking Bear said. "When the snows have gone, I will journey over into their lands and see if they have tried to send letters to Sitting Bull."

"In the meantime, I will travel to the other villages and tell them what I know," Shining Horse said. "It is important that all our people learn of what is to come."

Kicking Bear nodded. "It is good that you will do this. We have few provisions, but we will give you some to take with you. And, like Sitting Bull, I will give you something to wear that will distinguish you and let all those you meet know that you have my blessing as well."

"What are the feelings of the other Minneconjou camps?" Shining Horse asked.

"Hump and Touch-the-Cloud live in a camp at the mouth of Cherry Creek," Kicking Bear replied. "They are against taking the White Man's Road. But my uncle by marriage, Big Foot, has talked about schools and Black Robes. It would be good if you visited both villages before you went on to the others. Maybe you can talk some sense into Big Foot."

After the council adjourned, Kicking Bear gave Shining Horse four weasel tails to place with the eagle feathers on his vest. Kicking Bear touched the small pouch he kept behind his ear and then held the weasel tails in his hand for a time. He fastened them to Shining Horse's vest, singing an old song of the hunt.

During the singing, Shining Horse noticed a very pretty woman watching him, the same woman who had been watching him when he had first come into the village. Besides her beauty, he saw a strength in her that he could not explain.

Something in her eyes spoke to him of knowledge, the kind that could be gained only through extreme trial.

As he waited for some last words with Kicking Bear, the woman approached him. "My name is Fawn-That-Goes-Dancing. I have a younger brother who knows the trails very well. He could go with you and show you the easiest way to travel." She pointed to Catches Lance, who was leading his pony into the village.

Shining Horse smiled. "If you know the trails, I would rather have you along."

Fawn didn't smile. "I just wanted to offer you the help of someone who could do you good. I'm sorry if I bothered you."

"Wait," Shining Horse said. "Please. I would like to speak with your brother. I had intended to ask Kicking Bear if he knew of two warriors who would accompany me. I haven't been on these trails for a very long time. Some of them I have never traveled."

"The second warrior you should take is Tangled Hair."

"I thank you for your help," Shining Horse said. "Maybe when I return, we can talk again, the two of us."

"Maybe," Fawn said.

Shining Horse told Kicking Bear that he would like to take Catches Lance and Tangled Hair with him. Kicking Bear said he had no objections, if the two wished to go along.

Catches Lance realized that Fawn had spoken to Shining Horse for him. At first he felt angry, believing that he should have been allowed to speak in his own behalf. Then he reconsidered and thanked Fawn. He hurried to tell Night Bird good-bye.

Tangled Hair did not wish to go at first. Fawn took him aside. "It would be good for you as well as for Catches Lance," she said. "You could help one another."

Tangled Hair kicked the dirt.

"I thought you would want to go," she said.

"You should have asked me first," he told her. "You know that your brother and I are quarreling now."

"I hoped you could resolve that on the trail."

"That is between Catches Lance and myself. I believe that you want me to protect your brother."

"You are right," Fawn said "I do not want anything to happen to Catches Lance. I should not have said anything to the warrior about you. I will tell him you do not want to go."

Tangled Hair stopped her. "It is too late for that."

"Then why are you complaining?"

"I want no more trouble with Catches Lance," Tangled Hair said. "He will think I am trying to steal his glory."

"That will not happen. This is not a journey for glory."

"Yes, it certainly is. That warrior, Shining Horse—he will be considered strong and brave for telling the Lakota people what he knows. I saw you talking to him."

"Is that why you are angry?" Fawn asked. "You know that I care for you as a brother, and as nothing else. It could never be any other way."

"I wish you would think differently," Tangled Hair said. "I could make you a good husband."

"You know that I think you are a very good man," Fawn said. "But you have never learned that I cannot think of you as a husband. You have to understand that."

Shining Horse arrived with his pony, ready to travel. Tangled Hair, frowning, left to catch his best horse and prepare for the journey.

"I came to bring news that I hoped would unite us all," Shining Horse said, "but I find that there is a lot of disagreement among villages, and even within families."

"You are right," Fawn said. "When a people are left to die, with no food or clothing, they turn against one another."

Shining Horse looked into the distance. "I have been gone for a long time. I had no idea it was this bad."

"My brother and Tangled Hair can tell you how bad it is," Fawn said. "You can learn much from them."

"I feel that I could learn much from you as well," Shining Horse told her.

"While you are gone, think about your mission, not about me," Fawn advised. "If you can somehow unite most of our people, you will have greatly helped the Lakota nation. If there are many who want to take the White Man's Road, it will be harder for you. Then you will see how bad things can really get."

The wind blew lightly, subtly warm, softening the snow. God's breath, Father Thomas thought. God's breath had saved him from death. But how long had he been gone from the mission? He had lost count of the days.

His pony had gotten away the first night out. After a long, hard ride, to which he was not accustomed, he had fallen asleep without hobbling the horse. Dawn had brought him scrambling from his blankets to find that the pony had slipped away in the darkness.

He should have returned to the Rosebud. Instead, he had chosen to continue his journey and hope for the best. Despite his blunder with the pony, he would reach the people who needed him. God protects fools and small children; he had heard it said often, and now he prayed that it was so.

Luckily, he still had the blankets and some of the slim ration of food that had been given him, but there was no more than a two-day supply left. He was rapidly weakening from hunger, and his thoughts had begun to blur. With no idea of where he was or of how far he had yet to travel, Father Mark Thomas was utterly in God's hands.

His feet were too swollen for his shoes. He now wore makeshift moccasins cut from one of the blankets and fastened around his ankles with leather from the hackamore he had used on the horse. He knew they would wear through in time, but there was more blanket left and, hopefully, more warm days ahead.

Father Thomas worried most about the cold; its return could certainly deliver him to God. But the weather remained unusually mild. The sun continued to shine, warming him as he walked long, lonely distances hoping he was on a northerly course that would take him to the Minneconjous before many more days.

To survive, Father Thomas had begun a systematic approach to his travel. He spent his days walking until just past noon; then he would locate a sheltered campsite and gather wood until darkness fell. He usually found enough fuel to last through the night, but not always.

He had learned to eat slowly, thus using the rations more beneficially. He had also learned quickly how to find campsites that afforded protection against wind. He had matches, but not enough to squander. More precious than gold, these little sticks tipped with phosphorus and sulfur brought him the only light and warmth to be had when night fell over the vast open.

The darkness tried his nerves. He would stare into the flames, unable to understand his situation. The crackle of sagewood afforded him his only feeling of security against the shadows and held at bay the lonely wails and howls that echoed through the darkness.

Between the howls there came an overpowering flow of empty air. The silence was almost harder to bear. He could hear nothing in the vastness but his own thoughts, come to haunt him toward madness.

"Dear Jesus, why will you not show me the moon when I need it?" he said to the sky during a night when his fear peaked. The fire would not burn brightly enough, and the sky was black. The wind had been blowing harder than ever before, bringing strange sounds to his ears.

He was certain that the children were crying again, the ones he had heard during the storm outside the Brulé village. But no, it was the crying of his mother, who had worked to raise him and his seven brothers and sisters in their two-room city tenement. He could hear her plainly, weeping in the darkness just outside his camp, worrying about his father, who always came back with his hand raised against any who dared challenge him.

Father Thomas held his hands over his ears. Still he heard the weeping. His mother had wept most of the time. He had been just Mark then, attending school whenever he could find time between jobs. He had to be the man of the house when his father was nowhere to be found.

He remembered his twelfth birthday, when his father had kicked the door in and grabbed his mother by the hair. She had dared to lock the door against him. Mark would never forget the sickening thud of the bottle against the side of his mother's head, nor the shattered glass and blood that had sprayed across his own face.

More painful than the prickle of the sharp glass was the vision of his mother kicking and flopping her life away on the floor, never to rise again. Mark had grabbed a chair and broken it over his father's head. Then another chair, and another. But his father would not lie still. He had come to his knees, wiping blood from his brow with a forearm, yelling, "I'll kill you, too! I'll kill you, I will!" His father had been rising to his feet. There had been nothing left to swing at him. Mark knew that if he stayed, he would die as well. The kicked-in door was standing open, and he ran.

Mark had watched the tenement until he had seen his father leave, staggering away in a fit of rage. Then he had rounded up his brothers and sisters, leading them for days through the alleys, finding them what food he could. They had returned to the tenement once, but their mother's body had been taken away.

An orphanage took them in, and Mark had to learn to allow the nuns to care for his brothers and sisters. He found the nuns to be kind and loving, something he was not used to. Though the orphanage had little food to offer any of the children, there was peace. The nights of waiting for their father to come home were over.

Those years in the orphanage had planted the seed of

Father Thomas's desire to help others. From the orphanage, to the seminary, the boy Mark at last rose to the distinguished title of Father Mark Thomas, S.J. He'd felt that he had seen the worst, but now he fought again to survive. This time there were no streets or alleys but only bleak, open plains. Nothing, really, had changed at all.

Father Thomas took his hands from his ears. The weeping had finally stopped. Dawn was breaking, and the vast plains came into view once again. He got to his feet and began to walk.

He realized that if he didn't concentrate on what faced him now, he wouldn't live to even care about the past. He realized, too, that nothing from his early life had anything to do with his current situation; it only detoured his thoughts from the practical matters at hand. No matter how much he had sacrificed as a child and young adult, he would die out here if he did not soon reach the Minneconjou.

There came a night when his wood supply ran out and he had to walk to keep from freezing to death. His mind on survival, he hurried along a deer trail, his teeth chattering, aware of nothing more than his fight for life.

The clouds were a mass of stringy shadows fleeing before the moon, losing themselves in a deep and endless realm of glittering black. He fell repeatedly but each time picked himself up, determined not to give in. Finally, in exasperation, he lifted his head to the heavens and screamed in rage.

"Why do You make me suffer so?" he challenged. "I have come to do Your work and You place me in death's hands. What are You doing? What are You doing?"

Father Thomas turned in a circle, yelling, his fists raised to the sky. He lost his balance and fell, striking the side of his head against a large prickly pear. He sprang to his feet, yowling, his cheek and temple filled with cactus needles.

Jerking the needles loose, he found his hand soon sticky with warm blood, and his face felt like fire. The needles stung much worse than the broken glass from his father's bottle. He sat down, his head bowed, tears mixing with the blood.

"Forgive me for the blasphemy, dear Jesus," he sobbed. "I am not worthy to be your servant. I know nothing of grace, but only of sinning. I have disobeyed my superiors. I welcome any punishment you wish to deal me."

Father Thomas continued to weep. He felt more confused than at any time in his life. He had been so sure that he must come north to the Minneconjou, yet it seemed that all that awaited him was death. Perhaps that was God's will. So be it.

Just before dawn he was able to gather an armful of sage wood. He had learned to distinguish the older, more brittle plants; their branches broke loose much more easily and burned more crisply.

As the sky began to gray in the east, Father Thomas took from his pocket the book Shining Horse had given him and began to read. He had been avoiding the text. Something in its contents, conceived by St. John of the Cross while in a Spanish prison nearly three hundred years before, had frightened him. He realized now that he was meant to consume it, from beginning to end.

Father Thomas turned again to a poem entitled "Obscure Night."

> Upon an obscure night
> Fevered with Love's anxiety
> (O hapless, happy plight!)
> I went, none seeing me,
> Forth from my house, where all things quiet be.
> By night, secure from sight
> And by a secret stair, disguisedly,
> (O hapless, happy plight!)
> By night, and privily
> Forth from my house, where all things quiet be.

Father Thomas read through the entire poem, gaining a deep insight. St. John of the Cross had been abused and impoverished from the time of his birth. Yet out of his despair had come a vision of Creation. Through his writings, St. John sought to teach those who wished to travel the arduous pathway to God.

Father Thomas began to realize that in asking for God, he had himself been shown the pathway to find Him. He could look to no one for guidance; there was no one around now to lead him or to tell him what to do. He had placed himself in the endless open, where no distractions could interfere. Now was the time of his own test if his quest were to be fulfilled.

So strong the irony! Shining Horse, born of these open plains, a heathen in the eyes of Christianity, presenting him with the very gift that could explain all this to him. Father Thomas knew that as he read from this volume he would find himself drawing closer and closer to what the saint referred to as the "dark night of the soul."

Father Thomas read, stoked the fire, and read again. As the sun rose, he prayed. "Father in heaven, I beg You again, forgive me for my outburst. I am so small. I know so very little. If You deem me worthy, teach me Your ways, and help me reach those who need me the most."

During the following days, Father Thomas fought the pain of the cactus needles. He had not been able to remove all of them and some were beginning to abscess. He had to cut more from the blanket to make new moccasins. They did little more than cover the scrapes and bruises of hard travel over ground alternately warm and frozen solid.

Despite these problems and his constant hunger, he drew strength and courage from the conviction that he was meant to survive. He vowed to himself that he would learn from this journey, do his best to bring the teachings of Christ to those who would listen, and never challenge God's ways again.

Now only mental and physical suffering stood in the way of learning what he had been ordained to teach others. This was what he had always wanted. Now, in the middle of this vast open, he would be tested to the limits of his endurance, for the love of God.

FOURTEEN

TWO DAYS had passed since Father Thomas had finished the last of the rations. He had eaten a handful of sage leaves, but they were bitter and brought a dryness to his throat that left him worse off than before. Dried stalks of grass that he tried to eat caught in his throat, as did fallen leaves from the previous fall that he found along the bottoms. None of that would sustain him, he realized. He would have to find game to survive.

Father Thomas now clung tenaciously to his blankets, for he did not want to lose them again. Continually light-headed, he had twice dropped them and had had to retrace his steps to find them. Though one was only half its original size, he needed them desperately. Without cover, the chill of night would finish him.

Because of the cactus needles, his right eye had puffed badly and was now closing. It pained him terribly even to touch the area. He still had the small bag Little Buffalo Woman had given him. He told himself over and over that he would live to deliver it to the Minneconjou woman named Fawn-That-Goes-Dancing. He envisioned himself handing it to her, saying, "This is from a friend among the Brulé." He said it to himself over and over. At night he would place the little bag in the lining of his coat. He retrieved it each morning and repeated the words he would say to Fawn-That-Goes-Dancing.

He found an occasional mouse by noticing mice holes. The little creatures' squeaks did not bother him as he pinched their tiny heads. He devoured them, chewing quickly so that he would not lose a drop of blood.

Father Thomas set himself a schedule. Though death seemed ever closer, he had to keep moving. He realized that should he stop during the early daylight hours, he could become disoriented. He had to continue until the sun crossed toward the west. Then he could gather wood and whatever food he could find until darkness approached. He told himself that if he stuck to his schedule, he would survive.

He concentrated on the stretches of country before him, telling himself that the end of his ordeal lay just ahead. He learned to look straight forward so that he would not veer off course in search of food that was not there; rocks and fallen logs had fooled him more than once. He had to keep moving a little farther each day rather than wandering to appease his hunger. Wasted effort would only bring him to his end.

"Jesus will find me," he told himself. "I will not destroy myself with worry. I have faith that Jesus will bring me food. He will find me."

Father Thomas continued to look for Jesus. He cried out often, to a silence that seemingly ignored him. One afternoon, while stumbling along a well-used trail that led to a flowing spring, he surprised a male wolf. The wolf started sideways and dropped something from its mouth. It retreated and watched as Father Thomas stumbled over and picked up a freshly killed rabbit.

The flesh was warm. He ate ravenously and vomited

immediately. His stomach ached, and he drank water slowly until he could relax. The wolf started toward him, obviously irritated at having lost the rabbit. Father Thomas lunged, and the wolf backed away, snarling.

After gathering the meat he had lost, Father Thomas began to eat a morsel at a time. As he chewed, he watched the wolf, who had begun to howl mournfully. Father Thomas was delighted at keeping the meat down. He found a dry place under a tree and fell asleep, clutching the remains of the rabbit tightly.

More than once he was awakened by the snarls of the wolf pack that had come to see who had stolen the kill. He would widen his eyes at the wolves and snarl back. The wolves would retreat and circle, retreat and circle.

Finally, Father Thomas tired of defending his find. He rose and gathered enough wood to cook the rabbit. Again he ate slowly. When he had finished, he threw the skin and bones to the wolves and resumed his journey, renewed by the largest meal he had consumed in days. He saw it as a sign that he would make it to Kicking Bear's village.

The wolves followed him for the remainder of the afternoon. After a time, Father Thomas ignored them. Later, when it was time to begin looking for a campsite, he discovered that he was eager to keep going. He knew he must stop and rest, that to keep moving would drain all of his energy. Yet he gave in to his urgings to continue. The wolves followed, keeping a good distance, watching him curiously.

Just before nightfall he came to a little river. He drank his fill from a hole where the sun had melted the ice. He made camp, watching the sun descend toward the horizon, wondering how far he had left to travel. As he gathered wood, he noticed an odor in the air. The smell was sweet to him, and he fought the urge to seek it out. Darkness would soon be upon him.

After building a large fire, Father Thomas rolled up in the worn and tattered blankets. Exhausted, he immediately fell into a deep sleep. Sometime during his sleep he felt as though he were rising. The wolf who had dropped the rabbit stood before him, its eyes glowing in the firelight. Father Thomas did not feel the urge to growl or to defend himself in any way. Instead, it seemed as though the wolf had come to show its respect.

Father Thomas knelt on one knee, as if calling the wolf to him. The wolf trotted over and licked his face, then turned and moved away. It turned back, wanting him to follow. He called to the wolf, to ask it where it wanted to take him. The wolf whined and loped off into the night.

Father Thomas found himself on all fours, scrambling away from the camp fire. The wolf barked and hurried on ahead. Father Thomas asked himself how this could be happening. It somehow felt so natural that he had no sense of fear whatsoever.

Soon they were joined by the other wolves, all of them watching him. Still he felt no fear, but a sense of being one with them. The leader surged forward, and Father Thomas fell in with the pack. They loped in formation, their long legs striding in unison, drifting through the night like ghosts across the moon. His strength had returned and his mind was clear. He was no longer alone, but journeying with his own kind across the open wilderness.

They crested a hill and darted down among a large herd of buffalo. The herd took flight and surged across the plain, their eyes a blazing red in the darkness. Father Thomas felt the heat of the chase, the incredible power of the flowing herd. He heard the pounding hooves in his ears and felt the creatures' steamy breath against his face as he ran past them.

He found himself closing in on a young cow, tearing at her stomach and hamstrings. She bellowed in terror as the weight of the pack pulled her down and sharp teeth tore open her throat.

Father Thomas fed with the wolves, savoring the warm blood. He heard himself growling and snapping and striking at the others for position. Then suddenly the wolves moved away from him. The night grew to be day, and the sky turned blue overhead. A short way from the carcass, the wolves stared back at the hill behind; they were trotting back and forth, barking to one another.

Father Thomas turned his head to see what they were watching. A column of smoke rose from his campsite. The fire had moved into the cottonwoods.

Alarmed, he tried to rise from the buffalo carcass. He found that he couldn't stand, that his legs felt like rubber. He turned away from the fire and lay down upon the buffalo, his eyesight growing dim . . . until everything faded completely.

Shining Horse awakened to the faint scent of smoke. He knew that their camp fire had burned down well back into the night. When he looked to be certain, there wasn't even a single live coal.

He arose in the dawn and saw the thin, dark stream rising against the graying sky in the east. He awakened Catches Lance and Tangled Hair. They rose from their blankets, expressing surprise at a fire of that size at this time of year. Although there was little chance of a massive blaze developing, it bore investigation. All three agreed that the fire had to have been man-made.

They were a day and a half out of Big Foot's village, on their way toward Pine Ridge. Catches Lance and Tangled Hair believed that the smoke was coming from near Bad River. After catching their ponies, they veered off the main trail and reached the source of the smoke just as the sun topped the horizon.

Looking down from a ridge, they could see the patch of cottonwoods ablaze just across a river. They crossed the shallow water, frozen in places and open in others. On the opposite bank a strip of burnt grass led outward from a neglected camp fire to the edge of the river and the cottonwoods. Near the camp fire there were the remains of two blankets, but there was no sign of a human presence.

They dismounted. Catches Lance discovered a set of wandering tracks that led away from the fire and along the riverbank. "One man, wearing something other than moccasins on his feet," he said. "This is very strange."

"Whoever this is, he has to be in distress," Tangled Hair said. "No one travels alone at this time of year, no matter how good the weather."

After remounting, they followed the tracks along the bank to where they led across the river and out into the open. As they topped another ridge, all three stopped and stared down in amazement. In a small gully lay a winter-killed buffalo. A small pack of wolves paced nervously nearby. A man dressed in soiled black garments slept across the buffalo's hindquarters. As the three urged their horses down the slope, the wolves scattered.

"A Black Robe," Catches Lance said. "How did he get way out here?"

Shining Horse dismounted and bent over Father Thomas. "I know this man!" he exclaimed. "I rode the train with him."

Father Thomas awakened with difficulty. "Shining Horse!" he said in a cracked voice. "Have we both died and gone to heaven?"

Shining Horse laughed. "You are in a good mood for someone who appears dead."

"Oh, no," Father Thomas said. "I knew I would survive. But it is good you came when you did. You have saved me more suffering. You and this buffalo."

"What happened here?" Shining Horse asked, viewing the side of Father Thomas's face and head. "Those spines went in deep. You must have fallen pretty hard."

"Quite hard," Father Thomas admitted, touching his swollen face gingerly. "I had it coming."

"You had it coming?" Shining Horse asked.

"I can't explain it, really," Father Thomas said. He pulled

the book by St. John of the Cross from his pocket. "Suffice to say that this volume has answered a lot of questions."

Shining Horse smiled. "I knew it would." He helped Father Thomas to his feet. "What are you doing on foot way out here?"

"I didn't start out that way," Father Thomas said. "I must confess, I have a lot to learn about horses."

Catches Lance and Tangled Hair had dismounted and were standing over the buffalo carcass. They stared at Father Thomas. "He must be sacred," Catches Lance said. "*Wankan-tanka* has guided him. The buffalo are gone, yet he has found one."

Shining Horse translated. Father Thomas pointed to the wolves, which were watching from a good distance. "I don't know whether I found the animal on my own or the wolves led me to it," he said. "I can't remember how I got here, only that I awakened with a mouthful of flesh."

While Catches Lance and Tangled Hair butchered the remains of the buffalo, Father Thomas and Shining Horse caught up on events in their lives since they had parted. Shining Horse wasn't surprised to hear that the Brulé and the others on the Rosebud were having a hard time. All of the Lakota were suffering.

"But why did you leave there, on your own, at this time of year?" Shining Horse asked.

"I am not well liked by my superiors out here," Father Thomas replied. "It was a matter of leaving under cover of darkness or possibly being sent back East again. I didn't want that."

"You've saved yourself, that is what counts," Shining Horse said. "What you have come through will bring you very close to my people."

"Do you know any Minneconjou?" Father Thomas asked.

"Some of them," Shining Horse said. "The two men with me are Minneconjou. I have been to three Minneconjou villages in the last week."

Father Thomas reached into his coat and pulled out the small bag. "I have to find a woman named Fawn-That-Goes-Dancing. Do you know of her whereabouts?"

"Yes, I do," Shining Horse said. "That man over there is her brother."

Shining Horse introduced Father Thomas to Catches Lance and Tangled Hair. Catches Lance studied the small pouch and started to place it in his pocket.

"No, I have to give that to her myself," Father Thomas said.

Shining Horse told this to Catches Lance, who frowned and stepped back. "It looks to be sacred," he said.

Father Thomas held out his hand. Though he was hardly able to stand, his tone was gruff. "I brought it this far. I intend to find her and give it to her myself, as I promised."

"He promised the Brulé woman that he would deliver it in person," Shining Horse told Catches Lance. "He is determined. His medicine is good, so maybe he should have it back."

Catches Lance returned the pouch to Father Thomas. "Did you open it?" he asked.

Father Thomas addressed his reply to Shining Horse, who translated. "No, I didn't open the bag. I don't have any idea of what's inside."

Catches Lance nodded approvingly and spoke to Shining Horse and Tangled Hair. "He is a holy man. He knows what is sacred."

Father Thomas turned to Shining Horse. "What did he say?"

"He said you did very well by not opening the little pouch," Shining Horse replied. "He says you are a good man. You should take the bag to his sister yourself, like you promised."

"A good man," Father Thomas said. "I'm glad to hear that. Maybe I can talk to him about why I've come."

"Yes, maybe so," Shining Horse said. "We'll take you back up to Kicking Bear's village, where he and his sister live. Then

I must take Catches Lance and Tangled Hair with me again. I have urgent news to carry to all of the Lakota villages."

"I'm grateful," Father Thomas said. "I don't know how to thank you."

"Learn the Lakota tongue," Shining Horse said. "Then I won't have to be with you all the time when you want to know what's being said."

"That's a good idea," Father Thomas said. "Will you teach me?"

"I'll start you, but that is all," Shining Horse promised. "I don't intend to live with the Minneconjou. After my journey to the Lakota villages, I will be going back up to my father's people."

Father Thomas thought about the interesting stories Shining Horse had told him of Sitting Bull. "Maybe someday I will get to meet your father," he said.

"Maybe someday you will," Shining Horse said. "So far, you have had many lucky days. I am beginning to believe that anything could happen to you."

Shining Horse led the way back into Kicking Bear's village. Father Thomas rode one of the packhorses, sitting awkwardly. He was still very weak. Catches Lance had tied the buffalo's head to the front of Father Thomas's saddle to show the people he was sacred in *Wankantanka*'s eyes.

The villagers assembled to stare, pointing, holding their hands over their mouths. Father Thomas had no idea of the significance of the buffalo's head. He felt ashamed to be making his first appearance looking so worn and bedraggled. At the same time, he felt happy to be alive.

Kicking Bear stared along with the others, certain that this Black Robe who carried the buffalo head must have powerful medicine. This gave Kicking Bear even more confidence that his vision on the day the sun died had bestowed him with special powers. This holy man might be a *Wasichu*, but he had found a buffalo. This had to be a sign that the herds were coming back and that this special Black Robe had come to bring them to his village.

Kicking Bear invited Father Thomas to eat with him, and to smoke and speak in special council about his ordeal, and to tell of how he had found the buffalo.

"I am a dreamer," Kicking Bear told Father Thomas, "but no buffalo has lain down and died to save my life. I had to run them all down when I was younger. You are special."

With Shining Horse's help, Father Thomas told Kicking Bear that he would be grateful and honored to smoke and to eat with him. But first he must give something entrusted to him to one of the women in the village.

Catches Lance had already spoken with Fawn, and she stood waiting near her lodge. Shining Horse approached with Father Thomas.

"This Black Robe has seen death, but he has not crossed over," Shining Horse told Fawn. "He has come from our brothers, the Brulé, on the Rosebud. He has something to give you."

Father Thomas extended his hand, proffering the small bag. His eyes filled with tears as he spoke the words that had carried him across many miles of suffering: "This is for you, from a friend among the Brulé."

Shining Horse translated, and Fawn frowned with thought. "I don't understand," she said. "He has deep emotions about the bag, but I have no idea of what it means."

"She says that she can't take something sacred that she knows nothing about," Shining Horse told Father Thomas.

The priest continued to hold out the bag. "Tell her about the Brulé woman," he said. "You know, the one who informed her of her mother's death. I told you about her."

Shining Horse turned to Fawn. "The Black Robe says the pouch is from a woman who met you at Pine Ridge, when you were looking for your mother. She told you of your mother's death."

Fawn's mouth dropped open. She accepted the pouch,

remembering the small woman whom she had met near the front of the rations line. Still, Fawn had no idea why the woman would give her a present like this.

"Tell him I thank him for the gift," she said to Shining Horse. "Tell him, also, that he should have the cactus needles removed from his face or he will lose the sight in his eye."

"Do you want me to tell him that you will remove them?" Shining Horse asked.

"Yes," Fawn said, "you can tell him that."

"She says she will care for your face," Shining Horse told Father Thomas. "Go with her to her lodge. I will tell Kicking Bear that you will be ready for council soon."

"Go with her to her lodge?" Father Thomas said. "Will her husband be there?"

"She has no husband," Shining Horse said. "Her brother told me so. But I think your face will be too sore for you to make love to her."

"Why would you say such a thing?" Father Thomas asked.

Shining Horse smiled. "I saw the look in your eye. You might be a Black Robe, but you are still a man."

"No matter what you might think," Father Thomas said, "I could never do anything like that."

"Just make certain she understands that," Shining Horse said. "I think she likes you, too."

FIFTEEN

Fawn positioned Father Thomas so that the evening sun shone directly on his face. Hawk and Little Star nestled up beside her to watch, but she ordered them back. She needed room for this very important task.

Many villagers had gathered to watch. Fawn directed them to stand at one side so that she could see what she was doing. She placed a stick between her teeth and clamped down hard, then removed it from her mouth and handed it to Father Thomas. He placed it between his teeth, clamped down, and nodded that he was ready.

Fawn washed the side of his head and face once more with a strong herb infusion. The mixture included the powdered root of purple coneflower and the ground roots, stems and leaves of other plants that contained natural anesthetics. Father Thomas ran the tips of his fingers over his face. The numbness had taken as much effect as it ever would, and it was time to get the procedure over with.

He bit hard into the wood as Fawn began to dig through the

swelling with the sharp tip of a bone awl. The needles that had broken off weren't hard to find, as they had festered severely. Fawn worked around them with the tip of the awl and jerked them free with her fingernails.

The herbs had deadened only the outer layer of skin and Father Thomas had to fight to keep from passing out. His head and face throbbed with pain, and he felt sick to his stomach. He tried to think of something happy, anything to divert his mind from Fawn's work on the embedded needles. Nothing came to him but the scene where his father had broken the bottle against his mother's head.

In his mind he again saw the bottle explode, hitting exactly against her temple. Again he turned away as the slivers of glass shot like tiny arrows, stabbing his cheek and temple. He wanted to jerk away from Fawn, to scream and tear the scene from his mind, but he knew that he had to hold still.

Father Thomas breathed deeply and chewed hard on the stick. Sweat poured from him, mixing with the blood from the sores on his face and scalp. In his mind he once again sat on the ground in the alley four blocks from the tenement and gently plucked the glass from his face. Even now he wondered what he might have done to save his mother's life. So many, many times he had relived the incident, changing moments, talking his mother out of keeping the door locked. In fact, he had unlocked it, but he had heard his mother's demanding voice.

"Mark, you leave that door locked! Do you understand, lad? Your father's not to come back. Not this time. Not ever!"

So he had relocked the door, knowing it would not stop his father, knowing it would only drive him well beyond any rage they had yet survived.

"You'll just have to get used to being without a father, that's all," his mother had told him. "That's all."

He had tried to persuade his mother to stop talking about turning his father away, warning her of the trouble it would cause. Then his father's voice had come from behind the door.

"Open this up, woman! Open this up, I say!"

There had been a lot of shouting from both sides of the door, and a lot of screaming and crying from the smaller children behind him. Then everything had exploded when his father had kicked the door in.

Father Thomas closed his eyes tightly. Again the bottle was coming in a wide arc, the neck held fast in his father's hand. He bit the stick in half just as Shining Horse shook his shoulder.

"She's finished," Shining Horse told him. "She believes she's gotten all of them."

Father Thomas opened his eyes. He saw a number of bloody cactus needles on the blanket next to Fawn's knee. She wiped his face clean and smiled. "You can go to the council now and tell them of your journey here," she said. "A lot of people want to hear you."

Shining Horse translated, and Father Thomas replied, "I don't know how to thank you."

"Tell him that it is I who should thank him," Fawn told Shining Horse. "He has brought the sacred buffalo, and hope, to our people."

Father Thomas smiled. The sun's last light shone in the west. Fawn's eyes glowed every bit as brightly.

The villagers who had been watching made signs among themselves about Father Thomas's power. He took a deep breath and rose to his feet. Hawk and Little Star touched him and then looked closely at their fingers. Other children approached and felt of his worn and smokey clothing. Father Thomas welcomed them and held out his hands. The children came and clasped them, laughing and jumping about.

"Come with me," Shining Horse said. "A sweat lodge has been prepared. You are the honored one."

Father Thomas thanked Fawn again and then walked with Shining Horse toward the river's edge. "What is going to happen now?" he asked. "What is this sweat lodge you mentioned?"

"Didn't you see any on the Rosebud?" Shining Horse asked.

"Yes, but I was told to stay away from them. I spent most of my time in the school."

"The sweat lodge is for purification," Shining Horse said. "You could liken it to confession, if you want. My people use the sweat to prepare for spiritual events and special occasions. Everyone who sits in the council will partake of the sweat first, for it is a holy occasion to sit with a holy man such as yourself."

As they drew closer to the river, Shining Horse explained that they would sit in the sweat naked and then enter the river as the final act of the ceremony.

"You will hear prayers, and you may be asked to say a prayer for all," Shining Horse said. "You are the honored one."

"Isn't the water too cold?" Father Thomas asked. "There is still ice along the banks."

"If the spirit truly touches you, the water will be refreshing," Shining Horse said. "I know you don't understand what is going on, but believe me, the sweat is every bit as sacred as any ceremony you have ever attended. Treat it as such. And remember, you are the special one."

"I don't know what to do or how to act," Father Thomas said.

"I will help you," Shining Horse told him. "But you must remember, much of it is to be done on your own. Sitting in the sweat lodge and praying is a private matter. Things will come to you. It is up to you whether or not you want to share them. The buffalo will be in there, so you will get direction."

"What is all this about the buffalo?" Father Thomas asked. "These people are beginning to treat me like a god."

"In their eyes, you are very powerful," Shining Horse said. "They believe you performed something that can be done only by a very sacred medicine man. Finding a buffalo to save you from death is a sign that *Wankantanka* knows you well."

"What does that mean?"

"It means the people here believe that you might have actually *made* the buffalo yourself. When the council convenes, make sure to explain that you did not make the buffalo out of nothing, and that you did not bring the buffalo to save yourself. You must be sure to tell them that the buffalo had already died and you merely stumbled upon it."

"God brought me to the buffalo," Father Thomas said. "I have no doubt of it. There were some wolves, and I believe that God sent them to help me. It was God's will that I live. I have to tell them that."

"I can believe that your god wanted you to live and told some wolves to help you find the buffalo," Shining Horse said. "But you have to be careful of how you explain it to the council. You must let them know that you did not will that the buffalo be there for you. Do you see what I mean?"

"Well, of course I didn't *create* that buffalo myself," Father Thomas said. "It died before I got there. Surely they must know that."

"Be sure to tell them that," Shining Horse said. "Otherwise, you will appear as if you can bring anything you want to yourself, including buffalo, and they will want you to do it again. And again, and again. Do you understand?"

Father Thomas stopped. He stared at Shining Horse. "Are you saying that they believe I had the power to call the buffalo to me and that they will want me to call more buffalo for them?"

"Yes. That is it exactly."

"I couldn't do that!"

"The people here believe that you can," Shining Horse explained. "There once were medicine men among our people who could do that. My father has the power to call down rain."

Father Thomas stared. "No, I don't believe it."

"It is true," Shining Horse insisted. "Why shouldn't there be men among my people who can do such things?"

"That is up to God," Father Thomas said.

"Whose god?"

"The one true God, yours and mine."

"Then are you saying that the one true God doesn't allow miracles?" Shining Horse asked.

Father Thomas stuttered. "Of course I'm not saying that. But miracles are very rare."

"Why would you think only your people should be blessed with miracles? Aren't my people worthy of miracles?"

"Of course they are," Father Thomas said. "It's just . . . well, I don't know."

"They are waiting for us at the sweat," Shining Horse said. "You will find it hot. Try to stand it as long as you can. If you feel really bad, you should get up and leave."

Father Thomas followed Shining Horse to a round structure made of willows and covered with hides and muslin. A small door flap faced east, where a fire had been made to heat stones. Shining Horse explained that the lodge had been built for use just after the eclipse and that it was larger than most sweat lodges. He told Father Thomas that Kicking Bear had had a vision during the eclipse, one that he felt had brought him great power, and that Kicking Bear used the sweat lodge almost daily. He had built it large enough to contain as many as seven participants at a time. Kicking Bear felt certain that the Lakota world would soon be changing and that many things would be happening before the end of the following summer.

Kicking Bear and a number of other warriors stood near the entrance. Father Thomas smelled the familiar odor of burning sage, mixed with an unfamiliar scent. "Sweetgrass," Shining Horse said. "Sage and sweetgrass, the incense of our people."

Father Thomas began to disrobe with the others. They watched him and, like the children, touched his clothing. "What do your people think is in my clothing?" Father Thomas asked.

"It is the essence of your very being that they feel in those clothes," Shining Horse explained. "Do not wash them or get rid of them. Not ever.

"I must wash them," Father Thomas said. "I can't wear them the way they are."

"You will be given other clothing," Shining Horse said. "I would advise you to give a strip of cloth to Kicking Bear as a gift."

"I can't do that," Father Thomas protested. "I must wear the garments of my vocation."

"If your vocation is to God, then you will listen to me," Shining Horse said sternly. "You must forget that you are a *Wasichu*, and particularly that you are a Black Robe. This is your chance to see whether you really believe the things you say you do. If you believe that we are all one under the Father, then you will not worry about how you look. Do it, and show my people your faith. You will have taken a big step in reaching them, a much bigger step than you can ever imagine."

Father Thomas had never been so hot in his life. Sweat poured into his eyes and stung his swollen face. As he could not understand the Lakota prayers, he often drifted into his own visions, his thoughts, flashing back on his journey up from the Rosebud. He wondered what else might come to test him as a true man of God.

After a series of prayers by Kicking Bear, silence followed. Water was poured over the hot rocks, and steam filled the darkness. As the steam subsided into a thick haze, Father Thomas began to sense a change coming over him. As it had on the open prairie, fear reached deep into him. Though Shining Horse sat on one side of him and Kicking Bear on the other, he felt that something had come to see him, something from another realm, a presence that began to take form in the haze.

"So, you thought you could get away from me, did you?"

It was his father's voice; and from the steam came his father's face, slowly taking shape to hover directly in front of him.

"You won't ever get rid of me, lad. You know that."

Father Thomas lurched from his seat, stumbling over Kicking Bear and past two warriors to the door flap. The buffalo head sat just outside. Father Thomas lunged over it and fell to the ground.

Scrambling through the lodge, he had burned the soles of his feet on the hot rocks. He rolled in pain and yelled for his father to stay away, to leave him in peace. Tears streamed from his eyes, and his throat constricted with his shouting. Suddenly he felt embarrassed; he had made a fool of himself.

Father Thomas sat up and looked around. To his amazement, no one had followed him out. Not far away, two old women stood over the fire, heating more rocks to replace those that were cooling down inside the sweat. They paid no attention to him.

Father Thomas rolled over on his back and stared up into the early night. The clear sky was dotted with the first stars. The heavens were vast and open, endless, beyond imagination. In the distance a wolf howled. Father Thomas sat up again and listened to the mournful sound. Grunting in pain, he staggered to his feet.

He limped back to the sweat lodge. One of the women held the flap open and he entered again. The prayers had continued without interruption. No one, including Shining Horse, acted as if he had ever left. He took his seat again and immersed himself in the steam. Before long, he felt even hotter than he had before.

The fear returned. He vowed that he would not let his father get the best of him this time. He waited for the image of his father's face to return. The fear remained, but no image showed itself.

"He's waiting until I let my guard down," Father Thomas told himself. "He won't win. I won't let him."

The fear was gradually replaced by a deep sadness. It welled up in him no matter how hard he tried to force it back down.

"It was not your fault that your father killed me," he heard a voice say. He began to sob as his mother continued: *"You have done very well for yourself, Mark Michael Thomas. You will do even better. Remember that I am well and that I want you to do the best you can do with your life. Worry about me no longer."*

Father Thomas felt the steam washing through him, purging him of long-held guilt. He breathed deeply, the rush of relief leaving him light-headed. He had thought he had learned much on those plains. Now he realized that he had just begun his journey toward God and that there was a very great distance yet to go.

Shining Horse nudged him. "Kicking Bear is asking that you offer a prayer for all, if you wish to do so."

"I am not worthy to offer a prayer at this time," Father Thomas said.

"Do you want me to tell Kicking Bear exactly that?"

"Yes."

"I will tell him that you pray for everyone, and for all life," Shining Horse said. "We say it as All Relations."

"That will be fine," Father Thomas replied.

When the prayers were concluded, Kicking Bear led the way to the river. Father Thomas gasped as he immersed himself in the icy water. But as Shining Horse had told him might happen, he became awakened in a new way.

The darkening heavens appeared even more brilliant than before, and the early stars popped with light. The tops of the trees stood out individually, not as a large mass of greenery as he had seen them earlier. The wolf that had howled in the distance now seemed closer. Father Thomas was certain that he saw the wolf's outline on a hill above the river, its nose lifted toward the sky.

"Time to leave the water," Shining Horse said, taking his arm.

Father Thomas pulled away. "I feel fine. In fact, I feel wonderful."

"That's good. But you can't stay out here alone. And you have a council to sit in on."

Father Thomas left the water feeling light and detached from the ground. The air was warm, and Shining Horse and Kicking Bear were smiling, as were all the warriors who had been in the sweat. The two old women kept their heads bowed. Impulsively, he hugged them both.

"Here are your Black Robe clothes," Shining Horse said. "We will go to Kicking Bear's lodge now and smoke with him while others use the sweat. Then the council will begin."

"I feel the best I've ever felt in my life," Father Thomas said, adjusting his cassock. "I realize I have much to learn."

"If you respect these people and their ways," Shining Horse said, "they will respect you."

"I don't want to give them the idea I can perform miracles," Father Thomas said. "But I want them to understand that I will lead them onto the white man's path to God. That is what they must learn. That is why I am here."

"Until you have learned the Lakota tongue, I will tell them anything you ask," Shining Horse said. "But maybe it is you who should turn a new way."

"What do you mean?" Father Thomas asked.

Shining Horse touched Father Thomas's worn cassock. "You left the Rosebud as a Black Robe, without much knowledge of Lakota ways. You lose your horse and must walk up here to these people. You would have died along the way if it hadn't been for two of the strongest medicine totems that exist among all the plains tribes, the wolf and the buffalo. Maybe you should wait until you know what you are supposed to be teaching."

Shining Horse started for Kicking Bear's lodge. Father Thomas stared after him. More of the warriors who would be part of the council were gathering around the sweat lodge to begin their own ceremony. Among them were Catches Lance and Tangled Hair. They gestured a greeting to him before entering the lodge.

Even if he could have communicated with the council, Father Thomas wouldn't have known what to say. All of them saw him as someone who could help them, but not in the way that he had planned. He wanted them to learn the white pathway to God, and they believed that he already knew *Wankantanka* better than they did.

Father Thomas began to limp toward the lodge. Shining Horse was right: he had entered the village in the fashion of a medicine man, not that of a Catholic priest. But he believed that he would always be a priest, even though he might open his mind to learn the Lakota belief system as well. But to these people, he was a holy man in their own tradition. That had been their first impression of him, and it would be difficult to change it, if not impossible.

SIXTEEN

WHEN THE council convened, Father Thomas had lost his feelings of well-being. In addition to his head and face, his feet now hurt him considerably. He limped noticeably as he made his way to his place between Shining Horse and Kicking Bear.

Catches Lance and Tangled Hair had also been invited to attend. Neither had ever been in council before, and they felt themselves privileged.

Catches Lance had never trusted any *Wasichu* he had ever met, and yet this was the first time he had felt truly a member of the Minneconjou. He thought it ironic that this Black Robe and an Unkpapa who had gone into the East and learned the *Wasichu* ways would help him gain honor.

Catches Lance hoped that this would be the beginning of a time of power for him. He had been one of the three to rescue this special Black Robe, so people might listen to him more readily now. In addition, his sister had taken the cactus needles from the Black Robe's face. His whole family had been honored.

As the council got underway, Father Thomas studied all of their faces and realized that they were watching him carefully. He sat cross-legged, the buffalo's head placed before him. The orations began. When someone wanted him, especially, to know what was being said, Shining Horse translated. Many of them wanted to know if he could show them his medicine by bringing more buffalo to the area. If he could do that, he would be among the greatest of all holy men ever among the Lakota people.

"Maybe this is why you have come among us," Kicking Bear told Father Thomas. "Maybe you can bring back the buffalo and feed our children."

Shining Horse translated. He then added, "This is the time for you to tell them what happened and who you are."

Father Thomas began to tell of his ordeal, speaking slowly enough for Shining Horse's immediate translation. He told of how he had left the Brulé to seek this village and of how he had never had any doubts that he would reach it. Though the way had been hard, the trip had been worth it, for he had now made many friends.

He talked about meeting Shining Horse on the train and learning much about the Lakota before ever stepping onto the reservation. He said he wanted them to know that he had come to help them as best he could, and to teach them how to know God in the same manner as their white brothers knew Him.

Father Thomas told them that he had been ordained into the priesthood of the Roman Catholic faith and would never waver from that office. He could not be one of their medicine men or in any way deviate from the ceremonies he had been taught. He wanted them to learn a new way, a way that would help them see their white brothers in a better light and build hope among all the Lakota for a better future.

Shining Horse translated to the council, then turned to

Father Thomas and spoke curtly. "That would be a great speech to give to one of your bishops, but it will do little good here. My people will now ask you why you smell of our sacred sage and sit with a buffalo's head in front of you if you don't believe in our ways."

"I didn't say that I disagree with their ways," Father Thomas said. "I want them to know that I have a better way for them."

Father Thomas looked around the council. The firelight flickered on waiting faces. He turned to Shining Horse and shrugged. "What do you want me to tell them? I don't know any other way to say it. I'm a priest, and I can't convert to your religion. I came here to change *their* minds, not my own."

"Why don't you think about whether or not you really want to change their minds?" Shining Horse suggested. "You were brought here by the Powers that my people know. You can't deny that you were saved in a manner that you cannot explain. If you want to try to change their minds about this, you won't be able to."

Father Thomas stared at the buffalo's head in front of him. He lifted it by the horns and turned it over onto its top.

The council gasped in unison. Many began to shout at Father Thomas.

"What possessed you to do that?" Shining Horse asked.

"I want them to know that I can never adapt to their ways," Father Thomas replied. "I've come to learn that symbolism is an important part of your culture. I saw no other way to reach them."

"You've reached them, all right," Shining Horse said. "You did the same thing as spit on a consecrated host."

"I didn't mean to be sacrilegious."

"You turn a sacred object upside down, and say you didn't mean to be sacrilegious?"

Father Thomas grabbed the head once again and turned it back upright. Then he flipped it over once again, and back upright once again. The members of the council stared.

"Tell them that the buffalo takes me in circles," he said to

Shining Horse. "Tell them that I have become caught between what I learned in my own lands and what I have learned since coming out here."

Shining Horse smiled. "That is something they can understand. They have already seen that your feelings are torn. They will know that you speak from the heart."

Shining Horse translated, and the council nodded in approval. The pipes were passed once again, and Kicking Bear spoke. He said that his vision when the sun went dark had told him of special things to come. He considered Father Thomas to be someone very special, and he would now honor him with a name.

"From this time on, we will call you Two Robes," he said. "You wear the holy robe of your people, and you are also a holy man in the eyes of *Wankantanka*. You have learned the ways of the wolf and the buffalo. You are one of us."

The members of the council voiced their agreement. This holy man was now a brother of the Minneconjou people. His name, Two Robes, was fitting.

Shining Horse told Father Thomas to place his hand on the buffalo's head. "Among the Lakota people, you are now known as Two Robes," he said. "Soon there will be a ceremony to honor you and to officially give you the name. This is something you can be very proud of."

"Tell them that I accept the honor," Father Thomas said. "Tell them that I will do my best to teach them about Jesus Christ, the Son of the same God that watches over us all."

Shining Horse translated, and Kicking Bear began another oration. As he spoke, the council nodded and watched Father Thomas.

"You have shown to them that you have great courage to come from your lands and let *Wankantanka* lead you across our lands," Shining Horse translated. "Kicking Bear believes that you might be a prophet, similar to him. He also says that he has never before met a holy man of two races."

"A holy man of two races?" Father Thomas asked.

"Yes, of both the *Wasichu* and the Lakota," Shining Horse replied. "I believe that Kicking Bear is right. You came into the council to speak on behalf of your god. Your ignorance could have cost you your life. Instead, you showed with the buffalo's head that the sacred circle of life has cast you head-over-heels. They all see you in the middle of the worlds, where the holy ones dwell. From now on, you stand among the Lakota wearing two robes, as a special symbol of two worlds."

"I don't know what that means," Father Thomas said.

Shining Horse smiled. "It means, Father Thomas, that you have just become a saint."

Fawn sat inside her lodge stroking the hair of her sleeping children. The fire had dwindled, and the last small flames cast tender shadows against the canvas wall.

As she moved from her children's bed to her own, she touched the little bag around her neck, delivered to her by Father Thomas. She had looked into the bag before. She said a prayer to *Wankantanka* before opening it again.

Inside, a small breast feather from a snowy owl lay nestled with a tiny love charm: a doll-like figurine of a man and woman, carved from cottonwood and holding hands. Strong love medicine.

She was just beginning to see why Little Buffalo Woman had sent the bag up with Father Thomas for her. After her mother's death at Pine Ridge, Little Buffalo Woman had consoled Fawn, suggesting that she find a good man to care for her and her children. The snowy-owl feather held significance in regard to her mother's passing as well as to her own change in life. The figurine was to help her find the right man.

Fawn had told no one what was inside the pouch. No one spoke of those things unless to a holy man, who might help decipher the meaning of the contents. But Father Thomas was the only holy man associated with the pouch, and he was

Wasichu. He seemed to be a very good man, and he had had enough respect not to open the bag, but he would never understand the meaning of its contents.

Fawn lay back in her robes, thinking of the Black Robe, wondering what had made him decide to become a holy man. Among the Lakota, such an office could be handed down, or given to one who showed special attributes, but only after incredible trial. The person had to be unusually strong.

This was not always the case among the *Wasichu.* There were Black Robes and White Robes and others who had come to tell of the *Wasichu* god. Often they spoke against one another, even in hatred. This seemed a very odd feeling for one holy man to have against another.

It seemed, though, that Father Thomas was different from any *Wasichu* missionary she had ever known. She had seen the missionaries at Pine Ridge and also when she had journeyed, three summers past, with a number of other Minneconjou to visit friends on the Rosebud. The Black Robes she had seen thought themselves better and more knowledgeable about spiritual matters than the Lakota.

They had been insistent that their way was the only way and that the Lakota tradition of worship was evil and an offense to the *Wasichu* god. But Father Thomas had come up to the Minneconjou along a hard road, so maybe he knew about the wind spirits and the special songs of her people. Maybe he had learned them from the buffalo.

He was a gentle man, she knew, and perhaps one who could understand the plight of her people. Once he learned the Lakota tongue, he could do much good if he didn't try to push his own ways on the people.

Fawn knew that the *Wasichu* god would not allow a Black Robe to take a wife. That was their law. That was too bad. She stared at the figurine. Had Little Buffalo Woman been aware that the male in the figurine seemed to be wearing a long garment of some kind?

She put the owl feather and the figurine back in the pouch

and lay back in her robes. Maybe, if Father Thomas tired of being a holy man in the way of the Black Robes, he would notice her as a woman.

The council members talked day after day about Father Thomas. To them he was now Two Robes. They spoke endlessly of how he had turned the buffalo's head over and over to demonstrate where he had been placed within the sacred circle of life. They said that Two Robes was more than just a special Black Robe who had come among them. They said that he was a special holy man who knew many worlds and was accepted as gifted in all of them. When Two Robes saw fit, he could make wonders happen. It would be good to listen to his words about the Bleeding Chief, the one known as Jesus Christ.

Father Thomas was given a special lodge, built for him by a number of older women skilled in making sacred dwellings. The villagers came daily and left small presents near his door flap. This practice embarrassed him, and he wondered what they wanted of him in return. But he couldn't ask. Shining Horse was not around to translate. He had left again with Catches Lance and Tangled Hair to finish his mission.

Father Thomas discarded the ruined pants and shirt he had worn under his cassock during the journey. Though his cassock had become badly soiled, he would not part with it. The garment was the sole symbol of who he was and of his mission to bring Jesus to these people.

To wear under his cassock, Father Thomas accepted a dark pair of cotton pants presented to him by Tangled Hair and a deerskin shirt that had belonged to Catches Lance. Fawn gave him a pair of beaded moccasins, with tufts of buffalo hair sewn around the ankles. He did not realize that in making her gift, she was showing an interest in him as a man, and not just as a holy man.

Father Thomas was eager to begin his work toward converting Kicking Bear's people. He realized that he could not say mass in English and have them understand anything. At St. Francis, a number of the Brulé had learned English well, but it wasn't that way here. Most of the people had remained locked within the old customs, although some of them had attended mission schools elsewhere on the reservation.

Father Thomas was glad that he had come when he had. The season had changed, and there would be no more cold. Flocks of geese returning from the south passed over in long Vs, their wings gracing the pale blue skies. Small birds returned to the trees and shrubs along the river, flitting among the swelling buds. The people were spending more time out of their lodges. There was a sense of renewed hope.

While his feet and face healed, Father Thomas began to learn the Lakota language from Fawn and her children. Hawk and Little Star were open and unafraid. They brought their friends and danced around him, singing songs and competing for his attention, helping him learn Lakota by showing him items and pointing to whatever they were speaking about.

In turn, Father Thomas taught them the English equivalents. They picked up the language readily, eager to learn from a man whom they trusted and were growing to love. Father Thomas learned quickly himself. Hawk and Little Star worked with him faithfully. It seemed that they were more eager for him to speak their tongue than even he himself was.

Although the children were a delight, it was Fawn who most impressed Father Thomas. He never tired of seeing her face, and sometimes he felt guilty for the feelings that welled up within him. She was a woman of uncommon strength, and she was extremely pleasant company. Something about her touched him deeply.

After a while Father Thomas had learned enough Lakota that he could talk to her about beginning his ministry. One afternoon while walking along the river, they talked about how he would bring changes to the Minneconjou.

"I want to teach your people about Jesus," he said. "I've sat in the sweat lodge and watched various ceremonies. I've learned many things. Now it is time that your people learn new things from me."

"Do you have any special garments that you need for your ceremonies?" Fawn asked.

"My black robe is the only garment I really need."

Fawn wrinkled her face. "It is pretty badly worn. My people dress in their finest clothes for ceremonies. I could make something for you."

Father Thomas thought of the white chasuble often worn over the cassock at baptism and at other special times. Something white would look splendid over his worn cassock.

"I would like something white to wear," he said. "Thank you very much. It would be good to wear it when I talk to your people about baptism. I will wear it when I pour water over their heads and give them rebirth in the eyes of the *Wasichu* god."

"I will be honored to make it for you," Fawn said. "Are there sacred items you will use?"

Father Thomas told her that he would need the same things all Black Robes needed to say mass. He would need a supply of bread and a small supply of wine.

Though she herself did not have enough to eat, Fawn offered Father Thomas a supply of hardtack from her rations. But wine was something she wanted nothing to do with. "Wine is not good for my people," she told him. "I do not believe you should use it in your ceremony."

"But I must," Father Thomas said. "I don't give any of it to your people. I use it only to complete the consecration of the bread, to make it the body and blood of Jesus."

Fawn looked at him. "The body and blood?"

"Yes, as part of the mass, the bread and wine become the body and blood of Jesus. The bread is given to the people to bring them closer to Christ and to let them remember that He died for them."

"You *eat* the Bleeding Chief?"

"Yes. It is called communion."

"Is it the same as when our warriors used to eat the heart of a strong enemy?" Fawn asked.

Father Thomas's eyes widened. "What? Oh, no! Of course not. This has nothing to do with war or killing."

"You told me that the Bleeding Chief was killed by his people," Fawn said. "Did they eat him then?"

"No," Father Thomas replied. "Those who killed him did so because they did not believe in him. They might have felt stronger after his death, but they did not eat him."

Fawn sat down on a log and brushed hair from her face. Father Thomas sat down beside her.

"So why do you Black Robes believe that it is good to eat him now?" she asked.

Father Thomas thought for a moment. "Before he died, Jesus gathered the men who were to carry on his teachings into a room. There were twelve of them. He shared his last meal with them and told them that wherever they went, they should break bread over wine and give it to the people in remembrance of him. Those twelve men loved Jesus very much, and they did as he said. This custom has been passed on through the years, and we follow it today to remember the death of Jesus for all of us."

Fawn looked into the water. "The Bleeding Chief must have been a very loving man."

"No one could ever be more loving than Jesus," Father Thomas said. "I want to teach your people about him and how he came in person, as the *Wasichu* God, to save everyone."

Fawn turned. "How do you know he was *Wasichu*?"

Father Thomas hesitated. "Well, I don't know that he was. The point is, he represents *all* of mankind. He gave his life so that *all* might be saved."

"I had not heard of the last meal," Fawn said. "But I knew that the Bleeding Chief was nailed to a tree and died, so that everyone after him would not have to worry about how they lived."

"It is true, he was sacrificed for our sins," Father Thomas said. "He died so that we might have eternal life."

"Does that mean the Bleeding Chief likes the way the *Wasichu* treat us?" Fawn asked. "Does that mean they can starve us and drive us to extinction and that the Bleeding Chief will like them for it?"

"No," Father Thomas said. "It is not right to persecute anyone. Christ taught that all men are brothers. We should get along together and love one another."

"Then it seems to me that the *Wasichu* do not listen to the words of their own god."

"I am sorry to say that there are those who live selfishly," Father Thomas agreed. "But it was the same in Christ's time. He taught that we are to forgive the wrongs of others."

"It is hard to forgive," Fawn said, "when you are watching your children starve to death."

"If you have the love of Jesus in your heart, you will never feel hunger."

Fawn stood up. "It would be hard for me to tell my children these things. I will make the white garment for you, but I will not listen to your teachings."

Father Thomas, disappointed, watched Fawn walk back to the village. He realized that he would have the same difficulty in explaining the sacred mysteries to the rest of the Minne-conjou. Even though they respected him as a man of two worlds, they would not want to embrace anything their enemies believed in.

But he knew he was not considered an enemy. He was, in fact, considered to be very special. He thought about how he had been delivered to this place. During his trials, he had not seen the face of Jesus. Yet a miracle had taken place in the form of the wolf dream that had led him to the buffalo. Surely Jesus must know this country. But could Jesus be trying to show him another way to spirituality?

Father Thomas concluded that he should not be so deter-

mined to do things his own way. He would need to find a new
direction in order to reach these people. He thought of his
reading. St. John of the Cross must have had his own plans,
which had no doubt been dashed by his imprisonment. His
whole life had taken a different turn because of events he
could not have foreseen.

Father Thomas began to walk back toward the village. He
reasoned that he should remain open and allow God to direct
him. He had accomplished his first goal, that of reaching the
Minneconjou, and he had become close to them; but it hadn't
happened as he had planned. That didn't mean, though, that
Jesus wasn't still with him, or that he couldn't eventually bring
all of Kicking Bear's people to Catholicism.

Shining Horse's advice might have been wise; maybe he
should become a different Catholic. He wondered if he could
approach his theology in some other way, yet maintain the
substance of his teaching. Could he teach the Catholic faith
through a means the Minneconjou would more readily accept
and understand?

No matter how he decided to teach them, he would have to
acknowledge the image they had of him. Instead of coming to
them as the man he once was, he had been escorted past death
by God Almighty through the use of the very totems these
people held sacred. If it hadn't been for the wolf with the
rabbit, and the strange dream of the wolf pack and the dead
buffalo, he wouldn't have survived.

Although he still couldn't understand what had happened,
the Minneconjou seemed to comprehend it completely. In
their minds, Father Thomas had been given the power of the
wolf, to run with the pack and to eat from the sacred buffalo.
He had become a holy man of two nations, the *Wasichu* and
the Minneconjou. Now they were certain that he knew their
spiritual beliefs inside and out; otherwise, *Wankantanka*
wouldn't have come to him in that manner.

He would certainly do things differently than they had
been done on the Rosebud. There would be no pressure

through fear. Never. He would continue to wear the cassock, and he would use the chasuble that Fawn would make for him when he baptized and said mass. He would now call himself Two Robes, and he would begin his mission among these people with a prayer over the head of a dead buffalo.

SEVENTEEN

Two Robes began attending more Lakota ceremonies. Often he would just watch and listen; but whenever he was asked to speak, he would do his best to tell the people that Jesus was also present, watching over them with love, wanting the best for them.

Slowly, the people began to accept this. There was nothing forced about the way Two Robes asked them to listen to him. He merely stated his beliefs and allowed them to react in any way they pleased. That was the way of a true holy man: there was no judgment, no pounding or shouting. Each individual must find his or her own pathway. A holy man was there for guidance, not for domination.

Two Robes found it difficult for the people to accept the fact that Jesus had sacrificed himself for them as well as for the *Wasichu*. The *Wasichu* felt themselves to be far superior to the native peoples, so why would they want to believe their god saw the Lakota as equal? Furthermore, they could see that the teaching of the Bleeding Chief went, for the most part, unheeded. They couldn't understand why the memory of such a man wasn't more highly revered among his own people.

Many argued with Two Robes that they had never seen any signs of Jesus. *Wankantanka* spoke through the things of earth: the birds and animals, the trees, and the running water. Surely the Bleeding Chief must have loved the land he was born into. Two Robes could only tell them that he believed Jesus was as much a part of the land as *Wankantanka*, since they were one and the same.

After listening further to the people, Two Robes began to wonder if God didn't appear to different cultures in different guises. As a child on the streets of the city, he had led his siblings through garbage for whatever they could find. He had never known the open spaces, where people had to hunt to survive, like the animals around them.

These people, he saw, had learned to communicate with the animals on a higher scale than he had known was possible. Their religion was the land itself and the open sky, and all that lived there. They admired each creature for its ability to survive. They had, in fact, learned hunting tactics from the animals.

Two Robes understood that the Lakota did not consider their accomplishments the result of their own superiority. On the contrary, they considered themselves on an equal plane with all life: animals, rocks, trees, everything. All one. Those that could not see the oneness were beneath them. And the *Wasichu*, though conquerors, could not see it.

Two Robes thought of Kicking Bear, and of Short Bull, and of the Brulé. No doubt Shining Horse's father, Sitting Bull, was the highest symbol among those who would never submit to the white way of life. These men and their followers would live out their lives in rebellion. Nothing that the agents or the missionaries said or did would ever change their minds.

Two Robes was determined to be different from every missionary these people had ever known. He wanted to become one with them and to show them that Jesus accepts everyone as equal. This would be difficult, for the people knew that men like Kicking Bear and Sitting Bull had more power than they did. Though men like this were not thought of as total rulers, they were looked up to for guidance.

Among the younger warriors, Two Robes found a strong ally in Catches Lance. He could see that Catches Lance worked hard to establish himself as one of the more prominent younger men. Catches Lance's thoughts had turned gradually toward greater acceptance of the *Wasichu* ways. There were some who agreed with him, and many who didn't.

Fawn was among those who did not agree. The old ways would be hers until her last breath on earth. Despite this, she maintained contact with Two Robes, laughing with him, allowing her children to see him and talk with him whenever they desired.

Two Robes had discovered wisdom, simple and pure, within the heart of this woman. It seemed at times as if she could see through him, right into his very soul. He found himself thinking about her all too often, imagining the feel of her long black hair and the smoothness of her skin. He realized that these thoughts interfered with the planning of his mission, but he could not bring himself to push her from his mind.

He agreed with joy when she asked if she could walk along the river with him early one morning. Three days of rain had been followed by two days of sunshine, and the land was bursting with color. Bell-shaped flowers, dainty and yellow, coated the side hills, along with other small yellow flowers.

"Buttercups," Fawn said. "My mother told me this. She said that a *Wasichu* who studied plants told her mother this when she was a child. Before she died, my grandmother would talk of summer trade fairs among the Mandans. It was there that a group of *Wasichu* stopped to study the Indian people. One of them painted pictures, so my grandmother said."

Undoubtedly explorers, Two Robes surmised. There had

been many expeditions into these lands. Why couldn't they have reported back that these people should be left alone? Somehow, right now he was glad they hadn't.

"I have the white garment nearly ready for you," Fawn told him. "Then you can give the baptism and communion you talked about."

"That's wonderful," Two Robes said. "I feel I have come a long way in my dream to bring Jesus to your people."

"Do you ever have dreams that seem like life in another world? Dreams where you are with a loved one who has crossed over?"

"The Brulé woman who gave me the little bag for you, she told me of lost souls," Two Robes said. "I heard some children crying in a snowstorm one night . . ."

"No, I don't mean lost spirits," Fawn said. "I mean happy spirits that come to you."

"I don't really understand. Can you explain it better?"

"I scarcely know how to begin," she said. "It happened on the day the sun died. The experience was so real, yet I cannot seem to have another one like it. I guess it isn't something you can tell me about."

"It must have been a good dream if it was about a happy spirit," Two Robes said. He stooped, picked a cluster of buttercups and handed them to her. "These look like they're happy."

"They're so beautiful."

"I've never seen anything that could match your beauty," Two Robes said.

Fawn smiled and tilted her head. Two Robes leaned forward and kissed her gently on the lips. Then he took her in his arms and kissed her for a long time.

Fawn felt an excitement coursing through her, a feeling that had not been a part of her for a long time. She was letting it fill her with gladness when Two Robes drew back.

"I am sorry," he said. "I cannot do this." He covered his face. "Oh my, what have I done?"

"Don't feel bad, please," Fawn said. "You did nothing wrong."

"Oh, but I did. It is not fair to you, or to me."

"You can hold me and not break your vow," she said.

"When I hold you, I want to break my vow. That is the sin: wanting to make love to you."

"How can that be a sin?" she asked. "Is that not part of being a man? How do you take that away when you become a Black Robe?"

"It isn't something that is taken away," Two Robes said. "It is something that must be controlled."

"I cannot control my feelings for you," Fawn said. "You are truly special to me. I knew it when you first came into our village."

"You are special to me as well," Two Robes said. "But we can only talk with one another and no more. I can't let anything more than that happen."

"I know the promises you have made," Fawn said. "But I can't help what I feel as a woman."

"I am sorry," Two Robes said. "I shouldn't have come out with you. I let myself be tempted."

"Blame me if you want to."

"That is something I would never do. You're not to blame for any of my faults."

"Faults? Why should you call your natural feelings faults?"

"You don't understand."

"I do understand," Fawn said. "You have been told that you shouldn't feel what is natural and real. That is what is wrong with you *Wasichu*. You deny your feelings."

"I made a vow to never be sexual with women," Two Robes said. "That is part of what makes me a Black Robe. If I have a wife, I am no different than any of the other men."

"Why should you be so different?" Fawn asked. "You are a man denying what *Wankantanka* gave him. Do you think that by not taking a wife you are holier than the next man?"

Fawn watched Two Robes turn and hurry along the path

through the trees. He was headed away from the village, likely to be gone for some time.

It did not seem fair to her that he had made such a promise to his god. Why couldn't the *Wasichu* god see men for who they were? Little wonder that the Black Robes had a difficult time with life.

Fawn started back for the village, wondering whether Two Robes would forgive her for her words about his feelings. She didn't think it wrong to show feelings. Yet she realized that she shouldn't blame Two Robes for the attitudes he had been taught.

Although she wished he would, she feared that Two Robes would never change. This way of honoring his god had been demanded of him by those above him. He had likely agreed to obey when he first decided to become a holy man, but he certainly couldn't have understood then how difficult it would be to keep the promise.

Fawn wondered about Two Robes's past; he must have felt love and desire for a woman before he met her. After all, he was a little older than she. But surely he couldn't have wished for anyone as strongly as he wished for her. She could tell that. And as deeply as she had loved before, she knew that Two Robes had stirred something within her that she had never felt until now.

It was raining heavily on the night that Shining Horse rode back into Kicking Bear's village. His visits to the other villages had met with mixed success. Though a good number of Lakota wished to hold on to the reservation lands, there were even more who wished for some relief from their poverty and wanted to sell.

Two Robes, invited again to the council, listened to Shining Horse tell that the land commission had gained a lot of support. There was major dissension within the seven tribes, and more people were turning to the White Man's Road daily.

Each adult male's signature brought the land commission closer to its goal.

"Three Stars Crook says things will be better for the Lakota people," Shining Horse told the council. "He says that if we don't sell, the *Wasichu* government will take our lands anyway. He says we should have given in last year when they came. Because we didn't, there is much anger among the white fathers in Washington."

"Three Stars Crook is but one man among many who bite one another in the back," one of the council members observed. "How many of the other land commissioners will stand behind the word of Three Stars?"

Shining Horse reported that this had been the main question he had asked at every council meeting. In many councils, the people were so strongly in favor of the promises that none seemed to care that their lands would not be returned if the promises were not kept. They felt certain that Three Stars Crook spoke from the heart when he said he would do everything possible to make their lives better. They saw him as powerful enough to carry out his intentions.

Two Robes wanted to speak also, but he realized that his opinion would not be welcomed on this issue. Kicking Bear and the others knew that his allegiance had to be to his own people, even though his heart was divided.

Shining Horse seemed like a changed man. What he had experienced on his mission with Catches Lance and Tangled Hair had embittered him deeply. He seemed too sad and angry to envision anything but dark days ahead for his people.

"What is left for me to do is to go back up to my father and tell him the news," Shining Horse told the council. "I have done my best. I can do no more. All I can do now is to watch until the settlers start pushing onto our lands once again."

The somber council adjourned. Even though it was late in the evening, Shining Horse decided to start for his father's village. As he saddled and packed his pony, Two Robes spoke to him.

"Don't you think it would be better if all the people came together and united to become progressive?" he asked. "Then you could exert some political pressure for better conditions."

Shining Horse tightened the cinch on his pony and grunted. "It is odd that you have learned our tongue as well as you have in such a short time," he said, "only to say that you think my people should become *Wasichu*."

"I don't believe your people should try to be white," Two Robes said. "But they're going to have to take the White Man's Road to survive."

"The only way we will survive is to forget the White Man's Road," Shining Horse said. "I am convinced of it."

"How do you think you can survive if you do that?"

Shining Horse turned to him, his jaw clenched. "Why would you ask such a question? Did the buffalo not come for you?"

"There are many of you, Shining Horse. There are practically no buffalo, certainly not enough to hunt."

"If you were saved in a land that is not even your own," Shining Horse said, "*Wankantanka* will see to it that his own are cared for."

"What has happened to you?" Two Robes asked. "You act as though you would lead a war party if given the chance."

"If my people had any chance of winning," Shining Horse said, "I would certainly lead a war party."

"You impressed me when we first met as someone who wanted to do some good for his people," Two Robes said. "Getting them killed by soldiers is not a good way to help them."

"My people have always preferred to die in battle," Shining Horse said. "Starvation is not an honorable death."

"Maybe the money that comes from the sale of the land will help."

Shining Horse finished securing his saddle. He made certain his packs were tight and turned to Two Robes. "I do

not understand you," he said. "You have been pushed out of
your order by your own kind because you wanted to do things
your way. When I tell you I think that my people should live
their way, you tell me I am a fool."

"How can they live their way under these conditions?" Two
Robes asked. "There are no places left where there isn't a
white settlement. If your reservation is cut up into sections,
many more whites will be living around you."

Shining Horse mounted his pony. "Maybe it is time we took
back our lands."

"You don't mean that."

"I am too angry right now to know what I mean. All I can
tell you is that I am going back up to my father. He will not
give in, no matter what comes. I am Lakota, as he is, and I will
not change for anyone, either."

"Will I see you again, Shining Horse?"

"I would invite you up to meet my father, but he would not
like the word 'progressive' to be used around him."

"I would like to meet your father," Two Robes said. "I
suppose you are right, though. I have decided to try to help
your people adjust to the white culture."

"There will always be change, my friend," Shining Horse
said. "But the type of change I am seeing now both sickens
and saddens me. My father is deeply angered by what is
happening, and I can see why he believes the way he does. He
wouldn't want to hear any of your words."

"I would not want to anger him. If you think it is best, I will
not journey up there."

Shining Horse leaned down from his pony and shook Two
Robes's hand. "You are a good man, and I will always call you
friend," he said. "But we cannot agree on what's best for my
people. Maybe our paths will not cross again. Take care of
yourself."

Two Robes stepped back and watched Shining Horse ride
off. It saddened him to think he might never see this man
again. It had been Shining Horse who had given him St. John

of the Cross and who had found him lost on the open plains. Like the wind that came from nowhere, the events in this vast open seemed unpredictable. But there was one thing that Two Robes knew could be predicted: when the land commission had finished its work, the Lakota world would be forever changed.

PART III
August, 1889–January, 1890

My children, my children,
It is I who wear the
Morning Star on my head,
It is I who wear the
Morning Star on my head;
I show it to my children,
I show it to my children,
Says the father,
Says the father.

Wovoka,
Paiute Messiah Song
to those gathered
at Walker Lake, Nevada

EIGHTEEN

WITH THE sun nearing the horizon and the flag at half-mast, Sergeant Roscoe Betters took one last look across the parade ground. The men stood sullenly at attention. Taps had been sounded and the grave of Colonel Edward Hatch was just hours old. The Ninth U.S. Cavalry would not be the same.

The black fighting regiment, known as the Buffalo Soldiers for their buffalo coats, had lost their founder and supreme commander to old age. After his transfer from the Tenth Cavalry, Sergeant Betters had served under Colonel Hatch against the Apaches; the regiment had gained the respect of such strong Apache leaders as Victorio and Nana. Of all the Bluecoats the Apaches had ever fought, they said, the Buffalo Soldiers had possessed the strongest medicine.

Sergeant Betters had seen action throughout the Southwest, days tracking renegade Indians, nights with one eye open. He now found the slow passing of time at Fort Robinson hard to take. The country was settling fast. He did little these days but play cards and watch the sun fall into the west.

No one knew for certain what the fate of the outfit would be. It was Colonel Hatch who had organized the regiment and he who had fought for its recognition. With the colonel gone, the regiment would likely be disbanded.

There was talk, though, that the Indians on the Great Sioux Reservation to the north had been growing increasingly uneasy. Word had it that General George Crook and his land commission were up there gathering signatures from the various Sioux groups to sell a good part of their lands. He already had many signatures, and the issue was splitting the Sioux nation apart. There would certainly be those who wouldn't sign, no matter what was offered. These would likely become renegades before long.

Sergeant Betters knew that money wasn't what the Sioux wanted. They wanted the land back that had been taken from them. They needed to be allowed to roam free as they once did, and to hunt instead of to farm. Sergeant Betters knew that would never come to pass. If anything, the Sioux would be increasingly pressured to work the soil.

He remembered being detailed back in 1879 to fight the Utes over the same issue. That had cost the lives of everyone at the White River Agency. As far as Sergeant Betters was concerned, the Great Sioux Reservation could well develop into another battleground.

Few would listen to him. Most thought that the Sioux were far too desperate, physically and emotionally, to do anything about the certain changes that were coming. But there were those, like Sergeant Betters, who knew Indians well enough to believe anything could happen.

Roscoe Betters had been a solider from the age of fifteen, when he had enlisted in the Union Army. He had survived that conflict and his numerous campaigns in the West with only minor flesh wounds. Then came the Boomers, the homesteaders who insisted on the forced settlement of Indian Territory. The Ninth was called in to drive them out and send them back where they had come from. Roscoe Betters now walked with a limp, courtesy of a drunken Boomer who had shattered his right kneecap with a blow from a blacksmith's hammer.

"I've been in many a fight, Comanches and Apaches and all the rest," Betters told those who asked about his stiff leg. "Couldn't expect to get off scot free. I just didn't think it would come after the worst was past."

But maybe the worst hadn't yet passed, he thought as he marched with the troops from the parade ground, swinging his diamond willow cane close to his side to steady himself. Maybe there would be something more for the Ninth to do before everyone went out to pasture.

When the men had adjourned to their quarters, the nightly poker club assembled at a table in the corner of the barracks. Though Sergeant Betters lived with two other black officers in separate quarters, he frequently joined the enlisted men when they played. He often won and always broke even. Tonight, however, he couldn't keep his mind on the cards.

"You seem a mite itchy to me, Sergeant," Private Nathan Cort said. He had served under Betters for most of his enlisted life, even requesting transfer from the Tenth to the Ninth to remain under Betters. "You figure this dry wind we've been having might blow trouble in or something?" He shifted his small, lanky frame in his chair.

"Or something," Betters said with a grunt. He tossed two cards onto the table and motioned to the dealer. "Give me two, Jesse. Make them good ones this time."

The dealer flipped two cards across the table to Betters and dealt draws to the others. Jesse Lane was short and broad, with eyebrows that grew together over his nose. He watched Betters study the cards and shook his head.

"Hell, Sergeant, why you even botherin' to play? You done lost just tonight most of what you won this whole week."

"Don't you worry about *my* luck, Jesse," Betters told him. "I'll come through. I just don't know what's going to happen up north."

"One thing's for certain," Cort said. "They sure ain't going to give them Sioux any leeway up there."

"Who says you know piddle about it?" Jesse asked him.

Cort eyed Sergeant Betters before he answered. "I figure the Sioux will have a bad taste in their mouth once Crook and his land commission get done. Can't be nothing but an ill wind that blows after he leaves up there."

"That's General Crook to you, Private Cort," Betters corrected him. "You can think of him as you please, but he's an officer, and you can't forget that."

"Yeah, okay, Gen'l Crook, then," Cort said. "It don't matter what his name is, Sergeant, he's bound to bring trouble to the reservation. Don't you figure?"

"He ain't no worse than Miles," one of the men watching the game put in. "If it were up to Miles, the whole reservation'd be gone, and the Sioux with it."

"Listen, all of you," Betters told the men, "it's not our business to decide what should or shouldn't be going on up north, or who is in charge. We'd best all do our duty here and let Washington handle the Sioux the way they see fit."

"I ain't about to get into no discussion about Washington," Cort said. "No, siree. If I got into hot water talking about Gen'l Crook the way I did, then the sergeant don't want to hear nothing from me about Washington."

"You can't go to talkin' a lot against Washington, Cort," one of the other men said. "You been in this man's army for so long you can't count the free meals you got so far."

"Well, I can't count the ones I missed, neither," Cort said. "I figure it evens out."

"We going to play cards or dribble off at the mouth?" Jesse asked. "Cort, you opened. What you going to do?"

Cort picked up three matchsticks and put them into the pile. "I think a lot of my hand."

The men grunted. The other three in the game passed to the sergeant, who threw eight matchsticks into the center of the table. "See your three and up you five."

"We got a raise limit of three here, Sergeant," Cort said.

"Sergeants don't have a raise limit," Betters said. "Are you proud enough to call me?"

The men studied Betters. Cort said, "You're bluffin', Sergeant." He continued to study the sergeant, sorting his matchsticks with a nervous finger.

"What you going to do, Cort?" Jesse asked. "I'm ready to deal the cards, so figure it out. It'll be reveille before you get your brain to work."

"See those five," Cort said. "And here's five more. Yep, five more."

Everyone stared while Cort counted out ten matchsticks and laid them carefully on top of the pile. He had one stick remaining.

"You ain't got the cards for that, Cort," Jesse said. "Why'd you go and bet like that?"

Cort squinted at Jesse. "How do you know what I got?"

"I mean, you're playin' with the sergeant, Cort," Jesse said. "He's done this to you before."

"He's old enough to figure it out on his own," one of the other men said.

"I'd hope so," Jesse commented. "He's got more wrinkles than a whorehouse dishrag."

"I done it, Jesse," Cort said. "I sure ain't takin' it back. And quit makin' reference to my person. You ain't no prettier than a buffalo's ass your own self."

Jesse grunted. Betters looked hard at his cards. He smiled and tossed five more matchsticks in. "I'll call."

"I told you, Cort," Jesse said.

"Jacks and tens," Cort said, laying down his hand. "And an ace to boot."

Betters spread his cards on the table. Jesse leaned over and laughed. "See that, Cort? Three ladies. I told you not to mess with the sergeant. Weep, you poor bastard."

Cort slammed his fist into the table. "How'd you do that, Sergeant? Put us to sleep like that, all night, and then go and come up with a hand like that!"

Betters gathered his winnings. "Looks like I'm back to even," he said. "I think I'll call it a night."

"We ain't hardly started," Cort protested.

"I'm not up to any more," Betters said. "I'll see you boys in the morning."

Cort and Jesse and the others at the table watched Betters limp out, the tip of his cane knocking hollowly against the barracks floor.

"He didn't even worry about me paying him," Cort said. "Usually he'll put a string on my finger about seeing him come payday."

"His spirit is way down," Jesse said. "I ain't never seen him so low. You don't suppose it's because ol' Hatch just passed on, do you?"

"No it ain't that," Cort said quickly. "I tell you, it's what's happening up north that's gotten him worried."

"Why do you figure you know so much about it, Cort?" one of the men asked.

"You know that bullwhacker, Cullen, who brings freight through from Yates all the time?" Cort asked. "Well, I talked to him. He's heard that the commission ain't leaving 'till they get the signatures they need. There's bound to be trouble when them Sioux lose more land."

"The sergeant ain't afraid of no fight," Jesse said. "You ought to know that."

"Of course he ain't afraid to fight," Cort said, shuffling the cards. "It's just that he don't want to this time." He set the deck down on the table. "You see, he's got a son up on that reservation."

"What?" Jesse asked. "How do you know that?"

The others stared. Cort began to toy with his sole remaining matchstick. "Back when we was both with the Tenth," he said, "we got called out in the middle of winter in seventy-three to catch a bunch of whiskey peddlers workin' the Indian Territory. We caught them and was bringing them in for trial when two of them got away. It was damn cold, and the sergeant said he'd take two men and go get them. I was one of the two who went.

"We found them whiskey peddlers all right, but they put up a fight and we had to shoot them. Coming back, we got caught in a blizzard, and lucky for us, some Arapahos took us in. We stayed pretty near a week, until the weather broke. The sergeant slept three nights with a young woman who took a shine to him. He found out later she had a boy. Came to Camp Supply and put the little rascal in his arms. I saw it."

After a silence, Jesse asked, "What makes you say the sergeant's son is with the Sioux now?"

"Cullen's been driving rations around the agencies up there for over a year," Cort said. "He's seen the one that's the sergeant's son. Up on Cherry Creek, in Kicking Bear's camp. Says they call him Tangled Hair."

"In Kicking Bear's camp?" Jesse said. "If there's fightin', that Injun will be in it sure. What else do you know about it, Cort?"

"Ain't nothing else to know," Cort said, biting the matchstick in half. "Just that the sergeant's son is up there, and the sergeant knows it."

Jesse took a deep breath and looked at the others. "I seen enough of that kind of thing when the South took up against the North. Brothers and fathers and the like fightin' one another, killin' like there was no tomorrow. The sergeant don't deserve nothing like that."

"Ain't a thing we can do about it," one of the men put in. "It's like the sergeant told us, we're here to fight when we're told, with a 'Yes, suh' and no back talk."

Cort stared at the deck of cards on the table. He spit the broken match from his mouth and stood up. "I didn't feel like playing cards tonight anyway," he said. "I figure it's time I turned in."

After the kiss, Fawn did not see Two Robes for nearly a week. She was close to completing the chasuble she had promised him, but she had to take time out to gather roots while they were still available.

Fawn realized that Two Robes was avoiding her physically and emotionally. He spent time away from the village by himself without even saying good-bye. But there was too much on her mind for her to think about him continually. This was the season for gathering plants and roots for storing. Early rains had brought many plants into profuse bloom across the plains.

Very important was the digging of breadroots that grew on the sandy hillsides and bottoms. The large, starchy roots grew deep beneath the soil, at least the length of a small child's hand. They were best when dug during their period of early bloom. After the heavy outer layer was removed, the carrot-like root could be cut into sections or ground into meal and added to stews and meat dishes. Fawn had learned from her mother that this root was one of the most important for keeping the people healthy during the cold moons.

It was important to collect as many breadroots as possible this year. In the previous spring, the plains had received little early rain. The breadroot plants had emerged from the ground, stems and leaves covered with fine, heavy hairs, had flowered briefly, and then within only five or six days, had broken off at the base. The hot winds had dried them up and they had blown away across the hillsides. After that there had been no way to find the roots.

Other plant roots needed to be gathered as well. Hawk and Little Star played with the village children while Fawn worked with Night Bird, passing the tedious hours with conversation. One morning Night Bird left her digging and walked off by herself. Concerned, Fawn followed her. Night Bird was vomiting.

"Fawn smiled. "What would make you sick at this time of day? Is it the reason I suspect?"

"Yes, it is for that reason," Night Bird said. "But it is nothing to rejoice over."

"Why not?" Fawn asked. "A baby is something to be happy about."

"I don't feel happy," Night Bird said. "I believe this will only make things worse."

Night Bird headed past Fawn toward her root bag. Fawn touched her shoulder to stop her. "What is happening?" she asked. "Are you and Catches Lance having trouble?"

"We have had trouble since he traveled down to Pine Ridge," Night Bird replied. "He is changing even more now. He says he wants me to come off the hillside and help him start a garden. I am a Lakota, not a *Wasichu*. I will not do it."

"I did not know this," Fawn said. "When did he say that?"

"Last night," Night Bird replied. She picked up her root bag. "I am not feeling well. I believe I will go down to my lodge and rest."

"I can go with you," Fawn offered.

"You should stay and dig for your family. I will be fine. I just need rest."

Fawn watched Night Bird make her way down into the village. Then, instead of returning to her work, she started for a little bench of land above the river. There she found Catches Lance bent over a hoe, tearing grooves through a patch of grass.

"What are you doing?" Fawn asked him.

Catches Lance continued to work. "I got this hoe from the agency. And I got some seeds. I will learn to grow corn and squash and beans, and teach others who want to learn."

"When did you decide to do this?" Fawn asked. "When did you decide to become a *Wasichu*?"

"Last ration day," he replied. "I heard there was seed, so I asked about it. The agent said we should all grow gardens so we can take care of ourselves. Others are doing it."

"But I didn't know *you* wanted to do it."

"I can make up my own mind about what I want to do."

"But this is something important," Fawn said. "I didn't know you would ever do this."

Catches Lance continued to dig. "Everything changes," he said. "Now I believe that our mother was right. She decided to live where many were following the White Man's Road. She is gone now, but I can still do what she would want."

"Are you doing what *you* want, Catches Lance?"

"Yes, I am doing what *I* want!" Catches Lance slammed the edge of his hoe into the earth and tore out a chunk of grass. "And I will be very good at it."

"How are you going to make your vegetables grow up here?" Fawn asked. "Why did you pick this place?"

Catches Lance looked up. "This is a good place. What is wrong with it? I have a bucket, too, down at the river. I will bring water up to the vegetables." Catches Lance forced the tip of the hoe through another heavy clod of grass, sweat pouring from his brow. Bees buzzed around wild-flower blossoms.

"Don't you have to make a field first?" Fawn asked. "Don't you have to turn over the soil?"

"I don't want to turn the soil over," Catches Lance said defensively. "I don't want to kill the grass. I just want to grow vegetables beside the grass."

"The *Wasichu* turn the grass over first so that it will die," Fawn said. "Corn does not grow where there is grass. The vegetables will not grow without first killing the grass."

"I told you, I don't want to kill the grass," Catches Lance said angrily. "Didn't you hear me?"

"Then don't look for the seeds to grow," Fawn told him. "I don't think you should turn the grass over, either. But you have to if you want to grow corn."

"How do you know this?" Catches Lance asked.

"Don't you notice how those *Wasichu* who have gardens do it? They are very good at killing the grass so they can grow other things. That's why I will never get along with them."

Catches Lance stood back from his work. "Why can't I have both corn and grass together?"

Fawn spread her hand in a semicircle across the land in front of them. "How much corn do you see growing out there?" she asked. "*Wankantanka* made this land for grass, not for fat corn. When we want that kind of food, we can go get it from the Arikara and the Mandan. Remember?"

"That was long ago, Fawn," Catches Lance said. "What do you think, that they are growing corn just for us now? The Mandan and Arikara are like us. They are not the same any longer. The Mandan are mostly long gone from the spotted sickness. So what are you talking about?"

Fawn sat down and covered her face with her hands. Tears flowed from between her fingers. Catches Lance sat down next to her. "I wish the old times were back," he said. "But they are gone. We have to do things differently now. I am going to take the White Man's Road."

Fawn stared at him. "What is happening to you?"

"It is the thing to do," he argued. "Night Bird is not certain yet, but she will soon see that I have made the right decision."

Fawn rose to her feet. "Are you going to make Night Bird do what you want?"

Catches Lance stood up quickly. "She is my wife. She will want to do what I do."

"You are making a decision that she will never feel good about."

"She will learn to like it."

Fawn took a deep breath. "What good will it do? The White Man's Road will never be open to you. Many of our people have journeyed down that path, but the *Wasichu* still spit on them whenever they can."

"I will change that," Catches Lance said. "It will not be that way when I get a band together and we show them that we can live their ways as well they can."

"I cannot believe these are your words."

"They are my words, and many are listening to them, especially a lot of the younger men and their wives who feel as I do. They will follow me. We will have our own village. Catches Lance's village."

"You are not old enough to have your own people," Fawn said. "What is the matter with you? Why can't you be happy the way you are?"

"I will never gain honor in the old way," Catches Lance said. "I must make a new road and travel it well so that those who travel it with me will honor me. You should think about it. It would be wise if you followed me."

Catches Lance took up his hoe once again. Fawn watched him for a while. Then she said, "I think you had better find a spot along the river where the water has brought mud into a flat space. It will be wetter there, and no grass will grow to choke out your corn."

Catches Lance again slammed the hoe into the ground. "You have always told me what is best to do," he said. "I am not listening to you any longer. I know what is best now. I will grow a garden where I want, not where you say. Now go and leave me to my work."

"Please don't think about going to live somewhere else. It would not be good for Night Bird, and it would not be good for the baby."

Catches Lance turned. "The baby?"

"Yes. Night Bird is with child."

"How do you know this?"

"She was sick when we were up on the hill. I asked her and she told me. She went back to your lodge."

Catches Lance stared into the distance. "She told you first. Before me."

"Maybe she just realized it today," Fawn said. "It does not

matter. She loves you, but she does not want you to change so much. Don't start another village."

"I'm not going to stay around Kicking Bear," Catches Lance said. "He has always wanted to become as famous as his cousin, Crazy Horse. Now, since the day the sun died, he believes he has been given special powers. He will not want any of us to be here if we follow the White Man's Road."

"I wish you would stop this talk," Fawn said. "Who would give Hawk and Little Star pony rides? We would miss you and Night Bird, and the baby."

"You will not change my mind about the White Man's Road," Catches Lance said. "I have to get Night Bird away from you so you do not fill her head with silly ideas."

Tears returned to Fawn's eyes. "Catches Lance, you do not mean that."

"I asked you to go. Why are you still here?"

Fawn left her brother. She went back to where she had left her bag and digging tool. She was wasting time by not gathering roots. She would soon have to find someone else to dig with, for Night Bird would not be there with her.

She jammed her digging tool, a two-pronged stick, into the ground. Tears blinded her. She pushed and pulled on the tool, trying to work a root loose. Suddenly the stick snapped in half.

Fawn pulled the broken shaft out of the ground and stood up. A breeze tossed her hair across her face. To the west, a great thunderstorm was building. She looked at the darkening sky. Then she tossed the broken tool into the grass and started down the hill.

NINETEEN

THEY STOOD in front of Fawn's lodge while the sun rose to the open door flap. Hawk and Little Star had informed Two Robes that his vestment was ready. He had been awaiting this day. For some time he had been telling the people that when his sacred garment was finished, he would baptize them and say mass.

Fawn presented him with the garment, folded neatly. He took it, thanking her, and unwrapped a fringed and beaded chasuble made of white muslin.

"I sewed it like a war shirt," she said, "but with large, open sleeves. I hope it will fit you."

Two Robes tried on the vestment. He slipped it over his head and let it settle down around his shoulders and upper body. It fit very nicely. Fine blue beadwork adorned the sleeves and collar, and black horsehair fringed the sleeves. A large red cross had been dyed on the back.

"I thought the shirt should have something on it," Fawn

said. "Just plain white won't make you special in my people's eyes."

"It's beautiful," Two Robes said. "I can't thank you enough."

Hawk and Little Star, who sat near the door flap, stared at Two Robes. They saw his smile as he ran his fingers along the beadwork.

"I held the beads for sewing," Little Star said.

"I thank you, Little Star," Two Robes said. "And you, too, Hawk."

"Yeah, well, I didn't do too much," the boy said. "I'm not a sewer. I will make you a good bow, with arrows."

"I'll just let you do the hunting for me," Two Robes said with a smile. He turned back to Fawn. "I wish that you would consider being baptized."

"No, that will not happen," she said.

"Why are you doing this for me?" Two Robes asked. "If you do not believe in my pathway, why are you helping me?"

"Because you are a holy man and your pathway is sacred. Just because I do not choose to follow your vision doesn't make it less sacred than my own."

Two Robes removed the chasuble and smiled at Fawn. He refolded the beautiful garment neatly, wondering how he could ever repay her.

"If you decide to change your mind, I would certainly welcome the chance to teach you more about the *Wasichu* god," he told her. "You will find that He is no different than the *Wankantanka* whom you know."

Catches Lance approached, dressed in his finest garments. "The people are waiting," he said. "Are you ready?"

Two Robes turned to thank Fawn once again, but she had slipped into her lodge with her children. He left with Catches Lance for the place along the riverbank where he would perform the baptisms and say mass.

Over two hundred Minneconjou had gathered to listen to his words. Most of them had come as spectators, not as participants. They wanted to see how this man of two worlds presented himself before they made any decisions about changing their faith.

Two Robes looked for Kicking Bear, but Catches Lance told him that Kicking Bear had gone into the agency. Tangled Hair and two other young warriors had gone with him. Two Robes wished that Kicking Bear had come to watch, at least. Catches Lance was young, and a good influence; but if Kicking Bear were there, many would feel better about joining Catholicism.

With all of the people watching, Two Robes donned his chasuble. He said a prayer in Lakota with the people, then lit a large dish filled with sage leaves and sweetgrass. The people came in a single file and cleansed themselves with the smoke.

Two Robes explained the sacrament of baptism. He told the people about the man named John, whom the Bleeding Chief knew and who had baptized many in a river such as this. He told them they would become reborn so they could better understand how the *Wasichu* god and *Wankantanka* were one and the same.

Two Robes waded into the shallows, where a buffalo skull had been placed atop a large rock. He stood on the rock next to the skull and asked the people to line up in a single file so he might baptize them, one by one.

Catches Lance was first, an honor he had demanded for his help in organizing the service. Two Robes spoke in Lakota, pouring water over Catches Lance's head from a buffalo-skin pouch, making the sign of the cross as he did so.

After Catches Lance, nearly eighty people came—men, women, children, and small babies. Afterward they took their places back on the bank, touching their heads and singing their own spiritual songs.

Then a small boy presented himself to Two Robes.

"Hawk!" Two Robes said in surprise. "Does your mother know you are here?"

"Yes," Hawk replied. "I asked her if I could come and she said she wouldn't stop me if that is what I wanted."

"What about Little Star?"

"She decided to stay with Mother. She said she would not be angry if I went to learn the ways of the *Wasichu* god."

"It is a brave thing that you are doing, Hawk. What made you choose to do this?"

"I want to do it. Did you ask the others why they have come?"

"No, and I shouldn't ask you all these questions, either. You are old enough to know what you want. I am very glad you came."

Two Robes baptized Hawk and lifted him up for a long hug. The boy went back to the bank with the others, touching his wet head.

The people stood together while Two Robes began the mass. Again he spoke in Lakota and explained the meaning of each phase of the service. He talked as he had to Fawn, telling them about the Last Supper and of how the twelve apostles had wanted to carry the teachings of Jesus Christ to all the peoples of the world.

They watched intently while he raised a small piece of hardtack to the morning sky and told them that it represented the body of Jesus Christ, the Bleeding Chief, who had died for their sake long, long ago.

Catches Lance stood on the bank, watching the people, but he did not listen intently. Instead, his mind roamed to visions of leadership and grandeur. He had been working hard to establish himself as a leader among the progressives and thought it would be good to gain Two Robes' approval.

His garden, now located along the creek, had become a showpiece. Gardens on the uplands had begun to fade as the summer sun turned them hot and dry. There had been no moisture of any kind for nearly a full moon.

Catches Lance spent most of his time at his garden and had discovered that he could divert water from the creek over to his plants and thus keep the soil moist. Those trying to raise crops on the uplands were losing everything to wind and the blistering sunlight. Already a few of the progressives were looking to him for advice.

Though he had followed Fawn's advice about his garden, Catches Lance had not spoken with her except to say a few words whenever he brought the children back from pony rides. Nor was he speaking much with Night Bird. Her pregnancy was not discussed, nor their future together. Nothing about his personal life fared well, although he was certain that this would change as soon as he had a village of his own.

Catches Lance felt that he had progressed a long way by getting so many people interested in the first baptism and mass. He felt certain that in time Two Robes and those who converted would move with him down toward the agency to start a new village. Though he hadn't discussed the idea with Two Robes, he was confident that this holy man of two worlds would share his vision of a new community of progressives. Surely many more would gravitate to them in time.

To gain Two Robes' admiration, Catches Lance had secured the wine for the mass. He had gone into the agency, where he had traded some of the old medicine articles, used by the people in bygone days, to a storekeeper who was collecting them for easterners who wanted to have them for themselves.

A ceremonial rattle and headdress that had belonged to his father had bought Catches Lance four bottles of wine, although alcohol was prohibited on the reservation. "Let's keep all this between you and me," the storekeeper had said with a smile. "We can do one another a lot of good."

Two Robes had been glad to get the wine, but he was concerned about how it had come to him. Catches Lance had refused to discuss it. "It is a gift," he had said. "I can find more when you need it. I can find whatever you need."

Although Two Robes needed wine to say the mass, he had not known how to find any himself. Even if he'd had the funds, he couldn't go to the store. The agency people had learned about him. Though they had never come out to talk to him, they could easily ask him to leave if he ventured into the agency. They were Protestant in belief and had been working to keep both the Catholic and the Episcopalian missionaries out. For this reason, Two Robes had accepted the gift from Catches Lance without prying.

With communion at hand, Two Robes had those he had baptized again line up in a single file. He placed into each mouth a small piece of hardtack dipped into the wine. Hawk stepped forward. He opened his mouth and Two Robes placed a tidbit onto his tongue. The boy swallowed the morsel and looked into Two Robes' eyes.

"It didn't change me. I don't feel any different. I thought it would change me."

"Why would it change you?" Two Robes asked.

"You told my mother it would bring her close to your god. I don't feel any different."

"I will talk to you after I have finished with everyone," Two Robes told him.

"Didn't you say that this would help me touch the *Wasichu* god?" Hawk persisted.

"Please, Hawk, wait until the mass is finished."

Hawk moved into the group that had received communion. He watched Two Robes continue the mass for a short time, then left. When Two Robes began the concluding rites, he noticed Hawk's absence. Troubled, he told himself that he must find the boy as soon as the service was over. But as soon as Two Robes ended the service, he was approached by Tangled Hair.

"I have just returned from the agency," he told Two Robes. "Kicking Bear received a letter from his uncle. He wants you to see this letter and hear what you have to say about it."

Two Robes hurried with Tangled Hair to Kicking Bear's lodge. He wondered why Kicking Bear would want to have him, specifically, read the letter. This had never happened before. There were others who could read, even in English.

A number of warriors had gathered outside and were in

excited discussion. Two Robes entered the lodge and smoked for a time with a few of the most prominent warriors in the village. Then Kicking Bear reached into a bag and pulled out the letter.

"I was given this at the store where the letters come, and I had the man who gives out the letters read it to me," Kicking Bear said, handing the missive to Two Robes. "After the storekeeper read it to me, he smiled. He kept smiling as he handed it to me. Now I want to know what the marks tell you."

Two Robes noted that the letter was written in Carlisle English, the pidgin form taught most Indians of the time. He restructured it in his head and began to read aloud:

13 July 1889
Ethete, Wyoming

To Kicking Bear from Spoonhunter:

I write to you to tell you of something very good that has come to the Indian people. There is a man who is a Paiute who has died and been to Heaven and has learned from the Father. His name is Wovoka. He has come back to bring a new way of life. In this life there will be no white men living.

Wovoka is holy and speaks truth. He will teach all who will listen the steps to a holy dance. The Indian people will have their lands back once again and the whites will be no more. The buffalo are returning.

Come and see what we have learned.

Spoonhunter

Two Robes looked up, shock on his face. Kicking Bear reached for the letter and Two Robes handed it to him.

"I see you believe the letter is real," Kicking Bear said.

"I don't know whether it is real or not," Two Robes said. "I doubt it. Who is this man, Spoonhunter?"

"He is my uncle, an Oglala. He married an Arapaho woman

and moved to Ethete to live with his wife's people. He is an honorable man."

"I do not question his honor," Two Robes said. "But this man, Wovoka, is telling people some very strong things."

"If Spoonhunter believes he is real, then I do too," Kicking Bear said. "This Wovoka man is a *Wanekia*."

"A *Wanekia*?"

"Yes, a savior. A real, live savior. You have called the Bleeding Chief a savior, a Messiah. That is who this Wovoka man is, a Messiah."

"How can you be so certain of that?" Two Robes asked. "Maybe this Wovoka is just a medicine man."

"My uncle would not become so excited over that," Kicking Bear said sternly. "If Spoonhunter says something good is coming, I believe him. I want to meet this man he speaks of, this man who is going to save our people. I want to know who he is who is bringing us a new world."

Two Robes stared. His mind spinning, he searched for words.

"What is the matter?" Kicking Bear asked. "You have talked about a new world before. You have spoken about a second coming of the Messiah."

"Yes, I have told you before that Christ will return to save the just," Two Robes said, "but I don't believe the time is right yet. Whoever your uncle is referring to can't be Jesus."

Kicking Bear shook the letter at Two Robes. "You told me the marks from Spoonhunter mean there is a Messiah who has come to help the Indian people. Is that not right?"

"That is what the letter says," Two Robes replied. "But I don't fully understand. The letter says someone died and came back to life. That isn't possible."

"The Bleeding Chief did," Kicking Bear declared. "Yes, he died and came back. Or have you been lying?"

The other warriors listened intently. Two Robes felt trapped. "This letter cannot be about Jesus Christ," he told Kicking Bear.

"Why not? Maybe he has returned as an Indian. Why not?"

Again, Two Robes was speechless. He had heard the same thing from Fawn. He had no answer.

"This letter bothers you greatly," Kicking Bear said. "All the time you tell us that the Bleeding Chief, who was killed by his own people, will come back and make the world better. But you did not ever think that when he returned, he would be a red man."

Two Robes was offered the pipe by one of the warriors. He took it and smoked. Then he told Kicking Bear, "The God I know will not advertise his coming in letters or by any ordinary correspondence. No. When the real Jesus returns, he will show his coming in signs that must be read by the faithful. He won't just walk through some door and announce himself."

Two Robes passed the pipe to Kicking Bear. After smoking, Kicking Bear said, "But you have not told me whether or not you believe Jesus would return as an Indian."

"The savior who will come will not be of any one race," Two Robes replied. "He will come for the good of all mankind. God would send no savior who would make things better for just one race."

"Things are good for the *Wasichu*," Kicking Bear said. "They have taken everything from the Indian people unjustly. They will not give anything back unless forced to do so."

"I told you, that is not God's way!" Two Robes said. "I believe that your uncle wants to return to the old times, just like you do. So that makes both of you vulnerable to someone who says that can be so if you will only follow him. Maybe you had better listen to this man and ask him some questions before you start believing the world is going to change overnight."

"You are wise," Kicking Bear said. "But I know in my heart that the man my uncle speaks of is very holy. I want to go talk to my uncle, so he can tell me more."

"What do you think of my teachings of Jesus so far?" Two Robes asked.

"You speak of a man who is fair and just," Kicking Bear said. "And you have come to know my people very well. But the Bleeding Chief has always been known as a *Wasichu* god. This time it is different. If Wovoka has gone across and has spoken to the Father of us all, then I believe he will help the Indian people gain back what is rightfully theirs. If that's what the Father told him, that is what will happen."

The council broke up. Before long the entire village had learned of the letter and Kicking Bear's planned visit to his uncle. Villagers gathered to talk about the *Wanekia* in the West who had come to bring back the old ways. They would know more when Kicking Bear returned.

No one appeared to notice Two Robes any longer. It was as though he were not among them. He watched with a mixture of anger and concern as everyone discussed the possibilities of being saved from their despair. His entire mission among these people was now in jeopardy.

Two Robes had learned a lot since coming among Kicking Bear's Minneconjou. These people were among the last holdouts against the White Man's Road. They wanted no part of the reservation system, which had set the stage for countless feuds between bands and families and had caused old friendships to break into fragments. The Lakota people were torn to their very roots.

Now an Indian man claiming to be a Messiah stood to unite all Indian people who would listen to him. This man, Wovoka, would certainly appeal to anyone against the White Man's Road. He would have many followers.

Two Robes could easily see why the *Wasichu* were so hated among these people. Behind a string of broken treaties and agreements had come the power of the U.S. Army, quick to enforce regulations none of the tribes had ever agreed upon. Now the reservation agents were exploiting their positions, taking what they could and making profits on goods that had been shipped to the Indians.

The Indians had been left in the middle, forced to comply

with ever-changing codes and policies. Almost no one wanted the Indians to be allowed to live the way they had lived for centuries. Everyone was in a hurry either to civilize them or to exterminate them.

Two Robes vowed to do what he could to keep those he had already baptized and to add to their number. He would continue to say mass and explain his position on his God. He would even put in kind words for Wovoka, pointing out, however, that this Messiah was nothing more than a man with good ideas. It was still important that they look to Jesus Christ.

He knew that he couldn't change Kicking Bear's mind or the minds of his most ardent followers. But he knew, too, that there would be a number who would continue to listen to him. He had to keep his dream alive, even though it would be much harder now than he could have ever envisioned.

TWENTY

S HINING HORSE helped his half-brother, Crowfoot, groom an old gray horse that Sitting Bull
had ridden in Buffalo Bill's Wild West Show. Crowfoot, who
had just passed his sixteenth winter, had recently returned
from visiting friends in another village.

Crowfoot had been eight when his father had given himself
up to the Bluecoats for the last time at Fort Buford, Dakota
Territory. Crowfoot had taken his father's weapons to hand
over to the Bluecoat officer.

He told Shining Horse, "Since that time, our father has aged
with worry about our people. He has done much to appease the
Wasichu, though they won't acknowledge it. In the old days, he
would never have lived in a cabin and kept cattle and chickens."

"That does not mean he has taken the White Man's Road,"
Shining Horse said. "He is only doing what he can to keep
peace. We can still be proud of him."

"Yes, he will hold his head high until his death. Sometimes
I worry that he feels his days have passed."

"He has many years left. Our people want his leadership. He will not let those he loves fall into bad hands without fighting for what is right."

Crowfoot pointed to a Winchester rifle leaning against the corral poles. "Did our father give that to you?" he asked.

"Yes, when I returned from telling the other villages about the land commission. He told me I had done a very good job and not to feel that I had failed."

"If you let me shoot the gun once, I will show you a trick," Crowfoot said.

"Do you shoot coins out of the air or something?" Shining Horse asked.

"Just watch."

Crowfoot cocked the rifle and fired into the air. The old pony immediately dropped back on its haunches into a sitting position and began to paw the air with a front hoof.

Shining Horse watched, unamused. "The ponies I remember could outrun buffalo," he said. "The *Wasichu* have no better use for a horse than to make it act like a dog."

Crowfoot put the old horse back into the corral while Shining Horse sat on the corral gate and unfolded a newspaper Sitting Bull had given him. He read the article marked for his attention.

SHE LOVES SITTING BULL
New Jersey Widow Falls Victim to
Sitting Bull's Charms

A sensation is reported from the Standing Rock Agency, the chief participants being Mrs. C. Wilder of Newark, New Jersey, and Sitting Bull, the notorious old chief. Sitting Bull has many admirers and among them is numbered Mrs. Wilder. . . .

Shining Horse realized that the *Bismarck Tribune* meant Catherine Weldon, the representative from the National Indian Defense Association. His father hadn't said much about the woman, only that she had arrived and had gotten into a dispute with White Hair McLaughlin. The Lakota had named her Woman-Walking-Ahead in honor of her attempts to make things right for them.

Shining Horse could see that the press had taken McLaughlin's side. They wanted to make it appear as if his father and the woman were having an affair. The article said that Mrs. Weldon was not of good character, not to be trusted. McLaughlin had called her a "crank" and a troublemaker.

"That woman will not give up," Crowfoot said, seeing what Shining Horse was reading. "She has promised our father to do whatever it takes to help the Lakota people. She is now off doing what you did. She wants to keep the land commission from splitting the reservation."

"It will be hard for her. I wonder how much she knows about our people."

"She has read a lot about our father," Crowfoot said. "She believes he is the strongest Indian ever to live."

"Maybe she is in love with him. Does she talk about staying here?"

"I believe she does," Crowfoot said. "I believe the two wives will give her trouble."

Long Hand and Bob-tailed Cat appeared, riding hard through the village toward the corrals.

"Something has happened," Crowfoot said. "Silent Eaters do not become alarmed easily."

Long Hand and Bob-tailed Cat reined in their horses. Long Hand asked, "Do you know where your father is?"

"His wives are bathing him in the river," Shining Horse told him. "What is so urgent?"

"Three Stars Crook and the land commission will begin the council to get signatures today," Bob-tailed Cat said. "We heard the news this morning. I do not believe that White Hair wanted Sitting Bull or any of us Unkpapas to be there. The word is that Charging Bear, the one the *Wasichu* call John Grass, is acting as chief for the people."

Crowfoot grabbed a bridle and reentered the corral to catch the old gray pony. "Our father will have to ride up to the agency on horseback," he told Shining Horse. "He will not have time for his wagon."

"Tell the other Silent Eaters that we must all go up there as quickly as possible," Shining Horse said.

Long Hand left to alert the others while Bob-tailed Cat helped Crowfoot saddle the old pony. Shining Horse hurried to the river. Sitting Bull was being dried off by his wives.

"The land commission has started, and White Hair has not informed us," Shining Horse said. "He has put Charging Bear in to speak for the Unkpapa. Can you take a hard ride on the old gray horse?"

"You can tie me on," Sitting Bull said. "This is a meeting I will not miss. Ride with me."

Shining Horse and Sitting Bull arrived at the meeting in the middle of a speech by Charging Bear. They crowded past the Yanktonnais and Metal Breasts gathered in the doorway. Leading the Metal Breasts was Bull Head, with Shaved Head at his side.

"You are not welcome inside," Bull Head told Sitting Bull.

"Are you saying I cannot speak for my people?" Sitting Bull asked.

"They are no longer your people." With a cunning grin, Bull Head stepped aside.

Shining Horse and Sitting Bull took seats inside. Only one hundred or so were in attendance, not nearly enough for such an important meeting. Charging Bear, whose name tag read "John Grass," stood at the table reading from a prepared speech. White Hair McLaughlin and the members of the land commission listened attentively.

Shining Horse had never seen Three Stars Crook before. The graying general was a large man in a neatly tailored uniform. He had a trimmed beard, which he stroked continuously. No one in the room mistook the fact that he was in charge, even though he sat quietly.

Crook glared at Sitting Bull. No doubt the general had suffered a number of sleepless nights pondering their meeting in the Battle of the Rosebud thirteen years before, just eight days prior to Custer's defeat. At the Rosebud, Sitting Bull and Crazy Horse had stopped some thirteen hundred Bluecoats and Indian allies, sending them into disheveled retreat. Shining Horse surmised that Crook must have spent countless hours wondering what might have happened had he won that battle, and what might have happened on the Greasy Grass had he been there with Custer and his men.

Today there would be no defeat for Three Stars Crook. He had come to seal the land agreement. When John Grass had completed his presentation, Crook began to speak.

"Last year, when you refused to accept the bill, Congress came very near opening this reservation anyhow. It is certain that you will never get any better terms than are offered in this bill, and the chances are you will not get so good. And it strikes me that instead of your complaining of the past, you had better provide for the future."

Now McLaughlin was glaring at Shining Horse and Sitting Bull. It was hard to determine which he held in the greatest contempt. Shining Horse felt certain that McLaughlin wanted to have his Metal Breasts remove them, but there was too much at stake to begin something that could end in serious trouble.

Crook continued to address the gathering. "It strikes me that you are in the position of a person who had his effects in the bed of a dry stream when there was a flood coming down, and instead of finding fault with the Creator for sending it down, you should try and save what you can. And that when you can't get what you like best, you had better take what is best for you."

There was murmuring among those present. Many eyes

turned to Sitting Bull, who sat very still. Crook glared at him once again and resumed.

"Now we have understood that there have been some threats made against the Indians who sign this bill. You need not be alarmed, because no one will be allowed to interfere with you. And if any damage or injury is done those who have signed, we will ask to have it paid for from the rations of those who do not sign. So there must be no trouble. Now the tables will be moved down here and those who want to sign can do so."

Shining Horse wanted to stand up and challenge Crook's remark about taking rations from those who did not sign. But it was for his father to do the talking. Sitting Bull rose. "I would like to say something, unless you object to my speaking," he said. "If you do, I will not speak. No one told us of this council today, and we just got here."

Crook turned to McLaughlin. "Did Sitting Bull know we were going to hold a council?"

"Yes, sir," McLaughlin replied. "Everybody knew it."

Sitting Bull turned at the sounds of a scuffle outside. The Silent Eaters and the rest of his followers were still out there. McLaughlin quickly snatched the papers from the tables as Bull Head came in and marched up to McLaughlin.

"They will not be any bother to us," he told McLaughlin. "They won't get inside."

"It is only right that we be able to speak before the papers are signed," Sitting Bull said.

"The time for speaking is over," Crook said in a loud voice. "It is now time to sign."

A group of Metal Breasts, led by Shaved Head, came into the room and formed a circle around Shining Horse and Sitting Bull.

"You are like children," Shining Horse told them. "You must have many with you to handle but two people. What are you afraid of? You have already given away yourselves to the *Wasichu*, and now you are giving away our lands as well."

Bull Head squeezed his rifle tightly. "If it were not that White Hair told me not to shoot first, I would kill you both."

"It is time that we left," Sitting Bull said to his son. "We can do no good here."

Shining Horse followed his father outside. The Yanktonnais and the Metal Breasts had effectively sealed off the meeting from the Silent Eaters and Sitting Bull's other followers. There would be no way to enter the meeting without a gun battle.

"It is time to go," Sitting Bull told them. "It is too late. We have been tricked, and we have lost everything."

Shining Horse mounted his pony and waited for his father's signal to ride out. A reporter dashed up to Sitting Bull and asked him how he believed the Indians felt about ceding their lands away.

"Indians!" Sitting Bull shouted at him. "There are no Indians left but me!"

Following the letter from Spoonhunter, nothing felt right to Two Robes. Late summer brought no relief from the drought. The air was filled with dust, and the nights were as hot as the days. Certainly something bad was on the horizon, watching from the hills like the scattered packs of scrawny wolves that searched endlessly for game.

Word had it that the land commission had taken the reservation by storm and had secured far more than the needed signatures. The Minneconjou and the other branches of the Lakota nation would lose a great deal more land and would be forced to live within the white culture, whether they wanted to or not.

Two Robes' mission had faltered, also. Though the followers he had baptized remained with him, he had difficulty in gaining any more converts. Kicking Bear had gone to visit the Arapaho and many were awaiting his return before they would decide who the real Jesus was.

But Two Robes had one who worked hard in his favor.

Catches Lance talked endlessly about Catholicism and the virtues of seeing things from a new perspective. Based on the success of his garden, he advocated moving downriver, where the people could use the water more efficiently for irrigation.

But the plight of the Minneconjou grew worse. Crops dried up completely, and the deer and antelope were now being decimated by farmers and ranchers setting their own tables. The wolves themselves often fell prey to the homesteaders' rifles, leaving the nights open and empty without their lonesome howls.

Two Robes often wished he could bring a buffalo or two into reality for their survival. Whatever he did, whether he walked the river or sat on a hill, the wolves were there, watching him. At times he followed them, to see where they might lead him. Always they led him nowhere. Only out into the open, where he could see forever and ask the sky as many questions as he pleased.

The answers were always the same: change is constant, forever constant. He realized that he had changed, and would change even more. His past, still there to haunt him, kept its distance now. Instead of bad dreams about his childhood, he spent time with Hawk, who now spoke with the other children about Jesus.

Two Robes had discussed the baptism and communion with Hawk, convincing him that the feeling of being whole with Christ did not happen quickly. "It is a matter of determination," he told the boy. "If you are determined to know Jesus, he will eventually come to you."

In saying it, Two Robes had had a funny feeling within. How many times had he asked for Jesus? He felt certain that he had experienced Jesus many times, yet none of those previous events could compare with the wolf dream, or with the deep sense of fulfillment he had had upon entering the village with the buffalo's head on his pony.

The admiration in the eyes of the council when he had

spoken about being caught between two worlds was something he would always remember. In that brief moment, they had discovered more about him than he knew about himself.

It had been easy to admire these people who bore such deep feelings for the land and for one another. Never had he seen families so closely knit. Never had he seen people so willing to call every child their own and so ready to help any member of any family who needed care.

Two Robes was certain that few of his own race could exist on the meager rations of these people and still maintain the energy level they did. For the Lakota, a meal was a sacred event to be shared with honor. Two Robes had heard Fawn say that as a child, when the buffalo still roamed the plains, she could actually feel the strength of the animal coursing through her at mealtime.

Two Robes had begun to use this relationship in his discussion about the sacrament of communion. He told the people that they could feel Jesus the same way they could feel the buffalo, if they wanted to. Many felt that this would be a good strength to have. With the drought that now held the land, there would be less to eat than normal over the winter.

On a hot Sunday morning, Two Robes baptized fifty new converts and said mass at the river's edge. Hawk had become his helper, holding the vessels of water and wine while Two Robes said the required prayers. Catches Lance was there as always, talking with the people and asking them to be sure to bring more to be baptized for the next mass.

Two Robes was just consecrating the host when a group of angry men, led by Tangled Hair, came running to the creek. Tangled Hair yelled down over Two Robes' voice, his fist clenched, "Take your *Wasichu* god away from here! Our people will not listen to any more lies!"

"What are you talking about?" Two Robes called.

"We have just come from the agency," Tangled Hair shouted. "We have been told to get ready for less to eat. They told us our rations have been cut."

Two Robes stared in shock. The people gasped, and some of the women began to cry.

"The land commission lied, just like Shining Horse said they would," Tangled Hair continued. "I once had faith in you, but now I am glad that I didn't decide to follow your pathway. Only a fool would think the *Wasichu* god would want to help the Lakota people."

Catches Lance yelled up at Tangled Hair, "Do not attack Two Robes. It is not his doing. He has come to help. He had no part in the land commission."

"I am not so sure," Tangled Hair countered. "Why did he arrive in our midst so close to the time when the commission arrived? And why did he tell us that things would be good? I believe he wanted to soften us up."

The people began to mutter and then to yell in agreement with Tangled Hair. Catches Lance shouted his support for Two Robes, begging the others to listen. Instead, they began running their fingers through their hair, trying to rub out the baptism waters, screaming in anger.

Catches Lance accompanied Two Robes up from the creek and to his lodge. By now, news of the rations cut had spread throughout the village. Everyone was angry, especially those who had signed the agreement. Those who hadn't signed it ridiculed those who had, and fights had broken out everywhere.

Fawn approached Two Robes, her eyes hard. "If you had not come to us in the manner you did, you would be cast out," she said. "Do not tell any more to my children about your god."

"You are no better than the others," Catches Lance told his sister. "Two Robes has proved his honor. He has nothing to do with the land commission. You and the others cannot see past your anger."

"Do not say any more, please," Two Robes told Catches Lance. "It has been a strange day, one of rejoicing and, suddenly, one of sorrow and anger. No one can be expected to think straight."

"I can think straight," Fawn said. "I have no doubt in my mind that the *Wasichu* want to exterminate us. They have ruined everything. Anyone can see that, no matter what kind of day it is."

Fawn turned for her lodge, leaving Two Robes deeply sad. Catches Lance shouted after her, insisting that the only way to survive was to take the White Man's Road.

"Do not fight with your sister over this," Two Robes said. "Her feelings run deep, as do yours. In many ways, you are both right. What is happening is not fair to anyone, but we cannot judge one another."

"You speak good words," Catches Lance said, "but now no one will listen to them. I can no longer count on you to help me start my new village."

Catches Lance left without another word, and Two Robes retreated into his lodge. Even inside, he could hear the hum of desperate talk. The villagers who were not fighting were discussing what they would have to do now that rations had been cut. He read for a time from St. John of the Cross:

It makes little difference whether a bird be held by a slender thread or by a rope; the bird is bound, and cannot fly until the cord that holds it is broken. It is true that a slender thread is more easily broken; still notwithstanding, if it is not broken, the bird cannot fly. This is the state of a soul with particular attachments: it never can attain to the liberty of the divine union, whatever virtues it may possess. Desires and attachments affect the soul as the remora is said to affect a ship; that is but a little fish, yet when it clings to the vessel, it effectually hinders its progress.

The passage spoke to Two Robes with the power of thunder. He stepped out of his lodge and turned toward the west. He had heard the people talk of Bear Butte, where, it was said, many mysteries were revealed to those who sought the sacred way. He would go there and seek the answers he so desperately needed.

He ducked back inside and removed his vestments. He would go dressed only in a cotton shirt and pants. He placed his cassock and the chasuble Fawn had made for him at the back of the lodge. He gathered his book and a root digger Fawn had given him into a skin bag. Then he touched the top of the buffalo's head and left his lodge.

At the edge of the village, he set a course south by southwest and began to walk. A short way out, he heard Hawk calling from behind. "Where are you going, Two Robes?"

"I am seeking my God," Two Robes said. "I must leave your people and look for Him."

"But you do not wear your black robe."

"I will go as a man, nothing else."

"Do you have to leave?" Hawk asked, a tear rolling down his face. "My mother didn't mean to be angry with you. She cried afterward in our lodge."

"Your mother is not to blame," Two Robes assured him. "No one is to blame. I am only doing what I feel I must."

"Where will you go?"

"I want to find Bear Butte. I have heard your people speak of that place."

Hawk looked into the distance. "Yes, it is near the Sacred Hills, the Black Hills. That holy place must be calling to you. That is where you will find your answers. The old people always say that."

"I hope they are right, Hawk," Two Robes said. "Go back and tell your mother that I am more than grateful for all she has done and that I could never hold anger against her. Tell her that."

"I will tell her that," Hawk said, rubbing his eyes. "Will we ever see you again?"

"Yes, if I am led back here. I don't know when, but I hope so."

Two Robes watched Hawk run back to the village. When the boy was gone, he turned and began to walk again. The sun shone hot in a cloudless sky. Soon a thin film of dust had collected on his face, borne on the hot breeze that rustled the stalks of dried grass standing sparse among withered gray sagebrush.

The land was a haze in the heat, seemingly devoid of life. For a time Two Robes felt very alone. Then there appeared a familiar sight. A small pack of wolves assembled on a hill above him and began leading the way toward the Black Hills.

TWENTY-ONE

"WORK THEM horses! Work them out good!" Sergeant Betters' deep voice carried clearly over the fort grounds. Replacement horses had been delivered that morning, and the men were breaking them to ride.

"Stay on them!" Betters yelled. "Private Cort, get back on your horse!"

Cort wanted to yell back to the sergeant that he wasn't a bronc buster. In the old days he might have tried it, but no longer. His more agile days had passed. This exercise was dangerous to his well-being.

But Sergeant Betters wasn't to be questioned. The sergeant was a changed man these days. His relaxed attitude had been lost in the hot winds that scorched the grasslands. The Sioux problem was constantly on his mind, and now it was getting worse. Cort knew all about it; he gleaned every bit of information just as soon as he could out of the freighter,

Harley Cullen. Cort had come to be close friends with Cullen now. There was a lot happening on the reservation.

The agents were concerned about a dance that had been brought from the Arapaho by Kicking Bear of the Minneconjou. Kicking Bear had learned it from his uncle and had told many of the Lakota leaders that this dance would wipe the white man from the face of the earth.

Cullen had brought word that each branch of the Lakota nation had elected representatives to travel west to Walker Lake, Nevada, to see this Indian Messiah. Kicking Bear of the Minneconjou and Short Bull of the Brulé were among a dozen Lakota leaders taking the train across to Nevada.

"It won't amount to anything," Cort had told Betters. "There's nothing to get excited about."

Cort had not convinced Betters that there wouldn't be a problem. After all, anything that made the agents nervous would eventually make the army nervous. Cort, Betters said, should be certain he kept in close touch with Cullen now.

It was from Cullen that Cort had first learned that the sergeant's son was living with Kicking Bear's Minneconjou on Cherry Creek. Cullen had fought for the North until he had lost his right leg beneath the knee at Gettysburg. He wasn't averse to giving out information, and he even answered Cort's letters, especially if a few bottles of whiskey were thrown in to heighten his memory.

"It's mighty lucky for you that Harley supplies those agencies," Cort had told Sergeant Betters. "You can figure he'll give us everything he hears."

Sergeant Betters saw to it that Cort had enough money for whiskey from nearby Crawford whenever Cullen brought freight through. Although Cullen would likely keep up the correspondence without the liquor, the insurance didn't cost that much extra.

"That's enough for today," Sergeant Betters told the men. "Take the horses back to the stables and rub them down."

Drenched with sweat, the men gladly headed for the

stables. The heat hadn't let up since late June, and though it was now mid-October, every exercise and maneuver in the field was a taste of hell. There was no grazing for the horses, and trainloads of hay had to be shipped in from the mountain states.

Sergeant Betters found Cort rubbing down his horse at the far end of the stalls. "The freighter is due in tomorrow," Betters said. "I want you to give him a few bottles again, and I also want you to give him this."

Betters handed Cort a letter. It bore no address, but only the name "Tangled Hair" in large letters on the front.

"I don't trust the agents to deliver the mail properly," Betters said. "And if they saw one from the military, there is no doubt it would be opened."

"Oh, you can trust Harley," Cort said. "He'll deliver that letter right into your son's hands."

Cort met the freighter the next day in the front street of Crawford. Cullen was old and grizzled, a veteran of many years on the frontier. He ran a string of eight pairs of mules and three large wagons in tandem. He didn't travel fast, but he carried a lot of freight.

Cullen had just finished loading supplies at the train station for the trip up to the reservation. He stepped down from his wagon. "There ain't much news since last I saw you," he told Cort. "Nothing is likely to happen until the Sioux get back from Mason Valley."

"I've got something important for you to deliver," Cort said. "You have to promise to get it where it belongs. It's really important."

Cullen took the letter and squinted. "He's on Cheyenne River. I don't go up there with the wagons. They get served from Rapid City."

"Can't you go a-horseback?" Cort asked. "After you get done with what you need to do first?"

Cullen studied the letter again and stuffed it under his shirt. "I'll keep it close to my heart."

"This ain't no time for jokes. The sergeant wants that given to his boy. You won't forget?"

"I'll take it up. I'll give it to him myself. Don't you worry. And tell the sergeant not to worry none, either."

"I've got a couple of bottles for you."

Cullen raised his hand. "No. I don't need no bottles this time."

Cort noticed mist in Cullen's eyes. "What? Why don't you want the whiskey?"

"Let's just say this one's on me," Cullen said. He took a deep breath. "I might have lost a son, might have shot him myself, if it hadn't been for someone who took a letter for me once."

Cort stared at the freighter. "You fight against your son during the war?"

"That's right," Cullen replied. "I had a son who fought for the South, and we had a group of them surrounded in a little pocket of ground at Gettysburg. Come dark, a drummer boy looking to leave took a note from me to my son and brought him back out. We killed all the rest in that pocket the next day."

Cullen climbed into his wagon and took the reins. Before he coaxed his mules into movement, he turned back to Cort. "You just tell that sergeant that I'll see his boy gets the letter. And I ain't promising nothing, but I'll try to talk him into riding back down with me."

"The sergeant will be obliged," Cort said. "Have yourself a good trip."

"I'll surely do that," Cullen said. "I'll see you next time, or you can figure the wind blew me away."

Cullen drove his wagons out of the train yard. Cort hoped the freighter would hurry. There was no telling when the Sioux would be back from seeing the Messiah, but when they came, anything could happen.

From the trees, Shining Horse watched the flames in the distance. Long Hand and Bob-tailed Cat had done a good job of firing the pile of logs. The blaze would certainly alarm McLaughlin and the Metal Breasts.

The ploy worked. Before long, McLaughlin was out of his quarters, buttoning his shirt and yelling through the darkness for his Metal Breasts. Soon they were headed toward the fire.

When McLaughlin and the others had gone, Shining Horse eased through the shadows toward McLaughlin's office. The back window broke easily, and he quickly slipped inside. In a moment he was searching McLaughlin's desk drawers; using up several matches, he filled a small sack with letters addressed to his father, plus a small box postmarked "Yerington, Nevada." He fought the urge to strike another match and toss it onto McLaughlin's desk. Instead, he dropped the sack outside the window and climbed out.

Long Hand and Bob-tailed Cat were waiting patiently at the predestined meeting place. "Good fire," Shining Horse said.

Long Hand smiled. "You have a full sack."

"I wonder how much I didn't find. Has my father gotten *any* of his mail?"

"Only what White Hair wants him to see," Bob-tailed Cat said. "It will be interesting to look at what he hid."

The sun had barely climbed the horizon when Shining Horse and the others arrived back at Grand River. Sitting Bull was in the water, bathing with his wives.

"I told you not to cause trouble," Sitting Bull said. "I see that you have disobeyed me."

"I think you should open this," Shining Horse said, holding up the box from Nevada. "It comes from the Paiute Messiah."

"I'll see it when I'm ready," Sitting Bull said with disgust. "For now, you had better hide that stuff until the Metal Breasts are gone."

"They are here already?" Long Hand asked.

"No, but soon enough, thanks to all of you," Sitting Bull replied. "It is better not to make trouble. I am tired of telling Bull Head to leave me alone."

"We have time to look at the mail before anyone gets here," Shining Horse coaxed.

"I said no!" Sitting Bull blared from the water. "Wait until they are gone. The words will not change on the paper."

"They are important words, Father," Shining Horse said.

"Maybe so, maybe not," Sitting Bull said. "So there isn't bad trouble, stay in the cabin until they have gone. They will not go in there. Then we will see the mail."

Shining Horse buried the mail sack in a hole near the river and toyed with his Winchester. He knew that it would be some time yet before the Metal Breasts arrived. Shaved Head and the others would first go to Bull Head's cabin just upriver to drink whiskey and talk about brave deeds to give themselves courage.

Shortly before noon, Bull Head and Shaved Head and ten other Metal Breasts rode noisily through the village, holding their Winchesters above their heads. As his father had asked, Shining Horse had retreated into the cabin.

Sitting Bull sat in a rocking chair in front of the cabin. From the corner of one eye he saw Bull Head grab the saddle horn to keep from falling off his horse.

"You are becoming braver, or more foolish," he told Bull Head. "One or the other. And it looks like whiskey has made you that way."

"You know why we are here," Bull Head shouted. "Who did you send to break into White Hair's office?"

"I sent no one," Sitting Bull said firmly. "I had nothing to do with it. I don't want trouble. I want to be left alone."

Bull Head leaned over the saddle. "When are you going to give up, old man? Your time is finished."

"Did White Hair send you here to insult me?" Sitting Bull asked. "Or was this your own idea?"

"It does not matter whether or not White Hair sent me," Bull Head replied. "I want you to know that the day is coming when you will be taken out."

"I know White Hair did not send you to say that," Sitting

Bull said. "White Hair does not like me, but he would not send someone else to threaten me. If he were to do that, he would at least come himself."

Bull Head spat on the ground. "What is between us has nothing to do with White Hair."

"What you want is power." Sitting Bull raised his hand toward one of the police. "Just like that young Minneconjou who came up here from Cheyenne River to be a Metal Breast."

Catches Lance felt eyes turning on him as Sitting Bull pointed him out. He sat as straight in the saddle as he could, but the whiskey had made him dizzy and his stomach was churning. This was the first time he had tasted liquor, and he wasn't certain of what was happening to him. He had not seen Sitting Bull since his days as a small child. Sitting Bull appeared to have aged a great deal. What power was there in an old man who sat rocking in front of a log cabin?

Shining Horse could wait in the cabin no longer. Despite his father's request to stay out of the problem, he emerged and stared at Catches Lance. He could see no expression in Catches Lance's eyes, not even a glimmer of recognition. Though Catches Lance certainly recognized him, Shining Horse was aware that he had put every bit of his past behind him; he had no ties to anything whatsoever. That made for a dangerous man.

Bull Head pointed at Shining Horse. "Aha! That is the one who has done your work for you. You had better keep your little boy at home, Sitting Bull. Next time we will catch him and he will be sorry."

Shining Horse glared at Bull Head. "Maybe you have said enough."

"I don't think so," Bull Head shouted.

"How many do you think are hearing this?" Shining Horse warned.

Bull Head saw a number of Unkpapa warriors looking at

him from their lodges. Some had already started toward the cabin, holding Winchesters and Springfield rifles.

"Now what do you say?" Shining Horse asked.

"There will be a time," Bull Head said. "Yes, there will be another time." He turned and led the way out of the village.

When the Metal Breasts had gone, Sitting Bull stood up. "You do not seem to understand what kind of trouble is going on here," he said to Shining Horse. "Bull Head and the others have become crazed with power."

"I can only see that it is not fair to you," Shining Horse said. "I am like the others who are loyal to you and want to protect you. Only more so, for I am your son."

"I am grateful," Sitting Bull acknowledged. "I have other sons, and they love me as well. But they do not seem to want trouble as much as you."

"It is only that we should stand up for what is right," Shining Horse said. "You are not being treated with respect. Our people are not being treated with respect."

"All we can do is stand up for our rights. We cannot push into the *Wasichu* and spit into their faces, for then we look like the kind of Indians the papers write about. That is not good."

Shining Horse took a deep breath. "It is difficult to lie back and be stepped on."

"Yes, but when they see that they cannot rouse you, they are angered and do the foolish things themselves. Maybe some-day the papers will help us."

"I don't know when that will be," Shining Horse said. "Sensational stories make people buy papers."

"Maybe so," Sitting Bull agreed, "but you do not want to make their stories real."

"You are right. I will not do anything more that will bring trouble. I am sorry I came out of the cabin."

"I am glad to hear that. Now show me what you found in White Hair's desk."

Shining Horse quickly retrieved the sack from the river-bank. When he returned, Sitting Bull was rocking peacefully in his chair. Shining Horse opened the sack and pulled out the letters and the box from Nevada.

"Ah, letters," Sitting Bull said. "Read me those."

Shining Horse held up the box. "But this is the most important."

"Not to me," Sitting Bull said. "Tell me what's in the letters."

Shining Horse began to open the envelopes. All of them were from Catherine Weldon, who had left for the East earlier in the fall, after her confrontation with White Hair. Shining Horse realized in reading the correspondence that this woman felt a duty to help his father and the Lakota people. A passage in one of the letters hinted of her return. "I will be seeing you again, of this I am certain. I have not finished with the agencies and the way they handle their affairs."

Shining Horse said, "I would bet she comes back, and with a vengeance."

Sitting Bull smiled. "Maybe she will become a wife to me."

"Haven't you had enough wives?"

"What's another, especially if she wants to take care of me that bad?"

"*Wasichu* women do not think the same as Lakota women," Shining Horse said. "I wouldn't try to get too close to her."

"I am already close to her," Sitting Bull said. "Now I just want to get next to her."

Shining Horse chuckled. "Are you ready, finally, to see what's in the box?"

"You seem to think it will change the world," Sitting Bull said. "Open it."

Shining Horse tore the package open and discovered ocher in an old tomato can, a magpie feather, and two small cactus buttons.

He examined the cactus buttons. "Peyote," he said. "And here is a letter." Shining Horse unfolded the piece of paper. The letter was written in English.

November 17, 1889
Yerington, Nevada

To Sitting Bull:

I have talked to your brothers. Kicking Bear and Short Bull say that you would like to be here. You must come and learn good things. I, Jack Wilson, will teach you.
I am giving everyone a dance. I use sacred paint to wear in the dance. The magpie feather is sacred.
Jesus is like a cloud, and is now on the earth. Tell no white man. But be good to the white man. He is our brother, like all the rest. Work for the white man. Tell no lie.
Every Indian who is dead will live. They will come in fall or spring. I will shake the earth. Do not be afraid. The buffalo are coming.
That is all. Come to see me.

Jack Wilson
Wovoka

Shining Horse folded the letter. Sitting Bull had grunted often during the reading. He grunted again and continued to rock, staring out over the river.

"What do you think of this, Father?" Shining Horse asked.

"He thinks he is big stuff," Sitting Bull said. "I'm not sure. Maybe he is. He thinks so. I am too old to go looking for a Messiah."

"What do you think about this dance he talks about?"

"I hope it is true. I will wait to hear what Kicking Bear and Short Bull say."

"I would like to go and hear him for myself," Shining Horse said.

"You promised you would cause no more trouble."

"What trouble would that cause?"

"Do what you want," Sitting Bull said. "But I cannot go. And I don't want you to take anyone else from here with you. There is already too much trouble."

"I understand, Father," Shining Horse said. "I will tell you everything I learn."

"Yes, tell me everything," Sitting Bull said. "Be sure to look and listen closely. Maybe this man is sacred. Even so, don't be fooled. If this is real, it will change the world. If it is not, it may still change the world."

TWENTY-TWO

A HALF MOON had passed without Two Robes. Despite her earlier anger, Fawn missed him. Hawk kept telling her that Two Robes would be back, that he had left for only a while, to do what *Wankantanka* wished of him. Hawk had spoken of seeing him in dreams. There was no need to worry; Two Robes was taken care of by the Powers.

Fawn had talked once of going to find him, though she didn't see that as very practical. There was a lot of distance between the village and the Black Hills. She finally decided that if he were meant to return, he would. Otherwise, his pathway would take him elsewhere.

Yet she couldn't bear the thought of never seeing him again. Though his loyalty to the *Wasichu* god had come between them, she could see that he loved her deeply. She could only hope that the Powers would direct him back to her.

A lot had happened since Two Robes' departure. Kicking Bear had left with a number of other Lakota leaders to see the Messiah. Everyone was talking about the new dance and the new world it would bring. And just the day before, Shining Horse had come down from his home on Grand River. He, too, wanted to see the Messiah, and he had talked Tangled Hair into going with him.

They would be leaving in the morning. They would ride horseback to Rapid City and take the train across to Nevada. Tangled Hair had attempted to talk Fawn into going with them. He had been trying once again to gain her affections. He had watched while she had fallen in love with Two Robes and had been unable to understand it.

The afternoon before he was to leave with Shining Horse, Tangled Hair once more tried to reach her. "Two Robes has gone to a new life," he said. "The best has remained behind for you. I'm still here."

Fawn couldn't find it in her to laugh; too much was happening too quickly. Tangled Hair persisted, even after she spoke harshly to him. She didn't want to alienate him totally, though. He was now her sole link to Catches Lance.

"I only wish my brother would spend as much time with me as you do," she said.

"I cannot understand his behavior lately," Tangled Hair said. "He went off to catch all his horses earlier today and he wouldn't tell me why."

"He went to catch *all* his horses? He was supposed to give Hawk and Little Star a ride."

Fawn discovered the children on their way back to the village. They told her that Catches Lance would not give them a pony ride.

"Did he say why he wouldn't?" she asked.

Both children were in tears. "He said he had very important things to do," Hawk told his mother. "He said he wouldn't be giving us any more rides."

Fawn told the children to eat some of the broth she had prepared for them and to await her return. She stopped first at Catches Lance's lodge and found Night Bird curled up on her bed. She had been crying.

"What is wrong?" Fawn asked.

"I am sorry to say this," Night Bird told her, "but I wish I had never met Catches Lance."

Fawn leaned down. "Tell me, what has happened?"

Night Bird burst into tears. "Catches Lance has decided to become a Metal Breast. He does not want to work at this agency, but wants to move up to Standing Rock to work under the one they call White Hair."

Fawn straightened up in shock. "No, this cannot be so."

"Yes, it is so."

"But why?"

"He will say only that he is tired of being nobody," Night Bird replied. "He says that Two Robes ran away and that the people who once listened to him no longer see him as a leader. He says that White Hair wants young men who are progressive, who wish to be leaders. He does not care where they come from as long as they are brave. He wants them for his army of Metal Breasts."

"I would never have thought that Catches Lance could do that," Fawn said.

Night Bird sat up and dried her eyes. "He says that there is no use to stay with the old ways, that the *Wasichu* are too strong. In his words, only fools will live the old life from now on. He believes that if he goes the way of White Hair McLaughlin, he will be honored among the whites."

"What makes him think that he will be honored if he becomes a Metal Breast?"

"It happened at the agency," Night Bird said. "A few young men rode down from Grand River. They started talking to our young men. They said they did not want to follow Sitting Bull any longer. They were recruiting for White Hair's army of Metal Breasts."

"What does Tangled Hair think of this?" Fawn asked. "Has he spoken with Catches Lance about it?"

"Catches Lance will not talk with him about it. He does not consider Tangled Hair a friend any longer."

Fawn realized now why Tangled Hair had been distressed. She took a deep breath. "What is happening to my brother? What is happening to our people? We are growing more deeply divided all the time."

"I do not want to go up there with him," Night Bird said. "There will be trouble. I don't want Catches Lance to be in the middle of it."

"I must talk him out of this," Fawn said. "He will only make his life worse."

"I have tried many times," Night Bird said. "I get nowhere with him. He becomes angry and yells." She began to cry again. "I believe he wants to have pay so that we can eat and that is why he decided to become a Metal Breast."

"I see," Fawn said. "Perhaps you are right. It could be that he feels pressured to take care of you."

"But that is not what I want. I can't make him understand that. I wish now that I wasn't with child."

Fawn took Night Bird in her arms. "No, no, you shouldn't feel that way," she said. "*Wankantanka* has chosen to bless you with the child. You do not have to feel guilty for that."

"But I do not want to move up to Grand River," Night Bird said. "I do not want to live with the wives of the other Metal Breasts. I belong here, with you and my friends."

"Let me talk to him," Fawn said. "I will tell him that we will find enough food for you and the baby. He does not have to give in to the *Wasichu.*"

Fawn left Night Bird and roamed the edge of the village until she found Catches Lance. He had been packing and tying bags onto the back of one of his two ponies. "Since our mother died, it has been hard for us to talk," she began. "I wish things could become as they once were."

Catches Lance secured a strap under his pony's belly. "Did you come out here to try to make things better between us?"

"That is part of it," Fawn said. "Don't you feel bad at all?"

"I have to live my own life," Catches Lance said. "The only

way to make things better is to take the White Man's Road completely. I am tired of starving."

"Night Bird is having a hard time," Fawn said. "I wish you would take some time to be with her. She loves you."

"Did she tell you what I am going to do so that I can feed my wife and child?"

"Yes. She told me that you are thinking about becoming a Metal Breast."

"I have already thought about it," Catches Lance said. "I *am* going to become a Metal Breast."

"I tell you, that is not a good idea," Fawn said. "You will be going against those of us who want to keep the old ways."

Catches Lance turned from his pony. "It does not matter what you or Tangled Hair or any of the others think. I have made my choice. It is time that our people stop holding back from doing what is right."

"Oh, Catches Lance," Fawn said, "those are not your words. They belong to someone else. Not to you."

"I don't think you understand. Our people have given up most of the lands they once owned. The word is now that nothing Three Stars Crook and the others promised will come to pass. There are no gardens, even along the stream. Everything is dry and dead."

"We have always survived. We will continue to survive."

"You do not understand," Catches Lance said again. "The cold moons are coming. Many will starve. Many will die of sickness. I do not want to see my wife and baby die."

"I will help to keep you and your family from starving," Fawn said. "So will Tangled Hair. He is your best friend."

"What can either of you do? Tell me, can you make food out of the air? Do you have that kind of medicine? Not even Sitting Bull or Kicking Bear can do that. I have made up my mind."

Catches Lance reached down and lifted a saddle onto the back of the second pony. Fawn watched him tighten the cinch. "Night Bird cannot ride," she said.

"I will get settled and come back for her in a wagon."

"And if she won't go then?"

"Then she will stay here and I will live up there."

"You have heard the news about the Messiah," Fawn said, using her last hope. "They say he is truly a powerful man. He will be coming to make things better for all the Indian people everywhere."

"I believe what Two Robes says," Catches Lance argued. "There can be no peace or harmony until everyone joins together as brothers. When do you think Kicking Bear is going to consider the *Wasichu* our brothers?"

"Look at what they have done to us. Brothers do not treat one another that way."

"Two Robes says we must forgive our enemies before we can live happily and without worry," Catches Lance said. "No one wants to listen to him anymore, so he is gone. But I saw you crying because of it."

"Why don't you wait for him to come back? You can start your own village with him."

"And who else? No one will follow me now. Maybe as a Metal Breast, I will find those who can see my leadership."

Tears filled Fawn's eyes. "Do not go, Catches Lance," she begged. "Please. Stay with your family."

"I cannot," he said. "It is time for me to go."

Fawn watched Catches Lance ride his pony over a hill toward the north. She sank to her knees, crying, and felt small hands on her shoulder.

"We came to find you, Mother," Little Star said. "Night Bird said you were out here. Why are you crying?"

"It is a sad day," Fawn replied. "Catches Lance has left."

"Why did he leave?" Little Star asked. "Was it to be a Metal Breast, like the people are saying?"

"Yes, that is why he left," Fawn answered. She hugged Little Star, who began to sob.

Hawk spoke up, his voice trembling. "Don't cry for him.

Don't cry for any of the Metal Breasts. They are weak. They are traitors."

"Hawk, don't talk about your uncle that way," Fawn said. "Don't talk about any of them that way."

Hawk broke into tears. "But it is true. If Catches Lance loved us, he wouldn't go to them." He ran away, toward the river.

"Hawk, wait!" Fawn called. She turned to Little Star. "Hurry back to Night Bird's lodge. Wait for me there. I will go and talk to Hawk."

With tears streaming down her face, Little Star obeyed. Fawn hurried to the river, where she found Hawk throwing rocks into the current. She sat down on the bank behind him.

"Hawk, I am sorry Catches Lance left," she began. "He is doing what he believes is best. We each have to live by our own feelings."

Hawk picked up more stones and hurled them one by one into the water, throwing harder each time.

"I know you are hurt and angered by his leaving," Fawn continued, "but he has to think of himself and what he wants to do with his life. He believes that taking the White Man's Road is best."

"Is that what Two Robes told him?" Hawk asked.

"Two Robes does not try to tell people what to do," Fawn said. "Certainly he believes that we should go the way of the *Wasichu*, but he believes that we should go together, as a nation. That way, the *Wasichu* government will have to treat us better."

Hawk turned and sat down next to his mother. "Do you believe that Two Robes is right?"

"When he says that we must all stand together, I know that he is right," she said. "I just wish that all our people would unite to keep the old ways. Then we could make the *Wasichu* government leave us alone and let us live as we wish."

Hawk leaned against his mother. "Did Two Robes know Catches Lance was going to leave?"

"I don't know, Hawk."

"Do you think Two Robes will pray for Catches Lance?"

Fawn hugged her son. "You cannot worry about all these things," she said. "You are but a boy. You should be laughing and playing."

"But I will miss Catches Lance," Hawk said. "I didn't want him to go." Tears trickled down his face.

Fawn leaned over and kissed the top of his head. "I will miss him, too. I will miss him very much."

"Will we ever see him again?"

"I hope so. But we will have to accept it if we don't."

"What about Two Robes? You said once that you might go look for him. Are you going to do that?"

Fawn wondered if she could travel to Bear Butte and find Two Robes. The thought excited her. But the only way she would consider the journey would be if she were to go with Shining Horse and Tangled Hair when they traveled to Rapid City to catch the train. Even then, it would be risky if she didn't find him.

"I don't know," Fawn replied. "If Two Robes didn't go to Bear Butte, I wouldn't know where to look for him."

"I told you, I saw him there in my dream," Hawk said. "I know he got there. He was on top, praying."

Fawn looked off into the distance.

"You can find him, Mother. Just go to the foot of the butte. He will come down. If you can bring him back here, maybe Catches Lance will come back, too."

"Perhaps I will go with Shining Horse and Tangled Hair," Fawn said. "But I worry about leaving you and Little Star."

Hawk jumped up and pulled his mother's hand. "Don't worry about us. While you are gone, I will take care of Little Star and Night Bird. You had better get going, so you can tell Shining Horse and Tangled Hair that you want to go with them."

Fawn got up and hurried with Hawk back toward the village. Hawk would be right about Two Robes: He would be on the butte, praying. Hawk was right about his dreams. Hawk, the boy of eight, too soon becoming a man.

As soon as the two houses of the soul are tranquil and confirmed and merged in one by this peace, and their servants the powers, appetites and passions are sunk in deep tranquillity, neither troubled by things above nor things below, the Divine Wisdom immediately unites itself to the soul in a new bond of loving possession, and that fulfilled which is written in the Book of Wisdom: 'While all things were immersed in quiet silence, and the night was in the midway of her course, Thy omnipotent Word sallied out of heaven from the royal seats.' The same truth is set before us in the Canticle, where the Bride, after passing by those who took her veil away and wounded her, saith, 'When I had a little passed by them I found him whom my soul loveth.'

At the top of a mountain near Bear Butte, Two Robes sat back against the tree where he had been reading. He turned his eyes toward the late-evening sky. The heat, still oppressive, shimmered across the final bits of scarlet sunset. Far across to the south and west there hung a thick haze, no doubt from a range fire. The faintest lines of smoke, borne on the upper winds, had reached to the edge of sundown, blending deep orange and violet into the fading twilight.

He had been gone from the village nearly three weeks, as best he could calculate. It was hard to keep track of time in this vast open. He had traveled slowly across the plains, getting a few meals from farmers and ranchers along the way, digging roots wherever he found them.

The wolves had come and gone many times, as if checking up on him before they went about their regular routines. Two Robes took it to mean that they would not be caring for him in the same manner they had during his trip up from the

Rosebud. He must learn how to be all alone and feel comfortable.

Once he had met a rider bound for Kicking Bear's village, a freighter named Cullen, carrying a special letter. It had been hard to believe that the letter was for Tangled Hair.

"I seen some characters in my day," Cullen had told him, "but a Catholic priest on his way to Bear Butte, dressed like an Indian, is something I've never seen the likes of before."

Cullen had told Two Robes that Tangled Hair's father was a sergeant named Betters, with the Ninth Cavalry at Fort Robinson. Though the army had no immediate concerns about the Sioux and possible trouble on the reservation, it seemed that Sergeant Betters did.

Two Robes had also learned from Cullen of the Lakota delegation headed for Nevada to hear Wovoka's teachings. This hadn't surprised him. After receiving the letter from Spoonhunter, Kicking Bear had wholeheartedly believed in the Messiah. It was no surprise that he would bring the fever back with him from the Arapaho.

That Kicking Bear and other leaders would embrace a new religion was something Two Robes knew would never happen if the Lakota people were not in dire straits. But the people were on their last legs, and leaders like Kicking Bear and Short Bull were striving to hold on to the old ways. Anything that would help them do that would be welcome.

Cullen had told Two Robes that the story of their train journey was the topic of discussion everywhere and that the agents were going to keep a close eye on things when they returned. Most of the agents felt there was nothing to worry about; it was just a dance, they said, and there would be little that would come of it. Besides, the people were hungry and sick, incapable of uprising.

"My experience with these people tells me that they will gain strength from this new religion," Two Robes had told Cullen. "The white authorities won't be in favor of that."

"You're right. Trouble's brewing for sure," Cullen had

agreed. "I hope the boy listens to me and leaves the reservation. I don't know where he'll go, but I'd wager that the sergeant is real close to retirement and would like to have him along."

After the meeting with Cullen, Two Robes had felt even more need to reach Bear Butte. There was a change coming to the land, a change coming to the people who lived here. He knew that his answers lay in a holy place he had no reference to, save that which he had learned from the Lakota people.

Fear had begun to well up within him, and the closer he had come to the Black Hills, the more fear he had felt. He wondered what had moved him to make this journey, what kind of drive within him had brought him to look here for answers to who he truly was.

He realized that he, too, was changing, and that this change would accelerate once he reached the butte. Were it possible, he would turn back; he would return to his old self. But he couldn't do that. There was no place for him to go and be his old self. He could never be his old self again; the changes that had already occurred were permanent.

Two Robes realized that his journey toward spiritual evolvement was proving to be more than he had bargained for. And much different from his expectations. The higher he reached, the more difficult and terrifying the experiences. He was seeing someone within himself that he did not recognize. He was learning something he wasn't certain he wanted to know.

To date, none of his spiritual experiences had taken Christian form as he had read about and heard discussed in the seminary. Instead, they were of animals. Wild animals!

In all of his Christian life he had prayed for visions of the Sacred Heart of Jesus and the face of the Blessed Virgin. He had sought the assistance of saints and angels in finding his way and fighting his spiritual battles against evil. But nothing had come to him at any time. He had never seen or felt the presence of those he had sought so earnestly.

Then he came into a land where he had no identity but that which he wanted to believe was himself, and he found that identity shattered. He saw the Lakota people looking at him as if he had been among them forever, as part of their sacred structure; and he felt guided by a strength he knew was God, that he was certain was the same Supreme Power that looked over all creation.

Two Robes reached Bear Butte during a heavy thunderstorm. He remembered the older Lakotas warning him that lightning was a sign not to climb the butte. For three days he attempted to make the ascent but encountered lightning each time. He had not eaten or drunk at all, and so he climbed a mountain nearby to watch for a sign that would tell him when the time was right.

His reading had kept him occupied most of the time. He would sit under a tree for hours, searching to understand his feelings. St. John of the Cross had been of some help, but not enough. He felt lost and very alone, even more so than on his journey up from the Rosebud. He realized that once he climbed the butte, he would not come down as the same person.

Now, as darkness grew closer, fear touched him deeply. He saw a faint glow coming from the top of the butte, a glow of purple that seemed to be radiating out into the sky, mixing with the last light of sundown. From the summit of the butte, a large eagle circled out and descended toward him. The bird hovered overhead, then rose into the stillness of the evening and was lost in the shadows above the butte.

Two Robes rose from his seat under the tree. He looked across at the butte and saw a large orange moon ascending the sky. After a deep breath, he started down the mountain.

TWENTY-THREE

TREMBLING, Two Robes reached the top of Bear Butte. The night was as still as any he had known. Such peace should not be frightening, but within the silence lay the answers he had been seeking.

The moon had risen well above the horizon and now glowed whitely. The star-shot heavens glittered, alive with light. They held him spellbound. As he focused on one cluster of stars that glowed especially bright, he began to feel himself floating toward it.

Into his vision there came a huge white wolf, eyes deep and black, tongue a throbbing scarlet. It stood before Two Robes, its thick coat glistening like clear crystal sand.

"You have come far, you who search," the wolf said. "Now it is time to begin the real journey."

"I am going to learn my destiny?"

"You will see the path to your destiny," the wolf said. "What you make of it is your own choice."

"But I am going to learn how to reach God?"

"You are going to learn that reaching is dangerous. Instead, you will see how your god can come to you."

Two Robes felt himself flooded with joy, a joy so profound that it could not be described with words. He followed the wolf through a forest and into a clearing filled with men and women. They circled him, dancing gracefully, smiling, each one alive and vibrant, yet all as one. Each showed true rapture. Their faces beamed with light, their eyes glowed with profound peace.

Then Two Robes saw the men and women change utterly, becoming life forms he had never seen before. He was terrified. "There is nothing to fear," said the white wolf.

Those life forms changed into still others he had never seen before. They merged and separated and merged again. From the forest came wolves, coyotes, foxes, mice, rabbits, bears, bobcats, deer, elk, even buffalo, all of them walking together, merging themselves into an incredible spectacle.

"Do you know what this means?" the wolf asked.

"No," Two Robes answered. "It is a great mystery to me."

"Yes, it is part of the Great Mystery of life," the wolf said. "Swirling, ever changing, always working toward unity, always struggling against forces that would pull that unity apart."

The swirling, changing images formed a giant circle of all life. From the circle there emerged beings who came together in separate circles. Each circle contained many forms of life, united, turning slowly clockwise.

"What am I seeing?" Two Robes asked.

"Life is a circle, a sacred circle that must turn with the will of the Creator," the wolf replied. "Love is the will of the Creator. That and nothing else. The forces of hate and anger are forever searching for weak links in the circle. When the links fall to the powers that despise Love, the circle weakens and breaks into parts. Those parts form their own circles. But those circles are forever searching for the main source; ever searching, no matter the obstacles in the path."

The sight of the Great Mystery had so overwhelmed him

that Two Robes now felt the need to turn away. The impressions were too strong for him to assimilate.

When he turned, the wolf stared deep into him through its black eyes and spoke again. "You have begun a journey for knowledge, and you have undergone hard times. But I am here to tell you that the hardest of tests by far is before you."

"Haven't I suffered enough?" Two Robes asked. He was deeply afraid.

The wolf continued to stare at him, its eyes glowing with a profound knowledge. "You will stop suffering when you understand that the suffering you feel is of your own doing. You bring it upon yourself by separating yourself from the god you seek."

"I have known God all my life," Two Robes said angrily. "I have known him since I was a child. How could you say that?"

"Do you know, truly, who your god is?"

"I learned as a child who God is. I also studied a great deal to become a priest. Of course I know who God is!"

"Then why are you still searching?" the wolf demanded. "Why haven't you found him?"

"Maybe I haven't been looking in the right places," Two Robes replied.

"How many places do you know where God is not present?"

Two Robes gritted his teeth. "Are you mocking me?"

"You mock yourself."

"I am honestly seeking God, and you tell me I am a fool."

"I'm telling you that your circle is broken. Repair your circle. Look and listen; feel what it is that your god wants of you. Not what you want of your god."

Two Robes thought for a moment. "I believe that I have done what God wants of me. I have come to these lands to open the eyes of the Lakota people. I have suffered immensely, and now a great wall stands in my way. Someone who professes to be Jesus Christ reincarnated has come. I am not to fault for that."

"And you don't believe this Messiah is real?" the wolf asked.

"Of course he's not real," Two Robes answered.

The wolf stared at him. "And what gives you so much wisdom?"

"I have been taught."

"And what makes you think all teachings are correct?"

"The teachings are the word of God."

At this, the wolf began to change, quickly becoming a massive white buffalo. Two Robes stepped back, shielding his eyes from the light that surrounded the change. When the glare subsided, Two Robes focused on the huge bull standing just an arm's length away.

"Must you find all sacred things only from teachings?" the buffalo asked. "Can't you feed yourself?"

"Feed myself?" Two Robes echoed. "What do you mean?"

"You want sustenance. Go and find it."

Two Robes stared, dumbfounded.

"Why can't you see that your spiritual growth depends on life energy, as does your bodily growth?" the buffalo asked. "Go out into the land and seek that food which is right for you. There are teachings meant for you, and you alone. Though we are all the same, our pathways are different. We must, each one, learn what is right for us. In the end, we will all reach the same destination."

"I don't know how to break away from what I have learned," Two Robes said. "How do I start over and proceed forward?"

The buffalo moved to one side, and Two Robes again watched the whirl of images. As he turned to ask the buffalo what he was seeing, everything evaporated into an empty void. The buffalo was gone.

Two Robes felt heavy, as though in a space that held no bottom. Suddenly he was falling, unable to control himself.

Then he heard a sharp voice beside him: "Stop your screaming!"

A huge eagle was floating beside him, its wings outspread. "Spread your arms," the eagle commanded. "Let yourself go! Relax."

Two Robes spread his arms. He trembled uncontrollably, so great was his fear. But he continued to hold his arms out.

"Do you have faith in your god?" the eagle asked. "If so, let him show you the way. Fly! Let him support you."

Two Robes closed his eyes. As if by instinct, he began to breathe deeply. A warm sense of security flooded him. Instead of the terrifying feeling of dropping through space, he felt a cushion of strength just under him, buoying up his entire being.

"Now you know how it is," the eagle told him. "When you allow the Creator to hold you, you have no fear of falling."

Two Robes watched the giant eagle tilt its wings and drift away. He called for the eagle to wait for him, but the bird had already sailed out of sight. At first panic set in. Then he realized that his flight did not depend on the eagle; it was his own.

Two Robes soared high over forests and plains, far and near, studying rocky summits from above, cliffs and canyons from angles where the sun splashed the deepest colors.

Then a voice inside his head called him to return to the butte. When he did, he found that the wolf had returned.

"I told you the hardest part of your journey was before you," the wolf said. "Can you see now how you must change to face this pathway?"

"I realize I must let myself go in order to find my destination," Two Robes said. "I can't hold on to old values."

"That is wise of you," the wolf said. "You have felt the power of self-abandonment, the ability to allow the Creator to direct you. This is not easy, for the will is difficult to control."

"But I thought I *knew* my direction," Two Robes said.

"No one is saying that you are not on the right path," the wolf said. "But *you* must realize what is best for you, not what others believe is best."

"If I stay on the wind," Two Robes asked, "will I be able to reach my goals?"

"Be certain that your goals are the same as those the

Creator has laid out for you," the wolf replied. "You will be able to understand this from the air. For the first time, you have risen above all that stands before you. Now you can see what there is to experience when you rid yourself of the chains called human frailty. If you wish to soar above those things that mean nothing, you must continuously reach for that state of mind."

"Do you mean I cannot fly all the time?" Two Robes asked.

"You have much self-will left to dissolve," the wolf said. "You are still bound by the world you know. You are frightened by the deeds of others around you; the thought of those who speak against you causes you to tremble like the rabbit when darkness falls. When others tell you that you have done well, you burst with pride; when they tell you otherwise, you wither like a fallen leaf."

"How do I rid myself of such feelings?" Two Robes asked.

"Prepare to do battle," the wolf replied. "Prepare yourself for such inward thunder as you have never known. You will be held in contempt, abased by those whom you hold in esteem. Find yourself and go where you must, despite what your enemies wish of you. Never falter from that which touches you as Truth."

"This will be difficult for me," Two Robes said. "Before coming to these lands, I did nothing but what I was told."

"Your life has changed, Strong One," the wolf said. "Carry on with your life, and do not let those who come to help go unnoticed."

The wolf turned and trotted into the trees. Two Robes awakened on his back. Daylight had come, and the sky was a deep blue. He found water and drank deeply. Sleep returned to him, filled with songs and dancing that he had never heard or seen before. He saw himself with Fawn, shuffling in a circle, wearing his chasuble again.

But the chasuble looked different. Images of birds and animals had been painted on it. He could feel it in his hands, and it brought tears to his eyes.

When Two Robes awakened again, it was late afternoon. He felt as though he were still drifting as he made his way down off the butte and into a meadow, where a doe was nibbling on the tender shoots of wild honeysuckle. She was less than ten feet away, yet she showed no fear.

Two Robes walked up to her; she merely continued to graze. He reached out, and she raised her head. Her tender nose touched his hand, and he dropped to his knees.

Fawn knelt beside Two Robes. He had reached out to her and she had taken his hand. Then he had fallen to his knees, as if struck by an ax. He had been in another world, and it seemed that he had not yet returned. Fawn helped him to his feet. He was weeping. She could tell that he had been fasting. Perhaps he had seen something sacred.

"You must eat," she told him. "I will seat you beneath this tree and fix some roots and pemmican."

Two Robes was too dazed to understand what she had said. He followed her over to a cottonwood and sat down. He watched her while she took a small cook pot and a wooden spoon from a skin bag and began to mix food.

After gathering wood, she lit a fire and sat down next to him. Soon the mixture of beef and roots had warmed to a near boil.

Two Robes wanted the entire pot, but Fawn ladled small mouthfuls at a time. "You shouldn't eat too much too soon," she advised. "You don't want to hurt your stomach."

He sat obediently while she fed him bigger and bigger spoonfuls from the pot. When the pot was empty, he begged for more.

"That is enough for now. After you rest, there will be another potful."

Two Robes immediately fell asleep. Fawn prepared more food for when he awakened. She left him and climbed a nearby hill. The sun was falling across the open grasslands, heading into a thick bank of clouds that rolled up from the horizon. A damp breeze in the air meant that rain was coming. Soon the gold of the late sun would fall to darkness. By morning the storm would have come.

She turned to leave and discovered that Two Robes had followed her. "You shouldn't be on your feet," she told him.

"I feel very good," he said. "Thank you for helping me."

"You have had a hard time since I last saw you. I believe the Powers have blessed you with a vision."

"I did see a lot of things," Two Robes confessed. "I don't even feel like the same person."

"You aren't," she said. "You have become even more of a gifted and holy one."

"I feel like my whole life has changed. I can't seem to feel the same as I did when I wore the cassock. I don't think I would feel right wearing it again."

"Maybe you are not meant to wear it again," Fawn suggested. "Maybe you are not supposed to be a Black Robe any longer. Maybe you never were meant to be a Black Robe."

Two Robes sat down and put his head in his hands. "Oh, but I do believe in the Lord God! I believe that Jesus is my savior, the savior of the world."

Fawn knelt next to him. "There is nothing wrong with believing that, is there?"

"But I have seen the images of animals, not of the Christ, or of the saints. I have been a Christian all my life, yet I cannot bring my spirit close to Christ."

"Didn't you tell me that your god was with us always, just the same as *Wankantanka*?" Fawn asked.

"Yes, I did say that. And it's true."

"Then why can't you believe that you have seen your god in the faces of the animals that come to you? Are they not of your god?"

"It just isn't what I expected," Two Robes said. "But I have learned that I must open myself to God and allow Him to direct me in the manner He sees fit."

"I believe you are being directed in a manner that is very

sacred," Fawn told him. "I have heard many of the elders say they envy you. There are those among them who have not had the visions and experiences you have, yet they realize they are special in *Wankantanka*'s eyes."

"I don't mean to sound like I don't accept *Wankantanka*," Two Robes said. "But I have come from another culture, one far different than yours. I expected to be guided by the deity I was taught about as a child."

"Perhaps now you are being taught right and are having a hard time acknowledging it," Fawn suggested. "Maybe you should understand that you are being prepared for what lies ahead of you. Do you know what that is?"

"No. I have no idea."

"You speak a lot about faith. Where is your own?"

Two Robes studied her. He had been told by the wolf and the buffalo that his greatest challenge would be his own convictions. The biggest block to his progress would be himself. Now Fawn, too, was pointing this out.

"You are right," he said. "I am not certain of what God wants for me, but I will place myself in His hands and not question my destiny."

"Even if it means becoming someone other than a Black Robe?"

"Yes, even if it means that."

"I am glad to hear you say that. I knew that you would learn the truth someday."

Fawn then told Two Robes that she had come across to the Black Hills with Tangled Hair and Shining Horse. They had told her they would wait for her in Rapid City until she had gone to Bear Butte to find Two Robes. She could have three days to decide whether or not to journey on with them. They knew her feelings for Two Robes and would respect her wishes, whatever they might be.

The two had planned to journey by train to Nevada, where they would see the Messiah. Then Tangled Hair had received a letter from his father. It had changed his entire outlook. He

now wished to visit his mother among the Arapahos, in hopes
that she would go with him to meet his father.

Two Robes told Fawn of his meeting with Cullen and of
how he had learned from Cullen about the Lakota delegation
to Nevada. "Maybe I should go and see this Messiah, also,"
Two Robes said. "I have been wondering about this man ever
since Kicking Bear received that letter."

"Would you take me with you, so that I might learn as well?"
Fawn asked.

Two Robes again felt pangs of guilt. Fawn was certainly
special. The feelings he had always had for her suddenly
welled up within him again, stronger than he had known
them before. He remembered what the wolf had told him:
"Allow special people to help you." Fawn had been there right
after his vision. He realized that she was meant to be part of
his future.

Two Robes gazed into Fawn's eyes. "I don't believe I am
supposed to be afraid of you any longer."

"Afraid? When were you ever afraid of me?"

"You know what I mean," Two Robes said. He leaned
forward and kissed her gently.

Fawn smiled. "Your kiss is far sweeter than any I have ever
known."

Two Robes took her into his arms and they lay down in the
grass, their lips together, their hands caressing each other.
Warmth flooded Fawn from head to foot, building itself
within her.

Two Robes had longed for this moment for so long, always
in the guilt of his desire. Now the guilt had lifted. The voices
that had held him back before now told him that there was
nothing to be ashamed of; loving this woman was his destiny,
no matter what he had thought previously.

Fawn helped Two Robes out of his shirt. His arms were lean
and strong, the muscles taut and firm. She trailed her fingers
down his chest to the top of his pants.

She stood as he raised her dress off, and she delighted in

the wonderment he expressed at the sight of her body. He leaned forward and kissed her breasts, his lips eagerly searching out her nipples.

Fawn unbuttoned his pants and slipped them off his hips. He moaned as she touched him and wrapped her fingers around him, bringing him to full erection.

Two Robes placed his shirt and pants on the ground for Fawn to lie on. Entering her was the greatest pleasure he had ever known. As a teenager, he had learned of sex, but those experiences had never felt like this.

Fawn held him tightly, following his rhythm, her entire being filling with ecstasy, until they both reached the peak of their union.

They lay together for a time, feeling one another's closeness in the soft twilight breeze. Then they began to discuss his coming to the Minneconjou and what he felt lay ahead for him.

"Everything is changed now," he said. "But I still feel that I must teach your people about Jesus Christ. I just don't know the approach to take."

"Why should you change your approach?" Fawn asked.

"I am no longer considered a true Black Robe."

"Do you feel that because of our union you have lost the powers that were given you?"

Two Robes thought for a moment. "No, I do not feel that way," he said. "Many years ago, Black Robes were allowed to marry. If I had been born then, I would have had no concerns about our situation. But a law was passed in the Church saying that priests cannot marry."

"It seems to me that your coming among my people has taught you something about laws," Fawn said. "Has it not?"

"I have learned that the laws of God and those of man can differ greatly. I don't see why I shouldn't continue to teach your people as I have been."

"Then nothing has changed, really."

"I want you to be a part of whatever I do," he told her.

"That has changed. Now that I have learned what you truly mean to me, I want you to be my wife."

"I will gladly come into your lodge," Fawn said. "When we return from seeing the Messiah, we will be one with my children."

"Yes," Two Robes said, "we will become one with all the Minneconjou."

TWENTY-FOUR

R AIN FELL during the following two days, changing to snow in the higher elevations. With
Tangled Hair and Shining Horse, Fawn and Two Robes rode
the train from Rapid City toward Nevada. Two Robes sat in a
baggage car with the others, watching rolling hills of sagebrush pass by.

They would have preferred to have ridden the old trails
that had once taken migrating tribes, and later emigrating
settlers, across these lands. But the trails were now blocked in
many places by fences. Orchards and hay meadows served
those who had been born to the first white immigrants. The
land was no longer open and free.

The rain made it hard to see across the unfamiliar country.
The towering Wind River Mountains were shrouded in dense
cloud cover; even down in the river canyon area, the air was
thick with fog.

"*Wankantanka* has covered this journey with tears," Fawn
observed. "I don't know whether it is a good sign or not."

"Tears can be cleansing," Two Robes said. "That would be a good thing for our people."

"Tears are shed in times of bitterness, also," Shining Horse pointed out.

The train stopped at Fort Washakie, on the Wind River Reservation, where a number of Shoshone and Arapaho waited to board.

"We have reached the reservation where my mother lives," Tangled Hair said. "You can stop on the way back and tell me what you saw and heard."

The three wished Tangled Hair good luck and continued on, getting what rest they could in the baggage cars and eating food offered by the Shoshones and Arapahos who had just boarded. At Rawlins, Wyoming, they boarded the Union Pacific, whose baggage cars were larger but no more comfortable.

They thought little of the inconveniences and much of their destination. The Lakota delegation had already been gone for nearly two weeks and had undoubtedly heard Wovoka by now. Two Robes read in a local paper that people had come to Mason Valley from as far away as the East Coast to listen to the Messiah. During one of the stops, he noticed a conductor reading about Wovoka in the Chicago *Tribune*.

During the following four days, the train passed from the mountains into the deserts of Utah and Nevada. Two Robes read from his book most of the time, while Fawn slept against his shoulder. Disconcerted, Shining Horse concentrated on trying to get Fawn to pay him the right kind of attention and to forget this foolishness with Two Robes. He had learned from Fawn of Two Robes' trip to the Black Hills and his vision on Bear Butte. He couldn't believe that the two of them had become so close.

Though Two Robes' hair was long and he no longer wore his cassock, Shining Horse still thought of him as *Wasichu*. He could see that the man had changed from the Black Robe he had met and befriended on the train, but he couldn't bring himself to believe that Two Robes was fully Lakota in his heart.

Despite the obvious jealousy over Fawn, Two Robes treated Shining Horse as a friend. He tried to talk with him about the Lakota situation, but Shining Horse would not converse. Instead, he waited for a chance to talk with Fawn alone.

Shining Horse had the opportunity during a water stop. People were stretching their legs, and Two Robes was chatting with a group of Arapaho.

"I see that you are acting as if Two Robes will take you into his lodge," Shining Horse said.

"He will take me into his lodge," Fawn told him. "Why do you ask?"

"He won't even lie down with you as a man does," Shining Horse told her. "What kind of life would you have?"

"How do you know he hasn't lain with me?" Fawn asked. "That is not your concern."

"He *has* lain with you?"

"I said, that is not your concern. You can be angry if you wish, but you will never lie with me. It is for Two Robes and me to be together."

"I cannot believe he could leave his Black Robe teachings," Shining Horse said.

"It is for him to decide which teachings he will leave and which he will retain," Fawn told him. "He will never cease to be a holy man. That's what is important."

"You've always hated the *Wasichu*," Shining Horse said. "Now you are going to become wife to one of them? That does not make sense."

"A man can be any color and still have a good heart. I did not believe that before. Two Robes has shown me the truth."

"That first day I saw him on the train, I never thought he would stay out here. It was the day when the sun died. Maybe that changed him. It certainly changed a lot of things."

"I hope that I will not hurt the friendship you have with Two Robes," Fawn said.

"I cannot help but admire him," Shining Horse said. "He is a strong man. But I cannot feel that he is a friend."

"He considers you a friend. He talks about you a great deal. He says you have much wisdom."

"Wisdom will not help us with the *Wasichu*. We need something stronger."

Shining Horse kept his distance from Fawn and Two Robes for the rest of the trip. Two Robes soon learned what had happened from Fawn. "He has always wanted me," Fawn said. "And he has always known I wanted you. He will not get over that."

"Maybe he will find a good woman soon," Two Robes suggested. "That is what he needs."

"He is too unsettled," Fawn said. "A woman would not help him now. He torments himself over things that are not his fault. He spent a lot of time away from the Lakota people and now he wishes he had never left. He will not accept what has happened to us."

"But he cannot change that. He couldn't have stopped the changes had he been here."

"I don't believe he understands that. I feel that now he will try to make up for what he wasn't able to do long ago."

"And this Messiah will help him," Two Robes said. "Or so he thinks."

"Or so he thinks," Fawn said. "But maybe the Messiah *will* help him. Maybe he will help all of us."

Mason Valley was surrounded by dry hills covered with sage and rabbit brush. The leaves on the cottonwoods lining the Walker River shone a deep gold in the bright sunlight.

Two Robes helped Fawn down from the wagon. They had been escorted into the valley with seventy other people. For the last three months, the Paiutes had been making regular excursions from Mason Valley north to the railroad, to give people directions and rides. Nearly six hundred people were now encamped, representing tribes from all over the midwest and western United States.

Shining Horse remarked that the Paiutes and other western tribes acted and dressed like the *Wasichu.* The tribes that lived in the deserts and valleys of this land had more easily adapted to the White Man's Road. Their ways had always been more sedentary, more suited for agriculture. Cattle and sheep had been far more easily accepted in a land where the bison had been gone for so long.

The dwellings were nothing like the traditional plains tepees. Although the Lakota people had been forced into cabins and makeshift houses, they had never grown used to them. Many still lived in traditional lodges when materials could be found.

Here, towns of Indian peoples had become commonplace; groups of shacks or small cabins clustered together haphazardly. Tule lodges, called *wikiups*, were the traditional dwellings, but only the most traditional still lived in them.

While setting up camp along the river, Two Robes and Shining Horse were approached by a young Bannock named Red Shirt who spoke Paiute fluently, and could also converse in English and three other Indian languages. He told them that there were a number of men and women in attendance who could help them understand the Messiah.

"When Wovoka speaks, you will want to know what he says," Red Shirt told them. "He wants everyone to hear him. You will be treated well here. This is a place of peace and harmony. Stay as long as you wish."

Red Shirt told them that Wovoka made nightly appearances just before sundown. Over the past weeks, the crowd had grown considerably. There were even a number of whites, mainly of the Mormon faith, who had adopted Wovoka as their savior and redeemer.

Soon a number of Paiute women arrived to help the newcomers get settled. They wore brightly colored cotton dresses, and some wore bonnets. Their dark hair was cut in bangs in front and cropped off along the sides and back. Their faces were painted white, with small black spots.

Fawn and Two Robes listened to the women chat in their native tongue, laughing as though their world knew no sorrow or pain. They had brought cast-iron skillets of mutton stew with bread, and they handed out blankets and tule mats for sleeping.

"I do not feel comfortable around these people," Shining Horse said. "The men do not look like warriors should. As a boy, I dressed in *Wasichu* clothes. But I was never comfortable. These people look like they have never known anything else."

"Well, they must want something else," Two Robes said. "Otherwise, they wouldn't be gathered to hear talk about bringing back the old times."

"You must be looking forward to the changes now yourself," Shining Horse said. "You are a new person."

"I am new in some ways," Two Robes acknowledged, "but old in others. I do understand the Lakota people better than I had ever thought I would, though. I thank you for a good deal of that knowledge."

"I don't know whether you are really as much Lakota as you think you are," Shining Horse said. "I have learned since our first meeting that I can never be anything but Lakota, living free like my ancestors. If you believe the Indian people we have seen here are anything like us, then no matter what you think you have learned from me, you don't know us at all."

"I'm not comparing anyone to anyone else," Two Robes said. "I'm just saying that thanks to you, it has been easier for me to learn your ways of life."

"It is easier for you to become Lakota than for any of us to become *Wasichu*," Shining Horse told him. "You will not be persecuted for it."

"In my life, I have taken more abuse from the white culture than I ever have from your people," Two Robes said. "Maybe that tells me who my true people really are."

Shining Horse remembered Sitting Bull saying that the color of a man's skin does not make what's in his heart. Here in this valley, where men of all colors had gathered to hear the words of peace and harmony, everyone felt of the same race. Maybe that was how it should be for true peace. But men should still dress as warriors.

Shining Horse pointed to a group of Paiute men. "Do you think that Wovoka will be like these men?"

"I believe that a man's strength does not lie in his clothes," Two Robes said. "It lies in his heart."

Shining Horse grunted. "Wovoka had better have a very large heart, then, if he wants to show true power to my people."

Later in the afternoon, after some much needed rest, Fawn went with Two Robes and Shining Horse to find the Lakota delegation. It had come together with the Cheyenne and was now camped with the Arapaho representatives. The Plains Indians' manner and dress differed greatly from all the others. They were the talk of the encampment.

"I want us to move our camp with our own people," Shining Horse said. "All the others here have taken the White Man's Road. You can see that by how they dress and eat. Mutton stew! They think the Lakota and the others from the plains are wild and unsettled. That is the way it should be, always."

"Maybe so," Two Robes said. "Maybe that is the main reason all of you came here, so that you could find a way to bring back the wildness to your lives."

Kicking Bear greeted Shining Horse with enthusiasm and seemed surprised to see Fawn. He was most surprised, though, to see Two Robes. "You have finally realized that you have seen *Wankantanka* more often than the *Wasichu* god of your own fathers," he said. "I felt that someday you would realize that."

Short Bull was astonished. The man he had met on the Rosebud in the snowstorm in no way resembled the man before him. "You no longer wear the clothes of a Black Robe," he said. "And you speak the Lakota tongue as well as your own."

"I have seen many changes since we last visited," Two Robes said. "I came among Kicking Bear's people to teach them, and I have become my own man now."

"I see," Short Bull said with a smile. "Have you learned how to hobble a horse yet?"

"Yes, I know how to do that," Two Robes replied. "I won't make that mistake again, no matter the weather. How is Little Buffalo Woman these days?"

"She is well," Short Bull said. "She cried when my pony returned without you. We thought you had crossed over, or soon would. Then we heard of a *Wasichu* holy man who lived in two worlds among the Minneconjou. The Black Robes at the mission heard this news also, and the Black Robe named Lindebner became very angry. He did not like it that you went against him and made the journey."

"It is good that I left when I did," Two Robes said. "I have come to know the wonders of this land and your people."

Fawn then stepped forward and showed Short Bull the little bag Two Robes had brought to her from the Rosebud. "Tell Little Buffalo Woman that the medicine has served me well," she said. "Someday I hope to see her again."

"Oh, you will see her again," Short Bull promised. "She is alive and well. You will also see many who have passed on. You will see your ancestors."

Fawn stared at Short Bull. "My mother has crossed over."

"She will return," Short Bull said. "You will see."

Kicking Bear said, "He is telling the truth. You will see your mother, and even your grandfathers."

"This is why we have come," Shining Horse said. "We want to know how this will come to pass."

Kicking Bear pointed to a flat, grassy area nearby where a large circle had been fenced by hanging bedsheets on tall stakes. "The Messiah is to come again tonight to lead us in prayer and tell us of his visions," he said. "Then you will see how the world is to change and how all the tribes will live in the old ways again before long."

Short Bull turned to Two Robes. "You will soon be living only in the Lakota world," he said. "You will not need to live in both worlds. What do you think about that?"

"I am not certain that that will come to pass," Two Robes said. "Others have talked this way, yet nothing has changed."

"This is different," Kicking Bear said. "No one has ever had the strong medicine of Wovoka."

"I have a difficult time with a man who claims to be the son of God returned," Two Robes said. "I just hope he can live with himself when he lets many people down."

"He has not let anyone down!" Short Bull said hotly. "I cannot understand why you would talk that way. You have not even seen him yet."

"I will see him this evening," Two Robes said. "And as far as I am concerned, he will not be Jesus."

"Wait until you see him cross over and come back," Kicking Bear said. "His medicine is far greater than that of anybody who has ever lived before him. No one can touch his medicine, not even Sitting Bull."

Two Robes looked at Shining Horse and saw that he did not take offense at the remark. "Wovoka sent a letter to my father, because he knows who is the strongest among the Lakota people," Shining Horse told them. "When the time comes, my father will join with him and the medicine will triple in strength."

"But your father did not come," Short Bull pointed out. "It is for us who came to learn the dance and teach our people, not for your father."

"Make no mistake," Shining Horse said. "When the time is right for the Lakota people, it will be Sitting Bull who again leads them on the pathway to glory."

"There are others who can lead our people back to the old

ways," Kicking Bear said. "Maybe the old warriors cannot see what is happening."

"My father is always able to see what is happening," Shining Horse said. "He can see better than anyone else."

"Then why didn't he come?"

"You know why," Shining Horse told Kicking Bear. "He didn't want to make trouble with the agent."

Short Bull spoke up. "See? The old ones do not want to make trouble. That is not the way of one who wants to bring back the old ways."

"I will listen to Wovoka's words and learn the dance," Shining Horse said. "If the medicine is good, my father will see it. He will lead our people, and not even the mightiest of the *Wasichu* can stop this from coming to pass."

TWENTY-FIVE

A N HOUR before sundown, criers ran through
the encampment to announce that Wovoka
would soon appear. The many who had gathered to listen
became instantly excited. Everyone migrated to the staked-
out arena in the middle of the valley. A large fire had been
built in the center, and the people were asked to sit in a circle
around it.

Fawn and Two Robes sat together, not far from where
Shining Horse had joined the other Lakota and the Cheyenne. Shining Horse was proud to be considered one of these
wild Indians, and earlier he had gone around the gathering
proclaiming that the Lakota people would soon rise to the
power they had once known.

Suddenly the people began to talk and point toward the
outer edge of the arena. A Paiute man in a large black Stetson
was walking from a wagon toward a smaller fire just inside a
circle of flags.

The man walked slowly and deliberately, each step filled

with special meaning. He stood near six feet in height, built sturdily, with a thick neck and large head. He wore a rabbit-skin coat, striped vertically with skunk skins. The coat was open in front, revealing a light cotton shirt and dark pants. On his feet were beaded buckskin newopats, which told the gathering that his feet touched the earth in a traditional manner.

Two Robes felt an instant affinity with him. The man appeared to be caught between two worlds, and not just in his clothing: he was not as dark as most Indians, yet not nearly light enough to be a white man. He had no trace of beard or whiskers, but his eyebrows were heavy.

The Paiute removed his Stetson and paused for a moment. Then he sat down and gazed into the flames.

The crowd roared, "Jesus! Jesus!"

Wovoka had appeared.

Two Robes stared across the crowd at Wovoka. There was something very special happening here, he concluded. People felt good, and there was a sense of love in the air. He wanted to go and talk with this man. But now was not the time.

Wovoka's assistants worked their way through the crowd, quieting them so that Wovoka could pray. They handed out to each individual sacred red paint and a peyote button, along with a magpie feather.

A Bannock man appeared in front of Fawn and Two Robes. He welcomed them in English and motioned for them to dip their fingers into the red ocher. He showed them how to mark their faces, then handed them each a magpie feather and a peyote button.

Two Robes held up the peyote. "What is this?"

"It is sacred food," the man said. "You eat it and you will see the things Jesus talks about."

When the Bannock man had left, Two Robes asked Fawn what peyote was used for.

"It is a sacred food used for seeing," she explained. "Your

mind becomes open to Truth. Sometimes you will be scared at what you see."

Two Robes put the peyote into his pocket. "I'm not going to take it. I have learned a great deal about Truth, and I didn't need anything to help me."

Fawn handed him her button as well. "I also have seen much without the sacred food. I do not need it, either."

Wovoka was still gazing into the small fire at the edge of the arena. Shining Horse left the Lakota and Cheyenne and hurried over to Fawn and Two Robes.

"Has he already taken the sacred food?" Fawn asked.

"I learned from Kicking Bear and Short Bull that he takes the food at the place where he lives," Shining Horse said. "Then he comes and gazes into the small fire for long periods of time. Sometimes he will perform miracles afterward."

"What miracles has he performed?" Two Robes asked.

"They said he made ice come down the river in the middle of summer," Shining Horse replied.

"Ice in the summer?" Fawn asked.

Shining Horse nodded. "They say he dies and goes to heaven, then comes back with messages. They say he can make animals appear from hats and clothes. He brings white birds that fly away into the night."

Fawn had her hands over her mouth.

Two Robes frowned. Though he thought Wovoka might be doing good for the people, he did not agree with illusion to gain importance. "There are many who can do tricks like that," he told Shining Horse. "They are called magicians. You must have seen them when you lived in the East."

"What about the ice in the river?" Shining Horse asked.

"I don't know," Two Robes said. "I believe that this man is good, but I am beginning to think that he needs to do something to show great power to the people. He does not need to do that to talk of God."

"You will always think like a Black Robe," Shining Horse

said. "You will always believe that only your kind can reach *Wankantanka*. That is what is wrong with you."

Shining Horse got up and rejoined the Lakota and Cheyenne delegation. Fawn looked into Two Robes' eyes.

"You know that Shining Horse is right. In many ways you will always think of yourself as a Black Robe, and closer to the Powers."

"I do not feel superior to anyone," Two Robes argued. "I have learned more since I came out here than during all the rest of my life. I owe most of that to Shining Horse. He gave me the book that I have learned so much from."

"Then why do you mock Wovoka?"

"I do not believe he is Jesus," Two Robes said. "Wovoka is just a man, like I am."

"Can you make ice in the river, or white birds that fly from within clothes?" Fawn asked.

"No," Two Robes replied. "But that does not make a man Jesus."

The crowd began to roar. Wovoka stood up from his bench and walked among the people to the middle of the circle. They touched him and cried. He stood next to the fire and called the people closer to him. Everyone moved up, crying, "Jesus! Jesus!"

Then Wovoka raised both hands into the air. The crowd quieted.

"Peace," Wovoka said. "Peace to all of you."

The crowd cried, "Thank you, Father," and "We love you, Jesus." Many hugged one another and clasped hands.

"Tonight we all love one another," Wovoka continued. "We have no anger. Only love. Pretty soon we start our dance. The voices tell me it will be very good. Very good. Voices also say I will journey to heaven again and then come back. I will tell you more about the return of the ancestors and the buffalo."

At this the crowd cheered.

Wovoka looked through the crowd. "Do you have the sacred paint on your faces?"

The crowd cried, "Yes, Jesus!"

"Have you eaten the sacred food?"

"Yes, Jesus! Yes!"

"I hope also that many of you will join me in the Other World this night," Wovoka continued. "All of us can go. All of us can see what will come."

"Yes, Jesus! We want to go with you!"

He instructed them to hold the magpie feather with both hands and study it. "Look at the sacred feather closely," he said. "See the black and white merging together, so that the feather is black on white, white on black." Then he began singing in a loud and high falsetto:

> They are coming, all are coming,
> Says the Father, says the Father.
> The land will laugh,
> The mountains will ring,
> The rivers will sing,
> Says the Father, says the Father.

At Wovoka's command, the people stood. They began to form a circle and join hands, all singing together. They shuffled to the steps that Wovoka had taught them during previous gatherings, weaving together in unison.

Shining Horse and the other Lakota took their place among the dancers, singing loudly. Whites and Indians alike, people from many different tribes, mingled together, joining hands with one another.

Two Robes had studied the magpie feather and had felt good about Wovoka's words. His mind was open and relaxed, and he was anxious to dance. He took Fawn's hand and entered the circle. He sang with her in Lakota and soon was caught up in the power of the dance, swaying and swerving in unison with the others.

Suddenly Fawn began to cry. Two Robes caught her as she

fell. "I miss my mother so much," she said. "I want to see my mother again, but I am afraid."

"I am with you," Two Robes said. "You don't need to fear."

Fawn pulled herself up. "I must continue," she said. "This is why my mother returned to see me."

"What do you mean? Did you see her while you were dancing?"

"No. One time before. I will tell you about it later."

After dancing but a short while, Fawn again burst into tears.

"Let's sit down," Two Robes suggested. "We can rejoin the dancers later."

They sat just outside the circle, watching the dancers sing and sway. Two Robes noticed mothers placing their children, even small babies, in the center of the circle.

"Babies and children are closest to the spirit world," Fawn explained. "They are pure and holy. It is their power that allows *Wankantanka* to hear us."

Suddenly the dancers began to chant loudly. The circle opened to reveal Wovoka in the center, prostrate on the ground, his body shaking uncontrollably. No one touched him. All sang louder, and the dance continued without interruption.

After a little while, Wovoka lay still, his face to the sky. His wife, a woman named Mary, covered him in blankets. She knelt over him and prayed. It was said that she worried about his trances and believed that each time he left his body, it would be his last journey. She always sang songs to bring him back safely from the Other World.

"Look!" Fawn said. "Others are falling, too."

Many dancers fell to the ground. Those left standing clasped hands and danced over or around them, leaving them to visit the Other World.

"What if someone dies?" Two Robes asked.

"I know about this," Fawn said. "I did it myself, on that cold day last winter when the sun died. I saw different worlds. And

I saw my mother. Then I came back, and I believe these people will come back as well."

Fawn told Two Robes her entire story. When she finished, she was weeping loudly. Two Robes took her back to their camp and held her until she fell asleep.

He lay down next to Fawn and listened to the dancing and singing as it continued out in the arena. Wovoka's words and the dancing had excited him; then Fawn's emotional outburst had robbed him of all enthusiasm. He had spent many strange nights since coming to live with the Minneconjou, but this was the strangest. Maybe it would be best to sleep through the rest of it.

The dancing continued throughout the night. At dawn, those who had not fallen wandered to their camps, many in walking trances. There were shouts and songs and screams from those on their feet as well as from those on the ground. Many spoke of seeing loved ones long dead, while others claimed to have talked to the Father in heaven. All had been in a different world and wanted what they had seen there to come to their world quickly.

Two Robes watched from his bed. Fawn still slept soundly. He got up and went out and mingled with the people, asking questions of them. They seemed convinced that Wovoka would bring back the old days and allow their relatives to live with them again. He learned that many Mormons who had come saw no reason to think Wovoka didn't have the same powers as Jesus. "He may or may not be the same man," one of them said, "but that doesn't matter. He promotes peace and brotherhood. Is that not what Christ taught?"

There were also many gathered who wished Wovoka harm. They stood on the sidelines, some with cameras and some with guns, the latter perhaps waiting for a chance to open fire and call it self-defense.

There was a large number of law officers in attendance as well. Some of them stood with Indian agents and political figures, discussing means to stop all this. But since Wovoka and his guests were breaking no laws, the dancing went on.

Two Robes saw that Wovoka had not come back from his trance. He still lay in the middle of the dance area, covered with blankets, his eyes and his mouth half open, his body as rigid as stone. His wife lay in the back of their wagon, her tear-stained face partially relaxed in sleep.

Two Robes found Shining Horse with the Lakota and Cheyenne, listening to Short Bull talk of being in heaven himself.

"It is as the Messiah has said," he was telling everyone. "There are more buffalo than can be counted in many days. The rivers run high with sweet, clear water. Grass is thick everywhere, and many ponies can graze together. This is all coming back to us."

"When will that be?" one of the warriors asked.

Short Bull answered with conviction. "As the Messiah has said, within the passing of just one or two winters, depending on how well we do the dance. We must get everybody to join in."

Shining Horse noticed that Two Robes had joined them. "I saw you dancing," he said. "You told me you didn't think that Wovoka was Jesus."

"I still don't think he is Jesus," Two Robes said. "But I believe he has done a lot of good in bringing everyone together and in talking about loving everyone."

"That might be good for over here," Short Bull said, "but I am sure that the *Wasichu* in our own lands will not want to dance. I did not see any of them in heaven."

"I heard Wovoka tell everyone to love *all* people," Two Robes said. "How can the changes be just for the red race?"

"The red man is the only one who considers the buffalo sacred," Short Bull replied. "You know that. You had better decide to keep on dancing."

A messenger announced that Wovoka was up, calling

everyone together. "Jesus has risen!" he said, out of breath. "Tell all you see, Jesus has risen!"

The Lakota and Cheyenne started toward the gathering, and Two Robes hurried to Fawn's blankets. He tried to awaken her, but she slept so soundly that he could barely get her to move. Finally he gave up and joined the others.

Wovoka stood up and staggered for a short time until he gained his balance. He was still wrapped in his blankets. His face was drained of color and expression, his hair matted to his head with sweat. His eyes, wide and lit with a distant energy, stared out into the crowd.

"I told you about the earth and how I was made to walk upon it," he was saying. "That was after everything was made by the Old Man. When I came back to earth, I was treated badly. Very few listened. This is what they did to me."

Two Robes watched Wovoka drop the blankets and roll up his sleeves, exposing scars on his wrists. He took off his newopats and revealed similar scars at the top of his feet. The crowd gasped; some clapped their hands over their mouths. Many dropped to their knees. Again cries of "Jesus! Oh, Jesus!" arose. Many wept openly.

Two Robes became irritated. The scars Wovoka had revealed did not resemble any stigmata he had ever heard of. He wondered if they had been self-inflicted.

"Peace," Wovoka said to all. "Listen and be filled with peace."

When the crowd had settled again, Wovoka talked about his wounds. "I want you to know that when they did this to me, I did not fight back. I did not have anger. I had only love. You understand? I had just love. I was sad that all the children here knew was how to kill me. I went back to the Other World and left them.

"But I did not hate them. I told them I would be back in many hundreds of years. I would save them. When the time was right, the Old Man sent me back here to make the evil go away. Everything will be like it was when the land was good."

Again the weeping and the moaning began. But Wovoka was not finished. "It will begin before the snows of next fall. Youth will return to all good people. They will keep youth if they do not do bad. The ancestors will come back to live with us. Dance as I have shown you. Love your enemies. I tell you, this is the most important. Those who do not listen to me will wish they had never heard me."

The crowd watched in silence while Wovoka looked through them. He studied them as if he knew each one individually. His eyes hesitated on Shining Horse and the others among the Lakota and Cheyenne.

"All men must live as brothers," Wovoka continued. "All must dance. No more fighting! Then the world will come back to us. We will all be whole again."

This brought cheering from the people. They asked when they might dance again, as they wanted to hasten the coming of the New World.

"We will dance again tonight," Wovoka said. "It will take some time before those of you who just came can dance correctly. Each time we dance, I will watch you all. When you have learned the dance well enough, I will make special marks on your foreheads with the sacred red paint."

Wovoka then stepped to the back of his wagon and pulled out a large sack. Newcomers were asked to offer him gifts in order to better gain the medicine of the dance, the Dance to the Father, as Wovoka called it. A number of guests lined up to offer him gifts, mainly handmade items such as skin bags and medicine pouches. Each in turn was thanked and given a magpie feather from the sack.

Two Robes waited for the line to dwindle. He found Red Shirt, the Bannock, and asked him to interpret for him. Together they approached Wovoka.

"I believe your message is good," Two Robes told Wovoka. "But if you truly believe that you have returned as Jesus, you have to also believe that your life is in danger, as it was those nineteen hundred years ago."

Red Shirt translated the warning and then translated Wovoka's reply.

"I died when I was first in the world, but it is not for me to die this time. The Father has told me how to be protected." He held up his Stetson and pointed to a bullet hole in the crown. "See? Once a man tried to shoot me. He could not kill me, or even touch me."

"Don't you believe it will be tried again?" Two Robes asked.

"No one can harm me," Wovoka said.

"I have seen how the lawmen glare at you. I only hope that you will take precautions."

"It is kind of you to show such concern, but you didn't hear me. I wear a special shirt that makes me safe from bullets."

"You mean you wear metal?"

"No it is not metal. It is cloth. But I put special symbols on it."

"I would like to see this," Two Robes said.

"You will see it," Wovoka said. "Before nightfall I will again talk to the people. I will show it to everyone. Now I must go and prepare for when that time comes."

Two Robes and Red Shirt watched Wovoka walk out into the hills above the valley.

"There is no cloth shirt that will stop bullets," Two Robes said.

"Oh, yes. The Messiah has talked about the holy shirts before. He says they will protect the wearer from bullets."

"I never heard of such a thing."

"He is a holy man," Red Shirt said. "When he returns this afternoon, you will see."

TWENTY-SIX

I N LATE afternoon the crowd gathered once again. Fawn and Two Robes waited expectantly with the others. Red Shirt sat with them. He explained that tonight would be the most special night of all. The Messiah would wear a sacred shirt and show its powers for all to see.

Fawn was caught on every word. Two Robes listened with mixed emotions. When he had first seen Wovoka, had first heard Wovoka's words and his songs, he had thought them beneficial, bringing mankind together.

But now he realized that Wovoka was caught up in his own importance. Wovoka wanted to be just a little more powerful each time he preached to the people. It was too bad. The dance was a very good idea, but the desire to overwhelm his listeners with his own powers was creating an illusion, one that took away from the goodness of his teachings.

Wovoka appeared in his long coat and stood before the people, his arms raised to the sky. "We pray for peace this night," he said. "All men are brothers."

Again Wovoka led the gathering through prayer. The people again responded with, "Jesus! Oh, Jesus!"

After the prayers, Wovoka took off his coat. The people gasped. He turned in a circle to present his special shirt.

Two Robes saw that it was the top of what had once been a white-cotton undergarment. It had been cut off just above the hips and was covered with painted images. Magpies and eagles, as well as crows and turtles, were mixed with Christian crosses, as well as with the stars and stripes that represented the American flag.

"All things sacred are on this shirt," Wovoka told the crowd. "It is something holy that comes from the Father."

Red Shirt told Two Robes that the Mormons wore a special kind of long underwear as a defense against evil. He said that Wovoka had used only the top half so that it would be easy to put on and take off again for dancing. All those in attendance could then make the same garments for themselves when they returned to their people.

Wovoka told his listeners that he would now show them how the shirt worked. A man holding a shotgun took a position less than twenty feet from Wovoka. When the flame from both barrels shot out, the crowd gasped. Instead of falling forward in death, Wovoka remained standing, his hands in front of his stomach, shot spilling onto the ground.

"The shirt is sacred! It is sacred!" Short Bull declared. He and the other Lakota hurried forward to collect some of the shot. The shot, now sacred itself, would be placed in medicine bundles used for the dance.

Kicking Bear showed Two Robes his shot. "See, this is real! That man is sacred."

"Can you really believe that his shirt actually stopped him from being hurt?" Two Robes asked.

"You saw it for yourself. How can you have any doubt?"

"Maybe what you saw wasn't real, but only a trick."

"Ahhh! You have no faith!" Kicking Bear said.

Everyone was following Wovoka and watching as he pinned

another of the shirts to a rope strung between two cotton-woods. Two Robes stayed behind and searched the area where the shotgun had been fired. He found very tiny bits of paper on the ground.

"Paper wadding!" he said to himself. "The shotgun shells were loaded with paper wadding."

Two Robes told the Lakota that Wovoka had been holding the shot next to his stomach and had spilled it out at the sound of the shotgun blast. No one would listen to him; they were too absorbed in the next phase of Wovoka's exhibition.

Wovoka stood back from the rope and invited members of various tribes to shoot at the shirt. Each time the shirt would fly backward with the impact of the shot, but no holes appeared in it.

"He is real!" Fawn said. "His medicine is powerful!"

"These are tricks," Two Robes insisted.

"No, the shirts are real," Fawn said. "You are again the *Wasichu* you once were. You do not want my people to be free again."

"You can't be free if you insist on believing lies," Two Robes said.

"They are no lie!" Fawn said. "The shirts will protect the wearer from harm."

"The shirt moves on air currents made by the shot," Two Robes insisted. "The shirt is not harmed because the air pushes it out."

"No!" Fawn said. "I am going to believe this. On faith!"

Fawn hurried over to Short Bull and Kicking Bear, who were taking the target shirt off the line. Two Robes followed.

"This one is special," Short Bull said, tearing the shirt into strips. "We will divide it and we will all take pieces back to our people. We will make many shirts for everyone, and they will be our shield against the *Wasichu* bullets."

Two Robes asked Shining Horse, "Do you believe in these shirts?"

"Yes," Shining Horse replied. "There is powerful medicine in them."

"No," Two Robes said. "It is a trick, like the white birds that come out of his hat, and the ice in the river."

"You have no faith," Shining Horse said. "In the old days, we could make things come to us simply by knowing that *Wankantanka* would allow it. Many men had the power to do many things that the *Wasichu* will never understand. Everyone who has seen the dance believes it will help make those days come back. And the shirts will help us against the *Wasichu*."

"The dance is one thing," Two Robes said, "but it is not possible for cotton and muslin to repel bullets."

"You don't know the Indian way," Shining Horse said. "My father and many others among the Lakota have had great medicine in the past. They have shown that bullets could not hit them. They had this medicine because they *believed* they had it. There is no reason to think that Wovoka does not have such medicine himself and that he is willing to teach it to others."

"Shining Horse is right," Fawn said. "I saw with my own eyes."

Fawn and Shining Horse stood together. Next to them, Kicking Bear and Short Bull each held pieces of the torn shirt. Two Robes stared hard at all of them. They stood before him, determined to build their dream into reality.

"What if all this goes too far?" Two Robes asked. "What if you find there is nothing to it? Many could get hurt, or even killed."

"You have seen the medicine with your own eyes," Short Bull said. "You know that the world will soon change. What more do you need?"

"The world will not change because of shirts said to repel bullets," Two Robes said.

Short Bull turned his back on Two Robes. The others followed suit as a gesture of anger and defiance. Fawn blinked back tears.

"I had hoped that you were now fully Lakota and had thrown away the ways of your people entirely. I fully believed that was so on the night we spent together in the Black Hills. But I can see that you do not want what is best for me or for my people."

"It is not that," Two Robes said. "I *do* want what's best for you and your people."

Kicking Bear said, "I believe she is right. You have returned to the *Wasichu* and have lost some of your powers in the Lakota world. You should try to get back what you learned and then forgot. You cannot be one of us and talk against the dance."

"I am only telling you what I feel," Two Robes said. "I believe that the dance will make the world better, but shirts that are supposed to stop bullets will get you in trouble with the agents."

"They cannot stop us!" Short Bull snapped.

"Maybe not," Two Robes told him, "but the Bluecoats can. If the agents don't want you to dance, they will ask for help. The Bluecoats will be everywhere. Then what?"

"Then we will fight them!" Kicking Bear said.

"Now, see what you have said," Two Robes pointed out. "Wovoka has told you not to hold anger, nor to fight. What did you just say?"

"It is different with us," Kicking Bear said. "The *Wasichu* are against us more than they are against any other tribe. We killed Long Hair Custer. They want revenge."

"All the more reason to stay peaceful," Two Robes said. "If you do not, the Bluecoats will come in quickly."

"The dance will work," Short Bull said flatly. "We have already seen the dead, our loved ones. We have seen that the shirts will help us bring the ghosts. We will dance until they come to be with us again. We will wear the shirts of the ghosts and dance for the ghosts. Not you, nor anyone else, will ever stop us from living the way we are entitled to live."

Kicking Bear and Short Bull led the Lakota away. Shining

Horse waited for Fawn. Two Robes stopped her before she could leave with them.

"Where are you going?" he asked.

"She wants to be with her people," Shining Horse said. "Let her go."

"I will talk to Two Robes alone," Fawn said to Shining Horse. "I will join you later."

Shining Horse left reluctantly. When he was gone, Two Robes turned Fawn to face him. "You don't know what you're getting into."

"Yes, I do know. I want my people to live as they once did. You no longer act like you are one of my people."

"Your people are headed for trouble. What about the dream where you saw your mother? She warned you about this. Have you forgotten?"

"I have not forgotten," Fawn said. "But my mother did not see the Messiah. She did not understand what all this means. I will learn the dance with my people, and I will teach it to my children. Then we will all live as we should live, and never go hungry again."

"What about your children?" Two Robes asked. "Go back with me and be with them. If the dance is real, peace will come to everyone."

"I will go back to my children when the time is right," Fawn said. "Now leave me. I want to be with those who care about me and my future."

Two Robes watched her disappear into the crowd. He spent the night alone in fitful sleep. Fawn stayed up and danced with the others.

Just before dawn, Two Robes threw back his blanket and returned to the dance circle. He found Fawn lying unconscious on the ground.

"Don't try to wake her," Shining Horse said. "She has gone to see the ancestors. She will come back when she is ready."

"I am worried about her," Two Robes said, and he knelt beside her.

Kicking Bear and Short Bull pulled him up and held him back. "Shining Horse is right," Kicking Bear said. "Do not try to awaken her before she is to return. If you cannot leave her alone, we will keep you away from her."

Two Robes paced until late morning, when Fawn began to stir. He hurried to her side. She sat up and held her head.

"I need water," she said. "I am very thirsty."

Two Robes gave her water and helped her up.

"Do not try to take her back to your camp, Two Robes," Shining Horse said. "She wishes to remain with me."

"Do not make trouble, Shining Horse," Fawn said. "I will go and talk with him for a while."

Two Robes helped Fawn back to their camp. Her head had cleared, and tears were streaming down her face.

"I saw my mother again," she said. "I feel that she wanted me to dance."

"That is not what you told me before," Two Robes said. "You told me she warned you about the dance."

"She told me that the dance is good to do, just as long as it is done properly. She said the world will change and there will be happiness. I feel that she will come with the others to the New World."

"Fawn, I believe that you want to be with your mother again so badly that you are making yourself see all this," Two Robes said. "Come with me, back to your people. To your children. You can consider the dance and what you have seen here quietly, away from all this confusion."

"I am not confused!" Fawn said. "I know what I want. You can't tell me that I am wrong."

"It is time we go back," Two Robes repeated. "We should go today."

"No, there is more that I must learn here."

"It would not be good for you to stay. Go back with me. Hawk and Little Star must miss you. Then if you want to return here with them, I will not try to stop you."

Fawn thought about the idea. Finally she agreed. She told Shining Horse what she was planning.

"Stay here," Shining Horse said. "Have Two Robes go back and bring your children to you. There is much you can learn while he is gone."

"No," Fawn said. "If the Powers want me to return, I will be back."

"I believe you will return," Shining Horse said. "We will save a place for you in the dance circle."

Fawn and Two Robes sat with Tangled Hair in the Arapaho village near Fort Washakie, where Tangled Hair had visited with his mother. They watched dancers make a circle in the new-fallen snow. The dancers had been singing since early afternoon and would not stop until the following morning, Christmas Day.

A lot had happened to Tangled Hair since he had left the train to see his mother. He had been with her just two days when she died of what a *Wasichu* doctor had called influenza.

"I didn't really get to talk to her," Tangled Hair was saying. "She didn't even know me, she was so sick."

"It is still good that you came," Fawn reassured him. "Your mother knew you had come. Though her body was near death, her spirit sang for joy. She is waiting for the time when you will be reunited."

Upon their arrival, Fawn had told Tangled Hair everything she had felt and seen in Mason Valley. He could see that she believed the world would soon change and that all would be good again for the Indian people.

Two Robes said openly that he could not decide how to feel about the new religion. He felt good about the dance and the words Wovoka had spoken, but he could not bring himself to forgive the man for playing tricks on his followers. This precipitated another argument with Fawn, who insisted they were miracles, not tricks.

"Miracles are events that change your mind about life," Two Robes pointed out. "Tricks make you feel bad about life."

Among both the Arapaho and the Shoshone people, many had become excited about the possibilities of the dance, while others had their doubts. There were those who believed that Wovoka wished to be thought a great medicine man, the greatest who had ever lived. Others believed him to be the Messiah.

Tangled Hair had come to find himself somewhere in the middle. He knew that many things were possible, yet he couldn't get himself into the ritual of the dance. He worried that his mother would have wanted him to dance, for a surviving aunt was pushing him to believe.

Tangled Hair took his father's wrinkled letter from his shirt. "Do you think my mother knows that my father sent me this letter?" he asked Fawn.

"I am certain she knows," Fawn said. "And I am certain she wants you both to dance, so that you can be together. That is the teaching."

"What if my father does not believe in the dance?" Tangled Hair asked. "I feel sure that he will not."

"All who want to be a part of the New World must dance," Fawn said. "All those who wish to end the *Wasichu* ways must believe. Tell him to come among the Minneconjou, who will surely be dancing soon. If you don't, the world will change and you won't be here to see your mother return."

Tangled Hair turned to Two Robes. "I know you are a holy man. Why don't you believe?"

"I can believe in the goodness of the dance," Two Robes replied. "But the ghost shirts will ruin everything."

"Maybe it is the way you have been taught," Tangled Hair suggested. "The *Wasichu* do not believe in sacred things."

"Sometimes what men believe to be sacred is not," Two Robes suggested. "We are often deceived."

"I have seen you change many times, Two Robes," Tangled Hair said. "When I first saw you eating from the fallen buffalo, there was little life left in you. But *Wankantanka* wanted you to live. I thought you had become Lakota. Then came the day when you were baptizing the people along the stream. You were wearing the sacred shirt that Fawn made for you. I was very angry. You looked like part of the *Wasichu* government. But you had nothing to do with the land commission and the rations we lost. Now I see you thinking like the *Wasichu* again. I believe you will always have the heart of a Black Robe."

"Why aren't *you* dancing?" Two Robes asked.

"I have never been able to do it right," Tangled Hair said. "I have never crossed over to see my mother or any of my ancestors. Maybe I am not worthy."

"You are as worthy as anyone," Fawn said. "If you dance in the right manner, and believe, you will see your mother."

"I believe I will leave my mother's people, though," Tangled Hair said. "I believe I will go to be with my father. He will know what is right."

"I told you, if you and he do not dance, then neither one of you will see your mother," Fawn warned.

Tangled Hair held up the letter. "But my father is alive, and I want to see him. The letter says he will be with the army until the next coming of the cold moons. He will finish the day before Thanksgiving. He says that is a special day among the settled people and that we can spend it together. Then I will live with him."

"Do you think you could adjust to that?" Two Robes asked. "Life for non-whites is harder for people off the reservation than it is on."

Tangled Hair looked surprised. "How can that be?"

"People on the reservation care for one another," Two Robes said. "They share things to help each other get by. Once you leave, you're alone."

"I will have my father, though."

"Yes, but he is not white, either," Two Robes pointed out.

"You will have to move either among Indian people or black people. You won't be accepted anywhere else."

Tangled Hair stared at Two Robes. "Why do you care what happens to me?"

"I have come to know you as a friend," Two Robes said. "I have learned much from you. You deserve a good life."

Tangled Hair tucked the letter back into his shirt. "I have much thinking to do. I do not feel that I should live here among my mother's people. Maybe I should go back among the Minneconjou until my father leaves the army."

"You must go where you can dance," Fawn said. "That is important."

"Do you really think I am worthy of the dance?"

"Why don't you dance tonight?" Fawn suggested. "Then in the morning you will know what you want to do."

"All right," Tangled Hair said. "I will try it again tonight. Maybe I can see my mother and she can tell me what to do."

TWENTY-SEVEN

Two Robes sat on a hillside in the falling snow and stared at the mission chapel. The faithful of Wind River were attending Christmas morning mass. He could hear the choir, a mixture of Shoshone and Arapaho, singing "Hark the Herald Angels Sing," while out on the flat a short distance away, others were dancing in a circle, singing songs they had learned in Mason Valley.

Fawn was among them, her face lifted toward the falling snow. Two Robes looked from the dancers back to the church. He didn't belong in either place, he thought. He belonged only to himself.

He walked down from the hill and joined a number of people watching the dance. Tangled Hair sat off by himself, looking again at the letter from his father. He had danced well into the night, had fallen, and had awakened just before dawn. Two Robes walked over to him and sat down.

"I have made my decision," Tangled Hair told Two Robes. "I saw my father, not my mother. My father is alive and has not crossed over. It was he who called to me. I will do as he wishes."

"How will you meet him?" Two Robes asked.

"I would like to go back with you and Fawn to the Minneconjou. When Thanksgiving approaches, I will journey down to the fort where he lives."

"I will do all I can to help you reach your father," Two Robes said.

"Maybe I will walk over to the church," Tangled Hair said. "My father probably goes into one of those. Do you want to come?"

"No, thank you," Two Robes said. "I need some time to myself."

Two Robes left the dance and followed a deer trail along the river. Though the snow continued to fall heavily, the temperature was moderate. Behind him, the dancers and the church singers sang their songs. As he walked, the two sounds blended into one. Then, finally, into nothingness.

Two Robes brushed snow from a rock and sat down. An otter stuck its head out of the water and stared at him for a time before swimming downriver. Three deer meandered through the cottonwoods, pausing momentarily to study him. They drank from the river and stepped softly back into cover.

The snow continued to fall, thick and white. It felt warm to him, comforting, soothing. He closed his eyes and breathed deep of the clean air. When he opened his eyes, he noticed wolf tracks in the snow at his feet.

He stood up. They hadn't been there before. Deep prints, large and fresh. Two Robes followed them. They took him away from the river, out into the storm. Despite the heavy snowfall, the tracks remained fresh. He followed them to the base of a butte.

Though the snowy footing was treacherous, Two Robes climbed the butte with ease. At the top, he stopped to catch his breath and look out over the country. But the snow was dense and he quickly became disoriented. He sat down to keep from getting dizzy.

Then Two Robes saw a hole in the storm. He squinted and tried to understand. The hole began to swirl, and his mind took him through it. There he again met the wolf.

"I didn't expect this," Two Robes said.

"It is better that you weren't prepared," the wolf said. "Then you begin to guess what is coming. That is not good."

"I don't think I could do that, not anymore," Two Robes said. "I don't even know what to think or believe anymore."

"What is it that you want to think and believe?" the wolf asked.

"I want to believe that the power of good can overcome anything," Two Robes said. "I don't know anymore if that is true."

"What is the basis of your doubt?" the wolf asked.

"Wovoka and the new religion he is preaching. His words are good, but his actions are bad."

"If you can see the separation, what is your concern?"

"I know he is a good man at heart," Two Robes explained. "But he is destroying his own message. He professes to be Jesus, and he talks of brotherly love. But he plays parlor tricks and wears a shirt that is supposed to stop bullets. Jesus didn't do that."

"Didn't you say yourself that Wovoka is just a man, like you?" the wolf asked.

"Yes, I did say that."

"Then why are you being so hard on him? You are a man; he is a man. Men make mistakes. Nothing is perfect here, no matter how much you wish it were."

"But it isn't fair to the people who are listening to him," Two Robes argued. "They believe he *is* Jesus. The Lakota are going to have trouble because of it."

"Do you see anything different in that than in all the other events of the world?" the wolf asked. "Jesus asked men to love one another. Wovoka asks men to love one another. Still, nobody listens. So who are you going to blame?"

Two Robes stared at the wolf.

"All men are given free will," the wolf continued. "Where is it written that you, or anyone else, has to follow Wovoka?"

"But if he professes to be Jesus, he is saying that his word is law," Two Robes said. "That means he will have many followers who will do whatever he says."

"Do you believe you can change that?"

"I've already tried to. That's what frustrates me."

"Haven't you enough of your own problems to deal with?"

"I believe this is my problem," Two Robes said. "Fawn has come to believe completely in Wovoka. How can I help her?"

"Fawn has her own mind and her own destiny. You cannot interfere!"

"But I want Fawn with me always," Two Robes said.

The wolf stared hard at him. "If you are doing as you should be, you will not have to worry about anything. If you stay on your own pathway, only joy can follow."

"So why don't I feel joy?" Two Robes asked.

"Because you aren't looking for it," the wolf replied. "You are spending your time trying to change things that are out of your hands."

"But Fawn is my joy. I can't imagine being without her."

"When you started your search for God, you didn't know anyone out here," the wolf pointed out. "If it hadn't been for your journey, you would never have met her. Do not forget the journey. Stay on your pathway. All else will follow."

"Should I have faith that she will always be with me?"

"You should have faith in your journey. Along the way, you might see that certain places and people no longer fit. If this is so, do not fight what you see. Joy is found on your pathway. Confusion is everywhere else. Everyone must find his own pathway by himself."

Two Robes shook his head. "No, no. I don't like this."

"Do you see how the days are changing you?" the wolf

asked. "Do you see that your mind knows things, but you cannot tell them to others? Not even to the ones you hold dearest to you."

"I fear for those I love," Two Robes told the wolf. "If I can't share with them, then what good is knowledge?"

"Nothing will stop you from sharing," the wolf said. "But you cannot *make* them hear you. They must learn their own lessons."

"I don't know how to handle this," Two Robes said. "I feel that I am above some things that are happening, but I can't do anything about them."

"That is part of the learning," the wolf said. "You will see things, but you will be helpless to change them. Many are hurt by the fancies of a few. It is not for you to judge. You cannot stop something that begins to rise on the wind."

Two Robes thought for a moment: life's events were like the wind, and there was no predicting or controlling a force such as that. He remembered being on Bear Butte and hearing the eagle tell him to drift with the currents that suited him. No others. He could only hope that Fawn would choose the currents he did.

But what if she didn't? What if her pathway was elsewhere? There would be nothing he could do about it. He let out a tremendous sigh.

The wolf said, "Don't despair. You asked for Truth, and now you have it. Be strong, for you will need to help the others when the time is right. Many will look to you for guidance. Be ready."

"Will Fawn be among them?"

"There will be those who know you have wisdom. Then you can help them."

"But I want to know about Fawn," Two Robes insisted. "Tell me . . ."

But the wolf had turned and was fading into the storm, its white shape dissolving into the blur of the falling snow. Two Robes found himself falling backward through the hole he had entered. He tumbled, first through air and then along a slope. When he came to his feet, he was at the bottom of the butte. Someone was calling his name.

Two Robes answered and stumbled forward on the trail. Soon he saw Fawn running toward him. She threw herself into his arms.

"I thought you had walked away to lose yourself," she said, tears streaming down her face. "I thought you wanted to die."

"No, I didn't want to die," he told her. "I love you too much to walk away from you."

Tangled Hair appeared through the storm. A number of Shoshones and Arapahos who had been helping Fawn search fell in behind him. When they heard that Two Robes had been up on the butte, they stared with wide eyes, their hands over their mouths.

"You have come to a sacred place," Tangled Hair said. "No one comes back from there and is the same again."

"I was led there," Two Robes told them. "I followed the tracks of the wolf."

The Shoshones and Arapahos turned back for the village, exclaiming over what they had heard.

"Once again you have shown great medicine," Tangled Hair said. "Do you want to talk to them about the dancing? You could probably tell them to stop and they would."

Two Robes thought for a moment. "It is not for me to decide what is good and what is bad for anyone. Let those who wish to dance go ahead, and those who don't wish to can stand back and watch. Then the world will be right."

The sun shone like a ball of gold when the train left the station the following morning. The temperature hovered near freezing; it was quite pleasant for late December. Still, the Shoshones had given them blankets to wrap themselves in. The open plains would be much colder.

Two Robes settled with Fawn and Tangled Hair among the baggage. Fawn talked again with Tangled Hair about the new religion, advising him to join with the Minneconjou, who would certainly be dancing when they reached Cherry Creek.

Tangled Hair told Fawn that he wanted no more to do with the dance. He had made up his mind to go to his father. As the country went from mountains to plains, the temperature dropped. The snow along the tracks was swept up in the wind like fine white dust.

Tangled Hair studied his father's letter often, running his fingers along the lines of words. He had Two Robes read them to him time and again. He especially liked the part where his father had said, ". . . I can't tell you how hard it is for me not to have seen you all these years. I only hope you can forgive me."

Fawn spent her time in singing songs she had learned in Mason Valley. She sang them low, and with deep feeling. Two Robes no longer tried to dissuade her from thinking about the dance. She had been so taken by the events in Mason Valley that little else entered her reality. Whatever had happened, the dance had impressed itself upon her very strongly.

The Black Hills came into view, covered with snow. Two Robes recalled his experience there, and how Fawn had found him. It seemed that it had happened many years ago. The country had been struck with autumn then. Now it was locked in frost.

He thought also of what had happened on the butte above Wind River. He understood that the wolf had come to tell him he was progressing, and that he was separating farther and farther from those around him.

As they changed trains for the last leg up to Rapid City, Two Robes wondered how his life would progress with Fawn and her children. He had never felt so close to anyone in his life as Fawn. Yet he did not feel the same as she did about Wovoka. He wondered if this would eventually separate them totally.

Nightfall found them camped in a trader's warehouse near the railway station. The trader told Two Robes that Harley

Cullen was due in the following day to pick up a load of supplies for the agent at Cheyenne River. Two Robes was confident they could get a ride.

"Your luck's running pretty good," Cullen told them the following morning. "I wasn't going to make this haul, but I've got something special I was supposed to take up."

Cullen had two more letters for Tangled Hair from his father. At Tangled Hair's insistence, Two Robes read them out loud. Tangled Hair wept openly, overjoyed at the prospect of seeing his father.

Through Two Robes' translation, Cullen gave Tangled Hair a great deal of information regarding Sergeant Betters. "He thinks a lot of you," Cullen said. "And I can tell you, he's a damn good man."

That night, next to a warm fire, Tangled Hair fell into a pleasured sleep, wrapped in new spreads and bedsheets destined for the agent at Cheyenne River. Fawn also fell asleep early, leaving Two Robes to drink real coffee, the first in a long time, and to talk with Cullen.

"Sergeant Betters is more than a little bit worried about his son," Cullen said. "He's chomping at the bit to retire. The army won't let him bring his son on the post to live. They say he's too much Injun for their blood."

"Maybe Tangled Hair can live off the post," Two Robes suggested. "When his father retires, they can both move away."

Cullen scoffed at the idea. "That boy would find himself in a mess of trouble in no time," he told Two Robes. "People wouldn't allow him no peace."

"I had hoped he could be united with his father soon," Two Robes said. "But maybe it would be best if he stayed with the Minneconjou until his father sends for him."

"There's not much other choice," Cullen said. "But that's what worries old Betters. He figures trouble's coming for certain. He thinks it won't be long. Word is that come

February, they're going to open up the ceded land to settlers. That will bring on a pack of problems."

Two Robes then related what he had seen and heard in Mason Valley. He indicated to Cullen that the misery of the Lakota people, together with Wovoka's incredible promises, was certain to bring about a strong push for the new religion.

"Ain't none of that dance could be true, though," Cullen said. "I told you before that it'll fizzle out. I can't see why you'd get so worked up over it."

"You have to understand what kind of power this man, Wovoka, has," Two Robes explained. "There are a lot of Indian people who believe he is Jesus Christ, come back as a red man."

"Just the same, I can't see it as no threat to anyone," Cullen argued. "The agents will tell them to quit their dancing and they will quit. Just like they did with the Sun Dance."

"This is different," Two Robes said. "They believe this dance will bring back the old times. Then the Sun Dance, and all the old ceremonies, will be reintroduced."

Two Robes contemplated telling him about the ghost shirts. He dropped the idea. As it was, Cullen wondered why he was so adamant about the dance. It sounded as if he believed in all this himself.

"You get a bump on the head somewhere?" Cullen asked.

"No, of course not," Two Robes answered. "You just mark my words. This dance will change things."

Cullen got up from the fire and pulled a bottle out from under the wagon seat. "Here," he said. "This ought to help you get all that off your mind."

Two Robes declined, and Cullen popped the cork. "Makes me sleep better," he said.

Late the next day they crossed Cheyenne River. Cullen told them he could take them no farther. "You're on your own the rest of the way to Cherry Creek," he told them. "I've got to go straight to the agency or they'll accuse me of selling these rations on my own."

They thanked Cullen for the ride, turned their faces against the wind, and set out for the village. By midafternoon the following day, the village came into view. Fawn ran into the arms of Hawk and Little Star. They were thin and weak from hunger.

"Mother, it has been so long!" Hawk said. "We thought you would never come back."

"I won't leave you ever again, I promise," Fawn said. She wiped tears from her eyes. "You have both grown. Night Bird has taken good care of you. Where is she?"

"Her baby died and she is still sad." Hawk held up both hands. "All these suns have passed since then. She is very sad."

"She lost her baby?"

"It would not drink milk from her," Little Star said. Her eyes filled with tears. "When the little one died, Night Bird carried her in her arms for a full day."

"Where is Night Bird now?" Fawn asked.

Hawk pointed north of the village. "She goes into the hills to mourn. She sings and cuts herself. She will be back later. She always comes back before dark."

"Maybe I can find her," Fawn said.

"Don't go away again," Little Star begged.

"I must find Night Bird, and you must wait for me," Fawn insisted. "I will have lots of time to spend with you now. Stay with Two Robes until I get back, and he will tell you about the trip across the mountains."

Hawk, especially, was eager to hear what Two Robes had to say. He had missed him and felt happy that he had returned. Now there was hope that Catches Lance might come back, too.

Fawn walked into the hills north of the village. The air was crisp with frost, and the snow crunched underfoot. Few came up into the hills at this time of year, and Fawn had little trouble in following Night Bird's trail. She discovered Night Bird lying on a rock atop a high hill, staring into the sky.

"Night Bird!" Fawn said. "Are you alive?"

Night Bird blinked. "Is it you, Fawn-That-Goes-Dancing? Have I crossed over?"

"You have not crossed over," Fawn told her. "Are you trying to die?"

Night Bird closed her eyes. Tears ran from their corners. "There is nothing left for me in this world. I cannot even keep a child alive."

"You cannot blame yourself," Fawn said, taking her hand. "There is some reason that the baby did not stay with you. Just for now, though, for I can tell you that the child will return."

Night Bird's eyes remained closed. "I may go to the child," she said, "but it doesn't seem that *Wankantanka* will allow it yet. I cannot seem to die."

"I did not say you will die," Fawn told her. "I said the baby will come back to you."

Night Bird opened her eyes. She sat up. "Did I hear you say the baby would come back?"

"I have seen a dance," Fawn said. "I have heard the *Wanekia*, the man that Kicking Bear left our village to see. I know that you will see your baby again."

"How do you know this?"

"It is promised. The *Wanekia*, the one called Wovoka, has told everyone. The world is going to change. Our ancestors are coming back. All of our loved ones are coming back, just like the letter from Spoonhunter to Kicking Bear said. The buffalo will return. There will be no more hunger."

Night Bird came to her feet. She removed a little bag she had tied around her neck and handed it to Fawn. "I have worn this while you were gone, as you asked," she said. "I will give it back now, and hope that what you say will come to pass."

"If you and my children were not so weak, we would travel to see the Messiah," Fawn said. "We could all dance."

"No, I could not travel that far," Night Bird said. "I am not strong enough. I am sorry I couldn't give Hawk and Little Star more food. There wasn't enough."

Night Bird began to sob. Fawn held her tightly. "You must not blame yourself. You did the best you could. My children are fine." She pointed to the sun breaking through the clouds. "See, the sun comes. When Kicking Bear returns with the dance, all of our people will live again."

Night Bird shielded her face from the wind. "Will this really happen?"

Fawn was smiling. "It is promised. You will never have to cry again."

Night Bird stared at her. "It is promised?"

"Yes," Fawn replied. "It is promised."

PART IV
March, 1890–January, 1891

The whole world is coming,
A nation is coming, a nation is coming,
The Eagle has brought the message to the tribe.
The Father says so, the Father says so.
Over the whole Earth they are coming.
The buffalo are coming, the buffalo are coming,
The Crow has brought the message to the tribe,
The Father says so, the Father says so.

Lakota Nation Ghost Dance Song

TWENTY-EIGHT

I N THE spring Shining Horse returned from Mason Valley with the other Lakota full of enthusiasm. Kicking Bear and Short Bull stopped first at Pine Ridge to enlighten Red Cloud and his Oglalas.

Shining Horse did not remain with them, but hurried on to his own people, the Unkpapas, eager to share his experiences with his father. He was given a pony at Pine Ridge and rode first to Cherry Creek to tell those in Kicking Bear's village that the dance had come to the Lakota; soon the *Wasichu* would be gone and the buffalo would again roam the hills and valleys.

"It is called the Ghost Dance," Shining Horse told the council assembled to hear him. "Soon Kicking Bear will return to you and teach you how to welcome the Messiah."

The news was received with excitement. The winter had been extremely harsh, and many had died of sickness and malnutrition. The people longed for deliverance.

Shining Horse wanted to know why Fawn had not returned to Mason Valley, as she had promised. She told him, "I will teach my children the dance when Kicking Bear comes back and shows everyone what to do."

"But you told me you would return," Shining Horse insisted.

"Hawk and Little Star were weak and hungry. Two Robes would not go with me. I would have gone with a friend, but she had just lost a baby and was very weak. It was better that I stayed here."

"Are you no longer with Two Robes?"

"He does not believe in the dance, and I do. But that does not mean we aren't together."

"You should bring your children and come north to Grand River with me," Shining Horse said. "I believe in the dance. We would have a good life together. It will be even better after the Messiah comes and the old ways return."

"I have told you before that I do not believe we are supposed to be together," Fawn told Shining Horse. "I love Two Robes very much even though he does not believe in the dance. If I were to part with him, I would never love another."

"That's what you said before you met Two Robes," Shining Horse pointed out.

"I felt that way for a long time. But if Two Robes and I do not stay together, my words will stick. I will never love again."

"Maybe there are some things I can do to prove that I am worthy of you."

"It is not a matter of your being worthy," Fawn told him. "You are a very special man in your own right. But you are not the one for me."

Shining Horse looked into the north. "I will go up to be with my father. Maybe someday you will change your mind."

"There is one way that you could please me," Fawn said.

"How would that be?"

"Tell Catches Lance to come home. His wife misses him, and I miss him. Tell him he should come back and start his life over again."

"I will tell him if I get the chance," Shining Horse said. "As it is, he rides with the Metal Breasts. They all hate my father. One day the Metal Breasts will go too far and they will die. I will tell Catches Lance to come back down here before that happens."

Catches Lance sat on the steps to his cabin, toying with a whiskey bottle. He stared out across the dry bed of Oak Creek. It was now midsummer and the people were forced to get water from a couple of springs that had not dried up yet. If it did not rain soon, the springs would likely dry up as well. The drought was awful. Even the progressives believed that *Wankantanka* was punishing them. There were no crops, and many of the cattle had wandered off in search of grass and water.

Most of the people were nearing starvation. It was only because he was a Metal Breast that Catches Lance had food. And he had been given the cabin when he helped arrest its former owner. The man, a mixed breed named LaCrosse, had lost his wife to one of White Hair's Metal Breasts. She was now living up the creek with him. LaCrosse had held White Hair responsible.

Bull Head and Shaved Head had stopped LaCrosse before he could shoot White Hair. They had taken him out into the country and had come back without him. No one asked what had happened to LaCrosse.

These days Catches Lance had trouble living with himself. He had little else to do as a Metal Breast but watch the suffering around him. He still had difficulty making it through the long nights, fighting away the memories of Night Bird and his sister.

Every night when he closed his eyes, he saw Night Bird's tears and heard her voice begging him not to leave. He wondered about their baby. It was hard to cope with the knowledge that he had left her at the time she most needed him. And he had let Hawk and Little Star down. He knew how they felt about him. Now they likely would never look at him again.

But there could be no turning back. He had come to gain recognition for himself; if he left now, he would not be able to live with himself. Fawn and her children might like to see him back, and Night Bird would likely take him into her arms again, but there were many among the Minneconjou who considered him a traitor. He could not face these people without seeing himself as a failure there as well.

Catches Lance popped the cork on the bottle. He drained the last swallow, licking the drops of whiskey from the top before throwing the bottle down near the steps with the others. He had not wanted to use it all up, for now he would have to get more.

Whiskey could be found easily enough, but it took something of value to trade for it. Those items of value were increasingly hard to come by. As a Metal Breast, he could enter anyone's home at any time, and sometimes they had items that the traders wanted, like guns or boxes of cartridges. But usually he took horses. He could take them at night and have them hidden before anyone knew they were gone.

Catches Lance knew that he would have to take a full bottle with him if he were to go down to Sitting Bull's village after Shining Horse. The word had come that Shining Horse had finally returned. He had left the reservation without a pass, and Catches Lance had been given the assignment of arresting him.

Well, arresting Shining Horse would bring him a promotion. It bothered him that he would be taking a good friend to the stockade; but, after all, Shining Horse had committed a crime.

Catches Lance rose from the steps. Maybe he could find something to trade for a bottle. There was a man who lived a ways up Oak Creek, just off the reservation, who was always ready to trade. He kept a supply of bottles just to trade for goods.

It seemed like this man wanted more and more for one bottle. At first Catches Lance could get two bottles for a rifle and four bottles for a good pony. Now he had to have two rifles to get a bottle, and was lucky to get two bottles for each horse.

Night would be coming soon. He would have to hurry, for he should get Shining Horse before morning. But it was hard to walk; he kept staggering.

In a cabin up the creek from his own he found an old woman making fry bread.

"What do you want?" the old woman asked. She lived alone since her husband had died.

"Do you have any guns?" Catches Lance asked.

"There are no guns, but you are welcome to eat."

Catches Lance waved her off. "I don't want that. I have to find a gun."

"Who are you going to shoot?" she asked.

"I don't want to shoot," he told her. "I want to trade with the *Wasichu* rancher over here."

"Oh, that. You know that isn't good."

"I don't want you to tell me what is good. What do you have that I can trade?"

"Take my bed if you want. I don't know what you can get for it."

Catches Lance leaned against the door frame. "Ahh! Haven't you got a gun or a horse?"

"A bed is all I have. Do you want to try it out and see how good it is?"

"Maybe I will try it," Catches Lance said. "But I can't stay long."

The old woman handed him a piece of fry bread. "Eat this and then look at the bed."

"Who are you?" Catches Lance asked.

"I am called Crane Woman," she replied. "I once had a son like you. He has crossed over now."

"How did he die?"

"He became a slave to the medicine water that you trade guns and horses for. He said he felt trapped. One day he rode his horse over a cliff."

"I am not trapped," Catches Lance said and stumbled into the room.

She helped him to the small bed in the corner. She made certain that he swallowed the bread; then she helped him lie down.

"We are all going to be gone soon," the Crane Woman said as she put a blanket over him. "They will kill us all, or be certain that we kill one another."

"I am not trapped," Catches Lance repeated. "I will never be trapped. I am my own person." He drifted out of consciousness.

"If I can, I am going to see that you are no longer trapped," Crane Woman promised. "I will help you, and you will be whole again."

"I did not mean to make trouble," Shining Horse told his father. "I only wanted to see the Messiah, and I am glad I did."

"That is good," Sitting Bull said, "but you are the one they want. You should go up to them and not bring the trouble here."

"I won't let them throw me in jail," Shining Horse said. "I did nothing wrong. I will die first. I would be freer that way."

"You have to make that choice," Sitting Bull told him. "I wish you would go and talk to that Minneconjou before he comes down here after you. You promised me there would be no trouble."

"I will find him and talk to him," Shining Horse said. "I just want you to think seriously about the Ghost Dance."

"I will think seriously," Sitting Bull said. "Just take care of your trouble first."

"Maybe I should take the white woman, Catherine Weldon, with me," Shining Horse joked. "You said she moved back here to help us. She could help me by talking to White Hair."

Sitting Bull saw amusement in a lot of things, but this time his mouth remained taut. "She does not like me anymore," he said. "I don't think you would like her now, anyway."

"Why not?"

"She is against the dance coming here. She said it cannot be real."

"I thought she wanted to help our people."

"She has tried to help our people, but she does not know our ways," Sitting Bull said. "While you were gone, she would come down here often from her home on the Cannonball. But all the presents she gave me will not make our lives easier. Now go talk your friend out of arresting you."

Shining Horse rode toward Oak Creek. He knew that Catches Lance had been given a cabin there. When he arrived, he found an old woman helping Catches Lance up the steps. Shining Horse was shocked to see Catches Lance's condition. He appeared to have lost a great deal of weight.

Catches Lance pulled away from the woman, staggered, caught his balance, then called out to Shining Horse, "You are under arrest!"

"I want to talk to you about that," Shining Horse said.

"There is nothing to talk about. I am going to take you up to the stockade."

"Save yourself the ride and shoot me. I will not go alive."

"If that's the way you want it."

Shining Horse watched while Catches Lance pushed past the old woman and into his cabin. The old woman hurried after him, trying to get him to listen to reason. Catches Lance reappeared with the rifle and thumbed the hammer back with trembling fingers.

Shining Horse sat his pony and opened his arms to the sky. He closed his eyes and took a deep breath. He waited. There was no sound of a rifle being fired, nor the searing pain of a bullet.

When Shining Horse opened his eyes, Catches Lance had dropped his rifle and was on his knees, weeping.

"Get down and help me," the old woman said. "I am going to give him some herbs and place him in a sweat house."

Shining Horse dismounted. "He won't stand for it."

"Yes he will," she said. "You are going to help me tie him up."

Shining Horse looked at her; she looked back fiercely. "He has had enough grief," she said. "I will get the bad medicine water out of him and drive the evil spirits away."

Shining Horse removed Catches Lance's shirt and pants and held him while the old woman bound his hands and feet. Catches Lance was too weak to resist.

"Who are you?" Shining Horse asked.

"My name is Crane Woman," she answered. "I have seen too many good friends hurting one another. It is time that it stopped."

"Are you related to him?"

"We are all related," she said. "Or have you forgotten?"

"He and I were close friends once. I am Shining Horse, son of Sitting Bull. I am going to try to take him back down to Cherry Creek. His sister wants him to return home."

"You will not make his sister happy if you bring him back like this," Crane Woman said. "He will only make bad trouble. I will need time to get the evil spirits out of him."

Crane Woman nodded toward the dry creek and told Shining Horse that there was a pothole still filled with water from a spring just beside the bank. Shining Horse dragged Catches Lance down toward the pothole, where a small sweat lodge stood nearby. A little fire had been started, and rocks were heating in the center of the flames.

"It looks as though you had planned this before I got here," Shining Horse said. He had put Catches Lance in the lodge.

"I want to save somebody from all of this," Crane Woman said. "I have seen too much."

"Our people will be saved from this very soon," Shining Horse told her. "There is a dance coming that will bring back the old times."

Crane Woman added wood to the fire and turned the hot stones over.

"I have heard about it," Crane Woman said. "Is your father going to dance?"

"He is not sure it will work," Shining Horse said. "But he will not stop our people if they want to. I have seen the dance, and I know of its power. I will show him that it works. Soon everyone will be together with their fallen loved ones."

Shining Horse watched Crane Woman place stones inside the sweat lodge. She took a flask of water and poured it over the stones, then closed the door flap.

"Remove your clothes and get inside with your friend," she said. "Pray for guidance."

Shining Horse hesitated. "I do not feel right."

"If he is your friend, you should feel good about it," she said.

Shining Horse disrobed and entered the sweat. The ground was covered with fresh sage leaves, and a bowl of sweetgrass sat burning beside the door flap.

Catches Lance lay on his side, moaning. Shining Horse helped him to a sitting position and wiped his sweaty face in the darkness.

"There are more tears than sweat," Catches Lance said. "I have been so dirty for so long."

"You have not been dirty," Shining Horse said. "You have been living in filth, but we are not responsible for it."

"Oh, but I have wanted power," Catches Lance said. "To be honored was more important to me than life itself. I will have a hard time digging out of the hole I have made for myself."

Crane Woman opened the door flap and added hot rocks to the pile in the middle of the lodge. She went back out and returned with more water. The interior of the lodge thickened with steam.

"There is too much for me to see at one time," Catches Lance said. "Please, take me out of here."

"You should stay longer," Shining Horse said.

"No! Get me out of here!"

Crane Woman opened the door flap. "Who is yelling?"

"He says it is too much for the first time," Shining Horse said.

Catches Lance had fallen over on his side. He jerked and trembled and begged to be released.

"It is the herbs," Crane Woman said. "They are acting on him. He is worse off than I thought."

"Will he die?" Shining Horse asked.

"Help me take him out," Crane Woman said. "I will give him some water and some different herbs. Maybe I should go slower with him."

Shining Horse dragged Catches Lance out of the sweat lodge and over to the water. He loosened the bonds and helped Catches Lance into the pool.

"I would be better off dead," Catches Lance said.

"No, you must live," Shining Horse told him. "You must recover and go down to be with your wife and your sister. You can dance with them, and then you will be well forever. You will see your mother again, and all will be well."

Shining Horse noticed Crane Woman glaring at him. "What is the matter with you?" he asked.

"What is all this talk for?" she said. "How can you tell Catches Lance about his problems when you don't even have yourself taken care of?"

"What is wrong with me?"

"Go back into the sweat lodge and find out. Ask yourself what you should be doing. Ask if you should be pushing everyone toward this dance."

Shining Horse stood up. "It is time for me to go back to my father," he said. He turned to Catches Lance. "You tell me when you are ready to return to your village and I will go with you. I think it will be at about the time the Ghost Dance begins. We will all dance together and the world will change. Nothing will be the same again, ever. Nothing."

TWENTY-NINE

THE SUN rose over numerous sweat lodges that dotted the banks of Cherry Creek. Four moons remained before the start of the new year. Hundreds of Minneconjou had gathered to hear Kicking Bear address the people and lead them in the Ghost Dance. It was said that after the passing of the next cold moons, when the green came again to the land, the Messiah would appear and the world would again belong to the Lakota people.

Kicking Bear had returned in midsummer and had talked before about this. He had told the people that they would have to know the dance and take part in it; otherwise, they would perish, along with the *Wasichu.* "You will have to be dancing so that you can be uplifted when the earth changes come," he would say. "If you are not dancing, you will be buried or swept away, and you will never see the buffalo again."

Now Kicking Bear would speak to his largest gathering. In his mind he had become every bit as powerful as Wovoka, the

Paiute who had taught him. Maybe even more powerful. After all, the Lakota had always lived a different kind of life, so the dance should fit that life.

Since returning from Mason Valley, Two Robes had spent much of his time in contemplation. He sought the meaning of his life among the Minneconjou, but he could get no answers to his prayers. He prayed to the God of his childhood and got no response. It made him feel that he was being punished for having accepted the Lakota way of faith.

But he no longer found comfort in visions, either. When he searched for the wolves, they were not there. He had fasted and prayed and had gone into the hills. Yet nothing had come to him. Once he saw a solitary male trotting along a trail, but the wolf only glanced at him and continued on.

The people now saw him as nothing more than one of them. He was respected, but not seen as a prophet, not like Kicking Bear. All but a few of those who had been baptized now rejected the *Wasichu* god, looking instead to the end of the White Man's Road and the new beginning for the Lakota people.

When asked about the dance, Two Robes would say, "Do what you feel is best for you." He and Fawn remained close, but he could sense her disappointment at his not believing. His emotions were being strongly tested. It was not up to him to direct anyone else, yet it tore at him to watch Fawn grow ever more devout in the new religion.

Tangled Hair had decided to remain an observer as well. He would watch the dancing without opinion. He stared at his father's letters often and sometimes journeyed into the agency, anxious to find out whether any letters had arrived for him. Occasionally one had, and he would have Two Robes read his father's words to him.

Though the Ghost Dance religion had become known to the agents, they made no demands. Two Robes thought of the freighter, Cullen, and his attitude. "It won't amount to nothing," he had said. So far, none of the white authorities had become alarmed.

Two Robes knew that this would change. Though many of the Lakota had rejected the religion, those who had embraced it would hold on to their dreams until the end. He realized it would do no good to worry; what was meant to happen would take place, no matter how much he tried to alter it. He sat and watched, hoping that Fawn and her children would still be with him when it was over.

The morning had nearly passed, and the dance would soon begin. Specially appointed men, warriors of good faith from the old times, assisted Kicking Bear in preparing the people for the ceremony. Long lines of people waited to be painted with suns, moons, and stars, and to have crosses drawn in precision across their foreheads and along their cheeks and chins.

Dots of blue and black, and sometimes yellow, blended in with the main color of red that bonded each dancer with the next. Ghost Shirts, adorned with magpies and crows, eagles, crosses, stars and stripes, and also turtles and otters, covered nearly all of the men. Each dancer wore an eagle feather, the symbol that he or she would be united with the Father when the *Wanekia* arrived to change the world.

"You are ready for the dance," Two Robes said to Fawn. "I will pray that you see your mother and learn many things from her."

"I would ask that you do more than that," Fawn said. "Your heart is good and the Powers can see that. For this reason, I am asking that you paint the symbols of the dance on my dress. I feel that this will help me cross over."

"How can I do that?" Two Robes asked. "I don't believe in the dance."

"But you believe in the Creator, as one who wishes good for all," she said. "With all your heart, you try to reach Him. Help me reach out, also."

"Maybe you should wear my chasuble," Two Robes suggested. "I could paint it for you."

"I cannot," Fawn said. "The Ghost Shirts are for the men. Maybe someday you will paint it for yourself. I hope that day will come. But I must wear my symbols on my dress."

Two Robes agreed to paint her dress. She handed him a palette of various colored paints and sat down.

With mixed feelings, Two Robes began to draw symbols on the back of Fawn's dress. In the center of the back he drew a large red cross. Above the cross he drew a dark brown eagle, its wings spread wide. On both sides of the cross he added magpies, and on the bottom, a crow. He drew a turtle on each side of the lower back.

Fawn turned, and Two Robes saw the light in her eyes. He wanted badly to kiss her, but the moment was not right. Her joy was in the hope of seeing her mother.

Two Robes painted two chickadees above the right breast of the dress, and a woodpecker above the left. Then he handed the paints back to Fawn.

"I hope you learn what you wish to learn," he said. "Just remember that I love you very much."

"I love you very much as well. I already feel as if I have been touched by *Wankantanka*," she said.

Fawn left to take Hawk and Little Star to the dance circle. Two Robes almost ran after her to tell her that he, too, wished to dance. But he held back. He could not take part in something that tore him in two directions.

The sun reached its peak. The dancers grouped together, joining hands to form a huge circle around a massive cottonwood tree. Then all waited in silence.

Kicking Bear stood near the cottonwood, wearing only a breechclout. He held a sacred pipe to the Four Directions, then to Earth and Sky, and handed the pipe to an old man. Kicking Bear turned to the east, his arms outstretched.

"Listen, our Father, Great One, the Creator of all, to your children, who humbly ask your blessing this day. Our hearts sing for the old times, for the buffalo that grazed the hunting grounds of our forefathers. We who dance here this day humbly ask to be taken back there, to see the geese in flight and to sleep in the warm lodges we once knew. Show us our lost loved ones and teach them what is to come. Help them to see the good things and to know the returning world of our grandfathers."

The old man who had taken the pipe raised his head to the sky and began to sing:

> My pony is running, running as before;
> The buffalo are coming, coming as before.
> My bow is strong and my arrows fly straight,
> Says the Father, says the Father.
> I see a new light in the eyes of my mother,
> Says the Father, says the Father.

The circle began to move, a long, rhythmic flow of bodies and emotions. Women cried for their dead warriors; the old begged to be young again. Small children, their eyes wide with wonderment, weaved with their parents and relatives, singing the songs as best they could.

Two Robes sat a short distance away, his eyes on Fawn. She danced with Hawk on one side and Little Star on the other. Night Bird held Hawk by his other hand, singing for the return of her dead baby, crying for the life it had not been able to enjoy.

The circle moved steadily faster. Kicking Bear and his appointed warriors dashed around among the dancers, waving eagle-feather fans and rattles. They seemed tireless, coaxing on those who would falter, keeping everyone flowing in the circle.

Late in the afternoon, the circle began to break. Individually or in groups, dancers fell to the ground, some kicking, some lying motionless. Those still on their feet danced over their prone bodies and joined hands, chanting and praying, pushing themselves.

Hawk and Little Star broke from the circle and fell asleep in the center. By late afternoon, the circle had filled with children of all sizes, and many infants as well.

Night Bird fell and lay still. Fawn stepped from the circle and lay down next to Two Robes. She was weeping.

He placed her head in his lap and stroked her hair. "What is bothering you?" he asked.

"Though I try very hard, I am not able to see my mother," she replied. "Why not? What am I doing wrong?"

"I can't tell you," Two Robes said. "It seems to me that you are reverent enough. Maybe the time is not right."

"I know that my mother has nothing against the dance," Fawn said. "When we both stood near Wovoka in the dream, she agreed that he was a good man. I do not understand."

"What makes you so certain your mother will return to you? Perhaps she is not meant to."

Fawn sat up. "Why would you say such a thing as that? Certainly my mother is to return. All the ancestors will return." She stood up. "I will dance until I see my mother and hear her words again. She *will* come back to me. You will see, Two Robes, and one day you, too, will believe."

As another moon passed, the Ghost Dance rose to an even greater fever pitch. The weather remained warm and open, allowing the daily dances to continue late into the night. Kicking Bear's followers grew more devout, as did Short Bull's. Everywhere the Lakota danced, the people rejoiced in knowing that the time to be with their departed loved ones was close at hand.

Many leaders who had decided to take the White Man's Road now reverted back to their old ways. Hump, an older warrior who had held great prestige, decided to throw off his Metal Breast uniform and take up the dance. Big Foot, Kicking Bear's uncle, who had cried for schools and missionaries, was as excited as any of his young men at first. When he saw no immediate results, his enthusiasm lessened.

In most camps, the elders wanted peace. No dances. Nothing new that would cause problems. Gradually the young men took control, intent on living the lives the elders always talked about. There would be no stopping them.

When Red Cloud of the Oglala began to talk against the dance, he was labeled too old to lead and too influenced by the *Wasichu*. Big Foot, whose health had begun to fail, gave in to a medicine man named Yellow Bird, who, against Big Foot's wishes, brought the Ghost Dance to an even higher pitch.

Concern spread quickly among the agents. One of them, a man named Royer, from Pine Ridge, was new. He had had no experience with any of the Indian people, let alone with the Lakota, in a crisis. He was the product of a revised political system that allowed senators and representatives to fill positions from within their own districts.

The agents now visited the dances, expressing concern over the frenzy. Officials from various government agencies took trips to investigate. They were either frightened or amused. Some were worried, but most of them declared that the snow would return everything to normal.

The military waited, wondering what would develop. General Nelson Miles, commander of the region, kept a close watch. He thought little of Indian agents and saw no reason to allow them to make any important decisions.

The agents, well aware of Miles' attitude, were afraid of losing control. They ordered their Metal Breasts out to break up the dancing before the army could take over. The Metal Breasts were met by painted warriors brandishing rifles, and they reported back that there was no way to stop the dancing.

The agents pondered their circumstances, then reported that they had full control and there would be no need for the military to intervene. The agent on the Rosebud told the Brulé that they would receive no more rations until the dancing ceased. When he was called to Washington to defend his position, the Brulé went wild. A great number joined Short Bull.

Meanwhile, Kicking Bear gathered more and more followers. Other devout leaders strengthened their own camps. Everywhere the people exclaimed over how they had seen their lost relatives and talked of how there would be great happiness when the Messiah appeared.

Just over a third of the Lakota nation had now embraced the Ghost Dance. Soon labeled "fanatics," the devout made their own camps away from the agencies. They received no rations and began to butcher their own breeding stock for food, defying the agents to stop them. They sold their firewood for arms and ammunition and painted themselves for war. They scattered about the area so that there was no one place where the agents and Metal Breasts could go and demand the dancing to be stopped.

Nowhere was the dancing more frenzied than in Kicking Bear's camp. Two Robes had watched the escalation. He had questioned Fawn on many occasions regarding her mother.

"My mother will come when the time is right," Fawn would always say. "I will not stop dancing, for I know it is a good thing."

Night Bird remained hopeful of seeing her child. She and Fawn danced together, each insisting that they would be carried across when the world changed. No one was more delighted to see Fawn dancing so earnestly than Shining Horse, who rode into the camp one afternoon with two other Unkpapas. He had come to invite Kicking Bear up to Sitting Bull's village.

"White Hair will not let my father go anywhere," Shining Horse told Fawn and Two Robes. "He was invited to Pine Ridge by Short Bull, but he couldn't go. Now I will ask Kicking Bear to help me show my father the medicine of this new religion."

Shining Horse said that everyone had heard about how Kicking Bear had gathered many hundreds of followers to himself. There were those who now considered Kicking Bear a powerful prophet, perhaps every bit as powerful as Wovoka.

"What did you learn of Catches Lance?" Fawn asked.

"He has become sickened by the bad medicine water," Shining Horse told her. "But an old woman is caring for him now. In time, he will get well and return down here."

"Are you certain?" Fawn asked.

"I will see to it," Shining Horse told her. He looked at Two Robes. "I will help you and your brother to prepare for the coming Messiah."

Shining Horse talked with Kicking Bear and persuaded him to ride up to Grand River and help him teach his father. "In time, we will all be united, and there will be no one on these plains but ourselves," Shining Horse said.

Two Robes watched the dancing. The sun had set, and the evening was rainy and cold. Despite this, many still remained in the circle, singing and dancing, working toward a vision.

Kicking Bear had returned from Grand River and had told of how the Unkpapa had embraced the dance. "Even Sitting Bull joined in the circle," he said. "Some Metal Breasts came and they also were convinced. Then other Metal Breasts showed up and forced me to leave."

Everyone was encouraged that the Unkpapa had joined the dance. No one had known what Sitting Bull might do. Now the Unkpapas were also dancing to bring the sacred circle together again.

Tonight, Fawn danced with increased intensity. Then, at last, she slid to the ground and lay writhing. Two Robes hurried over to her, but he did not touch her. He awaited her return to consciousness.

Hawk and Little Star joined him, staring at their mother.

"I worry about her," Hawk said. "She does not seem the same since she came back from the valley where the Messiah lives. I wish she hadn't gone there."

"I wish she would wake up," Little Star added. "I don't like this."

Two Robes did his best to comfort them. "Your mother will be fine," he said. "I will move her into the lodge so she will be warm."

When Two Robes began to move Fawn, three of Kicking Bear's assistants hurried over and stopped him. "She is not to be moved," they said. "Do you want her to be trapped on the Other Side?"

"I'm afraid she will fall sick out in this rain," he told them.

They were persistent. "You must leave her alone. If you don't, we will force you away from here."

"What about the children?" Two Robes asked.

"We will have one of the women care for them," an assistant said. "Night Bird is also on the Other Side."

As the woman escorted Hawk and Little Star away, Two Robes greeted Tangled Hair, who had just come from the agency. Under his coat he held a newspaper.

"It is almost too dark for you to see the marks," Tangled Hair said, "but I believe that you should look at them. I saw a lot of the *Wasichu* reading the paper and getting excited. Something has happened."

Two Robes and Tangled Hair hurried to the lodge, where the woman had built a fire and was comforting the children. While she fed them broth and laid them down to rest, Two Robes unfurled the paper in the firelight.

It was a copy of the *Chicago Daily Tribune*. Two full pages had been dedicated to the "Sioux problem" in the West. The headlines read:

TO WIPE OUT THE WHITES

What the Indians Expect of the Coming Messiah

FEARS OF AN OUTBREAK

Old Sitting Bull Stirring Up the Excited Redskins

A WOMAN'S EVIL INFLUENCE

Mrs. Weldon Partly Responsible for Sitting Bull's Conduct

Reprinted was a letter that White Hair McLaughlin had sent to Washington, D.C. Two Robes skimmed through it, stopping at the most alarming sections:

Standing Rock Agency, October 17, 1890

Hon H.T. Morgan
Commissioner of Indian Affairs

Sir:

. . . *I trust I may not be considered an alarmist . . . but I do feel it my duty to report the present "craze" and nature of the excitement existing among the Sitting Bull faction of Indians over the expected Indian millennium, the annihilation of the white man and supremacy of the Indian, which is looked for in the near future and promised by the Indian medicine men as not later than next spring, when the new grass begins to appear, and is known amongst the Sioux as the return of the ghosts.*

. . . *Sitting Bull is high priest and leading apostle of this latest Indian absurdity . . . and if he were not here, this craze, so general among the Sioux, would never have gotten a foothold at this agency. . . . Sitting Bull is a polygamist, libertine, habitual liar, active obstructionist, and a great obstacle in the civilization of these people, and he is so devoid of any of the nobler traits of character, and so devoted to the old Indian ways and superstitions that it is very doubtful if any change for the better will ever come over him at his present age of fifty-six years. . . .*

Two Robes did not finish the letter, but turned instead to another bold headline and story:

SOLDIERS ARE READY FOR HIM
The Army in the Northwest Prepared
to Quell Any Uprising

Standing Rock Agency, ND, Oct. 27—Special—For the last four weeks, Sitting Bull has been inviting the Sioux Indians in this vicinity to an uprising. . . . Several hundred of them have agreed to go on the warpath at his bidding.

Two Robes put down the paper and stared into the fire.

"Tell me what it means," Tangled Hair said. "You look like you have already seen the ghosts returning."

"I see a great deal of trouble ahead," Two Robes said. "I must get up to Grand River and show this to Shining Horse. I don't know whether he has seen it or not, but his father is in grave danger."

"What does it say?" Tangled Hair asked again.

"Let me borrow a pony," Two Robes said.

They hurried through the rain toward Tangled Hair's lodge, where they picked up a pad saddle and a hackamore. Two Robes related what the articles said, and Tangled Hair grew angry.

"Why would they say that?" he asked. "No one here wants war. No one on Grand River would want to fight, either. Would they?"

"Of course not," Two Robes said. "This could be a way to get the people to stop dancing. But it won't be the Lakota who will read the papers."

Tangled Hair found one of his ponies along the stream, picketed with a number of others in the shelter of the cottonwoods. He helped Two Robes saddle the pony, thinking all the while that his father was part of the army.

Two Robes mounted quickly. "Take care of Hawk and Little Star until Fawn comes around, will you?"

"Yes, I will," Tangled Hair said. "I will take care of Fawn, too, as best I can. What do you think you can do up there?"

"I don't really know," Two Robes replied. "But I do want Catches Lance to come back with me. There is bound to be a lot of trouble now, and we should all be together to face it."

THIRTY

SHINING HORSE sat next to his father, asking him if he had seen anything during his time of dancing. Though a light snow was falling and his breath was a mist, Sitting Bull wiped sweat from his brow.

"I saw nothing. I felt nothing. Maybe it is because of all the crosses on the Ghost Shirts. And the stripes. I never did like those things. They remind me of the *Wasichu*."

"Don't think about the *Wasichu*," Shining Horse said. "Think about your youth. Think about the old days."

"No," Sitting Bull said. "Those times are gone. I am getting old."

"You will see the Other Side," Shining Horse promised. "You will fall down and see the world as you once knew it. Just have hope."

Sitting Bull then asked, "Have you fallen and looked across to the Other Side?"

"No, I have not," Shining Horse answered honestly. "I am

still waiting for that time myself. But I have faith that it will come."

Sitting Bull continued to wipe his brow. "The people certainly have faith. Ever since Kicking Bear was here."

"We should not have allowed the Metal Breasts to come and intervene," Shining Horse said. "They had no right to make him leave here."

"If we had killed them, the Bluecoats would have come from Yates and killed us," Sitting Bull said. "It is not right that White Hair does what he does, but we cannot stop him."

"Why didn't he accept your offer to tour the other agencies, and to go west to see the Messiah?" Shining Horse asked. "Surely he would see that if we were left alone, the dance would not hurt anyone."

"That is the kind of man he is," Sitting Bull replied. "He has decided that the Ghost Dance is something he cannot accept. It does not matter that it is part of a religion we have a right to believe in if we so choose. Instead, he wants our people to accept the *Wasichu* way of praying. That is something I will never do."

"Many of those who embraced the *Wasichu* god before are now dancing the Ghost Dance in this camp, and on Rosebud and Pine Ridge as well. We will be held responsible for that."

"Our people should be able to choose how they want to worship," Sitting Bull said. "The *Wasichu* are free to talk to their god however they want."

"Maybe Kicking Bear and Short Bull have the right idea," Shining Horse said slowly. "Maybe we should arm our people and show White Hair and the Metal Breasts that the Ghost Shirts have strong medicine."

"They should dance if they want to," Sitting Bull said, "but they should not be fighting. That is no good anymore."

"That is something that might come," Shining Horse said. "It would be wise to be prepared for it."

Shining Horse stood up with his father as a lone rider entered the village. Shining Horse stared in amazement. "It is

Two Robes, the holy man that I told you about," he told
Sitting Bull. "He has finally decided to come up here and
meet you."

Two Robes reined in his pony and dismounted. He greeted
Shining Horse and was formally introduced to Sitting Bull.
Shining Horse couldn't help but notice the rolled-up newspa-
per under Two Robes' arm.

"You must come smoke with us," Sitting Bull said. "I have
heard a lot about you. What brings you up to visit?"

"I have news that is very important," Two Robes said. He
handed the newspaper to Shining Horse. "Read this. I believe
you will see that we have a lot to discuss."

Shining Horse read the articles, his eyes wide with shock.
Sitting Bull wanted to know what the paper said that was so
bad.

"White Hair wants to get rid of you," Shining Horse said
bluntly. "He wrote a letter to Washington, and the press
printed it in the paper. It makes you look like you want to go
to war with the Bluecoats."

Sitting Bull stood in silence, watching the dancers. "I will
not tell them to stop," he announced. "I don't care what kind
of lies are printed about me, I will allow my people to do what
they want. *Wankantanka* will take care of them."

"How about you?" Two Robes asked. "It would seem that
your life is in danger."

"Maybe we should take you into hiding," Shining Horse
suggested. "We could find a place in *Mako sica* and stay there
until the Messiah comes."

"No, no, I am too old to go running anywhere," Sitting Bull
said. "That would just make White Hair happy and convince
the others that they are right. I will stay here."

Shining Horse read more from the paper. "Father, Two
Robes is right. Your life is in grave danger."

"My life has been in danger for a time now," Sitting Bull
said.

Shining Horse and Two Robes looked at one another.

"A man knows these things," Sitting Bull said. "Come now and we will smoke."

Two Robes followed Shining Horse and his father into the cabin. Sitting Bull lit a pipe and offered it to the Earth and Sky, and to the Four Directions. Then he passed it to Two Robes.

"I would like to hear about you," Sitting Bull said. "You have done much, and I would like to hear you tell about it."

Two Robes told his story from the beginning. Sitting Bull laughed at times, nodded in agreement, and often raised the pipe in an offering of thanks to *Wankantanka*.

"The Creator has wanted you to live," Sitting Bull said when Two Robes had finished. "You must have things left to do on this earth."

"I learned much after coming to these lands," Two Robes said. He pulled a worn book from his pocket. "Your son gave me this on the train as we rode out here. The marks in the book say that all people are the same, no matter how they are born. They tell how a man who was imprisoned learned how to meet God. He saw light from the darkness of his cell."

Sitting Bull took the book and closed his hands over it. "There is Truth here. And there is much good. Did this man suffer of his own choosing?"

"He was forced into prison," Two Robes said. "He was a Black Robe with new teachings. Other Black Robes who did not agree with his ideas persecuted him."

"Did you ever hear of our Sun Dance?" Sitting Bull asked. "The old Sun Dance, where the people offered themselves to suffer and to talk to *Wankantanka*?"

"I have heard some things about it," Two Robes replied. "I wish I could have seen it."

"The *Wasichu* made us stop," Sitting Bull said. "They called us savages and barbarians. Now they are starving us so that we will not dance the Ghost Dance."

"There has never been a time when people treated one another fairly," Two Robes said. "I believe that Wovoka wishes that time would come. But there is no shirt ever made that will save everyone from harm."

"I believe, too, that suffering makes one closer to the Creator," Sitting Bull said. "But some are made to suffer more than others, for the wrong reasons. One man should not be allowed to own another man. No one can own my spirit. I feel right with *Wankantanka*, and I have nothing to fear."

Shining Horse stood up and walked to the doorway. He opened the door and looked out into the storm. He bowed his head and began to weep.

Sitting Bull handed the book back to Two Robes. "The snow is falling," he said. "It is a pure night."

"I have never met you until this day," Two Robes told Sitting Bull, "but I feel as though I have always known you. The first time I met your son, he told me there were men among the Lakota people who were more holy than the *Wasichu* saints I had learned about. I know now that I have met one of them, and for that I am grateful to the God who watches over us all."

There was silence in the cabin. Shining Horse left the door open and rejoined them. Two Robes stood.

"You should stay and sleep here," Sitting Bull offered.

"Thank you," Two Robes said, "but I must find a young Minneconjou and talk him into going back to his family."

Sitting Bull nodded. "Good luck in finding him and in talking with him."

Two Robes and Shining Horse hugged one another tightly.

"I know we have always thought differently in many ways," Shining Horse said, "but we think alike in the most important of matters."

"I will leave the paper with you," Two Robes told him. "I have no more use for it."

"I will use it when I go to the outhouse," Sitting Bull said. "Send more up."

Two Robes rode up to Catches Lance's cabin on Oak Creek. It was nearly dark by the time he arrived, and the snow had begun to fall heavily.

Catches Lance was sleeping, a half-filled bottle of whiskey sitting near the bed. He came awake in a foul mood, but straightened up when he saw that it was Two Robes.

"How did you get here?" he asked.

"I came to warn Sitting Bull that the agents and newsmen are blaming him for the Ghost Dance," Two Robes replied. "The papers are filled with lies."

"I know what is happening," Catches Lance said. "I am a Metal Breast." He rose, dashed to the door and vomited off the steps.

Two Robes helped Catches Lance back to the bed. "I told Fawn I would try to bring you back down," he said. "It would be good if you left here."

"I want to go back," Catches Lance said, "but I am afraid."

"Everyone wants you back. You could get well down there."

"I want to get well before I go. An old woman here is doing her best to help me. I guess I just don't know how to make myself stop this."

"Do you want to stop it? I mean, to *really* stop it?"

"Yes. I want to quit in the worst way."

"Then let the old woman help you," Two Robes said. "Do whatever she asks of you. It will be hard at first, but you can do it if you really want to."

Catches Lance pointed to the bottle. "Would you take that and pour it out for me?"

"You should get up and pour it out yourself. That would be good for you."

Catches Lance got up from the bed. He reached slowly for the bottle. He studied the remaining contents for a time, then made his way to the door. Two Robes heard the splash of the whiskey in the snow. When Catches Lance had finished pouring, he turned back inside and sat down on the bed.

"The old woman uses herbs and a sweat bath," he told Two Robes. "It will take some time, but I will go through with it until I am healed."

"Just be sure to understand that you are a good person,"

Two Robes told him. "You have to care about yourself, or you can't care about anyone else."

"That is the truth," Catches Lance said. "I wish I could go back down to Cherry Creek with you now. But I want to get well. Then I will come. Tell Fawn and Night Bird that, and tell Hawk and Little Star. I will be back to give them pony rides."

"I will tell them," Two Robes promised. "Hurry, though, for trouble is coming. We should all be together when it arrives."

The sky was dark and overcast, yet the temperature was mild as columns of the Ninth Cavalry rode into the Pine Ridge agency just before dawn on November 20, 1890. The Buffalo Soldiers, in their buffalo coats and muskrat hats, were followed by the infantry: four companies of the Second Regiment and one of the Eighth Regiment. The three hundred and seventy men, a Hotchkiss cannon, and a Gatling gun brought the power needed to stop the reported uprising on Pine Ridge.

Leading them was Brigadier General John R. Brooke, whose orders had been to come to the aid of Dr. Daniel F. Royer, the new agent at Pine Ridge. Royer had not realized what he was getting into and had repeatedly wired the Commissioner of Indian Affairs for military assistance.

General Nelson A. Miles had assumed authority when Royer wired that "Indians are dancing in the snow and are wild and crazy. I have fully informed you that the employees and government property at this agency have no protection and are at the mercy of the Ghost Dancers. . . . We need protection, and we need it now."

Sergeant Betters, bone weary after the long train rides and night marches, watched to see that the tall Sibley tents were erected in straight lines and that the supply wagons were positioned so as to be protected by the troops at all times.

In his estimation, the whole affair had been blown way out of proportion. The Lakota who gathered to watch the army encamp itself showed no signs of getting ready to fight. In his many years of Indian fighting, he had never seen warlike Indians standing in huddled fear, their hands held over their mouths.

"Where are the dancers?" the men asked. "Where are the guns? We were told to be ready to fight right away."

General Brooke had given specific orders that fighting would be the last resort. Sergeant Betters prayed it would never come to that. He took little consolation from the fact that they had not been called north to the Cheyenne River agency, where Tangled Hair was still living with the Minneconjou. Reports held that matters there were far worse than here at Pine Ridge, or over at Rosebud, where soldiers had also been called in.

Though he had no idea of how much Tangled Hair was involved with the Ghost Dance religion, Sergeant Betters did know that his son lived in the same camp as one of the targeted leaders, Kicking Bear. The trouble could be the worst up there. Nearby Fort Bennett had been reinforced with troops from other forts, to prepare for the same time of march.

Word around the post held that the army intended to circle the reservations and force the end of the new religion, one way or another. The agents hadn't been able to handle the situation, even by cutting off rations, so no other alternative existed.

"What's wrong with letting them dance?" Cort had asked Sergeant Betters. He had wanted to see how honest the sergeant would be.

"Do I have to tell you that you don't mess with the laws made by the white folk?" Betters had asked him. "Unless, of course, you happen to be one of the rich white folk."

No one in either the Eighth or the Ninth had ever accused Sergeant Betters of pulling punches. Everyone knew that he was referring to the fact that the army, in marching onto the reservations, had broken treaty agreements once again. It didn't seem to matter that the commission that had taken the land from the Sioux had failed to fulfill its promises; as soon as the Indians took a stand, they were to be severely punished.

Of all the campaigns he had experienced, Sergeant Betters knew that this one would be by far the hardest. In all his years, he had marched straight ahead into any conflict. This time he wanted nothing more than to ride back down to Fort Robinson.

In just three days, Sergeant Betters would have become eligible for retirement, able to leave the fighting behind and move with his son to someplace nice and warm. Now he had been put on notice that his tour of duty would not end until a successful conclusion to the Sioux problem had been reached.

Sergeant Betters knew there would be no easy solution.

With dawn of the following day there came news that the uprising Indians would not give in to the army. Though many of the Indian people on the Pine Ridge and Rosebud reservations had moved their lodges to the agency grounds, Short Bull had taken his followers and fled into the Badlands.

They had taken a stand atop a mesa known to the local Indians as the Stronghold. Their camp was at the northern end of a large mesa called Cuny Table and attached to it by a small land bridge. There was but one trail onto the Stronghold, and it led in from the east.

Sioux messengers were even now taking word of the Bluecoats' arrival to all the other villages. Sergeant Betters worried that Tangled Hair might now be among the militants who had fled into the Badlands.

While the military sent peace emissaries to the Badlands, reporters arrived from all of the major newspapers in the country. Many of them discovered that bloodshed was not as imminent as they had hoped, and they amused themselves with shooting portraits of one another wrapped in cartridge belts, holding rifles and pistols. Many saw to it that their assignments to the conflict remained justified by creating inflammatory headlines. The November 25th issue of the *Chicago Daily Tribune* read:

GETTING READY TO FIGHT
The Indians Massing for a Stand
Against the Troops
Reds Ready for a Battle

At the same time, a Nebraska reporter for the *Chadron Advocate* wrote: "We left Pine Ridge Agency Wednesday afternoon . . . a peaceful, orderly, well-behaved place. . . . The smoke of a thousand tepees rose in the still, hazy air; twice a thousand ponies grazed on the sunny hillsides."

A reporter for the *Pierre Free Press* branded the situation a "stupendous fake" and a "grand farce." The *Rapid City Journal* reported, "Everything was quiet today at the agency and no trouble was expected."

Sergeant Betters was interested to read that Charles Moody of the *Sturgis Weekly Record* was tired of seeing "silly sensational reports." In his opinion, the Ghost Dance had been "worked up into a very wonderful and exciting matter by pinheaded 'war correspondents' and other irresponsible parties."

More peace missions were sent to the Stronghold. All of them failed. Matters grew worse as the Ghost Dancers raided nearby ranches for livestock and stole rifles and ammunition. Within a week, another company of the Ninth Cavalry arrived at Pine Ridge from Fort McKinney, Wyoming. Major Guy V. Henry led them into formation and announced that he had been ordered to assume full command of the Ninth.

Sergeant Betters flinched at the news. Major Henry had lost one eye and half of his face at the Battle of the Rosebud. He would no doubt be looking for some of the same Sioux warriors who had been in that fight.

On November 26, Sergeant Betters found himself feeling more depressed than he had at any other time in his life. To see his son would be very difficult, if not impossible, before a major outbreak took place, for on that day the entire Seventh Cavalry, under Colonel James W. Forsyth, came over from Fort Riley, Kansas.

Sergeant Betters watched them arrive with pomp and ceremony, riding in formation to the tune of "Gary Owen," each face hard with determination, each man with a single thought: "Remember the Little Bighorn! Remember the Little Bighorn!"

THIRTY-ONE

THE STORM had come and gone when Two Robes arrived back at the village. Kicking Bear had left with the most ardent of his followers. Less than half of the villagers remained.

He discovered Fawn sitting with Tangled Hair, watching a small Ghost Dance in progress. Night Bird shuffled in the circle, Hawk on one side of her and Little Star on the other, singing loudly.

When Fawn and Tangled Hair saw Two Robes approach, they rose to greet him. "Where is Catches Lance?" Fawn asked. "I thought you were going to bring him back with you."

"He made the choice to stay up there for a short while," Two Robes said. "He wants to come down, but he doesn't feel the time is right yet."

"I don't understand," Fawn said. "When will the time be right?"

"A medicine woman is helping him get rid of bad spirits," Two Robes explained. "He has fallen to the bad medicine water. But he is getting away from it now and wants to be cured before he comes down. He wants to be happy again."

"Can he be cured of the bad medicine water?" Fawn asked.

"He says he wants to be cured," Two Robes told her. "It is up to him."

"And what about his quest to become a noted leader?" Tangled Hair asked. "Has he forgotten about gaining power and recognition as the most important part of his life?"

"I believe he just wants to be with his family and friends again," Two Robes replied.

"Will he want to dance with us?" Fawn asked.

"He did not say whether or not he wanted to dance," Two Robes said. "There is already trouble up there about the dancing, and he fears that it will spread. He is worried that the Bluecoats will soon come in to stop it."

"The Bluecoats have already come to Rosebud and to Pine Ridge," Fawn said. "A messenger arrived two days ago. Kicking Bear led many into the Stronghold, but there were also many who did not wish to journey there."

"Big Foot and Hump are leading their villagers in the dance," Tangled Hair said. "The people here want to go to Big Foot's village."

"Maybe we should move to the agency," Two Robes suggested. "That way, we wouldn't be involved if fighting broke out."

Fawn pointed to the cross on her shirt. "I have no fear of the Bluecoats," she said. "Let them come. I am protected. And I will be protected until the time that we again see our ancestors."

Sitting Bull's cabin was filled with sacred smoke. Shining Horse sat with his father and a number of others, discussing White Hair's decision to outlaw the Ghost Dance.

"He does not care about the dancing," Shining Horse said. "He is using that as an excuse to punish you."

"I have not acted dishonorably toward him," Sitting Bull

said. "No matter what he tells others, he knows that in his heart."

"You cannot think that White Hair or the Metal Breasts care about your honor," Shining Horse said. "And we know how their hearts are. We have learned that they are to come for you soon. You must believe this."

"I believe it," Sitting Bull said. "Yes, I know it is true. But I am not going to worry about it. That will do little good."

A warrior named Catch-the-Bear rose from his seat. "You do not need to worry, Sitting Bull. I, for one, will protect you always. I have matters to settle with Bull Head. He will not have his way."

"You cannot stop what is meant to happen," Sitting Bull told him. "None of you can. It is best not to worry."

Shining Horse sat in a brooding silence. His father seemed to have changed. And this change deepened with each day that passed. Sitting Bull hadn't been the same for nearly a week, not since the old circus pony had gotten out of the corral and had run into the hills. He had been gone half a day catching it and had returned with a blank stare on his face.

"I heard a meadowlark speak to me of death," Sitting Bull had told Shining Horse at the time. "I do not need to fear the Bluecoats. It is my own people who are after me."

Sitting Bull seemed now to be waiting for the end. But Shining Horse, like the others in the cabin, did not want to give up. He refused to allow Bull Head and Shaved Head to have their way.

There were now a number of new Metal Breasts, Unkpapas who had decided to join White Hair's group. Many of the former Metal Breasts had resigned. When they had heard that they would have to arrest Sitting Bull, they had turned in their uniforms.

Shining Horse and the others were adamant against the new Metal Breasts. They would not let these traitors who had gone over to White Hair come down into the village as big as you please and take Sitting Bull. There would be a bitter battle before that happened.

The pipe was passed again, and the smoke in the cabin thickened. Shining Horse asked to hear stories of the old days. His father recalled long-ago events, some he had not thought of for many years. "The times were different then," he said. "These new times are not for me."

"But the times will change," one of the warriors said. "It is promised. We are dancing for that reason."

Sitting Bull took a puff from the pipe. "No one can say for certain how the times will be. It is hoped they will change, but I will not see it."

All in the cabin listened sadly, looking at one another, clutching their rifles.

"You should get some sleep," Sitting Bull told them. "We have been up all night. Now it is time for rest."

After the others had left, Shining Horse spoke to his father. "I do not know what to say. What is going to happen?"

"We know what is going to happen to all of us, sooner or later," Sitting Bull said. "I only wish I had died as a young man in battle. I would be an honored ancestor now."

"You will always be honored among the Lakota people," Shining Horse said. "Of that there is no doubt."

Sitting Bull rose and hugged Shining Horse. "You have seen two worlds, my son, and have learned much. Your heart is good. Do not be afraid of what is to come. *Wankantanka* holds us in His hands."

"But I am afraid for you," Shining Horse said.

Sitting Bull looked out the door of the cabin. A streak of light had broken in the east. "Do not be afraid for me. Do not be afraid for yourself. As long as you believe the light will always come to you, there is only cause for rejoicing."

"I don't want that time to be yet."

"Be happy with what comes. Now go and get some rest."

Shining Horse left the cabin and walked down to the river. He wasn't ready yet to rest. Sleep would be slow in coming, even after a long night. He stopped near the riverbank. The water gurgled beneath patches of shore ice. A magpie landed without a sound on a cottonwood branch just above and looked down at him. Shining Horse was startled. Magpies usually spoke continuously, especially at daybreak. But on this morning, the black-and-white storyteller was silent. The bird lifted from the branch and flew away on silent wings into the darkness of the west.

Shining Horse turned toward the cabin. He wanted to ask Sitting Bull what a silent magpie meant. But his father was outside, going toward the corral. Shining Horse watched while Sitting Bull fed hay through the corral poles, talking and stroking the old pony's nose.

Not far downriver, a group of warriors dressed in Ghost Shirts mounted their ponies and rode across the river, south, toward the Stronghold. While many of the warriors were afraid and were leaving for the protection of the agency, there were still many who wanted the return of the old times.

Among the riders were Long Hand and Bob-tailed Cat. They had heard about the coming of the Bluecoats to Pine Ridge and Rosebud. When word got around that Sitting Bull would not leave his home, they had decided it was time to join with the more active warriors and follow Kicking Bear and Short Bull.

Shining Horse noted that his father had seen the riders. There was a moment when it seemed like the old warrior wanted to saddle his horse and join them. But instead, Sitting Bull turned and opened his arms to the morning sun. Softly he sang a song.

Shining Horse looked at the dawn, just touching the eastern hills. The light seemed so pure, so radiant. The air smelled as fresh as he could remember it. He felt a movement above his head and looked up. An owl was gliding past on silent wings, headed into the darkness of the west.

Catches Lance was sleeping soundly when Bull Head burst

into his cabin at dusk. With him were three other Metal Breasts.

"Get dressed," Bull Head told Catches Lance. "This is the night. Hurry!"

Catches Lance looked groggy. Bull Head leaned over and pulled him up. His breath smelled of whiskey. "Get up, I said!"

"What is happening?" Catches Lance asked.

"We are going to arrest Sitting Bull," Bull Head told him. "White Hair got the order from the Bluecoat chief that it was to be done. We are all to meet at the agency. Shaved Head and the others are waiting."

Catches Lance gathered the blue pants and shirt of the Metal Breasts. Bull Head paced nervously across the floor. While he dressed, Catches Lance thought to himself that he had meant to turn these clothes in the day before. He had spent long enough with Crane Woman to feel confident in himself. He didn't know why he was dressing; he had intended to start out for Cherry Creek the following morning.

"Hurry up!" Bull Head yelled to him. "What is taking you so long?"

"I don't know if I want to go," Catches Lance said.

"What? You have to go. All the Metal Breasts are going."

"I decided today that I didn't want to be a Metal Breast any longer. I should have turned in my uniform."

Bull Head stepped in front of Catches Lance, his eyes wide with anger. "You are going to turn afraid, like the others?"

"This is not the right thing to do."

"Bahhh!" Bull Head yelled. "Why am I wasting my time with you?"

"None of you should go," Catches Lance said. "It is against the Powers."

"Now I can see who you really are," Bull Head told him. "You came up here to be strong, you said. But it was really to live with that old lady.'"

The others laughed. Without warning, Bull Head slammed

the butt of his rifle into Catches Lance's face. Catches Lance fell backward against the wall.

"You don't quit just like that," Bull Head yelled. "You who sleeps with old ladies."

Catches Lance was coming to his feet when Bull Head hit him again. Catches Lance rolled to his side and shielded himself with his left arm as Bull Head struck yet another time. Catches Lance heard a sharp crack and felt his arm give.

"Stop, Bull Head!" one of the other Metal Breasts yelled. "You will kill him!"

Bull Head raised his rifle again. "This one needs killing."

"No, we are supposed to go and listen to White Hair," the Metal Breast reminded him. "We are supposed to arrest Sitting Bull. We are wasting time."

Bull Head held up. Catches Lance was in a ball, awaiting the blow, holding his broken arm against his side.

"You are not worth killing," Bull Head told him. "You are like the others who quit. You are nothing but a scared child. Now I will go and do my duty."

Bull Head led the others out the door. Catches Lance heard them mount and ride off into the darkness. He came to his feet and ripped away the bloody sleeve of his shirt. A sharp piece of bone protruded from his forearm.

Holding his broken arm against his chest, Catches Lance made his way to Crane Woman's cabin. She was standing at the door when he arrived.

"Something bad is happening," she said. "I feel that death is coming."

"Help me make a sling for my arm," Catches Lance said. "I must get down to Grand River."

Crane Woman brought Catches Lance inside, sat him down next to a lantern, and looked at his arm. "Did Bull Head do that to you?"

"Yes. He hit me with his rifle."

"You are through for a time," she said. "You have to rest that arm."

"No, I have to go down to Grand River," Catches Lance protested. "They are going to arrest Sitting Bull."

Crane Woman went to her stack of firewood in the corner. "Who is going to arrest him?"

"Bull Head and the other Metal Breasts. I don't know whether the Bluecoats are going along or not."

Crane Woman returned with two flat sticks and a little branch. She gave Catches Lance the branch and told him to bite down on it.

"You won't have to go after this. Hold still."

She held his arm firmly and jerked. Catches Lance nearly blacked out from the pain. He toppled sideways, and the wood fell from his mouth to the dirt floor.

"You had better let me find someone to go down for you," Crane Woman said.

Catches Lance straightened himself and got to his feet. "I have to go. Please, fit me with a sling."

"You will be sick," she said.

"I will be sicker if I don't go."

Crane Woman ripped off a large piece of bedsheet and tied the splints against Catches Lance's arm. She fit him with a sling, trying again to talk him out of going to Grand River.

"Do you want them to take Sitting Bull?" he asked her.

"How are you going to stop them?"

"I will warn him, and he can get away."

Crane Woman took a deep breath. "You don't know Sitting Bull. He will run from no one."

"I have to tell him, though," Catches Lance insisted. "I owe that much to a friend. A friend who is Sitting Bull's son. I should have listened to him a long time back."

Hoofbeats pounded through Shining Horse's dream. They were yelling, Bull Head and Shaved Head and the others, as they rode into the Grand River village.

Shining Horse saw his father, resting beside his older wife, rise up in his bed and greet an eagle.

Bull Head and the others pounded through the village, their horses breathing fire. They circled the cabin, brandishing pistols and rifles. Their clothes were dark in the gray hour before dawn, but on each arm shone a ring of white. In Shining Horse's dream, each ring flashed from white to red, and back to white, dripping red.

Shining Horse thought he was awake, it was so real. He stood before his father's cabin, holding his arms up to stop his father. But the old warrior drifted past him, his arms held fast by unseen hands.

Shining Horse yelled in his sleep as Bull Head and the Metal Breasts formed a line. The arms with the white rings lifted, each with a rifle aimed at Sitting Bull. Shining Horse thrashed in his bed. He lunged out, trying to divert their rifles. But they were out of reach.

There was a giant flash of red, and the world exploded. Shining Horse saw Bull Head, his eyes afire, tumbling down a hill toward a black hole in the ground, firing his rifle as he went. Shining Horse cried out as flame from the rifle shot toward his father.

More flame erupted from behind Sitting Bull as someone shot with a pistol into the back of his head.

Shining Horse rolled from his bed, screaming. He hit the floor with a heavy thud. He staggered to his feet and struggled into his pants and shirt, grabbed his rifle and ran from his cabin.

Outside, the night was alive with gunfire. He cursed himself for having slept so soundly. He fought guilt at having spent most of the day near his father, even while his father slept, forsaking his own rest. He should have known they would come at night.

A tangle of fighting bodies milled in front of his father's cabin. He couldn't be certain who was lying on the ground, for everything seemed hazy and unreal.

The first thing he saw clearly was his father's old pony, back on its haunches, striking hooves into the air at the sound of the gunfire.

"Stay back!" someone shouted as he ran by. "We are all killing each other!"

"Where is my father?" Shining Horse yelled. "I must find him."

He started forward again. Shaved Head lay in front of the cabin, writhing on the ground, holding his intestines in his hands. Nearby lay other Metal Breasts, including Bull Head, who was calling for someone to help him.

Then Shining Horse froze. He saw the body of his father, lying still among the others. He was staring at his father when a sudden burst of flame spit at him through the dawn light. Suddenly his stomach was on fire, and he dropped to his knees. His belly felt like it would tumble out of him. All around, the yelling slowly died, and he turned on his side to rest.

The sound of rushing water replaced the chaos around him. He saw the river, and his father, who reached out a hand to him.

"We will cross together," he said. "You and I, my faithful son."

THIRTY-TWO

CATCHES LANCE stopped often to rest on his way to Grand River. His arm hurt so badly that there were times when he felt he might pass out. It had swollen considerably, despite the herbs Crane Woman had given him.

When he reached Sitting Bull's village just after sunrise, he yelled in frustration. The air was filled with mourning songs and cries of anguish, including those of Sitting Bull's two widows. A crowd watched soldiers dragging bodies toward a wagon and into a nearby stable.

Catches Lance learned that the Metal Breasts had come to take Sitting Bull and there had been a terrible battle. Then the army had arrived and had driven Sitting Bull's followers into the trees along the river with fire from their Hotchkiss gun.

No one knew for certain yet how many had fallen. In the words of one woman: "It does not matter. They have killed our leader, and the sacred hoop cannot be mended."

Catches Lance discovered that the fallen Metal Breasts had been laid out in a wagon. Soldiers had just finished fitting Sitting Bull's body in among them. The body was covered with blood and the face terribly disfigured. Relatives of fallen Metal Breasts hurled oaths at the body, and soldiers stood guard so that no one got near the wagon.

"Does anyone know Shining Horse?" Catches Lance asked. An old man pointed toward the stable. "He's not a Metal Breast. He'll be over there."

On the way to the stable, Catches Lances stopped near an army ambulance wagon. Inside was Shaved Head with a blanket over him, nearly unconscious. A trooper pushed Catches Lance aside to make room for two men who were carrying Bull Head to the ambulance. Bull Head was conscious and obviously in great pain.

"Was it worth all this?" Catches Lance asked him.

Desperately weak, Bull Head could turn only his eyes. Despite this, he tried to spit at Catches Lance.

The trooper who had pushed Catches Lance ordered him to back away. "I'll put you under arrest," he threatened. "If you have no business here, move on."

Catches Lance went into the stable. People stood over the bodies and talked, retelling the events of the fight.

"That one, Crowfoot, they just shot him for no reason," a woman was telling her husband. "They pushed him out of the cabin and the others outside just opened fire. He's no more than a boy."

The stories continued, each telling the events as they had seen and heard them. One woman believed that Sitting Bull would have gone quietly if it hadn't been for Crowfoot, who accused his father of giving in. Another one said that it had been one of Sitting Bull's wives who had caused him to resist.

All of them were certain that the fighting had actually started when Catch-the-Bear had come around from the side of the cabin looking for Bull Head. It had been Catch-the-

Bear, they all agreed, who had fired on Bull Head. Then the slaughter had begun.

Catches Lance saw no point in learning the details. It was clear that the tragedy had blown a terrible wound in the middle of the Lakota nation. White Hair must be happy. Now there would be no one among the Lakota on Standing Rock Reservation to stand against him and tell about his dishonorable deeds.

Catches Lance discovered Shining Horse in one corner of the stable. He was lying with his arms folded across his chest. Someone had closed his eyes. Except for the blood, he could have been sleeping. Catches Lance knelt down and placed his fingers gently against Shining Horse's cheek. It felt cold and unreal, completely unlike the warm tears running down his own face.

He asked two onlookers to help him with Shining Horse's body. One of them offered an old pony, and Catches Lance watched, holding his broken arm, as they put Shining Horse over the back of the horse and secured the body tightly.

"You are a Minneconjou," one of the men said to Catches Lance. "Are you going back to your people?"

"I will take Shining Horse with me," Catches Lance said. "He had good friends among Kicking Bear's people."

"Many of them have gone into the Stronghold," the man told him. "The others have joined Big Foot. Do you know where your friends are?"

"I will find them. My friend, he who has died, will help me find them."

Both men smiled. Catches Lance offered one his moccasins and another a blanket for having helped him.

"No, we do not need a gift for that," one of them said. "Just pray to *Wankantanka* for our people."

Catches Lance traveled all afternoon. The wind deadened the outside of his body, while the pain of the day's losses had an equal effect within him. He rode as if in a trance, leading the old pony laden with Shining Horse's body. The scattered, windswept clouds and the open plains drifted past him like dreams in deep gray.

Once in a while Catches Lance would turn and look at Shining Horse, fully expecting that he would come to life and ask to be untied so he could sit up in a comfortable position. But it never happened, and Catches Lance turned around less and less often, intent only on reaching his people again.

Just after dark, he came upon a settler's cabin, abandoned with the news that there was impending war with the Sioux. He hobbled the ponies and apologized to Shining Horse for having to leave him out in the cold. He would bring him inside the cabin but for his broken arm.

Inside, Catches Lance found a lantern and a bed. He also found a bottle uncorked on a small table, along with a plate of stale biscuits and a plate of frozen beef. After eating, Catches Lance blew out the lantern and lay down. He pulled a sheepskin over himself and tried to settle in against the cold night.

He stared at the dark ceiling, fighting the urge to get the bottle and drown everything he felt inside. The pain in his arm was tremendous, but it didn't compare to the pain of the terrible events at Grand River.

Maybe if he had quit the Metal Breasts sooner, none of it would have happened. He could have warned Shining Horse and Sitting Bull. They could have left and joined the other Ghost Dancers in the Stronghold.

He remembered Crane Woman's remark: "Sitting Bull does not fear anyone. He will go nowhere. How are you going to change anything?"

Catches Lance got up and relit the lantern. The bottle sat there on the table, nearly filled with an amber liquid that drew him closer and closer. He reached toward the bottle, then quickly pulled away. He clenched his fist tightly, fighting the desire to make everything he had seen and felt during the last year melt away with the long drinks that dulled the mind.

How could he even allow himself to think that way? Crane Woman had talked to him a great deal, and he had realized that her words were true. How had the bad medicine water ever helped him with his feelings? How had the terrible liquid, filled with bad spirits, ever made things change?

With a quick flip of his wrist, Catches Lance knocked the bottle off the table. It thudded to the dirt floor, the liquid spewing out and collecting as mud. He blew out the lantern and returned to bed.

Inside, Catches Lance leaped for joy. As he drifted off into sleep, he saw Night Bird smiling broadly, welcoming him home. He saw Hawk and Little Star jumping up and down, each one demanding the first turn on his pony. And Fawn, who had been so dedicated to doing what would help him. Now she, too, was smiling, waving to him as he rode down the hill into the village.

Catches Lance felt confident in his future. Now that he had overcome the pull of the bad medicine water, he saw no reason to succumb to it again. It would be better to face whatever bothered him and conquer it than to let the terrible whiskey flow into him and make him sick, making the problems he wished to forget only deepen.

With this knowledge came a calming contentment, a realization that he had finally become the warrior he had always wished to be. He could pass by one of the bottles without stopping. He could be with others who drank and not partake. The custom of accepting what was offered would make it hard, but he would make it known not to offer bottles to him.

He could now take pride in his achievements. He had gained honor, much honor. In pushing the drink away, he had counted as strong a coup as he ever could have struck on a battlefield. He could always walk with his head held high, knowing he had overcome something very difficult. It would be a continuous battle, a battle he would face almost daily, but he would never lose again.

He wished he could have shown Shining Horse that he had made it. He wanted to be able to tell him thank-you for his concern and help. As he fell asleep, he felt in his heart that Shining Horse already knew and was somewhere waving at him with pride.

The burial scaffold faced east. Two Robes had built it himself, tying cottonwood limbs together to make a platform for the body. Four poles planted in the ground supported the platform. Shining Horse, wrapped in blankets, would meet the Grandfathers in the old way, from the side of a hill that opened to the sky.

The sun had just risen, and the cold wind had stopped for a short time. Fawn and Night Bird sang a mourning song, while Two Robes stood gazing into the distance. Tangled Hair had placed a pair of moccasins on the scaffold as a symbol of the journey they once took together. He now looked off into the distance as well.

Catches Lance stood back with Hawk and Little Star, clutching their hands, their love coursing through him. A feeling had guided him and he had ridden directly to Big Foot's village.

"We knew you would come back," Hawk had told him. "We knew you were strong. How did you know where to find us?"

"There is someone watching over me," Catches Lance had said. "And for that, I am grateful."

Though both children were sorry about Shining Horse's death, it felt good to see their uncle again. They had sat in his lap the entire day of his return, while their mother and Night Bird had bathed Shining Horse in warm water and prepared him for his journey to the Other Side.

Now they all stood back from the scaffold and wondered how many of their people would be going across during the upcoming cold moons. It had come to seem like a common thing. Mothers of little babies awakened each morning wondering if the small life next to them could still move.

"You won't go away again, will you?" Little Star asked Catches Lance.

"I will never go away again," Catches Lance told them. "When the time is right, Night Bird and I will give you some little cousins to play with. But for now, we all have to hold together until the bad times have passed."

When Fawn and Night Bird had finished their song, Two Robes stepped forward. He took a worn book from his pocket and placed it under Shining Horse's clasped hands.

"I would keep it as a remembrance of you," Two Robes said, "but I will think of you much more without it. You are something special that I have lost."

After the others had left, Two Robes sat by himself on the top of the hill until the day passed and fell into evening. Below, in Big Foot's village, the people began the Ghost Dance. Two Robes could hear the songs clearly. The circle of humanity shuffled and twisted in the light of the sunset.

Fawn had Hawk and Little Star with her, and Night Bird had persuaded Catches Lance to try the dance. He shuffled with the others, singing loudly, his voice carrying above everyone else's.

Two Robes watched from the hill for a while longer. He had brought a small knife with him, and as the sun fell, he sliced three gashes across the inside of both arms and then raised his arms to the sky.

Tears flowed down his cheeks as he whispered into the twilight. "Shining Horse, wherever you are, I will always remember you. I can't tell you how many times I've wondered how I could have been so lucky as to have sat with you on that train. I can never thank you enough for all you have done."

He turned his hands over, palms down. The movement had come automatically. He had seen the Ghost Dance priests pray in this manner. He felt Wovoka's words reaching deep into him: "Pray for all. Do not fight. Love one another."

Two Robes realized that his time to begin the dance had come. He again invoked the memory of Shining Horse. "My time to become fully Lakota has come," he said. "I will dance and pray for the land you dreamed of. If that land comes, I will be waiting to thank you again for all you've done for me."

Two Robes came down from the hill and met Fawn at the edge of the dance circle. She smiled and handed his chasuble to him, along with a palette of paints. "I knew this time would come," she said. "Paint your shirt in a sacred manner and wear it. You will learn many things."

With trembling hands, Two Robes took the chasuble and paints. He sat down next to a fire and placed an eagle above the large red cross, then two magpies on either side of the cross and a crow at the bottom. He finished with a turtle and a woodpecker.

"That is nearly the same as my dress," Fawn commented.

Two Robes turned to her. "Are we not meant to be one, you and I?"

He stepped into the dance circle between Fawn and Hawk. Soon his feelings welled up from deep inside. The scene of his mother's death unfolded again, and he watched it as though it had happened to someone else. An understanding came to him: her death had been part of his preparation for this land. Had things been easy for him, he would never have understood the grief of the Lakota people.

As he continued to dance, Two Robes saw his father again. This time he felt no fear or anger, only a sense of pity for a man whose bitterness had controlled his life.

Suddenly his father's features changed into those of a younger man. "I wish I were you and had learned the things you have," his father said, his face sad. "I have a lot of trials ahead. Pray for me."

Two Robes felt strange at hearing those words from his father. "Pray for me," he said aloud. "Pray for me." He remembered that his mother's fondest hope was that people would pray for her upon her death. She had said any number of times, "You will always pray for your mother, won't you,

Mark, my boy?" And he had said any number of masses for her as a priest. But none for his father.

Tears poured from Two Robes' eyes. He swayed with the rhythm of the dance, releasing the guilt that he had never prayed for his father. Of the two, his father had certainly needed the prayers the most. But even as a priest, he had never forgiven his father—not until tonight.

Forgiven. The word echoed through his head. *You are forgiven.*

Two Robes stumbled. Fawn let him go on one side and Hawk released him on the other. He stumbled again. Then he was on the ground, looking up at the dancers, each of them drifting by just above him, hand in hand, singing and shuffling.

They turned upside down, still singing, still shuffling. Then they were gone.

Before him was a landscape he had seen from the train to Nevada, but he had never seen it this close, or this vividly: a scrambled land of high spires and deeply eroded clay peaks, breaking into steep coulees and draws; grays and browns and light hues of blue mixed with white, chalky hillsides and yellowish bottoms.

"You have come to *Mako sica*," he heard a voice say. "Remember the trail you stand on, for you should take it soon."

Two Robes knew the voice. Shining Horse was talking to him. He looked around, feeling the wind, seeing dusty clouds of alkali forming in the bottoms.

"Bring them all here," Shining Horse was saying.

"Where are you?"

"Look up."

Two Robes did and saw a figure standing on a hilltop nearby. The figure seemed almost transparent, but it was alive with the spirit of Shining Horse.

"Don't worry about what you see when you get here,"

Shining Horse said. "Don't worry about what you've heard. Just bring the people here. Bring all of them here."

"This is not the land that was promised," Two Robes said. "Bring people here? This is desolate and forsaken."

"Don't ask a lot of questions. You cannot understand the answers," Shining Horse said. "This is your time of learning, and you must go with what you feel, not with what others believe is Truth."

"Who am I supposed to bring to this place?" Two Robes asked.

"You will know when the time is right," Shining Horse said. "You will understand then." He pointed toward a large plateau in the distance. "Go to that place. It is called the Stronghold."

Two Robes stared at the plateau. It appeared to be moving, as though circles were lifting off the top into the sky. He realized that the circles were people joined together, dancing. It made him dizzy, and he felt as if he, too, were being lifted.

He turned back toward the hilltop and saw a wolf loping off of it and down into a steep coulee, where it was lost in the swirling alkali dust.

Two Robes felt himself turning and twisting upward toward the sky. The clouds were a mass of tumbling shapes, moving and surging across the thin winter blue. Buffalo. All of them white. Racing against the wind.

Two Robes reached toward the buffalo. The clouds stayed out of grasp, and the sky grew darker behind, until a maze of stars appeared.

"You have awakened," Fawn said. "Can you hear me?"

Two Robes sat up. The dancing continued around him, the singing loud in his ears. Catches Lance and Night Bird were on their knees next to Fawn. Tangled Hair stood just above them. A short way off, Yellow Bird looked on with intense curiosity.

"What did you see?" Fawn asked. "Did you see the Other Side?"

With help, Two Robes stood up. "I saw Shining Horse," he said. "He tried to tell me something."

"See! The ancestors are coming!" Fawn said with joy. "Now you know that."

"He didn't say anything about ancestors," Two Robes said. "He showed me the place you call *Mako sica*. Something is going to happen there."

"Yes, that is where Kicking Bear is with many of our people," Night Bird offered. "Short Bull is there as well, along with many others."

"Maybe that is where the Messiah is to appear," Fawn said. "Is that where we are supposed to go?"

"I know we're supposed to go there," Two Robes said. "I don't know about the Messiah. I just know that I saw the place where they are dancing. I don't know how we should get there, but we should go soon."

THIRTY-THREE

DURING HIS time among the Minneconjou, Big Foot had become one of the most respected of all leaders. Many called him Spotted Elk. They pointed not to his war record, but to his abilities to pacify quarreling factions among the Lakota people. He had often been asked to intervene in disputes, and had been successful in restoring peace the majority of the time.

The Ghost Dance had come, and he had embraced it totally. He did not see it as a war dance, but as a dance to bring back the old, sacred way of life. Though he wanted to keep the dance peaceful, there were those among his younger men who insisted that the only way to make certain the dancing would continue was to take up arms and prepare to fight.

"The word of the *Wanekia*, as I understand it," Big Foot had told the more militant dancers, "is to hold no anger in your heart. How can you hold a rifle and shake it without feeling anger?"

The medicine man, Yellow Bird, had assumed leadership

among the most avid Ghost Dancers. Though older himself, he taught ideas that pleased the younger warriors. He spoke sharply to Big Foot. "You have become old in thought, and now you are sick as well. You should allow younger men to make the important decisions."

Big Foot had indeed been coughing over the past weeks, and the cough was worsening. There were those who felt he was dying. Soon the younger leaders would be making all the decisions. Yellow Bird wanted to establish himself as the strongest among them.

Big Foot answered that he could lead his people as well as he ever had. No matter his health, he had not lost his sense of hospitality, and he welcomed those Minneconjou who had not followed Kicking Bear to the Stronghold. But he insisted that the level of warlike intensity be held down during the dancing.

Because of Big Foot's respected position, the dancers agreed to maintain a calmer atmosphere, even though the Bluecoats suddenly marched in and built a camp nearby. Nobody knew what the Bluecoats really wanted to do, but Big Foot was certain that their leader, a man named Sumner, had no intention of causing problems.

In council, an interpreter for the Bluecoat leader had told Big Foot that Sumner had been ordered to watch over the camp and see that no problems arose. Nothing else. No one wanted trouble.

But trouble had come from the north. After Catches Lance had come with news that Sitting Bull had been killed, a number of terrified Unkpapas had fled the Standing Rock Reservation and come into the village. Sumner had told Big Foot that he could not allow the Unkpapas to camp there. Big Foot must send them back north.

"If starving *Wasichu* women and children asked you for help, would you turn them away?" Big Foot asked the commander.

Sumner agreed that he would not turn away hungry

women and children. He told Big Foot that they could stay,
provided they made no trouble. But Sumner did not know
that his commanding officers had decided to arrest Big Foot.
He was, in their minds, the same kind of firebrand that Sitting
Bull had been. He needed to be incarcerated.

Now Big Foot's health had worsened, and his people were
starving. He had begun to move them toward the agency, as
rations were to be issued on December 22, but he realized that
if he marched into the agency, he would be walking into
shackles.

Again, Yellow Bird and the younger Ghost Dancers made it
plain to him that they did not intend to go to any jails. If he
went in, he would go in alone.

Fawn, along with many of the others, began to feel trapped.
She suggested to Two Robes, "We should move out to *Mako
sica* now, to be with Kicking Bear and Short Bull. You have
heard this from Shining Horse. This idea of maintaining
peace with the Bluecoats is not sound. All they want is to fight.
We should at least be joined together in strength."

"We could not march clear across to *Mako sica* by ourselves,"
Two Robes pointed out. "The weather has turned cold, and
storms are coming."

"Others will join us," Fawn said. "We cannot simply stay
here. Something bad will happen."

The next day the army drove five steers into Big Foot's
camp. Sumner told the people to eat, and sat with Big Foot in
council. "Your people will be taken care of," he promised.
"But you have to go back to your village and stop the
dancing."

"Can you promise that my people will be taken care of after
you get your own way?" Big Foot asked. "Or do you just bring
in beef so that you can get what you want? Later, everything
will be the same as always, and your words will be as empty as
the wind." Big Foot coughed. "Leave us in peace."

"You have no choice," Sumner said. "You can either go back

to your village and stay under my rule or I will escort you down to the agency and you will be put in chains."

With no alternative, Big Foot agreed. They started back to the village in the cold. Two Robes rode horseback, while Fawn and her children rode with Night Bird in a wagon driven by Catches Lance.

As Sumner's troops pushed them to go faster, the tension between the Bluecoats and the younger Ghost Dancers worsened. Fawn's wagon got caught in a gate and the Bluecoats became angry at the delay. Some of the young warriors brought up their rifles and drove the Bluecoats away.

Finally, the wagon was freed from the gate. After that incident, Sumner insisted that Big Foot take his people past their homes and on to Camp Cheyenne, where they would be kept under observation.

"You cannot tell us to leave our homes now," Big Foot said. "If you insist, the young men will certainly make war against you. Who would you explain to when some of your men got killed? You would be held accountable, as I am. So make your choice."

Sumner backed down once Big Foot promised to come into Camp Cheyenne the following morning for a council about the situation. During the night, many of the Unkpapas who were to be in the council took flight. Big Foot sent out some of his leaders to bring them back. The leaders returned to camp that evening without the Unkpapas.

"The Bluecoats will be angry that we did not go to council today," Big Foot said. "But they would have accused us of leaving the Unkpapas behind. We are in trouble no matter what we do."

Two Robes sat in camp that evening wondering if Fawn hadn't been right about leaving for the Stronghold. Now they were surrounded by soldiers, with nowhere to go. Earlier in the day, a rancher whom Big Foot and his people had named Red Beard had come into the village with the news that Sumner was worried about the Unkpapas and more people who might come down from Standing Rock.

"Sumner has decided that you should take your people down to the agency," the rancher had reported. "You must surrender at Fort Bennett or you and your people will be shot."

Tangled Hair was already considering going into the agency to wait until everything had settled down. But then Catches Lance had told him how the Metal Breasts operated and Tangled Hair had decided to stay and take his chances with Big Foot's people.

"Now we are going to have trouble," Tangled Hair said. "I can feel it, bad trouble."

The following morning, Big Foot called a special council. Many of the people wanted to join the Oglalas, who had offered a hundred ponies for peace if Big Foot would lead his people down there. Big Foot had many relatives among the Oglalas and knew he would be treated well there.

Those more adamant about the Ghost Dance wanted to go into the Stronghold and join forces with Short Bull and Kicking Bear. Big Foot did not want to go anywhere for a time. He hoped the crisis would pass, that they could stay where they were, in their homes, and leave the Bluecoats alone to watch them if they wished.

Yellow Bird and others argued that if they stayed, the Bluecoats would stop them from dancing. "We cannot give up the dancing now," Yellow Bird warned. "When the *Wanekia* arrives, he will not recognize us."

"The Bluecoats are just waiting for a reason to start shooting us," Big Foot told the council. "Any of you who don't believe this should stop and think about it. The *Wasichu* have wanted us to die off from earth for a long time. They have tried to starve us and to make us freeze in the cold. But we have survived. Now we should continue to survive. We should not give them reason to shoot us down. We can do the dance again when they have left."

Two Robes had been asked to sit in on the council. His reputation as a holy man was well known among all the Lakota now.

Big Foot turned to him. "You know the *Wasichu* ways," he said. "What do you think?"

Two Robes thought about his dream and wondered if he should discuss it. He quickly abandoned the idea. He realized that Yellow Bird and his followers would take his vision to mean that they should join Short Bull and Kicking Bear for military reasons. They would push Big Foot even harder.

Though Two Robes did not yet understand what his dream had meant, he didn't feel that fighting the U.S. Army had anything to do with it. He decided to tell Big Foot about his dream later and see what the leader felt. For now, he would take Big Foot's side, as it seemed the most logical.

"What is it you think?" Yellow Bird pressed. "Aren't you going to tell us what you believe we should do?"

"I feel that we have to be very careful," Two Robes said. "If we make any kind of trouble whatsoever, the Bluecoats will use the excuse to fight. Maybe we should do as Big Foot suggests and wait until the trouble passes before we move."

Yellow Bird became upset. "Why do you take Big Foot's side in this?" he asked. "It sounds like you do not want the old times to come back. You are a *Wasichu*, and it does not matter that you live with our people. If it were up to me, I would see that you were thrown out."

Many of the younger warriors agreed.

"I believe we should hurry and join with those at Pine Ridge," one of the council members suggested. "We have been offered a hundred ponies for peace if we go down there."

"What good will a hundred ponies do if you perish and cannot ride them?" Yellow Bird asked. "If we want the old ways back, we must join those in the Stronghold. Nothing less will help us. We must join and fight alongside those who believe as we do."

"I have told the Bluecoat chief that I do not feel good and

do not want to travel south," Big Foot told the council. "If we stay here, they will believe that we want peace."

"No, they will take us to the agency," Yellow Bird contended. "I will die before I become a prisoner."

"Most of the people do not want to fight," another council member said. "They want to be where it is safe. There is food and it is safe at Pine Ridge."

Yellow Bird and his followers continued to argue for the Stronghold. Big Foot listened to everyone and realized that the majority wished to go south and try to reach Pine Ridge.

"We will go south, then," Big Foot said. "I have heard what you want. It is not what I want, but I will lead you anyway."

Sergeant Betters rode in formation with the Ninth Cavalry, his face smarting from a cold wind. The sky was gray and flecked with intermittent snow. Some of the men were singing a chorus of "Silent Night," the only means by which they would celebrate Christmas Day, 1890.

A scout rejoined the column and reported that Harney Spring lay just ahead. The Ninth would camp at this eastern entrance to the Badlands, some ten miles from the Stronghold, until further notice. This was the only way into the Badlands, as cliffs blocked any other entry for nearly fifty miles in every direction.

At a council near the Stronghold, a number of Lakota who had given up the Ghost Dance were trying to persuade Kicking Bear and Short Bull to return to Pine Ridge. They argued through Christmas Day and for another two days after that. At that time a scout reported to the Ninth that the vast majority of the Ghost Dancers had struck their lodges and apparently headed into Pine Ridge. Only Kicking Bear and Short Bull remained, with two hundred of their most ardent followers.

"It's way too cold for anybody to last very long without food," Cort told Betters and the others sitting around the fire.

"I guess they figured as much. Can't call them stupid. You can call them real dangerous, but not stupid."

So far, the Ghost Dancers had not attacked anyone. However, a vigilante group had organized and had fought a number of skirmishes with the Ghost Dancers. Men had fallen on both sides, a fact that would not aid in constructive talks.

Sergeant Betters had no way of knowing whether or not Tangled Hair was among those now leaving the Stronghold. After Sitting Bull's murder, Kicking Bear had taken the most fanatical of the Minneconjou Ghost Dancers with him. A good number of the others were now with Big Foot, who had fled his village on Cheyenne River and was reportedly headed in their direction. The military surmised that Big Foot would try to lead his people to the Stronghold, to join Kicking Bear and Short Bull. This surmise was what had sent the Ninth to Harney Spring.

Sergeant Betters now prayed that Tangled Hair was among those in the Stronghold. Word had come that Short Bull and Kicking Bear were giving in to their people, who were too cold and sick to stand the oncoming winter. If Tangled Hair was among them, he would soon be safe at Pine Ridge.

The most serious problem now, as the military saw it, was Big Foot, but the units on patrol had yet to discover his whereabouts. Cort and Jesse, along with other veterans of the Indian wars, had a good idea that Big Foot couldn't be far away. The Oglala scouts working with them had reported sighting a scouting patrol watching the movements of the Ninth. Big Foot had to be considering entering the Stronghold or the scouts wouldn't have come to check out the entrance.

Sergeant Betters felt quite certain that none of the Indians wanted war, whether or not they were Ghost Dancers. Had the various factions wanted to fight, they would have done so already.

Two days after their arrival at Harney Spring, Sergeant Betters got orders to assemble the men under him and break camp immediately. When Cort and Jesse asked him where they were going, Betters answered in a reserved but hopeful tone.

"The scouts sent to check out the Stronghold came back with the news that all of the tepees were struck. It appears that Short Bull and Kicking Bear have decided to call it quits now as well."

Cort and Jesse cheered. "Do you think that means this thing is over with?" Cort asked.

Betters did not answer at once. When he did, he said, "I haven't got the feel that it's over. Everybody's been worried about those in the Stronghold, but no one's found Big Foot yet."

"Yeah, but it sounds like your son's out of trouble," Cort said. "That has to be good news."

"It should be good news," Betters said. "But I'll feel a lot better when I see him standing beside me."

The Ninth moved down to White River and camped at the mouth of Wounded Knee Creek. There another scout rode in and reported to the commanding officer that Kicking Bear and Short Bull were leading their people into Pine Ridge. They would arrive in but a few days. All that remained was to find Big Foot and his people and disarm them.

That evening a number of troops crowded into one of the tents for a poker game. Sergeant Betters could not sit still for more than one hand. He went out into the night and paced the campground.

Cort picked up the cards dealt to him. He couldn't keep his mind on the game, either. "Play or fold your cards," Jesse told him. "Ain't no good worrying about the sergeant. That won't change nothing."

"He has the jitters worse than any time I've ever seen him," Cort remarked. "I reckon he's got to be thinking that anything can happen. He's this close to seeing his son, and still, nothing says he ever will."

"If we go to shooting, nothing's final for any of us," Jesse said. "Big Foot could have a lot of warriors with their sights on us right now, just waiting for their chance."

"We ain't guarding the Stronghold anymore," one of the other men pointed out. "What's to stop Big Foot from slipping around us and getting in there? It'll be us who has to go in after him."

Cort said, "I just know there's trouble ahead. And the sergeant knows it, too."

A trooper burst into the tent with the news. A scout had just ridden into camp. "The word is that Big Foot sent scouts to Pine Ridge to tell them he wanted to go down and surrender," the trooper said. "But ol' General Miles figures that Sumner did things poorly, and he don't want Big Foot getting away again."

"Does that mean we have to ride after Big Foot?" Cort asked.

"That's what it means," the trooper replied. "We have to see if we can't come at him from the north. Miles is sending the Seventh out from Pine Ridge to go straight up at him."

"The Seventh is coming out?" Cort asked in alarm. The Seventh had come to avenge their fallen at the Little Bighorn; they had made no bones about that. They wanted to be in on the thickest of the action, expected to take place in the confrontation with Big Foot and his warriors.

Jesse slapped the deck down on the blanket. "I guess that means there'll be a fight. Those boys came for blood, and they figure to have it."

THIRTY-FOUR

Two Robes sat in council with Big Foot and a number of his warriors. Yellow Bird wanted to go into the Stronghold now more than ever. But Big Foot had no such notion.

"The scouts have told us that the Buffalo Soldiers are guarding the way into the Stronghold," Big Foot was telling Yellow Bird. "Now will you stop this idea of getting in there and joining Kicking Bear and Short Bull?"

"The Buffalo Soldiers are not as strong as they are said to be," Yellow Bird insisted. "If we struck them from three sides, with their backs to the walls of *Mako sica,* we could wipe them out."

"You say the Buffalo Soldiers do not have strong medicine," Big Foot argued. "When have you ever fought them?"

"I am saying we could wipe them out," Yellow Bird persisted. "I still do not think we should go down to Pine Ridge."

"Going to Pine Ridge is the best thing," Big Foot repeated. "You know that the Buffalo Soldiers have strong medicine.

You know that they will have the big guns that roll on wheels. How would we have a chance? That is not a good idea."

The question of fighting had come up often during the flight. "It is important to see that the Bluecoats want to fight," Big Foot continued. "If we try to fight them, we will lose. We are no longer strong enough to fight. We will die if we do not get down with our relatives at Pine Ridge."

For the first time, many of Yellow Bird's followers agreed with Big Foot. The people were starving; and even if they managed to get past the Buffalo Soldiers and into the Stronghold, there would be no food there, either. They would all surely die.

"But the Messiah will deliver us!" Yellow Bird shouted.

"It is a long time until spring," Big Foot told him. "Can you live without food until then?"

The council adjourned. Two Robes and Catches Lance helped Big Foot to his wagon. He wiped perspiration from his face and covered himself with blankets.

"I may never recover from this," he told Two Robes. "Even if we get to Pine Ridge, I may never be well again."

"They have doctors there who can treat you," Two Robes said. "You will recover."

"I want you to help Tangled Hair," Big Foot said. "Take Tangled Hair and two scouts. Go to the Buffalo Soldiers. If Tangled Hair can find his father, maybe he can tell them we do not wish to fight. Then they can come with us into Pine Ridge. I would trust the Buffalo Soldiers."

"That is a good idea," Two Robes said. "We will hurry. It should only take a few days. Can you hold out here?"

"We must keep traveling," Big Foot said. "Someone heard an owl. It is a bad omen. It will snow soon and grow colder. We have to keep going. You can catch up."

While Two Robes and Tangled Hair prepared to leave, Catches Lance told Fawn that their trip might bring the end to all the troubles. "Two Robes will talk to the Bluecoat leaders and tell them that no one wants to fight," he said. "That will be good for everybody."

"The scouts saw the Buffalo Soldiers two or three days ago," Fawn pointed out. "They might be gone by now. Then what?"

"We must hope for the best," Catches Lance said. "That is all we can do."

Two Robes, with Tangled Hair and two scouts, had been gone a short time when a scout rode his pony at full speed into the Minneconjou camp and dismounted at Big Foot's wagon. He was Oglala, and no one knew him. He held up his hand when surrounded by the younger warriors.

"I have come to do no harm but to bring a warning," he said. "Bluecoats are camped on Wounded Knee Creek. The leaders are paying scouts twenty-five dollars to find you. The *Wasichu* paper writers have offered much more. You are a target."

Yellow Bird and some of the others began to sing war songs. Big Foot called for silence, reminding them that the Bluecoats would be many in number, with the big-shooting guns. It would be suicide to begin fighting in a place where they could be so easily trapped.

"Tell the Bluecoats on Wounded Knee that we want no fighting," Big Foot told the scout. "We are traveling that way and will surrender to them when we get there."

The scout left immediately. Big Foot coughed blood into a scrap of blanket. At his request, Catches Lance tied a white cloth to the end of a pole and affixed the pole to the wagon.

"I don't want the Bluecoats to have any reason to shoot," Big Foot said.

"Why don't we stay here and wait for Two Robes and Tangled Hair to come back with the Buffalo Soldiers?" Catches Lance asked.

"We must get the women and children down to Pine Ridge," Big Foot said. "They are starving. The mothers have no milk for the infants. We need food and shelter."

"You are right," Catches Lance said. "We will hurry as fast as we can. Two Robes and Tangled Hair will find us. Then when the Buffalo Soldiers come, all will be well."

Two Robes sat his pony at Harney Spring. A cutting wind blew light snow over the trampled ground where men and horses and wagons had left the unmistakable marks of encampment.

Tangled Hair and the scouts were on the ground, inspecting camp-fire remains and horse droppings. Tangled Hair walked over to Two Robes. "They were here no more than two days ago," he said. "If we hurry, we can find them and get them to travel back with us."

"I doubt that Big Foot can wait for us that long," Two Robes said. "Perhaps Big Foot should bring his people over this way so that the Buffalo Soldiers can find them and escort them down."

"Big Foot does not want to come this way," Tangled Hair said. "He believes there will be fighting in the Stronghold."

"I can't understand why the Buffalo Soldiers left here," one of the scouts remarked. "It must mean that there is no one in the Stronghold any longer."

"How can that be?" Tangled Hair asked.

"Maybe they gave up," Two Robes said. "I can't imagine it. But it has been cold. With no food, no one can dance."

"We should go look for ourselves," Tangled Hair said. "Then we will know."

As they started up from Harney Spring, a column of warriors crested a hill just ahead. In but a few moments the warriors had surrounded them. Then Long Hand and Bob-tailed Cat rode down toward them.

"Ho!" Long Hand said to Two Robes. "What brings you out here?"

"We have been traveling with Big Foot," Two Robes replied. "We learned that the Buffalo Soldiers were here. We want them to take us down to Pine Ridge."

"We heard that Big Foot was coming here," Bob-tailed Cat said. "Kicking Bear and Short Bull have given up. We wanted to join Big Foot."

"It is not a good idea to fight," Two Robes advised. "There are a lot of Bluecoats moving into this country."

"What about the dance?" Long Hand asked.

"Once everyone is at the agency, we can worry about the dance," Tangled Hair said. "For now, we must find my father and the Buffalo Soldiers."

Long Hand pointed north. "You can see the trail. They are not going fast. I think they are watching for Big Foot to come this way."

"Do you still want to join us and Big Foot's people?" Two Robes asked Long Hand.

"I guess that is the only way," he replied.

"I will take the scouts with me and find my father," Tangled Hair said to Two Robes. "I will lead the Buffalo Soldiers down to you."

"That would be good," Two Robes agreed. "but you had better hurry."

Tangled Hair spotted the Ninth Cavalry encamped in a draw out of the wind. He rode to a hilltop and signaled the Oglala scouts with them, who came out and escorted him into the camp.

He jumped down from his pony and stood among the black troopers gathering around him. A middle-aged man emerged from among them and called an interpreter over.

"Did you come from the Minneconjou?" Sergeant Betters asked.

"I am Tangled Hair. Are you the one called Betters?"

Sergeant Betters began to tremble slightly. He bit his lip and reached out to his son. They held one another tightly for a time before Sergeant Betters led Tangled Hair to his tent.

There, Tangled Hair met Cort and Jesse, as well as others of the Ninth. Though it was hard for both Betters and

Tangled Hair at first, the two finally became comfortable and briefly discussed their lives with one another.

Tangled Hair then told his father that he wanted to have him escort Big Foot and his people down to Pine Ridge.

"Big Foot?" Sergeant Betters asked. "You know where he is?"

"I have been traveling with his people," Tangled Hair said. "He does not want to fight."

The commanding officer, Major Guy V. Henry, was resting in his tent, with explicit orders not to be disturbed.

"I believe he will see this as important," Betters told Cort, who then left to give Major Henry the message.

Major Henry sent for Betters and Tangled Hair, and the scouts who had come in with him. He wore a patch over one eye, and his face was hollowed from the bullet that had passed through both cheeks. The major was irritable but polite when introduced to Tangled Hair.

"Tangled Hair has lived among the Minneconjou for some time," Sergeant Betters said. "He has come to lead us to Big Foot. Then all this will be over."

Henry stared back and forth from Sergeant Betters to Tangled Hair with his one good eye. "How am I to know this isn't a trick?" he asked. "What if he leads us into a trap?"

"He is my son, Major," Betters said. "Would he come here like this if he meant to do us harm?"

Tangled Hair explained that Big Foot trusted the Buffalo Soldiers far more than he did any of the other Bluecoats.

"I'm telling you, sir," Betters said, "that we can put an end to this if you will just let him take us to Big Foot."

"You know my orders are to patrol this area, and this area only," Major Henry stressed. "If I lead the men out from here and Big Foot somehow gets around us, there would be a lot of explaining to do. Wouldn't there, Sergeant Betters?"

"Send a scout to Pine Ridge and have someone wire General Miles, if that's what it takes," Betters suggested. "I think we ought to act on this."

"Very well," Major Henry said. "Have the scouts that came in with your son report to Pine Ridge. If they come back with orders for my movement, we will pursue this idea of yours."

"But Major, it may be too late by then," Betters argued.

"That is all, Sergeant Betters."

Betters saluted and led Tangled Hair and the others out of the tent. The sun had begun its descent into the winter sky, and a chill breeze had begun to blow.

"I can't tell you how glad I am you came," Betters told Tangled Hair. "If we hold on here, this thing will be over. Then you and I will have a new life together."

Two Robes sat his pony with Long Hand and Bob-tailed Cat in the darkness above Wounded Knee Creek. Below, flames, from the Bluecoat camp fires danced in the chill air. Rows of tents overlooked the circled lodges of Big Foot and his people.

Raucous laughter echoed up from the tents as Bluecoat soldiers moved about, celebrating the capture of Big Foot and the last of the renegade Sioux. Officers moved back and forth from a wagon, refilling their tin cups from a keg of whiskey.

"What has happened here?" Two Robes asked in alarm. "The Seventh Cavalry was called out? I just hope Tangled Hair can get here with his father and the Buffalo Soldiers before long."

"I don't want to go down there," Bob-tailed Cat said. "I am afraid."

"I don't like it, either," Long Hand said.

"Neither of you have to go down there with me," Two Robes said. "Go back and find Tangled Hair and his father. The Buffalo Soldiers shouldn't be far behind us. Tell them what's going on here. Tell them they had better hurry."

"We should eat first," Long Hand suggested. "Then we can make the ride."

The three rode down into the village and were stopped by a trooper posted as a sentry. He leveled his rifle and ordered them to dismount.

"Who goes there?"

"We are of Big Foot's people," Two Robes said. "We have come to join them."

The trooper studied Two Robes. "Why, you're a white man. What are you doing with these savages?"

Two Robes stood with Long Hand and Bob-tailed Cat at a good distance from the leveled Springfield, yet the smell of whiskey was pungent in the air.

"I married a Minneconjou woman," Two Robes explained. "I would like to find her now."

"I'd reconsider if I was you," the trooper said. "They'll put you on that train with the rest of them. You won't see the light of day."

"What train?" Two Robes asked.

"They're all going to Omaha, and who knows where else," the trooper said. "We've got to lock them up. Sure you want to go along?"

"If you'll excuse me, I'll find my wife now," Two Robes said.

The trooper laughed. "Like them red women, do you?"

After they had left the guard, Long Hand and Bob-tailed Cat told Two Robes they wanted to go among the lodges.

"I am going to tell my people about the trains," Long Hand said defiantly. "I will not be taken away from my home like a beef cow. Maybe I will get a number of others together with Long Hand. Then we will all break out of here."

Long Hand and Bob-tailed Cat hurried away. Two Robes worried that there would be immediate trouble. Everyone who learned of the plan to herd them onto trains and ship them away would become defiant immediately.

Two Robes searched the Minneconjou camp until he found Night Bird and Catches Lance outside their lodge. "Fawn has been worried about you," Night Bird said. "Where are the Buffalo Soldiers?"

"Tangled Hair left us at the spring near the entrance to the Stronghold," Two Robes said. "I believe he must have reached his father by now. The Buffalo Soldiers should be coming."

Fawn had heard Two Robes' voice and she emerged through the door flap. Hawk and Little Star popped out behind her and rushed into Two Robes' arms.

"There has been trouble since you left," Fawn said.

"I can see that," Two Robes said. "What has happened?"

"They made us camp here and said they would council with the men in the morning," Fawn replied. "I don't know what will happen. The young men are angry."

"They will be angrier when they hear about the train." Two Robes told them what the sentry had said. He added that he should have been more forceful with Big Foot in discussing the Stronghold. Had they gone there, everyone would be marching out to Pine Ridge with the Buffalo Soldiers now, not with the Seventh Cavalry.

Bob-tailed Cat and Long Hand appeared and announced that they would have to stay in camp or fight immediately. Bluecoats were moving among the lodges.

"They are looking for those who are trying to leave," Bob-tailed Cat remarked angrily. "They say that if they catch anyone going for the horses, they will put them in irons."

"It seems to me that these Bluecoats are meaning to make it hard for us," Catches Lance said. "Big Foot is in the Bluecoat's camp, being treated by a *Wasichu* doctor. They say they want the best for us. But they don't fool me. It's just a way to try to keep us calm."

"Everyone knows about the trains now," Bob-tailed Cat said. "No one will want to obey them tomorrow. I don't know what will happen."

They talked late into the night. Though all of them were tired, only Hawk and Little Star could fall asleep. Finally, a few hours before dawn, the rest of them rolled into robes and blankets for a short time.

Reveille awakened the village. The sky was overcast, and a cold wind had invaded the valley. Two Robes left Fawn in the lodge with Hawk and Little Star and stepped out to see what the Bluecoats would do. Catches Lance and Bob-tailed Cat joined him.

Bluecoat soldiers took positions at the edge of the council square and around the perimeters of the encampment.

"Do you know what this means?" Catches Lance asked Two Robes.

"I don't really know," Two Robes replied. "But I am worried. Look up on the hill. Four Hotchkiss guns. More Bluecoats have come in during the night."

"I think we should get together with the others and break out of here," Bob-tailed Cat suggested. "I am not going on any train."

"You have to be careful," Two Robes told him. "There are women and children here. If there is trouble, those Bluecoats won't stop to see who they're shooting at."

"Then let's move the women and children away from here," Catches Lance said. "I know there will be trouble. I can feel it."

Two Robes could find no reason to argue. He hurried Fawn and the children out of the lodge and helped them into the wagon. Night Bird joined them.

"Stay here until we see what is going to happen," Two Robes instructed the women. "If we have to, we'll take the wagons out toward the road."

Already a crier was calling the men to council in front of Big Foot's tent. Big Foot had been brought back from the Bluecoats' camp. Bluecoats were passing out rations of hardtack to the women and children, while the commanders spoke through interpreters to Big Foot.

After some discussion, many Minneconjou men came forward and deposited old and broken carbines in a pile. The commanders shook their heads. One of them held up a new Winchester and pointed to a number of the younger men assembled at the edge of the square.

"That's pretty clear," Catches Lance said. "The Bluecoats want our rifles. They are not going to have them."

As Two Robes and Catches Lance watched, Bluecoat soldiers separated the men from the women and ordered the men to hand over any weapons they might have, while taking all axes, knives, and cooking utensils from the women, anything that could be used in any way as a weapon. They told women who were sitting down to stand up, and took rifles from under their dresses.

Yellow Bird was singing a Ghost Dance song, flinging dirt into the air. He pointed into the sky and then to the Bluecoats, and flung more dirt.

Two Robes saw a younger warrior raise a Winchester above his head. Nearby Bluecoat soldiers struggled with the young warrior, who held his rifle high, and suddenly the entire square exploded into gunfire.

The screaming began. Women dropped down over their babies to protect them from the sudden hail of bullets that flew in every direction. The line of young warriors fired on the Bluecoats, who returned the fire. In the smoke and confusion, the cavalry ponies broke loose and stampeded up the hill past Two Robes and Catches Lance.

More Bluecoats opened fire, while young warriors and old shot from any position they could find. A stream of bullets pierced the lodges, bringing more screams from women and children inside.

Then the Hotchkiss guns opened fire, and shells burst all through the village. Screaming women and children stampeded from the lodges and climbed frantically into their wagons, trying to escape up the hill toward the road.

Two Robes and Catches Lance jumped into Fawn's wagon. Two Robes slapped the horse with the heavy reins; a bullet zipped past his left ear. Bob-tailed Cat came running for the moving wagon, and Catches Lance reached over the back of the wagon to help him up.

"Get in!" he yelled. "Get down!"

"They have shot Long Hand!" Bob-tailed Cat screamed, scrambling aboard. "They killed him."

"Get down!" Catches Lance yelled again.

Bob-tailed Cat groaned and grabbed his side, slipping down onto the floorboards.

"They hit him!" Catches Lance shouted.

Hawk and Little Star began to cry. They were halfway up the hill now. Below, a large number of people cut off from the wagons began to break toward the ravine at the southern end of the camp. Men, women and children fell like rows of chopped corn as the Hotchkiss guns raked through their ranks.

Fawn screamed as a shell burst near the wagon. One of the horses fell in its traces. The remaining horse reared and lunged as the smell of hot blood flooded its nostrils.

Another shell hit the wagon ahead of them, blowing wood and body parts in all directions. Two Robes could not hold the remaining horse as it turned back on the wagon, its eyes wild, and lurched into the driver's seat.

Two Robes jumped over the horse and landed heavily on his right shoulder. A large chunk of hot shrapnel tore into the horse's ribs. The frantic animal shied sideways in harness as another shell hit nearby, and the wagon turned onto its side, dumping everyone out. In the dust and smoke, another shell screamed overhead and plunged toward earth.

THIRTY-FIVE

Two Robes curled into a ball as the shell exploded on the other side of the downed wagon, blowing shards of wood and metal everywhere. On his forehead a lump was already forming where he had been struck. He pulled free a splinter of wood that had been driven nearly three inches into his left breast. The wound filled with blood that spilled down his front like a small river.

Two Robes called for Fawn. Through thick clouds of dust hordes of screaming people were running and falling; some were shot, and others were trampled by horses and wagons and one another.

Catches Lance rolled from under what was left of the wagon, holding his bad arm. Somehow he had slid off when the horse had slammed into them, but he had landed on his broken arm and was now in great pain.

Night Bird had been thrown clear of the wagon. She got up and hurried to Catches Lance, a stream of blood running down her left cheek.

Fawn then crawled out of the wreckage, Little Star under her left arm. Little Star was crying loudly but seemed to be unhurt. Hawk scrambled out by himself and began running back toward the soldiers.

"Get him!" Fawn screamed. "He doesn't know what he is doing!"

Two Robes ran toward the boy. Bullets zipped past and thudded into the ground around him. He caught Hawk and carried him back behind the wagon.

"We're going to the ravine!" Catches Lance yelled. "It's the only place with cover."

"Just stay here!" Two Robes ordered. "You will be shot down if you're moving."

They took refuge behind the fallen horses and what remained of the wagon. Shells continued to fall nearby, and shrapnel buzzed through the air like huge, angry bees. As Two Robes crowded next to the wreckage, he could see Bob-tailed Cat's lifeless body under one of the dead horses.

The deafening sounds of the bursting shells, mixed with the constant crying and screaming, began to send Hawk and Little Star into a state of shock. Fawn held both children and rocked them furiously. They clung to her with all their might, crying loudly.

Finally the Hotchkiss guns ceased and the rifle fire slowed to sporadic popping. Two Robes stood up and helped Catches Lance to his feet. Catches Lance stared across the devastation and began to weep.

Below, the council square was covered with bodies. Angry Bluecoats were roaming what was left of the village, finishing off the wounded. Other Bluecoats tried to stop them, and they quarreled.

Down toward the ravine, Bluecoats fired into brush patches. Now and then a Hotchkiss shell would scream overhead and explode in the ravine, bringing cries for mercy. In the middle of it all was a Black Robe, administering last rites to the dead and wounded.

"Do you know him?" Catches Lance asked.

"No, but he isn't doing a lot of good," Two Robes said. "The Bluecoats haven't finished their killing. We had better find a way out of here."

A number of refugees had already assembled and were beginning to flee southward, toward White Clay Creek. Two Robes caught two ponies and helped Fawn up onto one, then handed Little Star to her.

He reached down to help Hawk onto the other pony. He stopped and looked closely at the boy's gingham shirt. "Bullet holes!" he exclaimed. "Hawk, are you hurt?"

"I am not hurt," Hawk said.

Fawn jumped down from her pony and frantically examined her son. It was obvious that a bullet had passed through one side of his shirt and exited the other. But he showed absolutely no signs of harm. Fawn held him tightly. "*Wankantanka* has watched over you this day," she said, tears streaming down her face.

Two Robes caught another pony and jumped on. He reached down and pulled Hawk up behind him. Catches Lance sat behind Night Bird on a pony she had caught. He held on to her with his good arm, fighting the pain that threatened to rob him of consciousness.

Two Robes rode over to them. "We should find a wagon."

"No, we must ride fast," Catches Lance insisted. "Kicking Bear and Short Bull must be told so that the same thing does not happen at Pine Ridge."

Two warriors rode by, one of them with a wound in the leg. The wounded one stopped and looked at Two Robes. "You had better hurry out of this place," he said. "The Bluecoats are looking for a *Wasichu* who wears a Ghost Shirt. They say he caused trouble among the Indians they were trying to disarm peacefully."

"What do they mean?" Fawn asked.

"It means that you had better get your husband out of here, fast," the warrior repeated. "If they catch him, they will put the blame for the battle on him. He will go to prison somewhere."

Tangled Hair talked anxiously to his father, trying to get him to understand the urgency of reaching Big Foot. They had spent the entire day scouting the Stronghold area for any holdouts who might be left. Now the weary troopers were turning in for the night.

"Why did Henry do that?" Tangled Hair asked. "Why didn't he let me lead the men to Big Foot's people? I don't understand."

"He had his orders to stay in this area," Sergeant Betters replied. "Besides, I don't know if he believed you."

"Don't take it so hard, son," Cort told Tangled Hair. "The army don't believe anybody, except those they want to believe."

Cort had spent considerable time with Tangled Hair, talking to him, and Tangled Hair had grown to understand that conditions had been difficult for his father during his life in the army. Though the Buffalo Soldiers had done a lot of fighting over the years, they had received little credit. Not one of them had ever been promoted to command their own.

"So you see," Cort had told Tangled Hair, "it's not that any of us love to fight Indians. It's just that we were born and raised in war and we don't know anything else. When this is over, you and the sergeant, neither one, have to remember any of it."

Tangled Hair now realized that his father had little influence with Major Henry. "We'll get out of this," Betters told his son. "It's cold, and it's not fun out here. But we'll get out of it. And then we'll live someplace else."

Two scouts from Pine Ridge rode in with the news of Wounded Knee. They announced that all of Big Foot's people had been wiped out. They reported that Kicking Bear and Short Bull had led their people back from surrender and were preparing to make war.

Boots and Saddles was sounded, and the men of the Ninth scrambled from their bedrolls toward their horses.

Tangled Hair saddled his pony in silence. He contemplated leaving his father and joining Kicking Bear and Short Bull.

"I'm sorry about your friends," Betters told his son. "But there's nothing we can do about it now."

"If only your commander had listened," Tangled Hair said angrily, "maybe it wouldn't have happened."

"I told you, it's in the past now," Betters insisted.

Cort then said, "Listen to him, son. You can't change any of it. Just stay with your father. You can't do better than that."

Tangled Hair fought the rage and grief welling up within him. His friend since boyhood, Catches Lance, now gone. Two Robes and Fawn, and the children, all killed by the Bluecoats. For what reason?

He finished saddling his pony and climbed on. "Maybe I won't fight the Bluecoats or your Buffalo Soldiers," he told Cort and his father, "but I won't stay here and fight the Lakota."

"What are you going to do?" Betters asked.

"I am going to ride out of here," Tangled Hair answered. "I don't know what tomorrow will bring. We will see."

Two Robes sat near the fire on White Clay Creek discussing the events of Wounded Knee with Kicking Bear and Short Bull. Behind them, a Ghost Dance ring circled another fire. The people sang louder than ever.

Two Robes and Fawn had made it safely with the children, even though they had had to stop often to let Catches Lance rest. He was down with fever. Fawn and Night Bird attended to him, keeping him covered and giving him water. Fawn had even placed Hawk's shirt with the bullet holes in it across Catches Lance's brow, in hopes that the medicine would help him.

Though the village on White Clay Creek was crowded, many others had chosen to go into Pine Ridge. They were being cared for there by doctors and clergy. Some who had left Pine Ridge to join Kicking Bear and Short Bull warned Two Robes that the Bluecoats were asking about him.

Two Robes had been branded a troublemaker, a scapegoat for a plan that the Bluecoats were preparing with haste so that the massacre at Wounded Knee would appear justified to the American public.

Two Robes was a fugitive now. Big Foot and Yellow Bird were dead. There were no survivors whom the Bluecoats could call leaders. Though Two Robes had not been a leader, the Bluecoats knew that he had been among those who sat in on important councils. And he was white. That made him suitable to place blame on. If he even tried to talk with the Bluecoats, he would likely lose his freedom, possibly his life.

As the fire blazed in a night filled with light snow, Kicking Bear smeared war paint across his cheeks and forehead. "The Bluecoats will pay for this," he said through gritted teeth. "Look at the women and children who have come to join us. There are so many who are badly wounded. They tried to kill everybody."

"Many of the younger warriors have already started fighting," Short Bull added. "Soon we will have little bands of warriors all over and the Bluecoats won't be able to stop us."

"How do you plan to fight the Bluecoats without food or shelter?" Two Robes asked. "There are a great number of them, and many more coming. They will have food. It will be hard for the warriors."

"We can hold off until the Messiah rescues us," Short Bull replied. "Our people have fought for a long time to save our lands. We can last a short time longer, until the spring brings an end to the *Wasichu*, forever."

Late that night Tangled Hair appeared in the village. Two Robes met him near the Ghost Dance circle. "What happened?" Two Robes asked. "I thought surely you would bring your father and the Buffalo Soldiers to Big Foot's village."

"Henry wouldn't believe me," Tangled Hair said with

disgust. "Scouts came and told us about Wounded Knee. I don't want to be around any Bluecoats again, whether they are Buffalo Soldiers or not."

"Don't blame your father for this. Certainly he must have wanted to follow you to the village."

"I need food and rest," Tangled Hair said. "I don't know what to believe any longer."

Later, Two Robes crawled into the blankets next to Fawn and tossed in fitful sleep throughout the night. Kicking Bear awakened him at daybreak. He was leading warriors against the Bluecoats.

"They have come back from Wounded Knee," he said. "We will take them up into the deep valley above the mission and get rid of them forever."

While the warriors readied for battle, Two Robes told Fawn that he was going to stop it.

"You can't stop it," she said. "Kicking Bear is determined to fight. Short Bull will stay here and lead the dancing and send more warriors out when they are ready."

"There is a way to stop this," Two Robes said.

"Don't try," Fawn said. "It is much too dangerous."

"I have to try," Two Robes said. "If I don't stop this, there will be nowhere that we can hide."

Two Robes rode with Tangled Hair down the slope toward the oncoming Buffalo Soldiers. Troops in the front ranks began loading their rifles.

Betters yelled, "Hold your fire!" He came out of the column, along with Major Henry and two scouts.

"Father," Tangled Hair told Betters, "we have come to help you, not to fight you."

Sergeant Betters took a deep breath, relief evident on his face. Major Henry pointed to Two Robes. "Sergeant Betters, I want that man placed under arrest. He's wanted for inciting trouble at Wounded Knee."

"Place me under arrest if that's what you want," Two Robes

told Henry. "But there won't be any witnesses against me if you don't ride up the valley, and in a hurry."

Henry's good eye squinted at Two Robes. "What are you talking about?"

"If you came down from the Stronghold to aid the Seventh Cavalry, you had better forget about me for the time being," Two Robes said. "Kicking Bear and his warriors have the Seventh trapped up there. If you don't stop it, there won't be a man left by the end of the day."

"Why are you telling me this?" Major Henry asked. "You just said that if they were all killed, there would be no witnesses against you."

"I'm tired of all the killing," Two Robes said. "I was once a Catholic priest. I'm supposed to save lives, not take them."

"Are you sending me into a trap?" Henry demanded.

"I'm asking you to put an end to all this," Two Robes said. "If you can save the Seventh, the fighting will stop that much sooner. If you don't save them, Kicking Bear and his warriors will rise in glory. You will have to hunt them down to the last man."

Major Henry ordered Two Robes and Tangled Hair placed in shackles and under guard until he returned. Four troopers stayed behind and took them to a cluster of trees along the creek while Major Henry led the rest of his command up into the valley, where shooting had already begun.

"I hope they aren't too late," Two Robes said. "If the Seventh goes down again, the government will kill every single one of the Lakota people. No one will be spared."

Firing could be heard from up in the valley for the entire afternoon. Two Robes told the curious troopers standing guard of his mission among the Minneconjou.

"I ain't proud of all this," one of the troopers said. "A lot of us folk don't have no means to make money, so we join the army. Then we get put places we don't want to be. But I don't see no end to that."

"There can be an end to it," Two Robes said. "The idea behind the dancing is not to make war, but to pray for peace. If everyone thought about peace for a change, there would be no need for armies."

"I'm afraid that ain't the way of things," one of the other troopers commented. "It seems that from the time you're born, there's nothing to look forward to but trouble. It don't matter who you are, you got to face some real hard times."

By late afternoon, Major Henry and his troops were helping the Seventh Cavalry back to the agency. Kicking Bear and his forces, plus others who had come to join the fighting, were on the run. There had been few casualties on either side.

Major Henry and Sergeant Betters dismounted near the trees where Two Robes and Tangled Hair were being held.

"Release these two men," Henry said. "I can't believe that either one of them deserves to be tried for anything."

He pulled a notebook out of his pocket and jotted on one of the pages. He tore it off and handed it to Two Robes.

"You were telling the truth," he said. "There could have been another tragedy up there in that valley. It would have been senseless. We would have all been in the field for a very long time. The army would have sent in enough men to wipe out the Lakota people."

Two Robes read the paper. It was an official order to whom it might concern stating that he was not to be bothered while taking people with him, wherever he wanted to go, on any of the reservations.

"You keep that with you," Henry said. "I will have an official letter sent to you at the Cheyenne River agency. Take your family, and anyone else you wish, back up there. I will see to it that a wagon of provisions awaits you at Pine Ridge. If anyone questions you, show them that note. I will vouch for you at any time in a court of law."

Two Robes thanked the major. Tangled Hair gave Two Robes a long hug. "I will go down to Fort Robinson with my father," he said. "Maybe someday I will come up to visit."

"You have to promise," Two Robes said.

"We promise," Sergeant Betters said. He then shook Two Robes' hand, and hugged him, also.

Two Robes watched the Buffalo Soldiers ride down the valley toward the agency. They might see more action before the crisis was ended, but it seemed likely now that Sergeant Betters would be allowed his retirement.

It was late evening when Two Robes reached the camp on White Clay Creek. Kicking Bear and Short Bull were fuming.

"It is known among us that you told the Buffalo Soldiers where to go so that the Bluecoats from Wounded Knee would not be wiped out," Kicking Bear said. "I cannot understand this. The Bluecoats want to take you prisoner."

"I have one Bluecoat who will not allow this," Two Robes said. "The leader of the Buffalo Soldiers was grateful for no more bloodshed. He told me I could go in peace and take whomever I wished back up to Cherry Creek."

"What good will that do?" Short Bull asked.

"We will have no weapons with us, and we will dance," Two Robes said. "No one will worry, now that we have no rifles to point at anyone."

"The Bluecoats will stop you," Kicking Bear said.

"Not any longer," Two Robes said. "Not after what has happened."

Two Robes left the council and rolled up in a blanket with Fawn. Everyone slept well that night, and in the morning they loaded their belongings on their ponies and in the wagon, where Catches Lance lay under a blanket. Two Robes tried not to think of Big Foot.

"I am feeling better," Catches Lance said. "Thanks to you, we now have hope, both for the dance and for our future."

"I am but one man," Two Robes said.

"There will be others like you," Catches Lance said. "One day the dance will bring happiness for everyone."

By now, more Minneconjou had packed their things and

were asking to join the procession. Two Robes welcomed all who would care to come along. He led the way out of camp, toward Pine Ridge, where they would pick up the wagon of provisions that had been promised.

With the number of people now joining them, they might need two, and possibly three, wagons of provisions. Two Robes smiled, while the children sang the song their mothers had taught them:

> See the buffalo, all returning.
> They roam forever, laughing.
> The river flows with warm rain,
> And the tree grows once again.

ABOUT THE AUTHOR

Earl Murray was born in 1950 in Great Falls, Montana. He grew up on a ranch in central Montana and has worked as a botanist and rangeland conservationist. He is the author of over twenty novels dealing with Native American history and the West, including *High Freedom, Free Flows the River,* and *Whisper on the Water.* He makes his home in Montana with his wife and family, and he is currently working on another historical novel for Tor Books.

BESTSELLING WESTERNS
BY RICHARD S. WHEELER

"No one does it better than Dick Wheeler."

—The Round-up Quarterly.

☐ 51071-2 SKYE'S WEST: BANNACK $3.95
   51072-0   Canada $4.95

☐ 51069-0 SKYE'S WEST: THE FAR TRIBES $3.95
   51070-4   Canada $4.95

☐ 51073-9 SKYE'S WEST: SUN RIVER $3.95
   51074-7   Canada $4.95

☐ 50894-7 SKYE'S WEST: YELLOWSTONE $3.95
                                             Canada $4.95

☐ 51305-3 SKYE'S WEST: BITTERROOT $4.50
                                             Canada $5.50

☐ 51306-1 SKYE'S WEST: SUNDANCE $3.99
   Coming in October '92   Canada $4.99

☐ 51997-3 BADLANDS $4.99
                                             Canada $5.99

☐ 51297-9 FOOL'S COACH $3.99
                                             Canada $4.99

☐ 51299-5 MONTANA HITCH $3.99
   Coming in December '92   Canada $4.99

☐ 51298-7 WHERE THE RIVER RUNS $3.99
                                             Canada $4.99

Buy them at your local bookstore or use this handy coupon:
Clip and mail this page with your order.

Publishers Book and Audio Mailing Service
P.O. Box 120159, Staten Island, NY 10312-0004

Please send me the book(s) I have checked above. I am enclosing $ _____
(please add $1.25 for the first book, and $.25 for each additional book to cover
postage and handling. Send check or money order only—no CODs).

Names _____

Address _____

City _____ State/Zip _____

Please allow six weeks for delivery. Prices subject to change without notice.